ORACLE

J.C. Martin

J. Taylor Publishing

ORACLE

Published by J. Taylor Publishing
www.jtaylorpublishing.com

Copyright © 2012 J.C. Martin

All rights reserved. No part of this publication may be reproduced, distributed, or transmitted in any form or by any means, including photocopying, recording, or other electronic or mechanical methods, without the prior written permission of the publisher, except in the case of brief quotations embodied in critical reviews and other non-commercial uses permitted by copyright law.

This book is a work of fiction. Names, characters, places, and incidents are either the products of the author's imagination or are used fictitiously. Any resemblance to actual persons, living or dead, businesses, events, locations, or any other element is entirely coincidental.

ISBN 978-1-937744-08-3

First Printing: July 2012

My eyes began to burn—an incredible, searing pain as if someone had shoved glowing hot pokers through both my eye sockets.

I cried out. My hands shot to my face as I tried to wipe the fiery chemical away, but every brush of my fingers left a blazing trail of hot coals across my corneas. My eyes watered. As my vision descended into a red haze of pain, my cheeks and lips started to tingle.

My whole face was on fire.

Something hit the back of my knees, like a boot—a heavy one. Arms flailing, I fell forward, sprawling onto the floor. Lost in my own world of pain, I was nevertheless aware of a presence beside me.

"J.C. Martin really knows how to throw down a scene. Well written, constructed perfectly, and boy does she know how to leave the reader hanging at the end of every chapter."
— Jocelyn Adams, author of Shadowborn

"From the very start, the story had me in its grips and didn't let go until the end."
— Lynda R. Young, author of Birthright, Make Believe Anthology

"A fantastic read that kept me on my toes, heart racing until the end."
— Aimee Laine, author of Surrender

"The plot is so well thought out, and unfolds at just the right places, with all the reveals bringing a twitch to the eyebrow."
— J.A. Belfield, author of Blue Moon

"Oracle has a unique and original premise that makes it a refreshing read. Its well-drawn characters and twists and turns will keep you turning pages compulsively. I couldn't put it down."
— Lisa L. Regan

*To my three biggest fans:
Nick, for your unswaying belief
Ma, for my love of reading
Pa, for the freedom to pursue my dreams*

1

The last of the theatregoers had gone, the place locked up for the night, but for Vincent the Magnificent, the entertainment had only just begun.

He stood between the thighs of his lovely assistant, Olga Petrov, his trousers pulled down around his ankles. Still dressed in her too-tight stage gown, her sequined skirt hitched up to her hips, Olga sat atop the dressing table, legs splayed, as Vincent thrust himself repeatedly into her, his face buried in her substantial bosom, intermittent grunts muffled by her yawning cleavage. The rickety old table creaked in rhythm to their clumsy lovemaking, and under the yellow light of the lone naked bulb, Vincent's thinning, black hair glistened, greasier than usual, slicked with the sweat from his carnal exertions.

Even as his lunges grew faster and deeper, and Olga moaned sexy but unintelligible Russian into his ear, and as his balls ached in anticipation of climactic release, a tiny voice nagged at him from the back of his aroused consciousness—one sounding disturbingly like his wife Debbie with a bad bout of PMT saying 'Where are you?', 'What are you doing?', and 'Who's with you?'.

Not only did wifey force him to replace Linda—his previous assistant, a buxom redhead with morals as loose as her pussy was tight—she'd since imposed a curfew on him, which was why he had to be both discreet and quick—especially that night.

It was Debbie's birthday.

Olga gasped as she raked her fingers down his back, her nails digging into his skin through his sweat-sodden shirt. The sensation pushed him ever closer to the edge.

As he prepared himself for discharge, Vincent lifted his head from the gaping chasm that was Olga's cleavage.

A reflection in the mirror behind her shimmered.

"What the fuck? Debbie!"

Quickly extricating himself from his assistant, Vincent spun round, hands cupped over his groin. Blood thundered in his temples, and his distended scrotum throbbed in frustration.

The figure in the doorway looked nothing like his middle-aged, overweight wife.

Olga pulled her skirt down, a small scream leaving her mouth, but stopped when the man trained his gun on her.

"H-hang on." Vincent snatched his trousers up. He extracted his wallet from his back pocket and tossed it at the intruder's feet. "W-we don't want t-trouble." His hands shook so much he had trouble zipping up his fly. "Just take the money. Please."

The man waved the muzzle of the pistol at the open door. "Out." No emotion in his tone. Only cool efficiency.

"C-can you wait ..." Vincent's fingers trembled as he continued to fumble with his trousers, his testicles about to burst from unreleased semen. The fact that he still had an erection made zipping up all the more difficult.

God, my nuts hurt.

The gunman jammed the pistol into Vincent's crotch.

"I said move," the man growled, every word dripping with malice, "*now.*"

A rush of warmth blossomed between Vincent's legs. For a brief moment, he thought he'd finally ejaculated, but there was a lack of euphoria, and the tightness in his gonads remained unrelieved.

Holding his urine-stained trousers up, Vincent walked out of the dressing room, a tearful Olga sobbing beside him.

"Where are you taking us?" The Russian woman sniffled, her shoulders jerking up and down as she hyperventilated.

No answer. No sign the man even heard her.

He led them onto the prop-littered performance stage. On a small table sat a top hat and a deck of playing cards, across two lightweight gurneys, a hand saw and a long box, garishly coloured despite its resemblance to a coffin in size and dimension, and in the middle stood a six foot tall, clear tank filled with water. A pile of iron chains and shackles, still dripping wet from Vincent's last performance, lay in a heap beside the massive receptacle. In the semi-gloom of the deserted auditorium, rows of empty seats stood like silent witnesses to the unfolding events.

The trio approached the Water Torture Cell, Vincent's *pièce de résistance*. A wooden stepladder remained propped beside the tank.

"Get in. Both of you."

"No ... please, don't ..." Vincent whimpered.

"Get in, or I will kill you and put you in myself." The muzzle of the pistol jabbed into Vincent's back left no room for further argument.

Blubbering pitifully, Vincent climbed the wooden steps on shaky legs. He hesitated at the top, staring down over the threshold of the acrylic tank into the clear, rippling water below. A mere few hours before, he'd stood at that very spot, feeling nothing more than supreme confidence and a mundane sense of boredom. Olga's warm body pressed into his as the intruder piloted her up the steps at gunpoint, her fleshy bosom heaving against Vincent's back.

"Get in," the gunman instructed again.

"C'mon, mate," Vincent pleaded, "Whatever it is, we can talk—"

Their captor reached up and roughly grabbed one of Vincent's legs, pulling him off balance. The magician pitched forward, tipping over the edge of the tank and into the cold water within.

The shock of the icy liquid made Vincent gasp, and he swallowed a mouthful of water. His frenzied mind barely noticed when Olga landed beside him in a hail of bubbles, wedging him up against the wall of their cramped shared space. The darkness around them thickened as the metal lid slid over the top of the tank.

Holding on to the scant breath he had left, Vincent propelled himself upwards towards the steel cover. He groped frantically along the underside of the solid sheet, searching for the hidden catch that opened the tank from the inside, the one he relied on during every performance.

Come on, come on! Where the fuck is it? A building pressure constricted his lungs like a steel band tightening around his chest. His pulse thundered in his ears, drums beating out a desperate cry for help.

Just as he could hold his breath no longer, Vincent's fingers found a reassuringly familiar sunken niche and inside, the smooth silhouette of the release handle. He gripped the knob in his fist and turned. A metallic chink signalled the unlocking of his watery prison.

With renewed purpose, Vincent placed both hands on the metal cover. One slight upward push would slide the lid back, and he'd be out, sucking in deep lungfuls of delicious oxygen.

Vincent shoved. The hatch rattled.

It stayed shut.

What the fuck . . . ?

He tried again, harder. Again and again, a gurgling tar pit of dread spreading through his stomach. Something caught his peripheral vision. On the outside of the tank, a pair of feet dangled in mid-air.

The bastard is sitting on the cover!

His lungs screaming for air, Vincent pummelled the lid with his fists. Olga flailed beside him, clutching and clawing at him, dragging him down.

At last, his oxygen starved brain triggered his inhalation reflex, forcing his mouth open. A freezing rush of water flooded his body, piercing his insides like a thousand needle-sharp icicles. His chest expanded, not with life-giving air, but with a cold, swelling torrent. As if realising its mistake, Vincent's body tried to expel the offending liquid by making him gag and cough, but the spasms only served to make him ingest more icy water, stretching his lungs to the point of bursting.

By the time a hazy gloom descended on his vision, Vincent begged for the merciful black void of unconsciousness.

2

"The beast ... pounced, and he thrust his spear into its side." Meghan squinted as she read the words before her. "It was as if the lion's hide ... was made of ... stone, and the spear snapped in two." Tiny fingers danced across the page, pointing out each word she recited aloud.

"Very good." I leaned in closer, adjusting my weight on the pink bed sheets plastered with pictures of Hannah Montana. Pale blue eyes magnified by thick lenses glanced up at me. I nodded, encouraging her to go on.

"So, Hercules took out his club and, with all his strength, struck the lion on its head. He grabbed the beast around its neck, and sk ... skoo ..."

"Squeezed," I said.

"Skoo-*eez*ed," Meghan parroted, "and squeezed and squeezed until the lion breathed no more. Since no weapon could pier ... pierce ... the beast's hide, Hercules used one of the lion's own razor-sharp claws to skin the animal, and he returned to the king wearing the pelt of the great Nee ... Nim ... Nemean lion."

"And, the end. Well done!" I held my hand up, and Meghan slapped my palm in a high five, chest puffed out with pride.

"I only needed help with ..." she tapped a count on her fingers, "... eight words this time!"

"I know!" I ruffled her russet hair, proud of her accomplishment. "Soon you'll be reading all by yourself!"

She crinkled up her button nose, an endearing habit of hers I loved. "Well, I'd still like you to read with me," she said. "And, I still need help with this." She lifted the clear plastic sheet, studded with tiny raised dots, layered atop the printed page of her book.

I forced my tone to remain light despite the pang in my chest. "We've got plenty of time to learn that together." I flipped to the next chapter, effectively changing the subject. The following page had another interleaved transparent Braille sheet, one I tried my best to ignore. "In the meantime, let's take a sneak peek at what we'll be reading tomorrow night. Now, what does the title say?"

Meghan tilted her head forward, focusing, I imaged, through the mini telescopes on her bioptic glasses. "The Second Labour: Slaying the Nine-Headed Hie … de … ra … Hydra." Her eyes twinkled. "I know what that is! That's the snaky, dragony monster in the movie, the one who keeps growing more heads! Oh, can we read it now, Daddy, please?"

I couldn't help but chuckle at her excitement. Meghan got her love of books from her mother. I'd wake up in the middle of the night to find Angie's bedside lamp still on, her freckled nose sandwiched between the pages of her latest literary endeavour. She read everything from the classics to contemporary fiction, from science fiction and fantasy to chick lit, even the odd memoir or biography.

The only words she refused to read were in crime fiction.

"I dunno, peaches, it's getting pretty late …" I shook my head, slowly preparing to close the hardback.

"Aww, but please? It won't take long …"

Crossing my arms over the storybook, I made a show of pursing my lips and furrowing my brows. Big Bambi eyes fluttered their lashes at me through thick plastic lenses.

"Please, with marshmallows on top?"

I laughed but relinquished the book. "Can't say 'no' to marshmallows. But, lights out right after. Promise?"

"Yes!" She all but snatched her precious tome from my grasp, the colourful cover depicting a man dressed in loincloth, wearing a lion's pelt and wielding a heavy club. Had Tarzan fallen for a Neanderthal instead of Jane, their lovechild would have been hairy, brawny, and wild like the picture. Above it, in embossed gold lettering, the title proclaimed the book to be *Greek Heroes Series: The Twelve Labours of Hercules.*

Meghan had been obsessed with Greek mythology ever since watching the animated movie *Hercules*. She'd gone through a Native American themed phase post-*Pocahontas*. Before that, Arabian legends, thanks to *Aladdin*.

I had a pretty good idea what her flavour-of-the month would be next week, having bought her *Mulan* on DVD for her forthcoming birthday.

A buzzing noise made us both jump. My mobile phone on the pink and white bedside cabinet lit up, dancing across the table to the tune of *Kung Fu Fighting*.

One glance at the caller ID, and my heart dropped.

Work calling at such a late hour was never good.

I let the phone ring a moment longer before reluctantly picking it up and pushing the green 'Answer' key. "Lancer." I clenched my jaw as the relayed information sank in. "I'm on my way."

When I hung up, Meghan faced me, duvet pulled up to her waist, arms around her favourite teddy bear. Through her glasses, pleading kitten eyes flitted back and forth between me and her book.

I sighed. I hated leaving her. "I'll call Uncle Reggie, see where he is," I said as I placed Meghan's book back on her bookshelf. "Sorry, kid."

The hopeful expectance on Meghan's little face crumbled, and so did a chip of my heart.

Again.

My blue Ford Fiesta cruised northwards up Mare Street, passing the Old Central Library on the right, its stone columns and circular balcony housing a music venue instead of shelves upon shelves of books. On the left, rows of interminable shops and offices gave way to the green expanse of Hackney Town Square. The gardens outside the town hall stood empty and dark, scantly illuminated by a smattering of streetlamps and the flashing lights from an army of police vehicles.

I turned into the narrow side street after the square and stopped in front of a barricade of traffic cones. A quick flash of my badge to the uniformed officer on duty, and the cones were removed, allowing me to pass. After manoeuvring my way between haphazardly parked vehicles and an ambulance, I double-parked beside a patrol car.

With a quick check in the rear view mirror, I frowned at each strand of grey hair twisted in with younger-looking black ones, all in tight braids that hugged my scalp like the ridges of a ploughed field.

Kurt, man, you ain't getting any younger.

A sharp rap on the driver's side window snapped me from my vanity check. My partner, Detective Sergeant Sam Blaize, grinned at me through the glass barrier.

I opened the car door and put my feet out, bending over to fuss with my shoelaces—an effort to hide my embarrassment at being caught in the act of narcissism.

"You can stare in a magic mirror all you like, Kurt, but it won't make you any prettier." The corners of Blaize's eyes crinkled her amusement.

"Actually, I was seeing how long it'd take for my face to crack the mirror." I stood up, towering over Blaize. Most women of her stature would cross the street when they saw me coming, but I'd seen Blaize take down enough men my size—one of them a knife-wielding maniac—to know my imposing physique didn't faze her one bit.

"Sorry for the shitty timing," she said. "You know how inconsiderate some people are, dying at the most inconvenient moment." In our line of work, a bit of morbid humour went a long way in preserving our sanity. "Did you manage to get a babysitter for Meg?"

"She's at home with Reggie."

Blaize gave me a wry smile. "Is that wise?" She'd met my brother a couple of times over dinner. In those meetings, he'd managed to set fire to the back garden—twice. Excessive alcohol consumption led to an overdose of lighter fluid in the barbecue grill.

I shrugged. "You know what they say, he ain't heavy…" Our forced laughter faded to an uneasy silence, and I shoved my hands into my pockets. Blaize's gaze fell to my shoes as she chewed on her lower lip. As soon as the small talk ran out, the veil of discomfort descended, hanging over our heads like a guillotine blade ready to decapitate any attempt at pretending that what happened between us two months before had never happened.

I cleared my throat, gestured at the hubbub around us. "So, what's gone down here?"

Blaize shrugged, all professionalism once more. "I just got here myself," she said, looking relieved to have broken through our barrier of awkward silence. "Your guess is as good as mine. The new guy gets credit for being the first one on the scene."

"Really?" Our latest addition to the Murder Investigation Team must have been eager to impress. "I've not met him properly yet." Aside from a five-second introduction before the Chief whisked him off on some grand orientation tour. "Have you?"

"No, but here's our chance." She flicked her head, her short red hair bobbing with the movement. "That looks like him now."

A small man with a slight build waited on the pavement. Despite the warm evening, the new Detective Constable wore a blazer, and the top button of his shirt remained steadfastly secured. Tie knotted right over his Adam's apple, he compounded his bookishness by donning glasses with thick black frames. Any stranger running into him in the streets would have dismissed the man as an accountant, a librarian, perhaps even something as exciting as a computer engineer.

They certainly would not have guessed homicide detective.

Then again, I should be the last person to judge someone by his appearance. With the size and stature of a rugby prop forward, I didn't so much as blend into a crowd as stand head and shoulders above it.

As we walked towards our newest team member, the man leant against the wall, arms wrapped around his midsection as if holding in the contents of his gut. At closer inspection, his complexion held a pale greenish tinge, and he was taking in gulps of air through slack jaws.

"I gather what he's discovered ain't too pretty," I remarked. Dealing with dead bodies on a near-daily basis was not everyone's idea of a day's honest work.

"Either that or he's not hacking it," Blaize added.

We introduced ourselves to Newbie.

"Detective Constable Thomas Holloway," he said, shaking my hand. "You can call me Tom." He enunciated his words with an air of formality. I couldn't be sure if it was a put-on or if he truly spoke that way all the time. His brows furrowed as he regarded us, particularly Blaize.

"*You're* Sam Blaize?" he asked my partner. "I was expecting a ... oh, it must be short for Saman—"

"No, just Sam." Blaize cut him off, green eyes flashing a stormy warning. There were two words nobody ever called her—*Ginger* was one. Her hair colour could be better described, in her own words, as "cinnamon." The other taboo word was *Samantha*. Considering her knockout record as an amateur kickboxing champion with the nickname *Firestorm*, most people were wise enough to respect her wishes.

"You seen the body then?" I asked Holloway.

"Bod*ies*." His gills turned green once more. He adjusted his glasses with trembling fingers. "We got two floaters."

"*Floaters?*" I blinked, not sure if I heard right. "Inside a theatre?"

"See for yourself."

We crossed the street towards an imposing red brick structure. Colourful posters dotted the wall, advertising a variety of acts: musicians, comedians, pantomimes, all slated to perform at some point at this cultural venue. Above the main entrance, proud, seven-foot tall letters announced:

HACKNEY EMPIRE

We continued past the modern, glass-fronted section of the theatre until we reached the original entrance, guarded overhead by an ornate statue of Thalia, one of the nine Greek Muses. Perched high atop a pediment in between carved terra cotta domes and arches, Thalia held court to the rooftops, a witness to the evolution of Hackney Central over the past century, yet she remained a beacon of enduring constancy. The Victorian facade of the Empire had remained largely unchanged since its completion in 1901.

Standing before the Empire was like stepping back through time, except for the bright yellow crime scene tape strung up across the glass double doors like a septic scar, and the horde of reporters and looky-loos swarming around the blocked off entrance like flies circling a rotting carcass.

Word had spread fast, and no one seemed fooled by the hastily scrawled notice reading: *Due to technical difficulties, tonight's scheduled performance is cancelled. We apologise for the inconvenience.*

Holloway cut a path for us through the crowd. We jostled past a news crew, ignoring the reporter's plaintive plea for information, and slipped under the cordon into the cool dimness of the theatre.

The foyer welcomed us with its magnificent lofty ceiling, elaborate chandeliers, and rich furnishings in hues of red and gold. A pair of staircases swept upwards to the auditorium. As we climbed, my feet sank into the plush burgundy carpet, solid marble underneath.

Inside the auditorium, the gilded ceiling arched high above us, a round skylight in the centre promised a peephole to the heavens. Row upon row of seats, arranged in tiers, faced a grand stage framed with marble and crowned on both ends by Indian domes. It was like being inside a maharajah's palace.

Amid the regal setting, I could imagine the Hackney Empire in its heyday, playing host to the likes of Charlie Chaplin and Stan Laurel.

Despite falling into disuse with the advent of television, the local community had rallied to its aid, refurbishing the theatre to its former glory. So well loved was the Empire, that the building had been featured on the official London 2012 pin for the Borough of Hackney. The coming Olympics had, in fact, played a major role in the variety hall's revival. With all the money pumped into the development of the city, particularly the East End, the Empire had regained its status as a centre for arts and culture.

In its one hundred eleven years in existence, the Empire had faced its fair share of challenges—closures, lack of funding, even the indignity of being turned into a bingo hall.

It faced yet another public relations nightmare.

My feet padded on the carpet as I walked down the aisle towards the stage where the buzz of activity appeared centred around two body bags and what looked like an oversized fish tank.

The dead, a man and a woman, were still dripping wet. Both bloated bodies had a greyish tint to their skin, with blue, wrinkled lips. The ridges on their fingers were swollen as if they'd spent too long in the bath. Their eyes remained wide open, features locked in an expression of abject terror.

We wouldn't need a forensics expert to determine the cause of death.

Drowning.

One of the worst ways to die. I glanced at Blaize. Even she seemed a bit subdued.

"Victims' names are Vincent Matthews and Olga Petrov,"

Holloway said, his gaze fixed on his notes, complexion turning a peculiar shade of blue-green. "They were a semi-successful magic act that performed here last night."

"The scratches on the man's face...?" I gestured towards the angry red slashes standing out starkly against the pallor of the dead man's skin.

"Probably Olga's doing as they struggled underwater. The autopsy will confirm that."

"Who found them?" Blaize asked, as white-clad forensic techs zipped up the body bags. Holloway's shoulders sagged when the corpses rolled out of sight.

"Caretaker, round six o'clock, when he came to open up for tonight's show."

"Any idea as to time of death?" Blaize cased the perimeter of the stage.

Holloway pushed the bridge of his glasses higher up his nose and flipped through his spiral-bound notepad. "A preliminary estimate places it between eleven p.m. and one a.m. last night. So, right after the end of their show."

I was genuinely impressed by his efficiency. "You don't really need us here, do you? You've done all the legwork."

Holloway's eyes flicked up from his notes before dropping down again.

My days, was he blushing at the compliment?

"There is one more thing," he added, "ol' Vincent was found with his trousers only partly done up, and Olga had no panties on." He gave what he probably intended to be a conspiratorial wink but which ended up more like a pained grimace.

Blaize and I exchanged glances. That one bit of information could rule out accidental death and suicide. If the victims were found partially dressed, it suggested something had interrupted them.

Or someone.

"Are the victims married?" I asked.

"Um, not to each other." Holloway scanned through his notes. "Olga is single, and Vincent is married to a ..." he stopped along the length of his pad, "a Debbie Matthews."

I turned my attention to the tank of water. A huge puddle pooled at its base, seeping between the wooden slats of the stage, the result of hauling two soggy bodies out from its depths.

"Is Mrs. Matthews aware of her husband's affair?" Blaize asked Holloway.

"I don't know, but from speaking with the employees round here, their extramarital relationship doesn't sound like a well-kept secret."

"Possible motive?" I climbed up the stepladder beside the Water Torture Cell.

"Maybe." Holloway scribbled in his notepad. "A jilted lover? Whatever the case, it begs the question, how did our perpetrator force not one but *two* people into the tank against their will?"

"A knife? A gun?" Blaize asked. "Some form of persuasion. But then, why not just shoot them?"

Holloway puffed up his cheeks and snapped his notepad shut.

I stood at the top of the ladder and peered over the edge of the tank, trying to imagine two people trapped in the casket-like space, thrashing against each other as their last reserves of oxygen expired. As *they* expired.

I shook my head to disperse the sobering image and something half-floating, half-clinging to the side of the tank caught my eye.

"Oi, look at this." I snapped on a disposable glove. Leaning over, I fished out the limp, green object.

Holloway cocked an eyebrow. "A leaf?"

"An *oak* leaf." I pointed out its distinct lobed outline as I descended the stepladder and proffered the dripping leaf to Blaize. "Bag it," I said, "and find out where the nearest oak trees are from here."

Holloway made a sceptical noise deep in his throat. "I doubt that's a worthwhile avenue to pursue. It's probably just detritus one of the DoA's tracked in."

"Perhaps." I watched as Blaize placed the soggy leaf into a clear evidence bag and turned my attention to Holloway. "Or perhaps, it's something their *killer* tracked in."

3

On a warm day, even for late June, the Oracle sat in the shade of the old oak tree, eyes shut, breathing deeply, steadily. A delicate breeze caressed the leaves overhead, their soft rustling like the gentle whisper of invisible voices. Sunlight shone through his closed eyelids, illuminating his self-imposed darkness with swirling hues of orange and yellow. He leaned his head against the ancient trunk, the firm, rough bark thrumming against his scalp, as he communed with the spirit of the oak.

He had completed his task and completed it well. The evil wizards were destroyed. No longer would they deceive the world with their fell magic. He had eaten well after—a celebratory banquet. Soon he would begin fasting again and await further instruction.

He had followed the news intently for reports of his deed. A two-minute slot on BBC identifying the victims of a "mysterious drowning incident" at the Hackney Empire, and a short article on page three of *The Sun*, beside the picture of the topless Daily Babe, had disappointed him.

He longed to be at the theatre when the police discovered his work. He yearned to see the officers' faces. Would they be puzzled? Shocked? Or would they see his work for the masterpiece that he intended?

He would not risk returning to the scene, as much as it called to him. He vowed to be stronger than Orpheus, who glanced backwards and lost everything he'd fought so hard to gain.

He would not risk losing his Eurydice.

Something prodded him in the shoulder, rudely bringing him out of his meditative state. His eyes opened to narrow slits, the brightness of the sunlight dazzling him. A small boy stood beside him, eyeing him with childish curiosity. He held a red plastic trowel in one hand, no doubt the offending weapon that had roused the Oracle from his meditation.

Before he could coax his relaxed body into any form of action, a young woman rushed up. Muttering something apologetic, she dragged the child away. Despite his annoyance at the unwelcome disturbance, the Oracle forced a genteel smile. As the woman returned to her gardening duties, her son proceeded to stab at a clump of dirt with his toy trowel.

Forget the urchin, the Oracle told himself. The child was but a minor inconvenience. His fate bore no consequence to the Oracle and his goal.

He made certain the boy was no longer interested in bothering him and shut his eyes once more, returning to the contemplation of his next task.

4

I peered into the office, hoping to find Chief Sutherland too busy to talk with me. Luckily, she was on the phone, back turned to the entrance.

Thank God.

I tiptoed my way past the open door.

"*Lancer!*" The shrill cry, like the wail of a banshee, tore through the air and ripped into my eardrums. Faces buried into computer screens peered up. Curious heads popped up from their cubicles, like meerkats sensing an approaching predator.

I winced, turned, and entered Medusa's lair.

With her tangled nest of hair coiling around her face, Detective Chief Inspector Kate Sutherland certainly resembled a gorgon, but her stare had never turned anyone to stone—at least not permanently. With eyes of gun-metal grey boring twin holes into my brain, I stood rooted to the spot like a petrified statue.

The Chief broke the spell by glancing down at her watch.

"It's twenty past eight," she said.

"I know. Traffic was busy on the school run."

"This is the third time in two weeks."

"I'm sorry."

"And you've requested an extended lunch break today."

I sighed and lowered my head.

"Kurt," she dropped the edge from her tone, "you know I sympathise with your situation. It's not easy being a single parent, and I admire your efforts."

Clenching and unclenching my jaw, I lifted my gaze. The scalpel-sharp glint in her eyes had softened—but not by much.

"But this cannot get in the way of your job."

"I understand."

"If you need to take some more time off..."

"I don't."

She nodded, signalling the end of the conversation. I stepped out from her office into the path of a dozen pairs of eyes. The fifteen foot journey to my cubicle might as well have been a trek across the Kalahari Desert, with the heat from curious stares burning into the back of my neck.

A cup of coffee waited for me on my desk, next to my Bruce Lee nodding doll. The space to my left—Blaize's cubicle—was empty, the desk cleared of paperwork. Holloway, newly stationed to my right, sat hunched over his computer, his face inches from the screen. He glanced up as I approached.

"Thought you could use a pick-me-up," he said, gesturing to a steaming cup.

I thanked him and fired up my computer, leaning over the wall as I waited. I sipped from the paper cup, the hot drink scalding my tongue. In the split second before my monitor sprang to life, I glimpsed my reflection in the darkened screen. Angie always said I looked like that boxer, David Haye. At that moment, I felt more like one of his opponents after twelve rounds in the ring.

I gestured towards Blaize's empty desk. "Where's Sam today?"

Holloway pushed out his bottom lip. "Dunno. Think she's on sick leave."

Blaize, sick? She was the healthiest person I knew. In the two years since she joined our Murder Investigation Team, she'd never taken a single day's medical leave. While the rest of us sneezed and coughed our way through flu season, she'd never had so much as the sniffles. Concern tugged at my throat, but I swallowed the lump down with another glug of coffee.

"How are you settling down?" I asked my new co-worker.

"Meh." He stuck out a hand, palm down, and wavered it in a so-so gesture. "Getting there."

"Miss your days in uniform yet?"

"Absolutely not. I've had more than enough of policing football matches and breaking up drunken bar fights."

"Amen to that." I remembered my uniformed days. The assignments may not have been glamorous, but we had great camaraderie. I still kept in touch with most of my mates down at the station. "But I bet you miss your fellow bobbies."

Holloway squinted at me as if I'd asked him if he believed in fairies. "No." He stared into his morning cuppa. "I wasn't ... really close with anyone."

Something in his tone told me he wasn't prepared to discuss the matter further.

Nothing wrong with being a loner, I figured. Some people preferred their solitude—like *I* had recently.

As long as he does his job well.

"I hear you had a successful stint in Narcotics," he piped up.

At least he was *trying* to make small talk.

"Three years. Then I applied for a transfer. It was all becoming too ... samey." For a youngish mixed-race officer in Narcotics, I only ever got one role—undercover.

"Any word from Forensics?" I asked, changing the subject.

Holloway sat back in his chair, took off his glasses, and proceeded to clean them with a handkerchief.

"They've got nothing." He blew on the lens and rubbed it. "Well actually, they've got absolutely shed loads. Just nothing we can use."

I nodded. No surprises there. With hundreds of people streaming in and out of the Hackney Empire every day, forensics would amass a treasure trove of hairs and fibres. Finding something remotely resembling a needle in the proverbial haystack would be nearly impossible.

"What about Pathology?" I fingered the Bruce Lee figurine on my desk, making his disproportionately large cartoon head bob back and forth.

"Working at a snail's pace as usual," he sniffed, squinting as he worked on his lenses. "But really, we don't need an autopsy to confirm cause of death."

"True." I pictured the pallid corpses with their distended bellies. "Although, I was hoping the coroner would find some clues as to *how* the drowning actually happened."

"There is some new information from the crime scene," Holloway said as he put his glasses back on. "They found Olga's panties. In the dressing room. Next to a puddle of piss."

"Whose piss?" I leant further over the wall. Cases of murderers or rapists wetting themselves from the thrill of the crime were not uncommon. Had our unsub left some DNA behind?

"Forensics are still on the case. But seems like the perp moved the vics all the way from backstage. That supports your forced-by-gunpoint theory."

I flicked Bruce's head again, sending him into a frenzied dance. Bruce Lee, head-banging with a pair of nunchucks.

Did the killer choose drowning because it doubled as a form of torture? What did that say about the mental state of the perp? The odd mode of execution suggested premeditation—and possibly a sick touch of sadism. In any case, the guy had done his homework and had left behind no incriminating evidence.

"Any leads on the oak leaf in the tank?"

Holloway pursed his lips. "It could have come from anywhere. Stuck to the bottom of someone's shoe. Blown in from outside. A stowaway in the magician's trunk ..."

"The leaf was fresh," I said. "Not brown, dry or brittle. And it didn't look trodden on. That tank was pretty well kept, the water clean and clear. The only thing out of place was the leaf." I rolled my chair out of my cubicle and into Holloway's before sitting down. "Humour me."

With a shrug, Holloway swivelled to his computer screen.

"Despite my scepticism, I have actually done a basic search. Within a three-mile radius of the Empire, Hackney Marshes would be your best bet for finding oak trees. However, there might be oaks on private land we don't know about."

"I think you can profile plant DNA the same way you profile human DNA. We need to get someone on leaf picking duty."

"Righty-o." Holloway grabbed a pen and wrote a quick note on a Post-it before returning all the stationery to its rightful place—pen in pot, nib pointed up, pad in top right corner of desk.

I would swear the man arranged his highlighters in order of colour.

"In the meantime," I said, "we need to interview some next of kin."

"Olga has no relatives in the country," Holloway said, "which leaves Mrs. Vincent Matthews as our best bet."

"We'll start with her. Then we'll canvass their neighbours."

"Okay."

"And seeing as Sam's out of action today, you can come with me."

"I can? Uh, I mean, sounds like a plan." Despite trying to hide his initial burst of excitement, Holloway's eyes shone like those of a kid who'd just found out he won a trip to Disney World. Grabbing his coat, he all but jumped up from his chair.

"Whoa, hold your horses, Tonto." I held up a hand while consulting my watch. "Let's get some paperwork out of the way first. We'll sit tight till after lunch."

"Why?" Holloway deflated, reminding me of a dog who'd been refused walkies.

I suppressed a sigh.

"Meghan's got an appointment with the eye doctor."

I cringed as Dr. Eisenberger removed the electrodes from my daughter's eyes. It wasn't Meghan's first electroretinography—nor would it be her last—and she'd assured me the device, though uncomfortable, did not hurt her. Still, no parent should ever have to witness his child's eye lids clamped open by metal clips, nor see wires sticking out from her eyeballs, as if she were a lab rat on some mad scientist's operating table.

Finally disconnected from all the machinery, Meghan stumbled up to me, rubbing her dilated eyes. When Eisenberger turned up the lights in the room, she blinked furiously and shook her head.

"Whoa," she murmured. "Spots."

"The spots will disappear once your eyes adjust to the brighter lights." Eisenberger rummaged in the pocket of his white coat and pulled out a lollipop. "Here. You deserve this for sitting so nice and still for me. Now can you be a dear and wait for your daddy in the play area?"

"Thank you, Dr. Eyes-on-Burger!" Meghan snatched the sweet with a grin before tottering off to the toy chest in the corner.

"Well?" I asked as soon as Meghan settled down with a musical picture book. The reedy tunes of *Old MacDonald* wafted across the sterile office.

Eisenberger sat across from me, propped his elbows on the desk and steepled his fingers, lips pursed.

Not good then ... From experience, I'd learned that the time taken for a healthcare professional to answer a given question is directly proportional to how bad the news is.

The ophthalmologist consulted the notes in front of him. "Her central and peripheral vision has continued to deteriorate, and the rate of degeneration shows no sign of slowing."

"Right ..." I mumbled, sinking deeper into my chair.

"At this rate, she will experience partial to total loss of light perception within the next four to five years."

His words were an auditory sucker punch to the gut. "So that means ..."

"I'm afraid so." Eisenberger nodded, his lips drawn into a grim line. "By the time she's thirteen, Meghan will be almost—if not completely—blind."

"But the diet... the carotenoids..." I heard the shrill desperation in my own voice.

"High lutein foods were never meant to be a cure, Mr. Lancer, merely an attempt at slowing down disease progression. But it seems your daughter has a particularly aggressive form of CRD."

Cone-rod retinal dystrophy. CRD. It amazed me how he could package something so sinister, so life destroying, into such a benign acronym.

I glanced at Meghan, sitting cross-legged on the floor, the stick of the lolly protruding from her puckered mouth as she punched away at the buttons on the interactive toy in her lap. Hair gathered up in twin ponytails. Crayon marks on her school uniform. Scabs on her knee. By all accounts, a *normal* child, save for the binocular-like lenses mounted on her head.

Meghan *should* be a normal child. She *should* watch too much television, not eat enough vegetables, play lots of games, live a *full* childhood in Technicolor vision. She should *not* be learning Braille or to walk with a cane. She should *not* be eating all those supplements, fish oils, the goji juice that smelled and no doubt tasted like cowpat.

Her world should *not* be plunged into darkness and shadows, but it seemed it would be, thanks to my dodgy genes and Murphy's Law of *Shit Happens*.

My daughter had been handed a life sentence, and the clock was ticking.

"Ooh! That sounds like the ice cream van!" Meghan trilled as we waited on the first floor landing of our house, a double-storey detached that had been converted into two flats. The one downstairs we called home. "Can I get an ice pop, Daddy, please?"

"Sorry, sweetie, but I gotta get back to work. I'm running late as it is."

"Did somebody say ice cream?" The main door opened, and a woman dressed in a strappy sundress appeared. "Lucy's just popping down to catch the ice cream man. Would you like to follow her, Meg?"

"Yesss!" Meghan cheered, as a sullen-looking teenage girl, hair dyed black with purple highlights, emerged from the flat. With a half-hearted "hi," she swept past us and headed out, an excited Meghan following close behind.

"Thanks, Helen," I reached out and plucked a length of curly ribbon from her hair. She ran a successful business designing handmade cards and wedding invitations. The fact that she worked exclusively from home and lived upstairs from us made her an ideal candidate for Meghan's fall-back babysitter, especially considering I'd been requiring her child-minding services on an almost daily basis.

I reached into my trouser pocket for my wallet.

"Don't even think about it." Helen had stopped accepting payment for watching Meghan weeks before, but we still went through the same ritual every time—me trying to push cash into her hands and she declining the offer graciously. I was hoping, if I persisted, she would cave in and take some money to help ease my conscience.

"I need to repay you in some way," I said.

"You can buy me dinner." She winked, leaning against the doorframe.

"Of course. You and Lucy can come down to ours. I can cook."

She shook her head slowly, one corner of her mouth hooked up in a wry smile. "I've heard about your cooking from Meg. Heard *of* it, as well, every time you set the smoke alarm off. No, I meant you can take me *out* for dinner."

"I could do that. We're celebrating Meg's birthday on Saturday. You and Lucy want to join us?"

Amethyst eyes glinting with mischief through her dark lashes, Helen crossed her arms, the action pushing her breasts together and deepening the cleavage peeking out from her low-cut dress. "I was thinking of a more ... *intimate* arrangement."

"Ah. Erm." I pretended to inspect the carpet runners on the stairs to avoid staring at her chest. "Sure ... I can't quite fix a date yet, though. Work's been kinda hectic lately."

She laughed, the sound of silk brushing against my ear lobe. "Well, you let me know after you've checked your diary, hmm?" She tossed her head, hair cascading in soft waves down her shoulders, framing her heart-shaped face in a chestnut coloured halo.

"Lucy not at school today?" I asked, changing the subject.

Helen shrugged her tanned shoulders, eyes casted skyward. "Managed to wheedle her way home—again." She sighed.

"What excuse did she use this time?"

"Period pains, what else? Classic. Reliable. Something she can use every month, and one that male teachers will never question."

"I suppose." I glanced downstairs, up at the ceiling, scrutinising the cobwebs gathering in the corner like lace curtains. "I ... need to get back to work," I said, finally, "I'll try to be back by seven."

"Take your time. If you're late, we'll put Meghan to bed." Helen had a set of keys to my flat for those long days at work.

"Thanks again. You know, I really appreciate all this." I touched her forearm, gave it a gentle squeeze. Her skin was soft and warm and started a quickened pulsing in the hollow of my throat.

"Anytime," she purred.

I loped down the steps, taking them three at a time. As I hit the ground floor, Helen's teasing voice floated down from the top of the stairs, "I'm sure you'll find a way to repay me."

"That lousy, good-for-nothin' *cunt*!" Debbie Matthews screamed through her tears. "I hope he rots in hell, the cheatin' bastard!"

Holloway and I squirmed in our seats as the newly widowed woman continued her profanity-laced tirade against her dead husband.

"No good lout! I knew he been fuckin' that cheap Russian slag, I *knew* it! But I can't believe he'd fuck her on me birthday!" She took one last drag of her cigarette before stuffing the glowing butt into one of a half dozen empty lager cans littering the coffee table.

"Mrs. Matthews," I began when I thought it safe to speak up, "we are very sorry you had to find out this way, but if at all possible, we still have a few more questions." Beside me, Holloway had his trusty notepad open to a fresh page, pen poised at the ready.

Debbie sniffed, shifting her heavy frame on the battered armchair, making the seat shriek in protest of its load. Judging by Vincent Matthews's slight frame, and his penchant for leggy women, I hadn't expected him to have married someone who resembled the mother of the Pillsbury Dough Boy. I waited while she produced a wadded up bit of tissue from her cleavage. Mrs. Matthews dabbed at her face, blew her nose, and gave a nod. She seemed calmer, more composed, yet behind her grieving, red-rimmed eyes burnt the fiery wrath of a woman scorned.

I cleared my throat. "So until today, you weren't aware of Mr. Matthews's affair with Miss Petrov?"

"Well, I had me suspicions," Debbie said, her Cockney accent dropping the H's from her speech. "After all, the cow was Vince's type, ain't she? All blonde haired and busty like. But nah, I ain't one hundred percent till now."

"May I ask where you were between the hours of eleven p.m. and one a.m. on Saturday night?"

Debbie gawked. "What? Ya thinkin' I had somethin' to do with it? Ya askin' me for a ... an—whatchacallit—an alibi now, izzit?"

"Just procedural questions, ma'am," I said. "We have to ask this of everyone we interview."

Debbie leaned back in her chair. "I was here." She extracted another cigarette from the pack on the armrest and lit up. Holloway made a face as she blew smoke out through her nose. Fanning away the cloud of nicotine wafting in his direction, he covered his nose with his sleeve. "I was waitin' for Vince to come home. He promised to bring back some o' me favourite takeaway for me birthday."

Nice, I thought. *Ol' Vince sure knew how to treat a lady.*

"Were you with anyone else at the time?"

"Nah, just me and Ben." She nodded in the direction of the cot in the corner where her two-year-old son lay sleeping.

"Is there anyone who can corroborate your whereabouts?" My question was met by a blank stare. "Anyone who can confirm you were home as you said?"

"N-ah," she began, "Oh, hang on, ya can ask the guy what delivers them pizza I ordered after I got sick o' waitin'." She gestured towards a discarded pizza box on the floor, spotted with grease. The remains of a stale pepperoni slice peeked out from under the lid.

"One last question," I said as the woman tapped cigarette ash into a crumpled beer can. "Can you think of anyone who would wish Mr. Matthews harm?"

Debbie snorted. "Hell, *nobody* liked Vince! He wasn't too popular round here. But no one would try to kill him … would they?"

"That's what we're here to find out. Did you know if Mr. Matthews had any enemies?"

The woman screwed up her oily face. "Well, them Slaters next door are always complainin' about the leaves Vince throws into their garden. But the shit comes from *their* tree anyway. We just givin' 'em back! And Lee Chivers down the road, he's still sore about Vince cuppin' a feel o' his missus. Other than that … can't think of any off the top o' me head."

"That's fine." I stood. Holloway followed suit. "If you can think of anything else, please give us a call."

"I'll show ya out." Debbie groaned as she heaved herself out of her chair. "Me back, ya see." She waddled towards the front door, leaving a trail of cigarette smoke in her wake. "Keeps me from workin'."

We stepped outside the ground floor maisonette, grateful for the fresh, smoke-free, outdoor air. Separated by low fences, the handkerchief-sized front lawns of the Matthews' neighbours stretched off to either side of us. A tall tree, too big for the patch of grass it inhabited, grew in the garden to our right, its fallen leaves collecting in dune-like mounds along the base of the fence.

"Is that the Slater household?" I asked.

"Aye."

I inspected the leaves littering the ground. "This is an oak."

"Aye?" Debbie looked mystified by the statement, but I ignored her as I reached up and plucked a leaf off a low-lying branch, bagging the specimen for later.

Perhaps there was something more to the neighbourly war.

5

The rain cascaded down in sheets, pelting the hapless commuters as they streamed in and out of Stratford station at rush hour. Despite the deluge, travellers marched on, undaunted, umbrellas up, heads down, impersonal and hurried as ever, Londoners through and through. Some sought shelter from the downpour in the nearby bus stand, its roof design resembling a sea of brollies turned inside out by the brisk winds—a typical British summer.

Except that day, Jesus Christ stood before the entrance to the station, dressed all in white, a cooking pot in one hand, a wooden cross in the other.

"Do you hear that?" The Messiah banged his crucifix on the pot. "Do you all hear that? That, sinners, is the sound of *thunder!* That is the voice of *God! My Father!* And do you know what He is saying?"

He whirled on the nearest passerby, directing the question at her. She hopped out of the way, glaring daggers over her shoulder as she marched on.

"He is not happy, folks. Daddy isn't happy. Why? 'Cause people, all of you, are forsaking Him. You are forsaking *Me!* And when the Day of Judgment comes, it'll be *Our* turn to forsake *you!*"

Eyes downcast, commuters continued on their way, trying their level best to ignore him. Like Moses parting the Red Sea, the stream of people entering and exiting the station moved around him, giving him a wide berth, an island soapbox from which to preach.

"Look at this rain!" Jesus hollered, raising his arms skyward. "What if this is the start of a second flood? What would you all do then? I'll tell you what you'd do. You'd be *begging* for salvation! But why believe in God only when your mortal souls are at risk? Why do we only pray to Him when we *want* something, when He is here *all the time*? Why not pray to thank Him for the food on the table? For the company of loved ones? *For another day of life?*"

A handful of people waiting at the bus stop faced him. A couple of religious heads nodded in agreement.

"*'Verily I say unto you, this generation shall not pass away, till all be fulfilled. Heaven and earth shall pass away, but My words shall not pass away.'* Luke twenty-one: thirty-two. It tells us that the end of the world is coming, and it's going to happen *within our lifetime!*"

At the mention of the end, a few of his listeners drifted away, a shake of their head or a roll of their eyes, dismissing him as yet another rambling doomsayer.

"What if the world ends tomorrow? The second coming of Christ could happen at any time! Thus says Mark, *'But of that day and that hour knoweth no man, no, not the angels which are in heaven, neither the son, but the Father. Take ye heed, watch and pray: for ye know not what the time is.'* It might be tomorrow! It could be today!" He bashed his cross against the bottom of the pot again, harder and louder as if driving the point home.

"Be honest now. If Judgment Day happened right now, how many of you can stand tall before the Lord, head held high, confident you've done enough to earn eternal life? How many of you will be grovelling at His feet, begging for mercy, as He sentences you to eternal condemnation in the fiery pits of Hell?"

A low rumble of thunder sounded in the distance. Jesus hammered out a response with his makeshift drum kit as if conversing with Heaven itself.

"Repent now, mortals! Do not wait! The end will come when you least expect it! Repent now, before it's too late!"

By then, Jesus had lost what little audience he had. Heads bowed once more, the sinners returned to their daily tasks, tuning out the ranting of the Messiah, saving the fears for their eternal souls for another, more apocalyptic day.

Only one man continued to watch and listen from the shelter of the bus stand, his simmering anger growing with each blasphemous word the preacher uttered.

"After all," the Son of God shouted amid his own loud clanging, "I did *not* die on the cross for nothing!"

A false prophet, thought the preacher's lone observer as he blended into the crowd. *A pretender to the throne, shamelessly imitating the holy thunder.*

He must be punished.

6

She waited in the deserted playground just inside the school gates. Hugging her satchel to her chest, she kicked at the dirt at her feet as she swivelled on the swing.

A lost, lonely little girl.

Needles of guilt pricked at my heart as I drove up to the gates, honking once. Meghan's eyes brightened, but she had her pout ready. She jumped off the swing and ran to the car. As I opened the passenger door for her, I glimpsed movement from beyond the gates.

She wasn't alone after all.

I tried to make a quick getaway, but Meghan fumbled with her seatbelt. As I reached over to help her buckle up, a shadow descended over the car. With brown hands planted on ample hips, a floral dress hovered outside my window, occluding the view of the school playground.

Hesitantly, I rolled down the driver's window.

"Hello, Mrs. Abiola."

"Good evening, Mr. Lancer," she said in her lilting Nigerian accent, placing deliberate emphasis on the word *evening*. "Busy day at the office?"

"Always," I replied.

She turned her watch toward her face. "School let out over an hour ago."

I held up my hands. "My brother was supposed to pick Meghan up. I only just got a text saying he forgot."

"He *forgot?*" Mrs. Abiola frowned, her pursed lips resembling a wrinkled prune as she scrutinised me over her tortoiseshell glasses—an errant pupil, wilting under her intent gaze.

"I understand how difficult it must be to cope, Mr. Lancer," she said, "but please, do not be late again. The poor child deserves better."

I offered Mrs. Abiola a meek goodbye as I pulled away, fingers already dialling on my hands-free kit.

"Yo, bruv," Reggie's voice, tinny with static, filled the car.

"Where the f—" I started, but caught myself, "—heck are you? Meghan had been waiting over an hour!"

"Whoa, hey, chill, bro—"

"Don't 'chill bro' me. You weren't the one that had to answer to Dragon Lady. She looked about ready to call Social Services! What was so important that you couldn't pick your niece up from school?"

"I got it, bruv," he said. I could hear the proud grin in his voice. "I got a promotion."

Cause of death: drowning. No surprises there. No other signs of trauma, apart from the scratches on the dead man's face, scratches Pathology quickly attributed to the dead woman when they found traces of his skin under her fingernails. The puddle of stagnating urine in the dressing room had been matched to Vincent, whose trousers also tested positive for high levels of urea.

What could have made a grown man piss his pants? Despite the opinions I'd formed of Vince Matthews in the course of my investigation, it would still have taken a lot to make that weasel wet himself.

They were scared into entering the water. Herded into the tank like cattle to an abattoir.

But by what? A threatening weapon seemed the most logical answer, but that only brought me back to the same puzzle. If the killer had a gun, why not dispatch the victims by shooting them? Why risk a struggle or one of the victims making a run for it?

Not a crime of passion.

A cold and calculated murder.

A jealous rival magician who wanted him out of the picture? Someone aiming to achieve a form of poetic irony—magician killed by his own prop *a la* Harry Houdini? Vince Matthews, though, was a struggling magician at the best of times. He performed at kids' parties and fun fairs, his greatest achievement being a half-capacity Sunday matinee crowd at the Hackney Empire. He relied on his wife's disabilities allowance for financial support.

Were the murders symbolic, ritualistic in some way? Did the element of water play an integral part in the killings? What psychotic tendencies and delusions did the murderer have?

If only I could get inside his mind.

"If only I could get inside his mind." The uncanny echo of my thoughts snapped me from my trance. Meghan, leaning on the table with her head in her hands, regarded me over an empty plate. Reggie, his grin rivalling the Cheshire Cat's, gestured to the plate before me.

"Ya gonna eat that, bruv?"

Glancing down at my uneaten dinner, I realised I'd twisted half my spaghetti around my fork. Like a ball of yarn covered in tomato sauce, it sat in the middle of the plate, fork protruding from the centre at a lopsided angle.

"Oh, my days!" Reggie laughed, flicking his wrist to make snapping noises, a gesture he knew I hated. "You's off wit da fairies, bro!"

I sat back with a sigh and pushed my food towards Reggie, who shovelled the cold pasta onto his own plate.

"Cheers," he said. "I'm a growin' boy, ya know." I rolled my eyes. Reggie was ten years younger than I, but twenty years more immature. He had a lot of growing *up* to do.

"Daddy," Meghan said, "you promised not to think about work

at dinnertime."

"You tell her, Goggles!" Reggie said between mouthfuls of pasta. 'Goggles' was his pet name for Meghan. She didn't mind it. I hated it.

"Sorry, peaches." I gathered up the empty dishes as Meghan jumped up to help. "I was just daydreaming." Dirty crockery crusted with stale food clogged the kitchen sink. I sighed. Definitely time to do the dishes.

As I turned the tap on and rolled my sleeves up, Reggie squeezed past and dumped his dirty plate on top of the teetering stack, sending water splashing over the front of my shirt.

"A bit of help would be nice," I said.

"Leave 'em there. I'll do it tomorrow." He burped and left the cramped kitchen. A few seconds later, the television in the living room blared to life.

"Can I dry?" Meghan asked.

"Of course you can. Just grab that towel there." I gestured to the dishcloth beside her and watched her grope for it, eyes squinting. "To your left ... bit lower ... there." I handed her a clutch of cutlery covered in soap suds, and we worked in an efficient silence.

On the last cooking pot, Meghan said, "Daddy, you've been daydreaming much more since Mommy went away."

My hands stopped scrubbing. The water from the tap ran cold all of a sudden.

"You've also been working harder at work."

I turned to her, drying my hands on the front of my trousers.

"It ... helps take my mind off things," I said.

"Like what?"

"Like ..." My eyes dropped to the wet handprints staining my thighs. "Like Mommy."

Her eyes widened behind her goggle-like glasses. "Why do you want to stop thinking of Mommy?"

Because it hurts. Because every time I think about what happened, a part of me dies all over again.

"Do you miss her?" Meghan pressed. I nodded. "I miss her too. And when I miss her, I get sad. Is that why you don't want to think about Mommy?"

Since when did my daughter become a therapist?

I knelt down and pulled Meghan in for a hug, one that I needed more than she did. My arms swallowed her tiny frame, a precious little bundle clutched to my chest.

"I'm sorry, peaches." I nuzzled her button nose with my big, unwieldy one. "I'll try not to work too hard."

"Good. You scare me when you work too hard."

"Why?"

"Mommy worked too hard, and the bad people didn't like it."

I chewed my bottom lip, considered explaining the differences between my work and Angie's in Serious and Organised Crime, and how a gang-commissioned hit on an officer was a far less likely occupational hazard in Homicide.

Instead, I kissed her on the forehead.

"I promise I'll be careful," I said. "And, I'll try not to work too hard. Especially not this weekend. Now, can you remind me what you'll be on Sunday?"

"Eight," she said proudly.

"What say we celebrate your birthday a day early by going out for a meal tomorrow?"

Meghan beamed. "Can we have Greek?"

I raised an eyebrow. "Do you even know what Greek food is?"

"Of course I do! There's wine, and grapes, and olives, and am-bro-sia ... is that like custard?"

I laughed. "I don't know about ambrosia, honey. It's reserved for the gods. But I can arrange for the rest, and more." I mussed her hair. "So, it's a date?"

"Yes!" She jumped into my arms and planted a loud smack on my cheek.

"Now, can you tell me what time it is?"

She made a face as she glanced at the clock. "Bedtime."

"Will you be a good girl and go get ready?"

"Only if you'll read a story with me." She fluttered her lashes and tilted her head.

How could I say no to that face?

After sending Meghan off to bed with a reading of Hercules's quest for the golden apples of the Hesperides, which Meghan pronounced *He-spur-rides*, I gave Blaize a call. She picked up on the fourth ring before I could convince myself it was a bad idea.

"How you doing?" I asked. "Missed you today." I masked the concern in my voice with some forced humour; she'd had two sick days in a week.

"I'm good ... I'm fine." Her voice sounded strained. "Think I ... think I ate something that didn't agree with me. Besides, I wasn't *off* off. The Chief agreed to let me work from home today. I'm sitting under a mountain of paperwork as we speak."

"Any joy on the double drowning?"

"Nope, but I got the unenviable task of breaking the news to Olga Petrov's family via a long distance phone call."

I grimaced. "Lucky you. How did they take it?"

"Their only daughter had travelled halfway around the world in search of a better life, only to end up brutally murdered. How do you think they took it?" Blaize made an odd noise, like the sound of air hissing between clenched teeth.

"Sam, you sure you're alright?"

"I'll be fine," her tone came through a little too abrupt. We lapsed into our usual spell of silence.

"Listen, about what happened back in May—"

"What about it?" she asked too quickly, her tone prickling with defensiveness.

"I don't want it to make things weird between us."

The phone line hummed with silence. "It won't. I mean, it doesn't. Nothing's weird between us, is there?" she asked.

"Come on, Sam. We used to hang out all the time. When was the last time we went down to the pub together?"

"When was the last time you had *time*?"

Touché. I scoured my brains for a rebuttal but found none. Sam sighed down the phone.

"Listen, I'm good, okay? You and me, *we're* good. What happened in May? I've already forgotten about it. Maybe you should, too." Another sigh. "I'll see you on Monday, Lancer."

I ended the call and returned to the living room. Reggie lounged on the sofa, feet stretched out on the coffee table. As brothers, we couldn't have been more different in appearance and personality, a testament to having different fathers. Reggie stood perhaps six inches shorter than me but weighed in at least a stone heavier. His complexion was more espresso than mocha, and while I inherited my white father's more streamlined Roman nose, Reggie got our mother's traditional bulbous African one. He was the carefree, impulsive one—the free spirit. I had always been more reserved. We only had three features in common: a leaning towards wearing our hair in braids, our deep-set, chocolate brown eyes, and our shared childhood trauma.

Reggie chugged a can of beer as he hollered at the news. "That Olympic infrastructure is jokes, man. They ain't never gonna get everything ready in time!"

I rolled my eyes. Twenty-two years old and still slanging like a pubescent street urchin.

"Oh, hey, check and see if there's anything in the mail for me today," he said, his attention riveted to the screen.

I glanced at the pile of letters on the side table beside the front door, no more than eight feet away from him, and gave him a quizzical look. "And you can't do that because …?"

Reggie affected an air of bone-deep fatigue. "Long day at work, man. Been on my feet all day. They're killing me."

"Oh, you poor thing." I retrieved the letters, joined him on the couch, and began sifting through the pile of advertising leaflets, junk mail, and utility bills.

"Here's one for you." I handed him a white envelope. He pocketed it straight away.

I arched my eyebrow. "You not gonna open it?"

"Hmm? Oh, I'll read it later. Kinda know what it is anyway."

I tossed the spam and leaflets into the wastebasket beside me. "Then why get me to fetch it for you now?"

"I like to keep it close to me, innit. Private and confidential and all."

"Private and confidential?" I nudged him with my elbow. "Is it from someone special?"

Reggie grinned, tapping the side of his nose. "Secret admirer."

"I see. Your Penthouse subscription is up, eh?" I received a lazy kick for my witticism.

"You're one to talk," he said. "You's the one gettin' it on with that Jaimeson lady upstairs."

"I am not." I laughed at the absurdity of the accusation.

"Maybe not yet, but it'll be a matter of time, bruv. I seen the way she ogles you. That lady's a cougar."

"Cougar? Reg, we're about the same age."

"Nah man, she's got at least a couple years on ya. You's her toy boy!" He took another swig of his beer. "Mind you, for her age she's pretty hot tottie. Mm, that woman's one fine MILF."

"Shut up." My rebuttal came half-hearted at best. Despite Reggie's rather unsophisticated vocabulary, I couldn't refute his comments. Helen had a timeless beauty, like Audrey Hepburn or Catherine Zeta Jones. She frequently received catcalls from some of the more charming young lads in our neighbourhood, and her full figure remained the envy of stick thin girls half her age. Helen Jaimeson was sexy, recently single—and seeking.

I wasn't sure if I was ready to be sought after.

"Oh, congratulations on your promotion, by the way," I said, moving on. "So, what do you do now? Supervise while others push trolleys?"

"Nah, man. I'm in charge of stocks."

"Shelf stacking, then." Despite my jibe, I was mildly impressed. Reggie had never lasted more than a couple of months in all his previous employments. His reasons for dismissal had ranged from falling asleep on the job and persistent tardiness, to being rude to clients, and in the case of one particularly short-lived appointment at the local cinema, consuming more popcorn than he sold. His tendency to start fights and to help himself to "gratuity" from the till did not help, either.

Four months without a disciplinary was a new record.

Perhaps my younger brother had finally matured.

Reggie belched, crumpled the beer can in his meaty fist, and dropped it onto the floor.

Then again, probably not.

7

"O Thou who camest from above
The fire celestial to impart,
Kindle a flame of sacred love
On the mean altar of my heart."

The imposter sang as he strolled through the darkened courtyard in front of the block of flats, his voice loud and clear as if he intended on projecting his praise to the heavens.

"There let it for thy glory burn
With inextinguishable blaze,
And trembling to its source return
In humble prayer and fervent praise."

He walked past a group of four young men, hoods pulled over their baseball caps, jeans hanging round their knees.

"God bless you, my sons!" he said to them. The youths eyed him with predatory disdain. One whistled a cuckoo's call, eliciting snickers from the rest, but the impostor sang on, undaunted.

"Jesus, confirm my heart's desire
To work and speak and think for thee;
Still let me guard the holy fire
And still stir up the gift in me."

As the impostor entered a dingy stairwell, the Oracle followed from a safe distance. He reached the group of boys, but unlike the impostor, the Oracle did not acknowledge the ruffians, instead strode brashly past them, unconcerned about being seen.

They do not yet realise who I am. They are sheep who have lost their way, sinners who have forgotten about our Lord.

The Oracle's task did not involve punishing the lost. It involved punishing the impostor—the false shepherd threatening to lead them further astray.

The lost might not have remembered His name, but by the time the Oracle finished, he would *make* them remember.

His quarry's song reverberated down the stairwell, making it easy for the Oracle to follow all the way to the lair on the fourth floor. The light above number thirty-seven was out, just like when the Oracle last visited. He waited in the shadows, his ear pressed against the thin wood of the door. From inside came the sound of the impostor humming and the slosh of running water. A crackling static followed by a tinny tune played from an old radio.

He easily overcame the flimsy lock. Stepping into the lair of the impostor, the Oracle closed the door behind him. Organ music and a harmony of choristers emanated from the old-fashioned radio on a table within the narrow corridor while the nearest door to his right stood ajar. From within came the sound of sloshing water and the song of the pretender:

"Still let me prove thy perfect will, my acts of faith and love repeat, till death thy endless mercies seal—"

"—and make the sacrifice complete," the Oracle finished for the impostor as he swung the bathroom door open. The false shepherd's eyes widened only briefly as the Oracle raised his arms skyward, and the shock of intrusion became full-blown horror.

"He shall smite all who oppose Him," the Oracle said.

And he smote him.

Before he left, the Oracle made sure to replace the false king's crown.

Let this serve as a warning to anyone who dare imitate the Thunder God.

8

I eyed Meghan's dress, something Angie had made her for Halloween last year. A garish explosion of lace and sequins, the pink get-up resembled a cross between a toga and a fairy princess gown.

"You know, peaches, when I said you could wear anything you wanted ..."

She jumped off her chair and did a little catwalk twirl. "We're at a Greek restaurant, aren't we? Don't you say, 'When in Rome, wear what the Romans wear'?"

Reggie and I laughed as the drinks arrived—beer for us, an apple juice for Meghan. I sipped the complimentary ouzo. The aniseed liquor warmed my throat, settling in my chest in the form of a comforting glow.

Reggie made a face. "Tastes like liquorice," he said, sticking out his tongue. "I hate liquorice." He pointed to the lunchbox Meghan carried, a pastel Dora the Explorer number slung across her shoulder in place of a handbag. "What's that?"

"This is my Pandora's Box." She held up the lunchbox so we could read the note written in multi-colour crayon and taped to the front: DO NOT OPEN.

"Ooh ..." I pretended to glance left and right. "What's inside? Can I see?" My voice came out a conspiratorial whisper.

She shook her head, making her curls bob. "I'm not allowed to open it. If I do, all sorts of bad things will come out."

"Well," I smiled as I produced the wrapped present from behind my back, "this is one box you *are* allowed to open."

With twinkling eyes and a massive grin, Meghan tore apart the gift wrap, revealing a plastic DVD case. She squinted through her magnifiers.

"*Mulan*? Oh, Daddy, thank you!" She squealed, throwing her arms around my neck. "I *love* it! I'm gonna watch it tonight! Will you watch it with me?"

I started to nod, but Reggie interrupted us by being Reggie. "I don't know about you, but I'm starving! Can we order now, please?" He picked up his menu.

Meghan tugged my sleeve. "Daddy," she said, her voice small. "I can't read the words. Do they have a Braille menu?"

I shook my head. "You don't need one."

"But I can't read this one."

"Most of the names aren't even in English. I'll read them out to you."

"But I want to read by myself."

I sighed, not wanting to draw further attention to Meghan's condition. We were supposed to be a normal family, out for a normal meal, celebrating the birthday of a *normal* child.

Reggie jumped up. "I need a piss." To my consternation, he said it loud enough for the neighbouring tables to turn our way. "I'll send the waiter over with a Braille menu for Goggles. Can you get me the souvlaki for starters and the swordfish for mains?" He gave me a discreet wink as he passed, the signal he was off to arrange the entrance of the birthday cake and the grand unveiling of Meghan's *main* present.

I returned to contemplating my menu.

"I wish Mommy was here." Meghan slouched in her seat, fingering the hem of her dress. "She made this for me, you know."

"I remember," I said. "And I wish she was here, too."

"Do you think maybe she is?" Meghan asked. "As an angel?"

I wasn't prepared to debate the existence of heavenly winged beings or to discuss the loss of my religious faith with my daughter.

"Mommy always said she'd love us forever."

"And I'm sure she does," I said.

Reggie returned to the table, a satisfied smirk on his face. He handed Meghan a menu in large print and flashed me the okay symbol.

I had never been more grateful for his intrusion.

A few minutes later, the waiter approached our table. "Are we ready to order?"

Meghan was reciting her choices when an urgent buzzing sensation ran up my leg. I retrieved the phone from my jeans pocket and glanced at the caller ID: *TOM H*

Christ, please, not now.

"Dude," Reggie mumbled, shaking his head. "Just leave it."

The phone rang a moment longer.

Does he have news of the case? Have we had a breakthrough? It must be important, for him to be calling at this time.

I gave in to the temptation. "I'm sorry, this is important." *More important than your daughter's birthday?* I pushed away the thought as I pressed the 'Accept call' button. "Lancer."

"Kurt," Holloway's voice quivered with excitement. "We got another body."

I took some details down and ended the call with a resigned, "I'm on my way." As I lifted the napkin off my lap, Meghan's tentative chewing of her bottom lip morphed into a full-blown pout. Avoiding her scowl, I stared instead at her makeshift Pandora's Box on the table. I wondered if she'd opened that forbidden chest, releasing evil, despair and suffering into my world.

It certainly felt like she had.

I shouldered my way through the crowds camped on the narrow landing of the block of flats and ducked underneath the crime scene tape into flat thirty-seven. Inside, paramedics, forensic technicians and uniformed officers bustled about in the cramped space, crawling over each other like bees in a hive. The focus of the drone of activity appeared to be the bathroom where I found Blaize and Holloway bent over a grimy bathtub complete with naked body.

"Whoa," I murmured as I pushed past a couple of EMTs. Rigor mortis had set in, locking the man's limbs in place, legs splayed, one foot hanging outside the tub. His head lolled lifelessly to one side, long hair and beard frizzed. A plastic circlet of thorns perched atop his crown at a skewed angle, and the pungent odour of singed hair lingered in the air. Pink and white blisters dotted the man's wrinkled, ivory-pale skin like some macabre version of chicken pox. A U-shaped, raspberry coloured burn adorned his collarbone, an imprint left behind by the heavy gold chain that still dangled from his neck. With morbid interest, I noticed that the large crucifix the victim wore had also been branded onto his skin, leaving a sign of the cross over his heart.

"Nearer my God to Thee, eh?" Blaize said, straightening and stepping away. Her complexion seemed a bit drawn, her features slightly pinched, but it was good to see her on her feet and on the job.

Pulling on a pair of gloves, I picked up a cigarette stub from the overflowing ashtray beside the tub. I brought the joint to my nose and sniffed.

"That doesn't smell like regular tobacco." Blaize held up a clear evidence bag. I dropped in the remains of the joint.

"I suppose getting high brings our DOA closer to God," I said.

"Sadly, 'thou shalt not smoke weed' is not one of the Ten Commandments." She sealed the bag for Forensics. As she moved away from the tub, I spotted a splash of emerald green in the water, floating just between the victim's legs.

Another oak leaf.

Damn. A signature could only mean one thing.

Serial killer.

"Neighbours called it in," Holloway said, his gaze landing everywhere but on the body. "Heard him screaming at around seven p.m. They found him in the bath with this." He tapped his pen on the chipped porcelain sink. It held a waterlogged radio, one of those older models, with wood panelling and fiddly dials. The black rubber insulation on its cable had been cut away, leaving the underlying copper wires exposed.

"Who disconnected it?" I asked.

"One of the neighbours turned off the mains to the entire flat."

I glanced down again at the victim, his clouded brown eyes wide open and fixed on the ceiling as if he'd been beseeching some divine being above in the final seconds of his life, asking—*demanding*—"*Why?*"

Victims of electrocution were never a pretty sight, but the cases I'd seen had always been *accidents*. To think someone would deliberately fry another human being befuddled me.

What's wrong with guns and knives?

We descended the dingy stairwell a few hours later, emerging onto a concrete landing that smelt of stale urine. I checked my watch and sighed.

Nearly midnight.

Meghan will never forgive me.

We crossed the courtyard, a small square of cement serving as communal ground for the blocks of flats hemming it in on all sides. A group of hoodies lounged round a low wall, all low-slung jeans, chunky trainers and gangsta attitude. They shamelessly ogled Blaize as we approached and made a show of glaring at the male intruders to their 'hood until I flashed my badge.

"We'd like to ask you some questions about what happened here."

Three of the four—all boys who couldn't have been any older than twenty—turned away. In their eyes, we would have ceased to exist. Folks round those parts didn't like talking to the Old Bill. The fourth thug, an older man who no doubt fancied himself the leader of the little gang, sneered, revealing a row of gold teeth gleaming in the twilight.

"Come now." Blaize seemed unperturbed by their open leering, although knowing her, she had to be dying to wipe the lascivious grins off their smug faces. "You look like the kind of fellas with a finger on the pulse. You must have heard something."

Golden Jaws smirked. "Ol' Kooky Christ in block D got done in, innit. Zapped by his own ghetto blaster."

So flattery works with these guys.

"Actually," Holloway butted in, "it wasn't a ghetto blaster *per se*, but a vintage Zenith model 319, made circa—"

I cut Holloway off with a wave of my hand. "That's right," I said. "Could you tell me where you guys were when it happened?"

One of the kids, a skinny hoodlum wearing a baggy, red Nike hoodie emblazoned with an ostentatious gold swoosh, drew his lips back in a snarl, hackles raised. "What is this, man?" He spat at my feet. "You thinking we iced the mothafucka? You think we'd waste our time on bible gimps like him?"

I raised both palms up. "Chill, bro. We just want to know if you saw anything."

Golden Jaws blinked, turning from me to Holloway to Blaize—mainly to Blaize. He rubbed the stubble on his chin as if deciding just how much to tell us. Police or not, there remained some element of trust between black brothers. Years spent in Narcotics undercover and having a gangster-wannabe for a brother had taught me more than I cared to learn about his kind. If I wanted to get anywhere with them—or to get away from them alive—I had to appease their alpha male mentality.

Sure enough, when he spoke again, Golden Jaws seemed visibly calmer. "For all we know, he could've wasted himself in some kinda hallelujah ritual shit. Man was like, one apostle short of an even dozen, ya know."

I had to grin at the colourful description. "So, did you notice any suspicious activity around here last night? Anything out of the ordinary?"

Golden Jaws hemmed and hawed as he scratched the fuzz on his chin. "I don't recall, officer." His voice dripped with sarcasm. "What did you mean by 'suspicious'? Gangs of hoodies hanging 'bout in the dark? Chavs with staffies out on a walk? Dodgy dealings on dark street corners? Shit like this ain't nothin' out of the ordinary round these parts." His compatriots sniggered.

"Any strangers, people you've never seen before, wandering the area?" Blaize asked.

"There was one man," Red Nike piped up, but his pack leader silenced him with a scowl.

"Could you describe him?" Blaize said.

"Yeah, he was a black shadow." Golden Jaws spoke for the group once more. "Gets dark here at night, and as you can see, babe, them streetlamps don't work."

"Tall? Short?" I prompted. "Fat? Skinny?"

The gang appeared to grow tired of our presence. "He was a dark, shapeless blob," Golden Jaw's tone grew shorter and sharper by the second. "You know what? Could've even been a woman. There, helps narrow things down, don't it?"

"Let's go," Holloway hissed.

We'd gotten all we could from the punks; they wouldn't be any further help. Colluding with a bobby amounted to fraternising with the enemy. No doubt the gang was packing some contraband—the cloying scent of marijuana smoke permeated their clothing—and the proximity of the cops had to unnerve them.

Did everyone on this blasted estate smoke that shit?

I handed them my business card. "Call me if you remember anything." As I turned to leave, Golden Jaws hacked a gob full of phlegm onto the card before tossing it over his shoulder.

"Well, that was a waste of time," Holloway said. "I'm surprised we got as much out of them as we did."

"He called me 'babe'. Did you hear that?" Blaize ranted. "As if all the mental undressing wasn't bad enough. I wanted to ram those gold teeth so far down his throat he'd have to start mining for 'em down under."

I chuckled, hunting in my pockets for my car keys. My hands closed around an envelope.

Goddamnit.

Meghan's big surprise. I'd forgotten all about it.

Holloway stretched his arms. "At least the weekend is still young ... well, kinda ..." He yawned. "You have any plans?"

"Yes," I told him, slapping my forehead with the envelope.

I've got a lot of grovelling to do.

9

> *"Most glorious of the immortals,*
> *Invoked by many names, ever all-powerful,*
> *The First Cause of Nature, who rules all things with Law,*
> *Hail!"*

The Oracle reverently placed the glowing joss sticks into a bronze urn atop the stone altar. Wispy trails of white smoke danced before him, enveloping him in a warm embrace, the sweet, intoxicating scent of the burning incense enfolding his mind in a dreamy haze.

> *"It is right for mortals to call upon you,*
> *Since from you, we have our being,*
> *we whose lot it is to be God's image,*
> *We alone of all mortal creatures that live*
> *and move upon the earth.*
> *Accordingly, I will praise you with my hymn*
> *and ever sing of your might.*
> *The whole universe, spinning around the earth,*
> *Goes wherever you lead it and is willingly guided by you."*

The Oracle decanted some red wine from an earthenware jug into a bowl and offered the libations to his Lord.

> *"Giver of all, shrouded in dark clouds*

and holding the vivid bright lightning,
Rescue men from painful ignorance.
Scatter that ignorance far from their hearts,
and deign to rule all things in justice
So that, honoured in this way,
we may render honour to you in return,
And sing your deeds unceasingly, as befits mortals;
For there is no greater glory for men or for gods
Than to justly praise the universal Word of Reason."

With eyes shut, he put the bowl to his lips and drank, the clear claret coating his tongue like velvet before slipping down his throat. The wine was light, fruity with a slight tangy note, and absolutely delicious.

A fitting reward for a task well done.

He rose from his kneeling position and entered the ablution chamber. Steam hung in the air like strips of gauze, enveloping his skin in a cool coat of moisture. He stripped off his clothes and admired his naked form in the flickering candlelight. Power coursed through him with every beat of his heart.

He climbed into the scalding tub, the hot water blushing his skin. Leaning back, he submerged his head, allowing the water to burn the tender flesh on his face. He resurfaced and picked up the sponge in the soap dish. Not a bath sponge but one of those green scouring pads used for cleaning pots and pans.

"*O great many-faced one, I prepare for you my humble body . . .*"

With long, firm strokes, he scrubbed himself with the abrasive pad.

"*See how I cleanse myself of my mortal sins . . .*"

He rubbed harder, faster, up and down his arms, legs, chest, even his face, leaving his skin an angry red-raw.

"*See me strip the layers of dirt and grime from my flesh as well as from my soul. See me purge myself of human desires, such that my only need is to serve Thee . . .*"

The Oracle relished the hot stinging of his inflamed skin as he stepped out of the bath. The chilling draught rapidly turned the hot film of water on his skin into an icy glacier sheet, but he ignored it as he stood in the centre of the room, dripping wet, a puddle forming at his feet.

"Behold, O God, my purified form, an empty vessel I offer up to Thee. Fill me with Thy blessing. Fill me with Thy bidding, such that I may fulfil Your wishes!"

An intense wave of euphoria washed over him, followed by an urgent ringing in his ears. His vision swam and danced before him, and his breathing grew shallow.

It is time.

The Oracle laid his wet body down onto the cold tiles. His eyes glazed over as he stared up at the ceiling.

"Enter me, my master."

He shut his eyes and communed with God.

10

I woke up to find Meghan watching *Mulan*. Alone.

"Morning, peaches."

Silence. Her eyes flickered at the sound of my voice, but she kept them fixed on the television screen.

"You had breakfast?" I poured myself a glass of juice and plopped down beside her on the sofa. She hugged the cushion tighter to her chest but refused to look at me.

"Happy birthday."

Her mouth remained drawn in a tight, determined line.

I picked up the card propped up on the coffee table. Pink foam bunnies with cotton ball tails frolicked around a speech bubble, wishing the recipient a "Hoppy Birthday."

"Cute." I opened the card and read the greeting inside. "From Mrs. Jaimeson. One of her homemade masterpieces. She must remember you like bunnies. Did you tell her?" I waited for an answer that never came. "Remember to thank her when you see her, okay?"

I deserved the frigid treatment. What kind of father would run off during his daughter's birthday dinner?

"Listen, Peaches, I'm really sorry about last night, but there was a major development in the case I'm working on." *'Major development'?* Who did I think I was addressing, a press conference? In response to my lame excuse, Meghan rolled her eyes but said nothing.

Time for plan B.

I pulled out the cream coloured envelope I'd been hiding behind my back, placed it on the coffee table, and slid it towards her. She tried to ignore me, but kept casting furtive glimpses at the envelope. Like a seasoned angler, I sat back and waited for her to take the bait. Sure, bribery might be an underhanded means of begging forgiveness, but I couldn't make things up to her without first getting her to talk to me again.

A few moments later, she pushed 'Pause' on the remote. A talking cartoon dragon that sounded a lot like Eddie Murphy stopped in mid-rant. She shot me a scowl that said, *'Don't think you're forgiven yet,'* and picked up the envelope, tearing it open. A stack of tickets slipped out. Tilting her head, Meghan focused on them, turning them and bringing them closer, mouthing words but saying nothing. Her mouth fell open. "We're going to the *Olympics?*" All traces of hostility evaporated.

I nodded. "We've got tickets to the Opening Ceremony and the gymnastics finals."

"That's my *favourite* event! Thank you, Daddy!" She nuzzled her face into my chest as short arms tried to encircle my waist. We sat in silence while I savoured the moment, stroking her downy hair, smelling the fruity fragrance of her shampoo. Holding her so close, I could feel the reassuring beat of her heart.

Moments like that had grown increasingly rare.

"I know this doesn't make up for last night," I said, "but I hope it's a start."

She jutted her dimpled chin at me. "It's a good start."

"You must try to understand. Daddy's got a pretty tough case at work right now."

"What's it about?" she asked.

"Well, there's a very bad man out there …"

Meghan rolled her eyes. "Dad, I'm eight. You're a homicide detective, and I know what 'homicide' means. You can tell me you're trying to catch a murderer."

I laughed, feeling more than a little silly. "I suppose."

"It's okay, I understand." She patted me on the knee. "Sometimes you have to work really hard to catch the bad guys." She turned back to the TV. "Sometimes you work too hard, and I miss you." Her voice dropped.

Ouch. Eight years old and a master of the guilt trip. I deserved that, too.

I wrapped my arms around Meghan and gave her a squeeze. "I will try *really* hard to be around more."

Another spell of silence followed as we sat staring at the frozen Eddie Murphy dragon on screen.

"Daddy, will you promise to come to the Olympics with me?"

"What? Of course I'm coming! It's my idea, isn't it?"

"But what if you get an emergency at work?"

I felt like a suspect being cross-examined. "Peaches, sweetheart, I'm taking the day off. *Nothing* is going to keep me from attending the Opening with my favourite girl." I gave her a reassuring hug.

"Pinky promise?" Meghan raised her hand, little finger extended.

I intertwined my little finger with hers. "*And* cross my heart. Now, how about we go for a walk in the park and see if we can find the ice cream van?"

"Okay." Meghan reached for the remote. "But let's finish watching the movie first."

I stared at the computer screen until my eyes glazed over, the pleasant afternoon at the park with Meghan already a distant memory.

A self-absorbed, adulterous stage illusionist and his equally horny Russian assistant. An eccentric street preacher who dresses up as the Saviour.

What could be the connection between these people? How were they chosen? Did the victims know their killer? Were the different killing methods significant in any way?

So many questions…

Forensics found nothing of use in the preacher's spartan flat. Interviews with neighbours turned up nothing. He was a loner, a loony religious fanatic but otherwise harmless. People generally left him alone or avoided him altogether.

No new leads meant the most frustrating time of any investigation. I called it TTT, thumb twiddling time, when an investigator feels most impotent. There were only two ways to progress the case from TTT. The first being if someone came forward with new information. The second was unthinkable.

Waiting for the killer to strike again.

Would an oak leaf be left at the next crime scene? It appeared to be the killer's calling card, but what did it signify?

I typed '*oak leaf*' and '*murder*' into Google. The search engine returned a list of websites, half of them advertising the services of tree surgeons.

Both murders had occurred in water. What role did water have to play?

I rose from the sofa and arched my back. My vertebrae clicked into place with a satisfying *crack*. I padded into the kitchen in my socks, got a can of Coke from the fridge, and cast a quick glimpse at the clock.

Maybe I can do a couple more hours before turning in.

The front door slammed. I cringed. *Then again, maybe not.*

Reggie swaggered into the kitchen with a shopping bag. "Wassup, bro?" He held up a fist, which I half-heartedly knuckle bumped.

"Off work early tonight?" I asked.

"Say what? Oh … yeah."

Either that or he's skiving. I reached up and yanked Reggie's hood off his head as he squeezed past. "Take that off. It's not raining in here." As he bent over the kitchen counter to unpack his groceries, I averted my gaze from his exposed underwear hanging out the top of his baggy jeans.

Reggie opened a large pack of cheesy Doritos and a bottle of Bud. He offered both to me. I shook my head 'no'. Everything on his shopping list either comprised some degree of alcohol or was laden with salt and saturated fat. Munching, he followed me into the living room and plonked down onto the sofa beside me. He picked up the set of Olympic passes from the coffee table.

"Gymnastics?" he said through a mouthful of crisps. "Fuckin' gymnastics? Of all the sports. Boxing, football, running ... you picked *gymnastics*? That's gay, boy!"

"Meg likes it. You don't have to come."

"S'pose I could tout my ticket, make some money." He snorted and tossed the tickets back, picking up the *Mulan* DVD case. "This any good?"

"Uh huh ..." I mumbled, eyes on my laptop screen, intent on keeping my brother from distracting me.

"Whoa, a cartoon with sick kung fu shit! Hey, is it anything like what you do?"

"Nah," I said, trying to think over his yammering. *Oak leaf ... magician ... drowning ... preacher ... electrocution ...* There had to be some sort of connection I wasn't seeing.

Reggie tipped the last of the Doritos into his mouth and crumpled up the bag. "You haven't been to trainin' in a while. Ya must be gettin' rusty. Bet I can beat ya now!"

"Mmm hmm ..."

He jumped up, head bobbing like a punch-drunk boxer. "C'mon, show me some of your Bruce Lee moves!"

"Not now, Reg, I'm bus—*ow!*" I recoiled as Reggie jabbed me in the shoulder—hard.

"C'mon, c'mon!" Reggie egged. "Show me what ya got."

I leapt up from the sofa and attempted a reluctant palm strike to Reggie's chest, but he slapped my hand aside.

"That all ya got? Six years of Wing Kun Do and ya can't even touch me?"

"It's called Wing Chun." I studied Reggie's movements as he

hopped back and forth like some gigantic, rabid rabbit. I concentrated on the rhythm—or lack thereof—in Reggie's shoulders.

The slightest twitch in his left shoulder telegraphed the oncoming punch.

I side-stepped the anticipated fist and countered by grabbing his wrist and twisting it behind him in a lock.

"Oi, let go of me, man!" The harder Reggie struggled, the more he painfully contorted his own shoulder.

"Say uncle first!" With my free hand, I poked him in the ribs, eliciting a rather un-gangsta-like squeal. "Jesus, will you keep it down?" I laughed. "Meg's sleeping!"

"Okay, okay! Uncle, uncle! You win!" Reggie relented, tapping the coffee table in submission. His trousers slipped lower, revealing even more underwear and a hint of arse crack. Something peeked out from one of his back pockets. Frowning, I fished out the brand new, latest-model iPhone and let go of his arm.

"What's this?" I said.

Still panting from our play fight, Reggie acted all nonchalant. "My phone, innit."

"Where'd you get it?"

"Jeez, man, it fell from the sky! Where'd ya think?"

I gritted my teeth. *Not again.* I thought Reggie had turned the corner.

"Don't fuck with me, Reggie. *Where* did you get it?"

"I bought it," he said. "It ain't stolen, I swear! I can even find the receipt to prove it."

"How did you afford this?"

Reggie raised both arms. "Fuck this, man, why can't you trust me? I saved up for it. Been savin' for time now. And it came cheaper with my contract upgrade."

I frowned, trying to decide if Reggie told the truth. My eyes held his as I tried to look into his soul.

Dude, he's your brother.

I ended the stare-off with a weary sigh and grudgingly returned the phone. What else could I do? Launch a full-scale criminal investigation over a single suspicious item? Render the man even more unemployable by padding out his criminal records? He already had a juvenile rap sheet that read like a "how to" manual on becoming the model criminal.

Reggie pocketed the offending phone. "I'll leave the receipt on the fridge tomorrow," he said. I made a move to wave the offer away, but he shook his head. "I have to, bro. If that's what it takes to get you to trust me."

Good God, what is this? Make Kurt feel guilty day? I collapsed onto the sofa with a groan.

"I'm through with petty crime, man," Reggie said. "Swear on my life. I ain't stealin' no more."

I glanced up at my brother. His eyes pleaded with me to believe him, to *trust* him, and I wanted to.

After all we'd been through together, I *needed* to. I was ten when our mother died. Reggie had only been a few months old. Mom had just left Reggie's father—her latest in a string of failed relationships. She was cursed that way, always falling for Mr. Wrong, starting with my father, a married English businessman who returned from his trip to Nigeria with Mom as a souvenir. He kept her as a mistress until my conception scared him off. Reggie's father wasn't much different except she decided to leave him after one drunken beating too many whilst pregnant with Reggie.

I recalled staying up late that night, waiting for Mom to return from work. I remember having my baby brother in my arms and singing *Itsy Bitsy Spider* while walking my fingers up his neck, making him squirm and squeal in delight.

Funny how you remember the little details.

The doorbell had buzzed. A couple of sombre-looking police officers greeted me with a sympathetic nod. I was old enough to know that when the Old Bill visited late at night, they never came with good news.

A mugging gone wrong, the police concluded. A bunch of

stoned youths with a knife, looking for an easy target. They panicked when Mom shouted for help.

The culprits were never caught.

Reggie and I moved from one foster home to the next, in constant fear of being separated. When I got too old for the system, I fought to gain custody of my little brother. Having lost both parents, I had vowed to cling to what family I had left, and I became Reggie's self-appointed guardian.

The protective mother hen in me had resurfaced.

"I trust you," I finally said. "And I'm very proud of you. I'm sorry I jumped to conclusions."

Reggie kept up the hurt puppy-dog look a little longer. "Say you're sorry for acting like a world-class arsehole."

I laughed. "I'm sorry I acted like an A-hole." I patted him on the shoulder, a gesture of truce. "You're old enough now to make your own decisions. I just have to get used to that."

Reggie smiled his lopsided grin. "Don't forget, big bro, the bad guys you huntin' are out in the streets, not in your own home."

Chief Sutherland smacked the tabloid onto the conference table and jabbed a clawed finger at the main headline.

"Read it," she said.

I scanned the title screaming at me in bold black letters: *OAKSECUTIONER STUMPS POLICE*. In smaller text, the subtitle read: *Oak leaf killer taunts Met by leaving signature*.

"*Oak*secutioner?" Holloway snorted. "*Stump?* Our friends at the Sun are really piling on the cheese."

Sutherland slammed her palm into the middle of the newspaper, making clear her lack of amusement. Even Blaize winced. "What I want to know is," the Chief growled, "how the hell did the press get wind of the oak leaf?"

Uneasy shrugs rippled around the table like a disjointed Mexican wave. Gazes shifted left and right as if playing eyeball tennis would expose the culprit responsible for the leak. Withholding that bit of information had been vital to our investigation by screening out the hordes of attention seekers and loonies claiming to be the killer.

It had also served to make the two murders appear unrelated.

I caught Blaize's gaze. She rolled her eyes, rubbed her thumb against the tips of her index and middle fingers. Money. Almost always the main reason a fellow cop would disclose critical information to the press.

"I've got the Mayor on my arse now," Sutherland continued her rant. "Serial killers are bad publicity for the Olympics, and he wants this bastard caught *now*." She hunched over the congregation, hands planted on the table, looking way bigger than her five foot five. "What I need now is *good* news. Sykes!" She directed her taloned finger at a young, brash Detective Constable. "Any news from Forensics about the DNA typing of the oak leaves?"

"Both leaves from the crime scenes came from the same tree." He stood with shoulders back, chest high, and nose in the air like a royal addressing his subjects. "However, we have yet to find this mystery tree. The oak leaf from the Slaters' garden—that's Vince Matthews's neighbours—aren't a match. So I'm afraid we may have to discount neighbourly rows as a motive."

Sutherland emitted a growl so vicious it could have come from Cerberus, the three-headed hound of Hades. "I said I wanted *good* news!" She thumped another fist on the conference table. Chairs inched backwards in response. Sykes sat back down, cowed. The Chief took a deep breath and ran both hands through her viper's nest. Snake-like curls stuck out from the sides of her head. Her flushed face, scowling eyes and general bad mood completed the demonic look. Sutherland's black hair seemed more shot through with silver than before, and I wondered if it was my imagination, or if the case had really been getting to her.

"We need a new lead," she said finally. "Some new development. *Anything.*" Her gorgon's stare was met by a room full of silent, petrified statues.

Holloway cleared his throat and raised a tentative hand—a schoolboy before the principal, owning up to a misdemeanour. "Um, this may be just another dead end, but I managed to find a link between our two cases. It's tenuous, to say the least, however—"

"Holloway," the Chief snarled, her message clear: *get to the point.* I could swear Holloway gulped.

"Um, it appears Olga Petrov was a religious woman."

"Religious? You mean she humped the preacher man, too?" Sykes cackled. The Chief silenced him with a glare steeped in venom.

"The link is even more obscure th-th-than that." Holloway pushed his glasses up his nose. "Olga attended a church in the East End, and Nicholas Kemp—Mr. Manic Street Preacher—used to crash Sunday service there."

"Crash Sunday service?" someone asked.

"He used to turn up in full Jesus Christ mode and try to take over the sermons. I guess you might say that he was ... one apostle short of an even dozen." Holloway winked at me. Scattered chuckles sprinkled the room, but Chief Sutherland's expression remained stormy.

"And you think someone at the church would know both vics?" she asked.

"Possibly the minister," Holloway said. "It's not a lot to go on, but perhaps it's a start?"

Chief Sutherland bit at her cheek, reminding me of a cow chewing cud. "Anyone else have any bright ideas?"

The room hummed with an oppressive silence.

"In that case, it's time to go to church."

11

"Bless me Father, for I have sinned." The woman's voice quivered above a whisper, the repentant squeak of a frightened mouse. "It has been ... three years since my last confession."

And nearly a year since I last attended church.

She hesitated, her shoulders stooped, weighed down by the guilt of her admission.

Through the confessional screen, the shadow of the priest leaned closer. "John chapter one says: 'If we confess our sins, He is faithful and just to forgive us our sins, and to cleanse us from all unrighteousness.'" His voice, like gentle waves lapping the shore, encouraged her to reveal her dark secret.

She took a breath. "My husband, he ... he had an affair, three years ago. With a temp at his office. Last month, she turned up on our doorstep with a two-year-old kid. Said it's his. She wanted nothing to do with the child, gave my husband custody. I—*we*—never wanted children. But now my husband wants to keep him." She pressed manicured fingers to her lips to stifle a sob.

"Thing is, the boy's got blond hair and blue eyes ... *just like his mother.* I see her face every time I look at him. He's a daily reminder of how she nearly destroyed our marriage. And he cries ... a lot. Says he misses his mommy. I've tried sweets. I've tried TV, but he just *won't stop crying* ..."

Covering her face with her hands, she began to weep. The shadow on the other side of the screen remained still, silent, as she fumbled in her purse for a tissue. She dabbed her eyes, smudging her makeup, and blew her nose.

"I... I don't hit him hard. I swear. Just a smack across the face. Or twisting his ears a bit. It... it makes me feel better. Vindicated, almost. And that scares me. What if I go too far next time? I know nothing is his fault, but I can't stop blaming him. And sometimes I just get so *angry*..."

Her words dissolved into tearful sniffles blown into the shredded tissue. Chewing on a French tip, she waited for the priest to respond.

"You are a kind woman to forgive your husband," the priest began. "It must be very difficult for you to be constantly reminded of his unfaithfulness. But do not forget that children—be it your own or someone else's—are a gift from God." There was no hint of judgment in his voice, only understanding and acceptance.

Almost instantly, a lightness overcame her as if her soul had been unburdened.

The rustling of paper whispered from the other side of the screen. "Pick up the Holy Bible beside you," he said, "and turn to the Book of Psalms, chapter one hundred thirteen."

The woman flipped through the yellowed book until she found the right page.

"Let us read verse nine together," he said. Her eyes scanned the short sentence as she whispered the words: "*He maketh the barren woman to keep house, and to be a joyful mother of children. Praise ye the LORD!*"

She sat in silence, letting the verse sink in.

"You think this is God's way of saying I *am* ready to be a mother?" she asked. "But why would He send me Frankie? Of all the children in the world, why him? Do you think He's testing me?"

"Perhaps," the priest said. "Our Lord's intentions may become clear in the future. Until then, all we can do is continue to put our faith in Jesus."

She heard the priest closing a book with a muffled clap.

"For your penance, you are to recite the Lord's Prayer five times and Hail Mary ten times."

"Yes, father." She bowed her head.

"Now, please say the Act of Contrition."

"My God, I am sorry for my sins with all my heart..."

He listened to the woman's voice, thick with tears and emotion as she beseeched divine forgiveness, purging her soul by paying lip service to God.

A preposterous charade.

That was the problem with the world. People lied, cheated, stole, and hurt others. They went to church to confess their sins, feign remorse, and after a couple of Hail Marys, they thought themselves free to continue sinning again, safe in the knowledge that their eternal soul had been redeemed by a benevolent, all-forgiving God.

What bullshit.

"I firmly intend, with Your help, to do penance, to sin no more..."

Liar, he thought, *you're not sorry at all. You're going to go home and sin again. You will abuse that poor child the next time he so much as coughs out of turn, and you will continue to do so, without remorse.*

"... my God, have mercy."

My *God will show you no mercy. He will not be appeased by empty repentance, and He will not stand by to watch you sin again.*

My *God will punish you for your sins.*

"I absolve you of your sins, in the name of the Father, and of the Son, and of the Holy Ghost. Amen."

He watched her exit the confessional, wedged heels clicking against the stone floor, Gucci handbag swinging from her shoulder, frilly mini-skirt at least four inches short of acceptable length in a house of worship. She checked herself in her compact mirror, taming her smeared makeup and red-rimmed eyes, making herself 'presentable' for when she left, he presumed.

With a final toss of her blonde highlights, she was gone, her vile sin already forgotten.

But not by him. Lord's Prayers and Hail Marys were not sufficient penance.

I shall administer the appropriate punishment.
In the name of my God.

12

"So how's your horticultural expedition coming along?" I asked.

Blaize groaned on the other end of the line. "Splendid. Sixteen oak trees approached so far, and not one of them objected to having a leaf sample taken. I'm beginning to think that perhaps plants are a bit more cooperative than humans when it comes to assisting in a police investigation."

I smiled. "Sounds like a walk in the park—pun completely intended. As for me, I'm not looking forward to church. Haven't set foot in one in … twenty-three years."

Not since Mom died.

Beside me, Holloway reversed into a parking space. We had decided to take his car, much to my regret; my size twelves took up what little leg room existed in the passenger seat, forcing me to sit with my knees folded up against my chest. "At least you're getting some fresh air," I said to Blaize, "it'll do you good."

The phone buzzed with silence. I wondered if she'd been cut off.

"What do you mean by that?" she finally asked, her voice taut, defensive.

"Um … nothing," I said, "just that, well, you haven't been a hundred per cent as of late."

"I'm *fine*," she said, cutting me off. We lapsed into another spell of static silence.

"Er, listen, we've just pulled up to the church. Gotta go. Speak to you later."

I ended the call. Having put the car in park and turned off the ignition, Holloway eyed me with waggling brows.

"What's up with her?" he asked. No doubt he detected the tension in the final seconds of our exchange.

"Dunno. She's not been herself lately."

Holloway sniffed. "Perhaps it's that time of the month."

We climbed out of his egg-shaped Smart, which looked more like a bumper car at a fun fair than a road-worthy vehicle. I groaned as I struggled out on cramped legs. "What possessed you to get a stunted midget motor like that?" I asked.

"Fuel economy, low carbon emissions, plus I can squeeze into the tightest of parking spaces."

I flexed my stiff calves.

St. Margaret and All Saints Roman Catholic Church was an oasis of spirituality and character in an otherwise drab neighbourhood. Nestled between a car workshop and a hostel for the homeless, the three-storey, brownstone structure boasted a pentagram on its rose window.

"Isn't that a pagan symbol?" I asked.

"Contrary to popular belief, the upright pentacle has actually been used in many cultures and religions, and not just in Wiccan symbolism," Holloway said as we crossed the road from the car park towards the church. "In ancient times, the five points of the star represented the five wounds of Christ. It's been referred to as the 'Star of Bethlehem', the guiding star that led the three wise men to baby Jesus. It was only during the Dark Ages that the pentacle became associated with witchcraft and morphed from a protective amulet to a symbol of evil."

"Huh," I said, impressed at his depth of knowledge. "My grasp of languages is pretty weak, but isn't the word *pentagram* Greek?"

"It's literally translated as 'figure drawn with five lines'. Pythagoras actually founded a sect based on his teachings of mathematics, philosophy and religion, and used the pentagram as a symbol for the organisation. You heard of the Masonic Order?"

"The Masons? Yeah."

"They trace their origin to the Pythagoreans."

"What was your major at university again?" I asked.

"Politics and Economics, with a Masters in Social Sciences. Why?"

"How the hell do you know so much about occult symbols?"

Holloway gave a noncommittal shrug, but his cheeks blushed. "I-I'm a ... naturalistic pantheist," he said.

"A *what*?"

"A naturalistic pantheist. It's a neo-pagan religion."

I regarded him with a grin. "I never had you down as the religious type. So what do you guys do, pray in the nude?"

"Not naturist, natur-*al*-ist," he said, a high-pitched tone of annoyance creeping into his voice. "We believe humans are but a miniscule part of nature, of the wider Universe. We don't believe in God in the sense of a greater being. Rather, we believe God and the Universe are one and the same."

The passion in Holloway's speech surprised me. "And you guys do witchcraft and stuff?"

"We're not Wiccan, and we don't believe in magic. To us, unexplained mysteries are merely facets of nature we've yet to explore and understand."

"That's a pretty scientific and logical view. I can see why this neo-nature thing is appealing." I was starting to experience a different side to Holloway, a side other than the bookishness and the obsessive-compulsive.

We walked up to the front door, painted the colour of fired brick. "You've got no qualms about entering the house of another religion, have you?" I asked.

"Not at all. We are tolerant of all faiths. Different people seek answers in different ways. What about you? Christian?"

"I was brought up as one," I said and left it at that. Past and present events in my life had not helped much in substantiating my faith in a greater omnipotent being. Holloway only nodded. I was grateful he didn't force the issue.

Just as I reached for the knob, the door swung open, forcing me to back pedal in order to avoid a face full of solid wood. A woman appeared at the threshold, blinking in the harsh sunlight.

"Oh!" she gasped. "I'm so sorry." She kept her gaze on me as she skirted past, fingers closing tighter round the strap of her handbag. Like a hunted deer, she tottered off on her ankle-breaking high heels, throwing glances at me over her shoulder as if to make sure I wasn't following.

Big black man, East London ... I suppose I can't blame her.

"Your type of girl?" Holloway asked, his voice strained.

"Huh?" I realised I'd been staring at the retreating woman. "She's pretty. Wears too much war paint for my liking, though. And a bit too negro-phobic." Holloway made a noise between a groan and a sigh as we stepped into the church.

Poor guy probably doesn't get much female attention, even of the negative kind.

I followed Holloway in, stepping out of the noonday sun and into the cool dimness of the church. It took a minute or so for my eyes to adjust to the lower light conditions. Wooden pews with threadbare cushions faced a raised pulpit and an altar draped in red velvet. Gold candelabra flanked the altar, and above it, in all its macabre glory, hung a wooden cross bearing the effigy of a suffering Jesus Christ.

The place was deserted, save for a cleaner mopping the floor. Dressed in a blue uniform, he whistled as he worked, the sound projected and amplified by the acoustics of the church interior. The tune had a certain pomp and splendour to it. I imagined trombones, violins and cymbals as suitable accompaniments, rather than drums, keyboards and bass guitars. If music was coffee, the rich notes made a full-bodied espresso, unlike the jaunty, watered-down lattes that were the pop songs of the decade. It sounded like it could have been a national anthem or some orchestral symphony.

"Hello," I said.

The cleaner turned. "Oh, hi." His cheeks coloured. "Pardon the racket, I didn't hear you come in." In his late twenties or early thirties, younger than I expected, considering his musical preference, and with his shaggy mane of blonde hair, he could've passed for a boy band member, but a pair of thick-rimmed glasses ruined the pop star image.

"No problem," I told him. "I quite enjoyed it. Debussy?"

"Er, no," he said. "Samaras."

"Never heard of him."

"He's relatively obscure, but I like his work." He shrugged.

I showed him my badge. "We're looking for someone in charge of the church. Do you know who that would be?"

"That will be the Reverend." He gestured to a corridor leading off from the altar. "He's just gone into his office."

"Refreshing to meet someone who seems to be enjoying his job, Mr . . . .?"

"Joseph. Joseph Peter." He smiled. "And I've been raised to be grateful for small blessings." As we left him to his duties, he began whistling that song again.

At least someone's having a good day at work.

We walked down the corridor until we found a door with a plaque reading:

THE REV. PATRICK MACKENZIE

I knocked.

A deep voice answered, "Come in."

We entered a small but tastefully decorated office with dark wood furnishings and a Persian rug. A framed print of Da Vinci's *Last Supper* hung beside a wall dominated by shelves of books on theology. Burgundy curtains framed a bay window with a view of the church courtyard. Underneath a small gold cross, the

Reverend Patrick Mackenzie sat at his mahogany desk, an open newspaper laid out before him.

He peered at us over the top of his glasses. "May I help you?"

I showed him my badge, introducing myself and Holloway. "We'd like to ask you a few questions."

Mackenzie rose from his seat. He stood almost as tall as me and surprisingly broad for a man his age. Wearing a black shirt with a clerical collar, he had a speckled beard and close-cropped hair. Despite the fact his salt-and-pepper contained more salt than pepper, there was a firm strength in his handshake.

"Anything I can do to help," he said, beckoning us to sit.

Holloway pulled out a photograph of Olga Petrov. "Do you know this woman?"

Mackenzie adjusted his glasses and perused the photo. "Yes, I believe I do. She comes to church here. Nice girl. All the way from Russia."

We showed him a photo of Nicholas Kemp, the street preacher. The Reverend's eyes narrowed.

"I don't know his name, but he comes round here occasionally, making a nuisance of himself. We've had to throw him out at least a couple of times." His frown deepened as his gaze shifted between the two photographs. "May I ask what the connection is between Olga and this man?"

"They're both dead," said Holloway.

Mackenzie tilted up at us. Back down to the photos. "I see," he said.

"Murdered," I added.

"Tragic."

Holloway and I exchanged glances. "You don't sound too sympathetic."

Mackenzie sat back and held his palms up. "What can I say? That Nicholas fellow was a blasphemer. Tried to pass himself off as the Son of God! How sacrilegious is that? He actually claimed to be the Saviour!"

"Reverend," Holloway said, "Mr. Kemp had a history of mental illness."

"He was ill all right," Mackenzie said. "His soul was sick. Matthew chapter seven warns: 'Beware of false prophets, which come to you in sheep's clothing, but inwardly they are ravening wolves.' This man disrupted my sermons, tried to lure my flock astray. I thank God he is gone—no doubt in Hell."

Holloway was scratching away at his notepad like a manic scribe. I clenched my fists under the desk. Religious fanatic types always rubbed me the wrong way, but the extreme narrowness of the Reverend's thinking was unbelievable.

"I take it you also have something against Miss Petrov?" I asked through gritted teeth.

The Reverend shook his head. "The poor child broke one of the Ten Commandments: 'Thou shalt not commit adultery.' I tried talking to her, but she wouldn't listen. She damned herself the day she agreed to consort with the foul magic of her married lover. *Magicians*," he spat the word, "they are false prophets themselves. Minions of Satan, tricking people into believing mere mortals can perform miracles."

"Miracles? You've got to be kidding me." Holloway fiddled with his glasses. "I'd hardly consider Vincent Matthews's parlour tricks divine miracles."

"You may be surprised how easily misled some people can be," Mackenzie said. "It is a sin to exploit this naiveté. Their punishment must be the Lord's will."

"Are you for real, man?" I couldn't believe what he said. "People are being *murdered*, and you're calling it an act of God?"

"Unrepentant sinners and non-believers must be punished," the Reverend said. "If you ask me, I admire this 'Oaksecutioner' for doing the Lord's work in ways I cannot. I can only guide my flock. He can cull the lost ones such that they no longer spread their disease." He regarded me with a smirk, fingers tented. "What about you, Detective Lancer? Are *you* a lost sheep?"

I stood up so abruptly my chair shrieked as it skidded backwards against the stone floor. *To Hell with lack of evidence.* I wanted to take the bastard down *right then*. If I stayed any longer, I was certain I'd face charges of physical assault on a man of the cloth.

"We'll be in touch." I quick-marched my way out of the church before I did something I'd regret.

Holloway hurried to catch up with me. "Talk about creepy," he said. "What do you think, Kurt?"

"I think he was taunting us, that's what I think." I flung open the door, stepping out onto the baking pavement, grateful to escape the oppressiveness inside the Reverend's office. "We've got nothing on him, and he knows it. Cocky sonofabitch."

"So you're liking him as our man?"

"Oh, I'm liking him," I said, "I'm liking him *a lot*."

"What should we do now?"

"Nothing much we can do without any evidence. We'll just have to keep an eye on him. In the meantime, we should canvass his 'flock'. See what we can learn about the good Reverend from them."

"Long shot, but we could also try running his name through the database," Holloway said. "On the off chance he has some previous criminal records."

"Good idea. Seeing as Sam's been confined to her desk recently, I'll call her now and get her on the case."

As I picked up my phone, I noticed I'd received a new text message. The sender's number wasn't one I recognised.

The message read:

I GOT SUM INFO 4 U

I eased my car into the driveway, turned off the ignition, and rested my forehead on the steering wheel.

What a long-arse day.

Interviews with members of the church had shed no further light on the eminent Reverend. He might have been a bit right-wing, a hard-line Christian, but he was an eloquent and convincing speaker. Most of his congregation seemed to like him.

I, for one, wanted to ram a crucifix up his sanctimonious behind.

Unfolding my legs, I climbed out of the car and checked my phone for the umpteenth time.

Still nothing.

Whoever sent me that text did not—or *would* not—answer when we tried calling back. A preliminary check revealed the message came from one of the many untraceable pay-and-go numbers doled out by mobile phone companies like complimentary sweets. Clearly, our informant wanted to remain anonymous, at least for the moment.

I composed my reply:

I'M LISTENING. TALK TO ME.

After pressing 'Send', I entered the communal front door of my converted house, navigating past the mountain of junk mail nobody had bothered to sift through. Strains of indie rock, thrumming with bass, drifted down from the flat upstairs, no doubt the musical choice of Helen's daughter, Lucy. I unlocked the door to my two-bedroom, ground-floor flat, making a mental note to notify the landlord of the mildew forming on the ceiling in the hallway.

Meghan sat on the couch watching TV.

Alone.

"Where's Uncle Reggie?" I asked.

"He had to run out."

"What? How long has he been gone?"

Meghan turned her head lazily toward the clock on the wall. "An hour or so."

Jesus, he left Meghan by herself.

I put Meghan to bed after a quick read of another one of Hercules's labours and set up station in the living room, working on my laptop whilst keeping an eye on the front door.

Reggie came home around ten o'clock.

"What were you thinking?" I leapt up from the sofa and towered over him. "You left Meg alone for over an hour! Why didn't you ask Helen to watch her?"

"I forgot! It was an emergency, innit." He held his hands up. "And I thought you'd be home sooner."

"Reggie, she's *eight. And* she has problems with her eyesight. What if something happened to her?"

"Like what? She's at home, bro. She's safe. Goggles knows not to play with fire and shit like that. She's sensible that way. Honestly, I thought you'd be home."

"Do you realise what would happen if Social Services found out about this?" I fought to keep my voice level, but an involuntary waver still managed to creep in. "I've already lost Angie. I'm not losing Meg, too!"

"Dude." Reggie placed a hand on my shoulder, squeezing me with his sausage-like fingers. "Relax. That ain't gonna happen. You're a great dad. And I'm a great uncle." He winked when I snorted at the last comment. "Hey, I know the last year's been tough, but we've worked most things out, haven't we? It ain't always gonna be easy, but you and me, boy, we'll get there in the end." He pulled me in for a hug, slapping me on the back. I caught a whiff of cannabis on his clothes but decided not to spoil the moment.

"Where were you?"

"At work, bro. Had to cover for someone."

"And you actually agreed to doing extra hours? I find that

hard to believe." I looked him up and down. "Why aren't you in uniform?"

He shrugged. "Changed out of it. Don't like wearing a supermarket's logo in public."

"Next time you need to run off, you tell me. Understand?"

He held up his three middle fingers. "Scout's honour." He turned and sauntered into the kitchen. I spotted the white edge of an envelope peeking out from his back pocket.

Was he fibbing about working an extra shift? Could he have been busy exchanging mysterious love letters again with his 'secret admirer'?

I returned to my laptop.

A beep from my phone interrupted me.

1 NEW MESSAGE

I accessed my inbox and frowned. The latest text looked to be just a jumble of letters and numbers:

E14 7JK

A car registration plate? A cryptic message?

It hit me.

A postcode.

Opening the browser window on my computer, I typed the code into Google. A map of the local area appeared.

My phone beeped again.

2MORO. 9PM. BEHIND THE CHIPPY.

"This is a bad idea," Holloway said, wide eyes flitting about. I'd seen those eyes before, on an antelope on the Discovery Channel as it drank from a crocodile-infested lake.

We stood in an alleyway reeking of spoiled food and old piss. A flickering fluorescent bulb cast long, dancing shadows, illuminating the neon graffiti adorning the walls, proclaiming endearing messages such as *J-Man likes 2 suck cock*. A rat the size of a small dog strolled brashly past us, gnarled tail swishing before disappearing under an overflowing wheelie bin. The greasy odour of chip oil flowed from a rattling vent, a promise of the culinary delights awaiting the discerning connoisseur at the Codfather fish and chips shop. Framed by the concrete walls of the alleyway, glittering office buildings soared in the distance. The distinctive pyramid crowning the Canary Wharf Tower twinkled, its aircraft warning lights beckoning like a beacon, enticing us to step into the fantasy world where corporate fat cats lived in high-rise condominiums, a mere bridge span away from the poorest slums in London.

"A bad, bad idea," Holloway repeated. "Today's Friday the thirteenth. Have you seen the movie? We should've called for backup."

"Hey, chillax, will ya? We're only here to speak to an informant."

"But why here? Why can't we meet up at a Starbuck's or something? Something fishy's going on here, and I don't mean at the chip shop."

"Shh …" I put a finger to my lips as the sound of footsteps bounced along the bare brick walls.

Lots of footsteps.

"Kurt," Holloway's voice dropped to a shaky whisper. "Exactly how many informants were you expecting?"

Before I could answer, a group of men—three of them—appeared at the end of the alleyway, hoods pulled over their heads. Golden Jaws, the guy from the dead preacher's crime scene, led them in.

He pointed a tyre iron at me. "What the fuck you doin' here?"

Guess he recognises me, too. "Official police business," I said. "You?"

Golden Jaws propelled a glob of spit in our direction. "That spineless cunt. Where is he?"

"Who's he?"

"Don't play games with us!" One of his thugs growled, fingers twitching above his waistband.

I held up my hands. "I honestly don't know who you're talking about. Now, if you'll tell me why you're here, we can go about our separate ways."

"Don't listen to 'em!" the antsy hoodie said. "It's a trap! B-Dawg must've ratted to the cops!"

Golden Jaws's eyes narrowed to dangerous slits. "Then let's find out how much they know."

The first hoodlum reached under his belt and pulled out a switchblade. Light glinted off metal as he flicked the knife open with a *click*.

"Aw fuck," Holloway squeaked.

All three gang members attacked at the same time, their combined width spanning the narrow alleyway, eliminating any avenue of escape. Golden Jaws swung at me with his tyre iron. I stepped into him, *inside* the arc of his swing, and grabbed his arm. Aided by his forward momentum, I flung him to the ground, disarming him with a twist of his wrist. Tyre iron in hand, I turned in time to defend a thrusting stab from the youth with the knife. My weapon hit him across the knuckles, knocking the blade from his grasp. It clattered into a pile of bin bags. I followed through by striking the back of his knees, sending him sprawling onto the garbage-strewn asphalt.

The third thug came at me with a broken bottle, hacking the air like some psychotic killer from a B-rate slasher film. One errant slice whizzed past, inches from my face. I forced myself to remain calm, to study his jerky movements, timing my counterattack.

I spotted my opening at the end of a clumsy lunge. Sidestepping him, I brought the tyre iron into his midsection. It connected with the soft tissue of his solar plexus, expelling the air from his lungs. With a loud *oof*, he dropped the bottle and collapsed in a groaning heap.

Something caught my ankle. As I stumbled, what felt like a

sack of potatoes—or a truck full of sacks of potatoes—hit me from behind. I landed face first on the ground, with a crushing weight on top of me. Kicking and squirming, I managed to twist myself round. Golden Jaws sat straddling my chest. He planted a right hook across my jaw. My teeth clashed together, a coppery tang filling my mouth. Fingers pried the tyre iron from my hands and pressed the cold hardness of the metal across my throat. I gasped as Golden Jaws constricted my windpipe. My hands groped at the rod, struggling to push it off, to relieve the pressure crushing down on my Adam's apple, but he had my arms pinned, and I couldn't get any leverage from my prone position.

Golden Jaws, the tyre iron, gravity... all worked against me.

My heart pounded against my ribcage as my lungs cried out for air. Black spots dotted my vision as my brain fought to function. The spots danced before me, swirling and condensing, until they formed an image of Meghan, dressed all in black.

Wearing the dress I got her for Angie's funeral.

Not again.

It can't end this way.

Just as the descending darkness seemed absolute, the pressure on my windpipe eased. Freed of obstruction, my lungs reflexively sucked in breath after breath of precious oxygen. I rolled onto my side, coughing and wheezing, gulping greedily, savouring the rush of wind in and out of my chest cavity. I didn't care that the air tasted and smelled like deep-fried trash. At that moment, it was the sweetest in the world.

As the black fog lifted from my vision, I propped myself up on rubbery arms. Golden Jaws lay slumped beside me, his face in a ketchup-stained Styrofoam box. Holloway stood guard over him, hugging what looked like a giant tin can to his chest—an empty barrel of vegetable oil no doubt discarded by the chippy. A skull-shaped indent crumpled the base of the container.

"You all right, Kurt?" he asked, his voice shrill, eyes wild.

"Could be better," I rasped, rubbing my bruised windpipe.

My spit tasted of blood, and my jaw throbbed with a pulse of its own. I glanced around the deserted alleyway, struggling to gather my senses.

"The other two got away." Holloway still wielded his makeshift weapon like a caveman carrying a boulder. He pointed his chin at the unconscious thug. "What should we do with him?"

"Cuff him." I dragged myself to my feet. "Then call for a squad car." My jaw cracked as I flexed it, lighting up my face with a flare of pain. Holloway barked into his phone, summoning backup, as I leant against a rubbish skip, waiting for my breathing and heart rate to return to normal. A whirlwind of questions tumbled through my mind.

What the Hell was that about? Where was my informer? I remembered giving Golden Jaws my card, recalled him spitting on it and throwing it aside. Did he send me the text? Was this a trap all along? If so, why?

Still keyed up from the encounter, I jumped at the sound of rustling behind me. I whirled, dropping instinctively into a defensive stance.

A fat, mangy rat climbed out from the Dumpster and plopped onto the ground before skittering away.

I straightened.

A flash of crimson appeared from behind the skip.

I launched myself at the hoodie, pinning him against the brick wall.

"Whoa, whoa, hey!" the guy cried, hands in front of his face. "Back off, man, I'm cool." I recognised his red Nike sweatshirt, the one with the gold swoosh logo.

One of Golden Jaws's goons from the council estate.

He wasn't one of our attackers.

I spun him around and patted him down, frisking him for weapons.

"Ow! Easy bro, I come in peace!" The wail of sirens punctuated the night—the cavalry on its way.

Grabbing him by his shoulders, I turned the punk back to face me.

"I'm not normally into police brutality, but you've caught me in a very bad mood. So talk. Now."

"Chill, man. Truce! White flag!" He waved an invisible pennant in his hand. "I is the one who brought you here. I's the one who texted you."

※

"I came as soon as you called…" Blaize's words trailed off. "My God, Kurt, are you all right?"

Alternating an ice pack between my temple and my fat lip, I waved my free hand. "None the worse for wear."

Blaize looked a little drawn, her honeyed complexion a bit pale. A faint knot creased her forehead. She kept taking in deep breaths through her nose before blowing them out, long and slow, through her mouth.

I kept the observation to myself.

Olive eyes clouded with concern, Blaize reached out to touch the swelling on my jaw. I winced. My bruises were so tender, even the softest caress sent pain radiating across my face.

"How's Tom?" she asked.

"He's fine. Came out of it better than me. A little shaken up, though. Was the first fight he's ever been in—can you believe that?"

"Where is he now?"

"Back at the office, writing up an incident report." No doubt trying to justify beaning someone with an oil barrel, Donkey Kong style. I jerked my head towards the interview room where we'd left the punk in the red Nike sweater to simmer. "Our mystery informant has revealed himself. Let's go say hi."

We entered the claustrophobic space. The pounding in my head rivalled the throbbing in my jaw. Blaize introduced herself to the nervous-looking hoody as we sat down opposite him at the table. She pushed 'Play' on the voice recorder. "Please state your name for the record," she told him.

"B-Dawg."

Blaize arched her brows. "I need your *real* name?"

The kid—he looked around the same age as Reggie—stared at the recorder on the desk, the whirr of the device the only sound audible in the silent room.

That and the pneumatic drill in my head.

"Yo, can you turn that thing off?" he asked. "I ain't too comfortable with it on."

"This is standard procedure," Blaize said. "Don't worry, your answers will be kept strictly confidential."

"I'd rather speak off the record," B-Dawg said, arms crossed. "Y'know, be like an anonymous tipper?"

"No offense, kid," I said, placing the ice pack over my tender jaw, "but you were at the scene when two officers got assaulted. And, you're linked to the attackers. I don't think you have much of a bargaining chip. You're lucky we're not trying you as an accessory to GBH."

"They twigged that I was going to the cops and followed me," B-Dawg said. "I had no part in the attack. Swear on my life!" Leaning his elbows on the table, he wrung his hands together, his street attitude gone, leaving just a scared kid—one who'd gotten himself into a load of trouble. "Thing is, the stuff I got to tell you is ... how you say, 'sensitive' information. I don't want nobody finding a tape of me ratting on no one."

"B-Dawg," Blaize rolled her eyes in an "*I can't believe I just called him that*" expression, "we've been through that. No one but the police will hear this tape."

"Nah, man." B-Dawg shook his head. "This guy has connections, innit. There be even rumours he got people on the inside. Cop friends." He slumped back in his chair. "I ain't takin' no chances, mate."

Blaize's eyes flitted towards me, her hovering eyebrows asking me for guidance.

"Turn it off."

The eyebrows dropped, crumpling into a frown. "You sure about that?"

I nodded. With a defeated sigh, Blaize reached out and stopped the recording. The whirring ceased, and a blanket of silence descended on the room.

Ice pack to my head, I turned to face B-Dawg. "This better be good."

The kid took a deep breath before letting it out in a long *whoosh*. "They gonna kill me, man. They gonna hunt me down and kill me."

"Who is?"

"The gang, bruv. The Ghetto Souljaz."

Blaize and I exchanged glances. The Ghetto Souljaz was one of the big players in gang-related crimes in the East End.

What links a street gang to a horny magician and a mad preacher?

"What is your involvement with the Ghetto Souljaz?" I asked.

B-Dawg's gaze darted between Blaize and me. "I'm not, like, discriminating myself here, am I?"

"I believe you mean *incriminating* yourself," Blaize said. "And no, you won't be."

"I ain't been with 'em long. Only a few months." The kid spoke slowly. "Maybe a year. I ain't done nothin' *too* illegal. Some spray-painting. Got in some fights. Sold some weed. Mostly I'm a runner." He glanced up as if expecting us to put the cuffs back on him.

"Thing is, I been given some weed to run, and kept half of 'em for myself. Mixed the rest with tobacco before delivering 'em. And the gang found out."

"Right," I said. "All very interesting. But when do we get to the part about the *information* you promised us?"

"I'm just getting to it," B-Dawg said. "I just thought y'all should know about my situation, innit. I'm in a bit of a shithole, which is why I thought, you and me, we could do a deal, like."

My eyes narrowed. The pneumatic drill in my head became a pile driver. "What do you mean, 'deal'?"

"A written statement or somethin', promising you'll put me on Witness Protection or some such like."

I slammed the ice pack on the table. B-Dawg jumped. "Listen, you slimy little prick. Don't play coy with me. I don't give a flying fuck about your problems. You contacted us offering information on a *murder* investigation. I'm not one of your junkie homies you can do deals with. So, unless you have some useful information forthcoming, you have wasted shitloads of police time, and I'm gonna make sure you go down for assault with the rest of your mates. Whatever beef they have with you, you guys can sort it out together in prison."

B-Dawg cowered in his chair as I loomed over him, but his chin jutted out, resolute. "I-I have plenty of information and names. Swear on my life, this is connected to the fried preacher man." His tough guy bravado dissolved once more. "I got in too deep, man, y'know? And I dunno how to dig myself out. There be only two ways to get out of the gang life, innit. Sure, I'm takin' the coward's way out. I admit it." His eyes misted over, and a childlike squeak crept into his voice. "But I don't wanna consider the other option."

"Kurt." Blaize motioned for me to step outside. I gave B-Dawg one of my best evil-eye looks before exiting, leaving the punk to stew alone.

"If this kid truly has useful information worth knowing ..." she began, shutting the door behind us.

"He's a sly little weasel who's holding information for ransom! I'm not bargaining with him."

"Listen. What he has to say might be complete claptrap, or it might be a new lead. We won't know which unless he talks. He's just a kid, and he's scared for his life. It won't take much to make him spill."

I listened to the logic in her words, my frustration ebbing. "Fine, but you do the talking."

We re-entered the interview room. B-Dawg had taken off his baseball cap, revealing a buzz cut with zigzags shaved into his temples. He fiddled with the Velcro strap on his cap as he angled up to us—a mixture of hope and fear in his mud-brown eyes.

Blaize pulled a chair up to the kid and sat down. I remained standing, leaning against the door with my arms crossed.

"Now before we can begin," she said, "I need a real name. God help me, I cannot keep referring to you as B-Dawg."

The kid grimaced but complied. "Bernard. Bernard Douglas."

I bit back a laugh. No wonder he stuck to B-Dawg.

"Well, Bernard," Blaize went on, "do you realise the police cannot authorise Witness Protection?"

"Er, really?"

"That is the job of the Crown Prosecution Service. Lawyer types. And I'm afraid they don't work overtime like us coppers."

B-Dawg, *a.k.a.* Bernard's mouth dropped open. "Huh, they never mention that in them TV cop shows."

"It's too late for us to get CPS to speak to you tonight. Tomorrow's unlikely as well, being the weekend. Monday would be your best bet. Thing is, we can't hold you till then. Legally, we have to charge you or let you go. Should you decide not to talk, well, with no evidence of any crimes against you, you'll be free to walk." She winced as if Bernard's freedom was a bad thing. "This Ghetto Souljaz gang ... how many more are there? How many know you watered down their cannabis? How many knew about your little meeting in the alley?"

Bernard shrunk before our eyes, caving in on himself like a deflating balloon.

"Now, I can follow procedures and go through CPS for a written promise of protection before you give evidence, but without anything to go on, that will take some time. However, if you divulge some information first, and if the quality of the information provided is deemed relevant, we could ... expedite the process." She placed a hand on B-Dawg's shoulder and rubbed his arm in an almost maternal sort of way. "Frankly, mate, this is the best deal you're gonna get."

B-Dawg worked at his lips, looking like he was about to cry. Finally, he said, "The Ghetto Souljaz supplied the preacher man."

I recalled the spliff in the dead man's bathroom.

"So you reckon a gang member offed him?" Blaize asked.

Bernard shrugged. "I dunno, man. Two people visited him that day. One was this guy with a grey beard. The other was one of ours."

"Can you describe this bearded gentleman?" Blaize asked.

Bernard sighed. I could almost hear his street cred crumbling as he became a police snitch.

"It was dark, man. I couldn't see much. But he was tall."

Blaize shot me a glance.

Tall. Bearded.

The Reverend.

I nodded, signalling to Blaize that we had the information we needed.

Blaize hadn't finished. She patted Bernard on the back. "Thank you," she said. "We appreciate the information, and we'll do everything in our power to ensure your safety. Just one more question. Who is this gang member who also visited the victim?"

Bernard opened his mouth, but no sound came out. After a brief hesitation, he said, "He the one I'm talkin' about. One with the connections. He'll kill me for grassin' him up."

"Bernard," Blaize said, "If you want us to be able to protect you, we'll need a name."

The kid chewed on his bottom lip again. "His name is Reggie Lancer."

13

Night had quieted the houses in Tudor Gardens. Situated at the end of a leafy cul-de-sac, concealing it from the main road, the gated community was an upper middle-class oasis in the gritty heart of the East End. Residents slumbered behind wrought-iron bars and red brick walls, blissfully cut off from the 'undesirables' of inner-city life.

Yet, not all appeared well in the isolated patch of utopia. From within one of the few homes whose lights remained on, the perceptive observer would detect the shrill but muffled sound of yelling. The shouts were followed by a dull thump, one that brought a stunned but short-lived silence, shattered soon after by a high-pitched wail.

A woman, her hair wild, face streaked with tears, rushed out of the house, slamming the door behind her. Sobbing, she pulled her terry cloth robe tighter around herself, her grip whitening grazed knuckles that had already begun to swell. The cries inside the house went on, long and banshee-like.

What have I done? What have I done? What have I done?

The very air seemed to oppress her, condemning her, making it hard to breathe.

Why couldn't he just stop crying?

She couldn't stay in the open, in plain sight of the judging eyes of her neighbours.

She had to get out.

I need a smoke.

She jangled loose change in her pocket. Satisfied she had enough for a small pack of cigarettes, she started walking, fuzzy slippers making shuffling noises as she went. She approached the black iron gates of her prison and touched an electronic fob to a security panel. The gates swung open, but as she passed through, no relief, no liberating sense of freedom took hold. Invisible chains shackled her to the place, and she knew that no matter how many times she ran away, she would always return, back to the daily grind of the same living nightmare.

Her footsteps quickened as she padded through the streets, scuffing her slippers over discarded beer cans and vodka bottles. Head down, she scurried past a pair of black youths loitering under a flickering streetlamp, eyeing her with predatory eyes through a fog of marijuana smoke. One of them shouted at her, something about 'gettin' it on'. The other laughed. She hurried on, wishing she had driven instead. She rarely ventured 'outside' after dark, especially not in a partial state of undress. Without her clothes and makeup, the costume and mask for her role in life's play, she was effectively naked, vulnerable, and purposeless.

The stark neon glow of the late-night convenience store welcomed her. A bell over the door chimed as she entered. The place was empty, save for an old Indian man at the till reading a newspaper. She purchased a ten-pack of Silk Cut and a cheap plastic lighter. Back outside in the humid summer night, she lit up a cigarette and inhaled, filling her lungs with comforting fumes. She sighed as she exhaled through her nose, twin streams of smoke trailing from her nostrils. Nicotine always made life marginally better. She took another drag as she headed for home.

I hope he's stopped crying. Perhaps the promise of an ice cream cone would buy his silence.

She'd have to make up another story about him falling over.

The youths at the lamppost had gone, no doubt off terrorising a different street corner. She flicked the ash off the tip of her cigarette. Glowing embers faded into the darkness like dying fireflies.

She jumped when a figure stepped out from a small side street. The man smiled, and she hesitated.

Where have I met him before?

Her brain plumbed the dark recesses of her memories, but it suffered the frustrating confusion of meeting someone out of context.

Before she could remember, he lunged forward. Strong hands grabbed her, pinning her arms to her side. Before she could scream, a cold, damp rag pressed to her face, filling her nose with a sharp, sweet scent, like the acetone in her nail polish. Despite the adrenaline surging through her veins, her limbs grew leaden. The ground beneath her seemed to give way. Her eyelids drooped.

Life moved to nothing but blackness.

14

A white van blared at me as I veered into its path, committing no fewer than four traffic offences as I took a turn on squealing tyres. If my mind had a speedometer, it would probably have displayed the same speed I drove.

Breakneck.

Reggie was at the crime scene. He might have been the last person to see the victim alive. What was he doing there? How long had he been involved with gang crime? Why hadn't I realised? What kind of big brother was I?

What else is he hiding from me?

More car horns swore at me as I ran a red light and came within inches of being blindsided by a freight lorry. I turned onto the residential road leading to my flat. Thankfully for me—and for unsuspecting drivers everywhere—the street stood quiet.

I screeched to a stop in front of the house. The odour of burnt rubber stung my nose as I opened the car door. A square of light from a ground-floor window illuminated a patch of gravel on our driveway.

Reggie was home.

Now what?

I hesitated at the door. After my cross-city death race, I wasn't exactly sure what to do. As I reached for my keys, my fingers brushed the smooth, cool metal of the handcuffs on my belt. The angel and devil on my shoulders battled, engaging in a furious tug-of-war with my heart.

My internal conflict was not the main cause of the ache in my chest.

He'd *betrayed* me.

The lounge sat in darkness. Across the hall, a shaft of light crept out from under the door to Reggie's bedroom. I walked as if in a dream, the hallway stretching on for miles as I trudged through the tunnel in my vision. In the absence of all other sounds, a faint, high-pitched ringing filled my ears, increasing in volume and urgency as I stood right outside Reggie's room.

With a deep breath, I pushed the door open.

"The fuck!" Reggie shoved his hand under his pillow before jumping up from his bed. "Jeez man, can you knock first?" Topless, his gut sagged over the waistband of his Homer Simpson boxer shorts. Two chains hung from his neck, one with his signature gold 'R' studded with cubic zirconia. On his feet, he wore mismatched socks. His big toe peeked out from a hole in his left one. Under any other circumstance, he would have been a funny sight, but at that moment, a cocktail of fear and anger left a sour taste in the back of my throat. The sensation of having lost all control fluttered in my gut like the death throes of a dying bird. I couldn't have smiled even if I wanted to.

I walked up to him without a word.

"Yo, bruv, wassup?" He followed my eyes as I looked from him to his unmade bed. "Dude, you okay? What happened to your face?"

I ignored him, not so much because I wanted to, but because my body had been set on auto-pilot. Like a puppet on a string, I moved involuntarily, detached from my own consciousness.

I stepped past him.

"Hey man, leave that alo—"

I whipped his pillow off the bed. A handful of twenty-pound notes fluttered to the floor. Wads of others, stuffed into white envelopes, stayed put.

At least a couple thousand pounds.

Fists clenched, I turned to Reggie. He opened and closed his mouth like a goldfish.

"H-hey man, it's not what you think—"

My fist hit him square in the face. The force of the punch shuddered up my arm. Reggie fell back onto his bed, knocking yet more money to the floor.

"*Fuck!*" he clutched his face, wiping at the blood gushing from his nose.

My throbbing knuckles brought me out of my trance. "There was never a supermarket job, was there?" My voice stayed mere decibels above a whisper. I flexed my fingers, restraining them as they itched to strike again.

"W-Whatcha talkin' about, man?" His bleeding nose gave his speech a nasal quality. "I-I can explain this."

I laughed, a dry chuckle that held no mirth. "Right, just as you can explain why you visited a dead man's flat?"

Reggie blinked. Several times. "W-what?"

"You know, Mr. Manic Street Preacher. Over in the Cumberland Drive estate. Stomping ground for the Ghetto Souljaz." I spat the name of the gang out like a curse.

He frowned. A drop of blood broke off his chin and spattered on his belly. "Who told you that?"

"Does it matter?" I asked, my voice rising. "Does it matter who the fuck told me my own brother has been stealing and dealing drugs behind my back? So tell me, what else do you and your crew get up to? Vandalism? Extortion? *Murder?*"

Reggie cowered on the bed. "N-no. I don't ... I don't do them things."

"Really? Now how can I be sure? You've lied to me about everything else."

"W-waitaminute. You ain't ... arresting me, are ya?"

"You tell me what other options I have!" I snapped. "We've been through this before. You *promised* me you're not involved in shit like this anymore!" I glared at the pile of money on the bed as if my gaze could set the loot alight. The envelopes taunted me with their whiteness, their purity, despite containing so much dirty money in their gut.

They looked like the envelopes Reggie had been getting in the mail.

I whirled back on him, incredulous. "You had your shit *sent* to our place!?" I half asked, half shouted. "These people *know* where you live?"

"Hey, they're cool, man. They cool."

"Are you stupid or something?" I jabbed my own temple so hard my head began to throb again. I wanted to yell at him at the top of my voice, but I didn't want Meghan to be roused from bed to such a scene. "Did you even stop to think about Meg or me?"

"Of course I did! Why'd you think I did it in the first place? You guys struggling as it is! And I was being an extra burden. The useless, unemployed brother! How'd you think that makes *me* feel?" He wiped his nose with the back of his hand, smearing blood across his cheek. "You always been the lucky one, man. You got the looks, the body, the brains, the girls ... Me, I ain't got nothin'. If that ain't bad enough, I got you breathing down my neck all the time with your holier-than-thou attitude, constantly reminding me how badly I fucked up my life, of how much better you are than me."

His words hurt more than any sucker punch to the gut.

Ungrateful son-of-a ... How could he say that, after I'd been caring for him all my life?

I'd have preferred physical retaliation.

"You think you're something special, don't you?" he went on. "A high-ranking cop who picked himself off the streets. You think you better than the rest of us!"

I pounced on him, silencing him by pinning him to the bed by his throat. The warm stickiness of his blood clung to my skin. Rage threatened to choke me. I was angry, not just at Reggie, but at myself for having let everything get so out of hand, for validating his accusations against me by reacting in anger.

"Did you kill those people?" I asked him through gritted teeth. "And for once in your goddamned life, you'd better be telling the truth."

He glared back at me. "I. Did. *Not*. Kill those people." I searched his face for the truth, gazing deep into brown eyes so much like mine. There didn't seem to be any hint of deception, but then again, how many times had he fooled me before?

I didn't like the lilt in his tone when he said the word '*those*'.

I let go, stood up, and turned away. Sheets rustled behind me. I kept my back to him. We stayed that way for God knew how long, unspeaking.

"What do we do now, bruv?" Reggie broke the stifling silence.

What do we do, indeed? I knew what I should've done. I should've read him his rights. I should've taken him down to the station, slapped the cuffs on him if I had to. I pictured my baby brother dressed in standard-issue grey overalls, sitting in a sparse prison cell, yet another victim of the system, of our fucked-up upbringing. I pictured him as a plump, cherubic toddler, sitting in my lap as I sang *Itsy Bitsy Spider* to him, laughing as I tickled him under his dimpled chin.

He said he didn't kill those people.

I picked up his backpack from the floor. Without looking at him, I tossed the bag in his general direction.

"Start packing."

"Wha-? You serious, bruv?"

"Take your dirty money and go. And stop calling me 'bruv'." My voice dropped to a rasp.

"I have no brother."

"So that's it?" Reggie said, a baseball cap pulled low over his brow, twisted shred of tissue plugging up his bleeding nostril. "Over twenty years of brotherhood. Gone, just like that?" When it became apparent I wasn't attempting a response, he brushed past me on the way out. "Don't think you can get rid of me so easily." An edge crept into his voice. "I'll be watching you." His hunched silhouette melted into the night.

I was still staring at the empty road Reggie had disappeared down when Holloway's Smart Car pulled into my driveway. He climbed out, followed by a flustered looking Blaize, hair dancing around her head like a ball of fire.

"Kurt ..." Climbing the three steps leading up to the porch, she tried to look past me into the house. "Is he here?" she asked.

I shook my head, my eyes fixed on the empty road.

"Where is he?"

I crossed my arms and shrugged, meeting her gaze.

"Christ, can somebody tell me what is going on?" Holloway said. "First, you take off on a hell ride like some kamikaze drag racer, and now you look like you've been in another fight—*ow!*" Rubbing his upper arm, he glared at Blaize, who still had her elbow sticking up.

"Our informer never mentioned a name," I stated, my voice hollow, robotic.

Blaize's eyes widened. "Kurt ..."

"Our informer never mentioned a name," I repeated a little louder. "Our main suspect remains the unsub with the beard."

"What are you talking about?" Holloway's jaw went slack as I figured realisation dawned. "Your brother? The one with the criminal record?" He received another none-too-gentle nudge from Blaize but seemed too outraged to back down. "Man, you can't do that! You'll get the sack when you're found out. We *all* will."

I glanced from him to Blaize. "No, you won't, Tom. You were never in the interview room with me. Neither were you, Sam. Neither of you are aware of my motive."

Blaize's mouth tightened into a grim line. I noticed the most imperceptible nod of acquiescence. We'd been through enough together for her to trust my judgment and to turn a blind eye to my sometimes ... *unorthodox* ways. As for Holloway, I didn't think it possible for his eyebrows to rise much higher. No doubt my decision went against every single principle in his rule book. My gaze held his, silently beseeching. He could get me off the case, probably off the force, with a single phone call. What I'd done could severely compromise the case.

I'd asked a lot of them.

Holloway's expression remained a mixture of horror and indecision, tempered perhaps with a touch of sympathy. "You do realise your brother is a key witness in a *homicide* investigation?"

"He had nothing to do with it."

"How can you be so sure?" *Good question.* I thought I knew my brother, but it seemed obvious I didn't. Yet, something in Reggie's tone of voice, something in the way he stared back at me during our confrontation let me know. "I trust him."

Holloway chewed on his lip. "I have a feeling I'm going to regret this."

I exhaled my relief. I needed their support, knew they were sticking their necks out for me.

I was about to utter my deepest gratitude when Blaize said, "If this ends up stirring up a disciplinary shit storm, I'll *kill* you."

"Lookin' good, Lancer," Chief Sutherland said as I entered her office.

I rubbed the swelling on the side of my face. "Trust me, this looks a lot better than it feels," I groaned.

"My friends from Organised Crime tell me your back alley antics have earned you an almost celebrity status in street gang circles. Understandably, the Ghetto Souljaz are not happy with you taking down three of their crew all in one fell swoop, with more biting the dust once we get your whistle-blower to talk. I don't know how much clout the gang's got, but word is you'd better watch your back."

It's great to be so popular.

"In any case," she continued, "you gave Organised Crime a bit of a breakthrough in their work. Now let's hope you can do the same for our case." Sutherland's Einstein-like hair seemed more bedraggled than usual as she nursed an extra large cup of coffee. She stared at the stack of reports before her as if they would magically provide her with an answer. The Mayor had called again, demanding answers. All the murders had happened near Olympic venues, which did not bode well for publicity.

"My informant talked," I said. "He said a man with a grey beard visited the preacher the night of the murder."

"Useful, but not *key* information," Sutherland murmured, sipping her caffeine brew.

"Chief, the Reverend's got a grey beard."

"So do ten thousand other men in the city of London."

"Ma'am," I said, "This guy is a Christian fundamentalist. He was openly scornful of the victims. Viewed them as sinners who must be punished. He actually stated he was glad they're dead."

"Which makes him a class-one dickhead," Sutherland said, "but *not* a murderer." She put down her mug as she sat forward in her chair. "Kurt, the Reverend Mackenzie is a highly respected member of the local community. Who just so happens to share a common feature with the killer. And who just so happens to have made some politically incorrect, and rather unfortunate statements. But you and I both know they're not enough grounds for a search warrant."

She skimmed through the topmost document of the pile.

"Do you think your informant can provide us with a facial composite?"

"I don't think so. He said it was too dark. All he could make out was a beard. And that the guy was tall."

"He didn't see anything else?"

My eyes flitted down to the desk. "No."

"Strange," Sutherland mused. "Your informant wants to provide information in exchange for protection from the Ghetto Souljaz, yet nothing in his statement implicates the gang in this."

I shifted in my seat. The faux leather chair seemed to be growing more uncomfortable by the minute. "He did say the gang supplied Kemp with drugs."

"In that case, has he revealed the names of fellow gang members?" Sutherland's eyes drilled into me like some superhero power—laser x-ray vision capable of reading my darkest thoughts and secrets.

"He ... he said he would only do that once he's been promised protection," I lied.

Sutherland nodded. "Then we'll get CPS to speak to him as soon as we can."

"Okay."

Please, B-Dawg, don't grass up my brother.

"We could also interrogate those thugs who assaulted you. See if they have anything to add."

"Right." I fidgeted with the collar of my shirt, wondering if the Chief noticed my discomfiture. A clammy sheen of sweat developed on my forehead and upper lip. I prayed for something, *anything*, to interrupt the awkward meeting.

The door to Sutherland's office flew open as Holloway all but tumbled in.

"Ch-chief," he started, eyes shining.

"What is it?" Sutherland asked, looking annoyed at the intrusion.

"Just got a call," he panted. "There's been another victim."

I released the breath I hadn't realised I'd been holding, feeling a measure of guilt for my relief at the news.

"Jesus Christ." Sutherland groaned. "This bastard's working fast."

Holloway practically bounced with excitement. "That's not all," he said. "This one's *alive*."

"Name's Sarah Quinn, twenty-six," Holloway said, flipping through his notepad while I drove. "She was discovered by a dog walker in Hackney Downs this morning. Found her hanging unconscious from a tree in the park—yup, you guessed it, it was an *oak* tree."

"Hanging?" I asked. "How did she survive that?"

"This is where things get really weird. She was chained to a branch by her *wrists*. And she had anvils—yes, solid hundred kilo *anvils*—tied to each foot, like some makeshift medieval torture rack."

"A hundred kilos? On each leg?" I whistled. "That's over four hundred pounds!"

"Yup, so as you can imagine, she suffered multiple dislocations: shoulders, wrists, knees…"

"Ouch."

"God knows how long she'd been hanging there before they found her."

I shook my head. "Fucking *anvils*? Who does our guy think he is, Wile E. Coyote?"

"You haven't heard the best part."

"What, better than anvils?"

Holloway nodded. "The chains our perp used had been spray painted gold."

We arrived at the Royal London Hospital and badged our way into the A & E Trauma Centre. I hated hospitals, hated the smell of disinfectant on everything, the grim-faced nurses and attendants, hated the sterility of it all.

A doctor dressed in green scrubs, a surgical mask pulled down to his chin, greeted us outside Sarah Quinn's door.

"I hate to disappoint you, but I seriously doubt you'll be getting anything coherent out of her today," he said.

"Is she in a bad way?" I asked.

"She's resting and pretty heavily sedated."

"May we see for ourselves?"

He led us into the room where a woman lay hooked up to a multitude of beeping machines and glowing monitors. My breath caught when I glimpsed the halo of blonde hair radiating across the pillow, but the sight of her exposed, dark roots shattered the illusion.

Not Angie.

"Kurt," Holloway said, "isn't that . . . ?"

The woman I bumped into outside St. Margaret All Saints.

I could picture her wearing a tight top, miniskirt, and wedged heels. I saw her flipping her peroxide hair as she clutched her handbag to her chest, eyes hooded with suspicion as she hurried past me.

The Reverend Mackenzie knew all three victims.

"Keep us posted on her status," I told the doctor. "We'll need to interview her when she's awake."

"There is one thing, Detective." He gestured to a nurse, who promptly disappeared on some errand. "Mrs. Quinn regained consciousness briefly when she arrived. She kept muttering the same thing. 'Take it out.'"

"Take what out?" I asked.

"Precisely my thought," he said. "Considering the circumstances, I decided to run a rape kit."

"None of the other victims was sexually assaulted," Holloway said.

"And neither was Mrs. Quinn. However, while swabbing her vagina, we found this."

The nurse returned with a clear Ziploc bag. She handed the plastic pouch to me.

"You found this *inside* her?" I asked, incredulous.

The doctor nodded.

I shook my head. "Fucking lunatic," I muttered, staring at the olive green nut with a brown cap within the plastic bag.

An acorn.

15

The early rays of the rising sun filtered through the window, bathing him with the warm promise of a bright summer's day. He sipped his coffee—black, no sugar—as he read the morning paper. On the front page, beneath the main news *OLYMPIC TORCH NEARS LONDON*, a smaller headline announced:

OAKSECUTIONER VICTIM SURVIVES

Sarah Quinn had suffered no fewer than six dislocated joints, but she was recovering in hospital and 'in a stable condition'.

Sarah Quinn. The woman who abused an innocent child. It was no more than she deserved.

His only disappointment was that she still lived. How he had wanted to tear through the screen of the confessional when she revealed to him her travesties, to beat her like she no doubt beat the poor child.

The Book of Psalms proclaimed, "Lo, children are an heritage of the Lord: and the fruit of the womb is His reward." Any woman who refused to bear children acted against the will of God. Any who harmed the beloved sons and daughters of the Lord deserved to go to Hell.

Just like the other sinners punished by the Oaksecutioner.

The magician and his Russian whore made no effort to conceal their adultery. Corinthians chapter six clearly stated, "Neither fornicators, nor idolaters, nor adulterers, nor effeminate, nor abusers of themselves with mankind ... shall inherit the kingdom of God."

Neither will false prophets.

Of all the sinners, he felt most glad to be rid of that one. Satan disguised himself as an angel of light. It was no wonder his servants also disguised themselves as servants of righteousness.

But the Bible tells us that, in the end, they will get the punishment their wicked deeds deserve.

With an offered blessing to the Oaksecutioner, the archangel of vengeance, for performing the will of God, he downed the rest of his coffee and prepared for Sunday Mass.

16

"... and Mrs. Rawlins told Charlie Towner off for putting glue in Patty Grayson's hair. But Patty started it by flicking paint at Scott during art, but she didn't get caught ..."

I half-listened to Meghan twittering on about her day at school as I pushed the cold, half-eaten sausage around my plate. On TV, an anchorwoman droned on about the torch relay that neared the outskirts of London, the Chinese team—all four hundred and eleven members—arriving at Heathrow, and a status update on a boxing medal hopeful's shoulder injury. It looked like he'd be well enough to contend after all.

"In other news," the poker-faced presenter said, "the serial killer dubbed 'the Oaksecutioner' continues to evade authorities. Responsible for the murder of three people, the Oaksecutioner also appears to be linked to the recent attack on a woman in Hackney."

I grabbed the remote and changed the channel. A man with a fat black caterpillar for a moustache spoke above a ticker tape of news headlines.

"So far, there seems to be no pattern to his killings, and he appears to be selecting his victims at random."

I groaned and switched channels again.

"A public outcry has erupted over the Metropolitan Police's handling of the case. With the Olympics only eleven days away, the last thing the city of London needs is a serial killer on the loose."

I turned the TV off.

"That Oaksy guy sounds pretty dangerous," Meghan said around a mouthful of starchy mash.

"He's just one guy."

"Wasn't it just one guy who took Mommy away?"

I started to explain that, technically, the 'one guy' who ordered the mob hit on Angie was the leader of the largest triad organisation in the country, with a legion of illegal immigrants clamouring to do his bidding in exchange for falsified visas. That when he ordered the hit, over a dozen assassins probably had Angie in their sights.

That the bastard continued to live freely off his ill-gotten gains, thanks to a lack of evidence against him.

In the end, I only shrugged.

"Will you promise to be careful?" she asked.

"I promise."

We carried on eating in silence.

"I miss Uncle Reggie," Meghan said. "Did he say when he'll be back?"

"No."

"I can't wait. I prefer the dinners he makes." She fluttered her lashes and shrugged at me as if to say *'No offence.'*

I gazed down at the meal of burnt bangers floating like blackened logs in a sea of lumpy gravy, streaked with the sludge of even lumpier mash. An island of green peas with still-frozen centres sat untouched.

As much as I hated to admit it, I missed having a decent cook around the house, too.

My phone went off, Carl Douglas singing about kung fu fighting again.

"Lancer."

"You want to hear something juicy?" Blaize asked, her tone conspiratorial.

"You know me," I said, excusing myself from the table with an apologetic grimace. "I'm a sucker for gossip."

"We've pulled something from Criminal Records. Looks like our good Reverend had a colourful past."

"How colourful?" I walked into the living room.

"Thirty odd years ago, he had a couple of sexual assault cases against him."

My initial optimism deflated. "That's not enough for a warrant, is it?"

"Not on its own, but I've got more news. Sarah Quinn has come round enough to speak. She can't remember much of anything, but she's pretty sure the guy who abducted her had a grey beard."

"So the Rev has a history of sexual violence, knows three of the victims, and could possibly be placed at two of the crime scenes." Elation, like a bloodhound when it finds a scent and closes in on its quarry, flooded me.

"The Chief's given the go-ahead to bring him in for questioning. He's being picked up as we speak."

"I'm on my way. See you there." I prepared to hang up but stopped when I sensed a hanging hesitation on her side of the line.

"Uhm ..." she said after a brief silence, "you're going ahead without me."

"What? Why?" I realised the reason as soon as I uttered the questions. "Sam, are you feeling okay?"

"I'll live." Her tone came out sharp with frustration.

"Christ, have you been to a doctor?"

"What are you now, my mother? Of course I have. And like I said, it's nothing life threatening. Nothing to worry about." A waver shook her normally confident voice, something I'd never heard before, a kind of vulnerability.

"Are you sure?" My heart tugged with concern. "I mean, what did the doctor say?"

"It's ..." She sighed. "You don't want to know."

"Come on, Sam. You can tell me."

"No. It's embarrassing."

"It can't be that bad." Even I noted the lack of conviction in my own voice. "What is it, flatulence? Worms? A third nipple? Try me."

After a moment's hesitation, she said "It's ... um ... lady problems," in a reluctant mumble.

"Oh. I see."

"See? You didn't want to know that."

"Of course I did," I lied. I still didn't know what was wrong with her, but I wasn't prepared to ask for further details. The physiology of the female body was about as familiar to me as alien anatomy, and much less desirable.

"Anyway," she went on, "The Chief's been pretty understanding, hence all this working from home. *And* she's keeping everything confidential, so don't you go around blabbing to everyone."

"My lips are sealed."

"Thanks." She sounded genuinely grateful I'd sworn myself to secrecy. "Anyway, you'd best be going now. Tom's already on his way."

I stared at the phone after Blaize hung up. The secrecy around her illness made sense as she was the only female member of the Murder Investigation Team, DCI Sutherland notwithstanding—the Chief had more balls than half the men on the team. From day one, Blaize had had a lot to prove. Talk of gender equality in the workplace was all well and good, but in reality, policing remained a largely male-centric profession—Chief Sutherland was a rare female leader in a male-dominated field, a fact I admired and mildly resented. Blaize had to work twice as hard to get half as far as the average male officer. Admitting to being encumbered by health issues of the feminine kind would compound her career prospects.

I returned to the kitchen to face a pouting Meghan, a glob of congealing gravy on her chin.

"Let me guess," she said, crossing her arms and glaring at me through her magnifying lenses. "You have to go."

"I'm sorry, peaches." I wiped the gravy off with my thumb. "I'll get Mrs. Jaimeson to put you to bed."

She pulled away from my touch.

"What else is new?" she grumbled.

17

He watched the dark figure race across the front lawn, ducking to avoid the low-hanging branches of the apple tree. The frizzy afro on the man's head bobbed as he climbed into his car. *He must be in a hurry.* He wouldn't normally leave the house without first braiding his hair into careful cornrows.

Vanity is such a sin—like Narcissus, it can be your downfall.

The car shuddered to life and pulled away from the curb. Headlights glanced off the lone observer, concealed in the bushes, before fading away into the distance.

He moved from his hiding place, creeping up to the window of the house. Through the wooden slats of the vertical blinds, a little girl with wavy hair the colour of burnished copper sat. Dressed in pyjamas adorned with teddy bears, she held a book up to an older girl. The teenager made a face, popped her bubblegum, and shook her head. The child pouted, thick lenses of her glasses making her eyes saucer-round like a puppy dog's. As she climbed into bed, the teenager turned off the lights and left the room.

He followed, moving to the next window. In the living room, the teenager switched on the TV, left it on a music video channel, and entered the kitchen. She scavenged through the fridge, emerging with a can of Coke and bar of chocolate. She scoffed as she picked up the house phone and dialled a number. Her conversation, no doubt to her boyfriend, judging by her smile and the way she twirled her hair as she spoke, lasted over a quarter of an hour.

When she hung up, the teenager checked her nails and the wall clock. Her shoulders moved up and down in a sigh as she tapped her fingernails on the arm of the sofa. She got up and wandered through the flat, peering behind every door. She turned the light on in the master bedroom.

Crouching low, the observer snuck to the base of the bedroom window. He watched the girl opening and closing cupboard doors. She pulled out the top drawer of a chest, rummaging through underwear and balled-up socks. Her eyes glinted as she picked up a jewellery box. She opened it and extracted something small and silver, something that fractured the dull yellow light in the bedroom into a spectrum of rainbow colours.

With a smirk, the girl stuffed her prize into the pocket of her jeans.

He had seen enough. He tiptoed back to the front of the house and rang the doorbell.

18

The Reverend Patrick Mackenzie sat with his arms crossed, glaring at me as though wishing the wrath of God on my soul. Beside him sat a man in a pinstripe suit with a leather briefcase.

With his balding hair, hooked nose and sagging jowls, Mackenzie's lawyer resembled a cross between a vulture and an English bulldog. "I must say, Detectives, that your case against my client is rather insubstantial."

Chief Sutherland leaned forward. "You have to admit, Mr. Frederickson, it is quite a coincidence that your client happens to know all four victims."

"Three, actually," the lawyer said. "He never personally knew the magician, Mr. Matthews. And like you said, Detective, it is merely a coincidence."

I twisted a tuft of my hair self-consciously, wishing I'd had time to braid it instead of turning up at the station looking like a Harlem Globetrotter. *Damn the Reverend for being so quick to cover his arse by setting his attorney on us already.*

Sutherland read out the dates for each Oaksecutioner murder, including the day of Sarah Quinn's abduction. "We need you to account for your whereabouts on those specific days."

"Inspector Sutherland, I am not a man who enjoys what the city offers in terms of nightlife," Mackenzie said. "After a long day at the church, I prefer to stay home and read from the Good Book."

"Will your neighbours be able to vouch for you?" I asked.

"Unlike some people," Mackenzie said, making it clear by his expression which 'people' he referred to, "my neighbours respect my privacy."

"The Reverend enjoys his solitude, Detective," his lawyer interjected, "which is why he lives in a quiet neighbourhood where people keep themselves to themselves."

"So you're saying nobody can vouch for your alibi," Sutherland said.

"I just don't want you to end up wasting your time or the neighbours'," Frederickson said.

"With all due respect, Mr. Frederickson," Sutherland steepled her fingers, "your client is the only link in this string of unrelated murders. He has been placed at the scene of two of the crimes, and he has two previous records of sexual assault."

Frederickson shook his head with a smirk. "Your eyewitnesses comprise of a street thug and a woman under the influence of heavy medication. I highly question their reliability. Besides, there are hundreds of tall men with grey beards in the city of London. My client's past record is an unfortunate blemish on an otherwise distinguished life and career. We all make mistakes, Inspector. It is unfair for you to judge the Reverend on a crime he committed over thirty years ago. After all, we were all young once." His voice rippled with an undertone of smugness. "With all due respect, I think you are grasping at straws here."

Sutherland fixed Frederickson with a withering glare. I could see the storm clouds gathering in the Chief's eyes. With her scowl directed at him, it amazed me that Vulture Man hadn't yet turned to stone.

The stare-off ended when a muffled buzz hummed from the Chief's jacket pocket. With a parting glower, Sutherland stepped out of the room.

I returned my attention to Mackenzie.

"So, Reverend, I can understand your dislike for the adulterous Ms. Petrov and the blasphemous Mr. Kemp. What I don't get is, why Sarah Quinn? She seems a good Catholic, a churchgoing woman. In your eyes, what sin did she commit?"

"Not in my eyes, in *God's* eyes," Mackenzie said, rising to my bait. "Mrs. Quinn is the lowest form of scum—a cowardly bottom feeder who takes her frustrations out on an innocent boy. Anybody who raises her hand to a child, for any other reason apart from discipline, deserves to rot in Hell!"

Frederickson silenced his client with a hand on his shoulder, but I'd detected the scent of blood in the water.

"Interesting how you can be privy to such intimate information, Reverend," I said, "information even the police weren't aware of. Where did you get it, may I ask? Perhaps when she placed her trust in you, her pastor, during a confession?" I leaned forward, looming over him. Using my physical bulk to full intimidating effect, I stared into Mackenzie's eyes. "Is this how you repay her trust? By punishing her outside the confines of the law?"

Mackenzie held my gaze, features reddened and twisted in a self-righteous scowl.

"You don't have to answer that," his lawyer whispered before fixing me with a glare of his own. I'd ruffled Vulture Man's feathers. "My client has nothing more to say to you about this matter, and unless you intend on formally charging him on the grounds of your paltry circumstantial evidence, you cannot detain him for any longer than twenty-four hours." He turned his Rolex towards his face. "Correction. Make that twenty-three."

I wanted to wipe the Reverend's self-assured smirk all over the walls of the interrogation room. As Mackenzie and his lawyer stood to leave, Sutherland returned, looking harried.

"Lancer," she said, concern lining her brow. From the alarm clouding her grey eyes, I knew at once that something was wrong.

"It's Meghan."

Weighed down by the lead lining my stomach, I parked beside

the two police cruisers on the front lawn of my flat, their domed lights bathing everything in a surreal blue, like the interior of a disco nightclub. I hauled myself from the car on shaky legs. The unwelcome familiarity of the scene punched a hole in my chest. I'd seen lots of crime scenes in my days, but for the second time, I'd seen my own home transformed into one.

That was twice too many.

My mind flashed back to the year before when I had gotten the call at work. I remembered my dream-like state as I arrived at our rented maisonette to find spinning lights everywhere. A bright yellow ambulance blocked the driveway, its back doors flung open. I moved as if underwater, at an excruciatingly lethargic pace. Police officers spoke to me, their voices garbled, distant. In their eyes, I saw the raw emptiness of pity.

I remembered Chief Sutherland being there in person.

"I'm so sorry, Kurt." Everything else she'd said drowned out by the roaring in my head as I concentrated on the dark pool of blood on the front porch, its edges smeared by thrashing limbs like the imprint of some gory snow angel.

The attacker had surprised Angie at the door, stabbed her six times in the chest and abdomen. All while Meghan slept upstairs.

Angie had lain there bleeding for half an hour before someone dialled nine-nine-nine. She died in hospital a few hours later.

We'd moved after that, to escape the memories, to escape the nightmare.

It seemed the nightmare had followed us.

Different house. Same scene.

The air once again took on a treacle-like quality as I sprinted towards the front porch in agonising slow motion. I badged the policeman at the door. He said something in reply as he let me through, but his speech sounded low and drawn out as if someone had messed with the speed controls of a recording device, leaving the slider on super-slow.

Meghan sat in the living room, watching a DVD with another

uniformed officer. She glanced up at me, looking nervous and confused, a little girl overwhelmed by the commotion around her. Other than that, she seemed unharmed.

Relief washed the lead filings from my gut. I scooped her into my arms, holding her close to my chest. I kissed the top of her head, savouring the smell of her shampoo, all the while blinking back a film of tears. For one brief moment, I feared I'd lost her just like I lost Angie.

She's okay.

"Inspector Lancer," an officer called from the kitchen. He led me to the dining table, where Lucy Jaimeson sat slumped in a chair, eyes red, cheeks streaked with tears. Mascara smudges around her eye sockets gave the illusion of two black eyes, accentuating her distressed victim look. Helen sat beside her daughter, holding the girl's hands. Her complexion had lost its normal healthy glow, replaced instead by the chalky sallowness of shock and fear.

"Helen. Lucy. You all right?"

Lucy gave me a weak nod.

"What happened?"

"I don't know," the girl said, her lower lip trembling. "Someone rang the doorbell. When I opened it, he attacked me. Pushed me up against the wall and started touching me..." Her voiced quivered with each word before collapsing into a blubbery sob. She buried her face into her mother's shoulder, leaving a black smear of makeup and a darkened patch of wetness on the sleeve of Helen's satin robe.

"Did he hurt you?"

"Not really. He was just real rough, like." A blackened tear rolled down her cheek, leaving a sooty trail.

"Then what happened?"

"I-I don't remember. I screamed. I think he just left."

"Where was Meghan when it happened?" I ignored the pang of guilt at the selfish question.

"She was asleep."
Thank God.
"What did he look like?"

Lucy shrugged as she chewed at a strand of black-purple hair. "He had a hood over his face. All I can say is he was black. Like you."

So are over half of all criminals in London. And I'm only half black.

I nodded to the police officer standing guard over the Jaimesons. "Take them home." I paid Lucy for her babysitting time plus extra for her troubles. Unlike every other time, Helen didn't decline payment. I walked them to the door.

"Oh." Lucy hesitated on the stairs leading up to their flat. "The guy might have stolen something. From your room. I think it might've been a ring."

I frowned. "He went into my room *after* he attacked you? I thought you said he ran off."

The girl's eyes dropped to the threadbare carpet lining the stairwell as if admiring the patterns formed by the colonies of fungi growing on the damp fabric. "I-I'm not sure," she mumbled, not looking up. "I was panicking, y'know?" Gaze fixed on the mouldy carpet, she tapped at the banister with purple fingernails.

I'd interrogated enough criminals to be an amateur body language interpreter. My internal lie detector homed in on the restless hands, the quickened breathing, eyes looking everywhere but at me. Telltale signs of someone trying to hide something.

Give her a break, Kurt. She's confused, and no doubt in shock.

I bid the Jaimesons good night, thanked the other officers, and put Meghan to bed. Afterward, I went into my bedroom and opened the top drawer of my chest. From a glance, I knew someone had rifled through it. I took out the small purple box, the one that held Angie's engagement ring—nothing fancy, just a simple, white gold hoop with a speck of a diamond. It was all I could afford at the time, but Angie absolutely loved it. She never took it off, not even after we married, not even when she went to bed or had a bath. Not even the time when she was elbow deep inside a monster turkey as she prepared Christmas dinner for her entire clan.

Maybe I should have buried the ring with Angie, but I couldn't bring myself to do that. To me, that ring was a part of her as much as her grass green eyes and honey wheat hair. Her clothes, her underwear, her perfume… they all changed with the seasons, but the ring remained a constant. I had clung on to it, like a man lost at sea would cling to a piece of driftwood.

The ring kept me from drowning in an ocean of despair—and it was gone. The jewellery box was empty. No ring nestled on the black velvet cushion inside. I sighed, tossed the container back in the drawer and fell backwards onto my bed—the king-sized one I used to share with Angie, a bed that always seemed too big, too empty, on cold winter nights.

As long as Meg's all right, I should be thankful. A lost ring should be the least of my worries.

The buzzing of my phone compounded my thoughts.

1 NEW MESSAGE

Another unknown number. Tendrils of dread seeped back into my blood as I retrieved the text.

I'M WATCHING U

Helen's eyes were rimmed with the dark shadow of sleeplessness, but she still managed a brave smile when she answered the door. She wore a ribbed tank top that gently hugged her curves, and khaki cut-offs that showed off her bronzed pins.

"Meghan, your daddy's here." A few seconds of bustling later, Meghan appeared in the doorway, beads and sequins stuck to her fingers.

"I helped Mrs. Jaimeson make some wedding invitations today." She held up a sticky index finger with a small horseshoe affixed to the nail.

I gave Meghan my keys, giving her strict instructions to go downstairs, lock the door behind her, and wash her hands. "I'll be down in a sec." As she stampeded down the stairs, I turned back to Helen. "How's Lucy?"

"All right, I think. Got the day off school today, of course, citing post-traumatic stress. But she's gone out now with friends."

I leaned my shoulder against the doorframe. "I'm really sorry about what happened last night. It must've been quite distressing for you."

She waved a hand, a layer of dried PVC glue on her fingertips making them all shiny and puckered as if they'd been shrink-wrapped. "We'll survive. Why are you apologising, anyway? It's not like it's your fault."

"I think it might be." I filled her in on my suspicions without going into case details, on how I suspected the attack was in retaliation to my role in bringing a criminal organisation to its knees.

"Huh," she muttered, inching closer towards me. "In that case, I suppose it is kind of your fault."

I gave her my best look of contrition. "I'm sorry Lucy got involved."

"It's not Lucy I'm worried about." She gazed up at me, her face so close to mine that the flecks of darker purple ringing her violet irises came into view. Like twin mountain lakes, her eyes dragged me under, threatening to drown me in their hidden depths. I caught a whiff of her perfume, sweet yet spicy, like the woman herself. Before I knew it, I found myself leaning forward, drawn towards those eyes like a moth to a flame, knowing full well I'd be burned for my troubles but not giving a monkey's.

Helen's lips yielded to mine, moulding to the contours of my mouth. I tasted the sugar and cream from her last cup of tea. The scent of her perfume, a mix of vanilla and cinnamon, mingled with the smell of PVC glue filled my head with intoxicating vapours. My hands snaked around her waist just as hers slithered up my neck and into my hair. Her fingers traced a trail of electric heat along my scalp, sending a shudder along my spine and down between my legs, awakening a long dormant desire.

Our lips still locked, we stumbled into her flat. I pushed her back against a table, lifting her as I sat her on the edge. Strips of coloured ribbon and glitter from Helen's craft projects fluttered to the ground. A plastic bottle of adhesive bounced off the linoleum and rolled across the room.

I drew in a sharp breath as her tongue pushed against mine, warm and moist and supple, probing me, tasting me, hungering for me like I did for her.

"Kurt ..." she sighed as my hands burrowed under her top to rub the smooth skin of her stomach. A seed of doubt nagged at me, but I pushed it to the back of my mind. I kissed Helen's neck, her earlobes, the hollow of her throat, tasting her, breathing in the scent of her. She moaned again, and the feeling of something being not quite right grew stronger—my seed of doubt had sprouted into full bloom.

Helen's normally throaty voice sounded distinctly light and tinkling.

Like Angie's voice.

I snapped my head up. Wavy dark hair, unusual yet compelling purple eyes, high cheekbones ... definitely Helen, but overlapping her features like an afterimage seared into my retina from staring at something for too long, I glimpsed flashes of a daintier, more elfin face, eyes the colour of dew-kissed grass, hair of frosted wheat, a light dusting of freckles across the bridge of an upturned nose.

The mirage lasted a mere nanosecond. I blinked, and Angie disappeared. Helen reappeared, hair tousled, cheeks flushed, pupils so dilated that her eyes appeared almost black. Her vest top had been gathered up around her breast, one strap hanging limply off her shoulder.

She must have caught the haunted expression on my face. "Is

something wrong?" she asked. Her hands stopped their fumbling with my half-unfastened trousers.

With a defeated huff, I pushed away from her. A fleeting glimmer of disappointment passed on her face, and she dropped her head, busying herself with straightening her top.

"I'm sorry." I tucked my shirt back into my trousers. The top buttons had mysteriously come undone, and my tie dangled in the hollow between my pectorals. "I shouldn't have ... I don't know what came over me ..."

"Shut up." There was no anger in the statement, but she gave me a resigned smirk as she perched at the edge of the table, arms across her chest. "It takes two to tango. I was being stupid. Should've known you're not ready ..."

I stood there mutely, unsure of what to say or do. My groin throbbed in painful frustration. I knelt to pick up the craft materials I'd knocked off the table, managing to retrieve all the bows and ribbons, but scattered everywhere were sequins and beads so small they refused to gain purchase in my unwieldy fingers. I tried pinching one, but it only popped out of my grasp and skittered away. We'd also knocked over a sachet of purple glitter powder. Twinkling specks floated and shifted across the floor with my every move. My efforts to scoop up a handful of glitter resulted in my hands being coated in sparkles.

"Leave them," Helen said, her tone defeated, "I'll vacuum later." She dropped to her knees, joining me on the floor, and took the ribbons from me. Even the slightest touch left my skin buzzing. Her gaze, bubbling with unfulfilled longing, seemed to penetrate my soul.

"Sometimes you just have to move on, without picking up all the pieces."

※

"A monster, a half-man, half-bull called ... Me-no-tore ..."
"Minotaur."

"My... *My*-no-taur... lived in a... guy, no, gigantic, twisting ma... maze, the... Baby-rinth."

I consulted my Braille translation chart. "Try the last word again," I instructed.

Meghan ran her fingertips across the raised studs again. "*B, A* ..."

"*B*'s got two dots, one on top of the other. How many dots has this letter got?"

She bit her lip, her smooth brow etched with concentration. "Two. No, three. There are three dots!"

"Good. So which letter is three dots in a row?"

"*L*," she said. "La-bye-rinth..."

"La-*bee*-rinth," I corrected.

"La-*bee*-rinth," she repeated. "Labyrinth!" With a loud exhalation, she slumped against her pillow, took off her glasses, and rubbed her eyes. "This is too hard!"

"Well, *you're* the one who insisted on reading a book with all these big words." My retort came out sounding harsher than I meant it. I'd been cranky since the night before, and I was sexually frustrated on top of that. The fact I was still picking stubborn glitter off my body didn't help, either.

"Sometimes you just have to move on, without picking up all the pieces."

Somehow I didn't think Helen was talking about spilled glitter. I'd been trying to move on for over a year, but I kept trying to pick up the pieces of my old shattered life. At times, it seemed I was constantly on my knees, trying to gather fistfuls of dust, the shifting remnants of my past, only to have them trickle through my fingers, torturing me with their incessant twinkling, beckoning me towards a life I'd lost forever and could never regain.

"Can't I just read the words on the page?" Meghan asked.

"No. You *must* learn to read Braille," *to prepare yourself for the inevitable.*

"But it's so difficult!" Meghan said. "I can't feel the dots right.

I'll *never* be able to read with my fingers!" Crossing her arms, she sank deeper into her bed with a huff.

"Don't be silly. You'll get there. In a couple of years' time, you'll be an expert!" I stroked her downy hair, chucked her chin. "You can't give up. It's like learning to ride a bicycle."

"In a couple of years, I'll be too *blind* to ride a bicycle."

It hit me then that the night's events had affected Meghan just as much as it affected me, if not more. After all, she'd lost her mother the last time an intruder came into her home.

Helpless, I watched my daughter, eyes shimmering with tears. Bright, sparkling, *healthy* looking eyes, the colour of polished aquamarine gems, flecked with darker strips of sapphire radiating outwards from the pupils. Eyes that were, in fact, dying inside, rotting and degenerating until all that would remain were their pretty blue outer casings as unseeing and lifeless as empty seashells scattered on a deserted beach.

Before I could even begin to dream up some form of uplifting response, my phone rang. I groaned. "Now is not a good time, Tom."

"Sorry, Kurt, but I thought you'd want to know this. I'm afraid it's not good news, either."

I had a feeling I knew which bad news Holloway was leading up to. "It's the Reverend, isn't it?"

"The only way we can pin this guy is to match him to the oak leaves. Unfortunately, the Rev has no oak trees in his garden. And we've typed the one in his churchyard. I'm afraid the tree is from a completely different species. We don't have a match."

"Damn."

"Which means we can't detain him any longer. He's walking."

"Damn!"

I ended the call, tossed the phone onto the bedside table, and laid down beside Meghan, my legs hanging off the end of her bed. Tucking an arm under her head, I joined her in staring up at the glow-in-the-dark stars on her ceiling.

19

The Reverend Patrick Mackenzie extended his hand to Detective Sergeant Holloway, the short, bespectacled one.

"It's been a pleasure," he said with a smirk. The detective frowned at the offered hand as if it had wiped some bottoms without washing.

"I will see you around. God bless you." With a wink, Mackenzie turned and walked out of the police station, immune from the venomous glares of the officers he passed. He knew they couldn't detain him; they had nothing on him.

After all, they were all barking up the wrong oak tree.

How he wished the tall, mixed-race cop had been around to see him walk. It was so easy to rile him, to get under his skin. That man was a lost sheep, a *black* sheep, blind to the workings of the Lord. In return, God would be blind to him on Judgment Day. For all his stoic principles and self-righteous morals, his soul was as damned as those of the criminals he pursued.

One cannot swim with shit and not get soiled.

Once outside, Mackenzie took a deep breath, inhaling the humid, smoggy air of the late East London evening.

Beats the smell of stale piss in the cell.

He shook his lawyer's hand, thanking him for his help.

"Will you be doing anything special tonight?" Frederickson asked.

"Oh, I intend to celebrate," Mackenzie replied. "I am going to paint the town red."

A murmur of appreciation rippled through the crowd as the woman on stage wrapped her legs around the top of the pole, leaned back, and spiralled her way downwards. A solitary cheer sounded as she settled on the floor on all fours, her skirt hitched up her thighs, her cowl-necked dress revealing more than just a glimpse of cleavage.

Rising to her feet, the woman shrugged off the straps of her dress and, with a naughty smile, wiggled until the garment fell down to her waist. The soft, pale skin of her exposed breasts glowed pink, purple and blue under the flashing lights, her nipples, dark cherries crowning twin mounds of creamy, erotic flesh, heaved from the exertion of her performance.

In time to the music, the woman dropped to her knees at the edge of the stage and leaned forward, dangling her tits in the face of the salivating men in the front row. Her body pulsing to the beat of the booming music, she jiggled her hips, working her dress lower still, until the lacy string of her panties peeked out from beneath the folds of clothing. The well-practiced tease elicited the desired response as whoops of admiration rang out through the audience.

Time for her grand finale.

She jumped up, leaving her dress in a heap on the floor. Naked except for a sheer G-string and silver skyscraper heels, she stood up tall, chest jutted out, legs parted. As instructed, she held the pose for a few seconds, allowing the punters to drink in the sight of her. She scanned the sea of gawking faces, making sure to make eye contact with each and every one. Her job was to make every customer feel special, to make it seem as if she danced and stripped only for him.

Her gaze fell on a familiar figure lurking in the shadows by the bar. For a brief second, her plastic smile faltered. The throbbing of the bass took on a sinister tone. The man downed a double whiskey, fixing her with an unblinking stare.

The eyes of a predator.

Fighting down the rising tide of unease, the woman forced herself to get on with the performance. She strutted up to the pole and climbed on, her body on auto-pilot as she twirled and danced. All the while, the man's eyes burnt into her, prickling the skin at the nape of her neck, tightening her stomach with an illogical sense of self-consciousness. The man's icy glare unnerved her more than all the goggle-eyed attention from the rest of the audience.

What really worried her was how much he'd been drinking—two empty shot glasses sat before him, and he was signalling the bartender for another one.

After what seemed like an eternity, the music stopped.

"Now was that a glimpse of Paradise or what? Let's give a hand to the divine Persephone!" the emcee announced to a smattering of applause. With a short curtsy and a faux smile, she retrieved her shed gown before scurrying backstage. She dressed in a hurry, her mind cycling through a list of possible excuses to get off work early.

Headache ... stomach cramps ... twisted ankle ... that time of the month ...

Scared for my life.

"Persephone!" A colleague, dressed in denim hot pants and a midriff-baring varsity top, patted her on the shoulder. "Christian's here. He wants a private."

No, I'm busy, she wanted to say, but she knew she couldn't turn him down.

He would destroy me.

With a weak nod, Persephone smoothed down the front of her dress and made her way to Private Room Two, where she would wait for Christian. Her high heels dragged along the floor, suddenly weighing a ton each. Her stomach fluttered, and mouth ached for a drink as she approached the aluminium door with the glittering number *2*.

In the pulsing light-darkness of the club, sinuous silhouettes gyrated to the thumping beat of music turned up way too loud. Nubile nymphs, all in various states of undress, ground their hips against metal poles, seducing the men with their dance in the same way the Sirens enchanted sailors with their song.

The women were nothing but a passing fascination for the Oracle. He came on a quest, and he would remain focused until he completed his task.

The girl who had been dancing on the central podium just minutes earlier wore a white toga with gold trim, looking as pure and breathtaking as the goddess of love and beauty herself. He had watched her cavort and weave around the pole, moving with a serpentine grace. Her strenuous performance had flushed her cheeks, leaving her with a rosy glow and giving her an almost divine aura.

Like a satyr stalking a nymph, his gaze shadowed her as she moved across the room, hands wringing in front of her. She hesitated before a metal door, luscious lips drawn into a tight line. She looked mortal again, vulnerable.

With a deep breath, his goddess disappeared behind door number two.

The Oracle moved into position.

20

Angie wore my favourite nightdress, a strappy turquoise number that brought out the colour of her eyes. The silk caressed her curves in all the right places, and a lacy slit ran up one side, offering me a teasing glimpse of alabaster skin.

I sat at the edge of the bed and unbuttoned my shirt. She helped me undress, her fingers brushing my skin and leaving blazing trails of goose bumps. She started rubbing my back, kneading the knotted muscles between my shoulder blades.

"You seem tense today," she said, her warm breath feathering my ear and neck.

I tilted my head back with a sigh, leaning into the valley of her soft bosom. I savoured the heady scent of her bath soap—jasmine and sandalwood.

"Meg and I went to the park today. We saw a fox. Well, at least I did. You know how much Meg loves foxes."

"Mmm hmm ..." Angie's hands wandered to my chest and began massaging.

"It was a little one. A cub. It came right up beside us, sniffing at our ice cream before Meg's squeal scared it away."

"She was excited to see it then." Hands on my stomach.

"That's the thing. She didn't see it. She was squealing 'Where? Where?', and it was right beside her." I sighed, interlocking my fingers with hers. Ebony and ivory. "I mean, I know her peripheral vision is deteriorating, but bloody Hell ... that fox was right next to her!"

Angie kissed the top of my head. "Meg told me she had a wonderful time at the park. She seems to be coping with her condition better than you are."

"But don't you think it's kinda unfair? For a kid to lose her vision before she's had a chance to see most of the world? To live in darkness for the rest of her life?"

Angie traced her finger along the planes of my stomach. "It is sad, I'll admit, but you know, Kurt, her disability will not *make her life any less rich or fulfilled." She walked her fingers lower.*

"Did you know what she told me yesterday? She said she wished Uncle Reggie would stop hanging out with his 'homies'. She never sees you arguing with him about his mates, never sees the trouble they get up to ... Hell, when you had to 'bail him out' the last time, she thought you were helping him drain a flooded boat! Yet somehow, she knows that it's Reggie's association with these people that's affecting the relationship between the two of you." Her hands settled on my thighs, and I could ignore them no longer.

"All I'm saying, Kurt, is that you don't need twenty-twenty vision to experience the world. Meghan sees more than you think."

She eased my back onto the bed and bent over me. I looked up at her, an upside-down vision of beauty. Her frosted blonde hair, cropped in an endearing pixie cut, reflected the ceiling light, creating a golden aura round her head. Her nipples poked their curious heads out against the flawless material of her nightie. Emerald eyes smouldering with desire, she leaned forward, her lips parting as they prepared to dock mine ...

"Daddy!"

I woke with a start, momentarily confused. As the fog of sleep evaporated, I found myself sprawled on the kitchen table, my head on my open laptop. I sat up, rubbed my cheek and wiped the drool off the touch pad. A string of gobbledegook ran across my screen where my face had rested on the keys. Meghan stood in her pyjamas at the kitchen entrance, mouth twisted into an expression of amusement, tempered with a dash of concern.

What's happened? What am I doing here? Where's Angie?

I remembered my dream, where Angie *really* was, and my heart broke all over again. Slumping back in my chair, I stared at my lap.

That was when I noticed my monster hard-on.

Meghan moved to stand beside me. I bolted upright, hands flying to my groin to conceal my erection.

"What are you doing?"

"Working." Legs crossed and hands clasped on my lap, I sat demure as a Victorian schoolgirl.

Meghan squinched her eyes. "I heard you snoring, Dad."

"What time is it?" I tried to stifle a yawn, but my mouth cracked open so wide my jaws creaked, and tears sprang to my eyes. I glanced at the wall clock. Nearly midnight.

I hadn't been out long.

"What are *you* doing up so late?" I asked.

"I needed a glass of water." Meghan padded over to the kitchen sink and filled a tumbler from the tap. "I thought I'd try to wake you. You'll sleep better in bed."

"Thanks, but I think I'll stay up a bit longer. Get some more work done."

She pursed her lips together and clucked her tongue, hand on hip. "You're gonna make yourself ill."

I ruffled her hair. "I'll go to bed in an hour. Promise." *Dear God, has my daughter actually imposed a curfew on me?*

"Fine." She sighed with a roll of her eyes. "But on one condition—double reading time tomorrow night."

I laughed. "It's a deal. More *Theseus and the Minotaur*?"

"Oh, I finished that after you put me to bed," she said with a mischievous wink as I mocked an appalled look. "The rest of the story was easy. I want to read this next …"

Before I could say, "Sweetie, you can show me the book tomorrow," Meghan darted off, bare feet slapping against the laminate flooring. She disappeared into her room, reappearing seconds later with a thin book in both hands. The jacket cover depicted a bearded man wearing a toga and a laurel wreath, brandishing a crackling lightning bolt. I recognised it as one of the books in her *Tales of the Greek Gods* series. In a font style inspired by Greek symbols, the cover read: *ZEUS, KING OF THE OLYMPIANS*.

I put the book on the table. "Fine, we'll read that tomorrow."

"Thank you, Daddy!" Meg gave me a peck on the cheek before tottering back to bed. I checked my erection. The swelling in my pants had subsided somewhat. I briefly entertained the notion of rummaging in Reggie's room for one of his 'hobby' magazines.

Angie, I miss you. My right hand just can't compare.

I got up to fix myself a cup of coffee, my mind running through the details of the case.

Four victims. Three dead. One survivor. A lucky escape? Something in my gut told me Sarah Quinn's survival was no accident. Hanging from a tree with weights tied to her feet had to be painful, and no doubt traumatic, but it was unlikely to cause death.

Sarah Quinn was meant to survive.

But why? Why let her live while the others died? Did it depend on the extent of their sin within the killer's twisted mind?

The Reverend accused her of being a child abuser.

Why gold chains? What did they symbolise? Being weighed down by material needs, perhaps? And why put an acorn into the woman's vagina? An acorn's a seed. Could he be sowing a seed? Why? Could he have been attracted to her? Maybe he was a secret admirer? A rejected suitor?

So many questions.

I sank back into my chair with a mug of coffee, the bittersweet aroma already sharpening my senses. As I blew on my drink, my eyes fell on Meghan's book.

Something about the cover made me take a second glance.

I put my mug down and picked up the book. The frilly leaves making up the Greek god's crown did not look like laurel leaves.

They were oak leaves.

I flipped open the book, swiping aside the plastic Braille overlays as I read the text.

One of the symbols of Zeus is the oak leaf. The Oracle at Dodona is a temple to Zeus where priests read fortunes by listening to the rustling of the leaves on a sacred oak tree.

My heart raced, all traces of drowsiness gone as if I'd received an intravenous transfusion of pure caffeine. I turned the page, skimming through the information and the colourful pictures.

I stopped on a page depicting a woman bound with golden chains.

Zeus loved his wife, Hera, but when she angered him, Zeus's punishments could be harsh. Once, to punish her for tormenting his son Hercules, he bound her with gold chains and hung her from the heavens, with heavy weights tied to her feet.

I sat back, shaking my head. I was right about the acorn inserted into Sarah Quinn being a 'seed'—one he sowed because he saw her as his 'wife'.

That bastard. He thinks he's Zeus!

I thumbed through the book, ignoring the light sting as one of the glossy pages sliced into my fingertip, and reached the last page.

There must be more to it.

Turning to my laptop, I called up my Internet browser. In the search engine, I queried the terms '*Zeus*', '*drown*' and '*magician*'. It returned a list of websites. I clicked on the first one.

In Greek mythology, the Telchines [pronounced 'Tel-she-nes'] were a race of beings that lived on the island of Rhodes. Skilled sorcerers, they used their magic for malignant purposes. This angered Zeus, who cast them into the sea to drown them.

"Son of a bitch."

I tried another search with the terms '*Zeus*', '*preacher*' and '*electricity*'. To my surprise, nothing useful came up.

Hold on, Nick Kemp was hardly a bona fide preacher. He dressed up as Jesus, for Christ's sake. Let's try a leap of the imagination.

I revised my terms: '*Zeus*', '*impersonator*', '*lightning*'

I hit 'Enter'.

Salmoneus was a mythical king of Elis in ancient Greece. He ordered his subjects to worship him as Zeus. He imitated the god's thunder by tying cauldrons to the back of his chariot before racing it across a brass bridge, and he used torches to impersonate the god's lightning. For his pride and blasphemy, Zeus struck him down with a thunder bolt.

Hera. Salmoneus. The Telchines. My head spun with the revelation. The pulse in my neck throbbed against my skin.

I called Blaize. The phone rang for nearly a minute before she answered with a sleep-choked, "Hello?"

"Sam, it's Kurt. I have big news."

A muffled yawn carried through. "Do you know what time it is?"

"I couldn't wait. You have to hear this. This bastard is unbelievable. And you know what?" I scrolled through the information on the new webpage I found.

"I think we may be able to predict his next move."

21

The darkest hour is just before the dawn...

Wasn't that what Thomas Fuller wrote? Standing alone in the deserted car park, the words rang with a haunting truth. No moon or stars punctuated the homogenous darkness of the sky. It was black, as black as the ink of dread dripping into her blood.

A gust of wind rushed into the walled parking lot, bearing dancing paper bags and twirling food boxes. Summer or no, London nights could be chilly. She wrapped her cardigan tighter around herself, the lightweight knitwear doing little to shield her from the cutting breeze.

Headlights pierced the grimy shadows as a car turned into the enclosed lot. The passenger door swung open, and a dark figure behind the wheel beckoned. She shuddered again, but not from the cold.

Reluctantly, she entered the car.

"Close the door," a low voice rumbled, "you're letting in a draft."

She did as he told her. As soon as the door slammed shut, the headlights went off, and the locks slid into place with an ominous *clunk*. Almost instantly, a pair of hands grabbed at her, groping her, pulling at her clothes and kneading her breasts.

"Stop," she pleaded, her voice a squeaky whisper. The stillness that followed came thick with foreboding. Eyes, shining in the semi-darkness, narrowed dangerously.

She fumbled in her purse with trembling fingers, pulling out a roll of cash fastened with a rubber band.

"Here's two hundred pounds." She proffered the money to the shadow beside her. "More than half my wages. I can give you this much ... maybe even more ... every week." Her fingers shook so much, she feared she'd drop the money into the limbo that was the inaccessible gap between the car seats. "Just ... just please, don't do this to me anymore."

The figure snatched the wad of cash from her and stuffed it into a coat pocket. He smiled, teeth gleaming in the dark like the Cheshire Cat's.

For a split second, her heart lifted on underdeveloped wings of hope.

The slap rang through the claustrophobic confines of the car, loud as a thunderclap. Her head snapped to the side, hitting the dashboard. Supernovas exploded in her darkened vision. Her cheek burned. She tasted the warm, metallic tang of her own blood. Rough fingers entwined themselves in her hair. She gasped as he pulled her head off the dashboard, ripping tufts of hair from her scalp by the roots.

"Insolent *whore*!" he roared in her ear, making her wince. "You *dare* to buy my silence with petty cash?" He smashed her head into the dashboard. A sharp *crack* echoed through her skull as her nose exploded in a crimson blossom, filling her eyes with instant tears.

"Do you know who I am?" he demanded, forcing her to face him again. "*Do you?*"

Her vision danced, making it hard to focus on his twisted features. Choking on her own blood, she managed a weak nod and a gurgled whimper of submission.

"Never forget that it is my word against yours." He leaned forward, sniffed her neck, nibbled her earlobes, and made her squirm with revulsion and pain. "Your parents are good Christians. Imagine their disappointment if they found out their beloved, seemingly wholesome daughter is nothing but a cheap, two-bit tramp."

He threw her back. The base of her skull struck the window on the passenger side. Hot tears came, tears of shame and guilt and helplessness. They trickled down her cheeks until they mingled with the scarlet dripping off her chin. A metallic chink sounded as he undid his trousers, pulling them down to his knees. His breathing grew louder, deeper—an overweight bear about to have a heart attack.

With a grunt, he climbed over her. His face loomed over hers, terrible in its carnal ferocity. His breath rolled across her chest, wave after wave of soured alcohol. She turned away, but vice-like fingers clamped around her jaw, jerking her neck back to face him. He glared at her in contempt; she was cowpat that dared soil the bottom of his shoe.

"You look a right mess," he said as if that was her fault. He grabbed her by the shoulders and turned her around, pushing her face right up against the passenger side window. Streaks of red transferred onto the clear glass. A chill tickled her bottom as he lifted up her skirt.

"Please . . ." she begged, "no . . . don't . . ."

"Shut up!" Another blow from behind sent her forehead crashing into the window. Reduced to mewling sobs, she shut her eyes, fingernails digging into the seat upholstery.

Please, God, don't let this happen again.

The door locks popped up with a *click*. A whoosh of cold air rushed into the car as the driver's door flew open. A dull *thump* followed with the weight of her tormentor disappearing.

The door on her side opened, and she tumbled out onto the gravel, landing before a pair of shoes. Three feet above the shoes hovered what looked like a mallet, the kind seen in slapstick cartoons.

It gleamed with a sheen of sticky blood.

Staggering onto all fours, she didn't know whether she should be thanking her saviour, her dark angel, or if she would be killed by some mallet-wielding psychopath.

The figure spoke, the words like an injection of drugs into her system, breaking her out of her paralysed shell.

She stood on unsteady legs and ran out of the parking lot, away from the car, turning her back on the unfolding punishment being meted out by her avenging angel.

22

Chief Sutherland looked miffed by the evidence before her. Exhibit A: a children's picture book with Braille inserts. Exhibit B: a sheaf of computer printouts of various web pages, all run through with a neon yellow highlighter.

"You still liking Mackenzie as our man?" she asked.

"I'm liking him *more*," I said. "A religious fanatic with a god complex. It makes so much sense."

"Well, he definitely won't be the first," Blaize said.

"Hold on," Sutherland said, "Mackenzie is an ultra-right-wing *Christian*. Why would he be worshipping an essentially *pagan* god?"

Holloway spoke up. "Actually, considering the Greek gods predated Jesus by several thousand years, one can find striking similarities between Greek mythology and the stories in the Bible, a possible result of Christianity borrowing from ancient legends. The most cited example is Pandora's opening of her forbidden Box, compared with Eve's eating of the Forbidden Fruit. In fact, some people believe the name 'Jesus' is actually a contraction of the Greek phrase '*ie Zeus*', which literally means 'O Zeus' or 'Hail Zeus'."

Sutherland gaped at Holloway and turned to me, her eyes wide. "How the *hell* does he know all that?"

I shrugged. "He's a naturist panty-ist."

"*Naturalistic pantheist*," Holloway said. "Anyway, the point I'm trying to make is that the influence of ancient myths in

Christianity is not uncommon knowledge." Sutherland, Blaize and I raised our eyebrows in unison. "Okay, perhaps not common knowledge, but there's information all over the Internet if you know where to look. Perhaps worshipping Zeus to serve Jesus makes some sort of convoluted sense in our man's twisted mind."

"That's not all." I located my handwritten notes from the pile of paperwork. "This is all the information I managed to find on Zeus, origins, worship, mythology, everything. Mostly background information. He's head honcho of the Greek gods, lives on Olympus, wields thunderbolts, yadda yadda. There's also some juicy details of his promiscuity and incest. But here's something that might be useful..." I flipped through the pages until I came across a line I'd written not only in block capitals, but also underlined multiple times.

MAIN FESTIVAL IN HONOUR OF ZEUS: OLYMPIC GAMES!!

"So all these murders in the run-up to the Games might be no coincidence." Blaize said.

"No coincidence," Holloway said. "He seems to be punishing all sinners in the eyes of Zeus in honour of the Olympics."

"Right, so we've established a motive, albeit a rather far-fetched one." The Chief sifted through the rest of the papers on her desk. "Now you're telling me we can predict the unsub's next move?"

"We could try. There are a lot of mini-legends involving Zeus. The drowning of the Telchines, the smiting of Salmoneus, and the hanging of Hera are just a few." I riffled through the stack and pulled out a printed sheet with a list in bullet points. "If our man is deriving his inspiration from these stories, maybe we can find his next target before he does."

Sutherland focused on the list as if trying to read something in a foreign language. "Zeus turned King Haemus and Queen Rhodope into mountains to punish them for their vanity," she read.

Holloway snapped his fingers. "He might be hunting professional models to bury them under a mound ... of ... something ..."

Sutherland returned to the list. "Tantalus was condemned to sit for eternity beside a pond under a fruit tree. The low-hanging branches grew out of reach whenever he tried to pluck a fruit, and the waters in the pool receded whenever he bent down to drink."

"That's an easy one," I said. "He'll try to starve someone to death."

"Tantalus's crime was cannibalism and infanticide," Blaize said, reading over the Chief's shoulder. "He fed his own son to the gods as a sacrifice."

Holloway shrugged. "We've got all kinds of people out there."

"And what about this one?" Sutherland slapped the page with the back of her hand. "Zeus transforms a nymph into a tortoise for turning down his wedding invitation?" She tossed the sheet down as she sat back. "How is *that* going to help us?"

Holloway and I exchanged bemused glances. "I suppose it's how you interpret it," I managed.

"Listen." Sutherland shoved the paperwork towards us. "All this guesswork and reading of tea leaves is all well and fun, but the fact remains that we still don't have a suspect."

"We can bring Mackenzie in for questioning again," I said.

"You can try, but I doubt he'll reveal much. As it stands, we still have no evidence to implicate him."

I chewed my lip, deflated. The Chief was right. Identifying the pattern had been thrilling, but that was all it was. Problem-solving. Even if we had an idea where and how the killer would strike next, we couldn't run with it. There'd be thousands of possible victims, and we had no feasible way to warn them without causing undue distress.

Hello, ma'am, we believe you have a one in ten thousand chance of being the next victim of the Oaksecutioner. Would you care for a police escort?

We simply didn't have the manpower, the resources, or the

time.

What we needed was a breakthrough in the case.

The phone on Sutherland's desk jarred. She answered, grey eyes grim. When she replaced the receiver in the cradle, she glared up at us.

"Time for a road trip, guys."

Someone—God, Jesus, Zeus, *Je-Zeus*—seemed to have answered my prayer.

23

The Oracle sat beneath the sacred oak, hands clasped in prayer around a string of wooden beads. He placed both thumbs on the opening bead, the one which held the knot in the string, and began to chant.

"All hail Zeus, God of Thunder, Lord of Lightning, Father of Gods and men! Hear me, all-seeing son of Cronos, O many-faced one, as I lay this prayer before you."

His fingers started moving, rotating the beads, pausing on each smooth bead in reverence. His lips fluttered as he whispered, his mind focused on projecting each word into the embrace of the leafy branches above, into the very trunk of the tree itself.

> "Great Zeus, much wandering, terrible and strong,
> To whom revenge and tortures dire belong.
> Mankind from thee in plenteous wealth abound,
> When in their dwellings joyful thou art found;
> Or pass through life afflicted and distressed,
> The needful means of bliss by thee suppressed.
> 'Tis thine alone, endued with boundless might,
> To keep the keys of sorrow and delight.
> O holy blessed father, hear my prayer,
> Disperse the seeds of life-consuming care,
> With favouring mind the sacred rites attend,
> And grant to life a glorious blessed end."

Knuckles gripped white from the fervour of his worship, the Oracle's fingers lingered on the final bead.

"Zeus was the first. Zeus will be the last. All things are from Zeus."

With a deep breath, he opened his eyes and gazed heavenward. Fragments of sunlight filtered through the leaves, dappling his skin in warm, golden rosette patterns. The patches on his skin danced as a breeze whispered through the branches.

The Oracle rose, flexing his legs. He pressed a hand to the gnarled trunk, the powers of the sacred oak channelling into his body. Running his palm down the coarse bark, his fingers memorised the grooves and knots, each one placed there by the supreme creator with meticulous care.

If only he could stay forever, basking in the company of the Almighty One.

He had to go, fulfil his mundane earthly duties, mind-numbing work mortals perceived as important.

Nothing is more important than serving our Father.

He looked forward to work. That day, his job would have a divine purpose—to double as a reconnaissance mission.

He must plan carefully for his greatest conquest.

In the name of Zeus.

24

We had descended into Hell. Either that, or Hell had risen up to meet us.

With handkerchiefs held to our noses, Blaize, Holloway and I shouldered our way past a couple of EMTs. The centre of the back alley parking lot had been transformed into a raging inferno. Flames licked at the air. Plumes of smoke rolled upwards, satanic black cumulus clouds rising to join their pure white cousins in the sky. Burning embers pulsed as they floated up, carried aloft on smoky wings. I coughed as fumes—the oily-smelling kind that seemed to tar the inside of my lungs—tickled my throat.

A team of soot-covered firefighters in their bright yellow helmets battled to bring the blaze under control, spraying a thick, white foam over the fire to asphyxiate it. Through the tangle of dancing flames, I glimpsed the heart of the roaring bonfire—a blackened shell of twisted metal.

A plainclothes detective introduced himself as Detective Inspector David Addams from Serious Crimes.

"We got an anonymous nine-nine-nine tip-off about suspicious activity at around four thirty-two a.m.," he said. "By the time officers arrived on the scene, this place was Hell on Earth. You should've seen the fire when we got here; what you see now is a baby version."

"Any idea who made the call?" Holloway asked.

"All we know is it was a woman. Made the call at a payphone just a block from here."

I scanned the lot that flanked the back of a row of shops. Brick walls lined the other three sides, save for a narrow alleyway leading out onto the road. Above a back door with peeling paint, a neon sign depicted a stylistic representation of a skimpily clad woman, bent over with her legs spread wide apart. In between her shapely pins, the words *NYMPHO MANIA* was spelt out in unlit light tubes.

All in all, the perfect spot for committing a crime.

"No security cameras in this lot," Addams said, answering my unvoiced question, "customer discretion and all that. But there is one on the street outside, overlooking the entrance into the lot."

"Have you analysed the footage?" Blaize spoke for the first time. She stood a little hunched over as if trying to mask some pain or discomfort. Addams's eyes travelled up and down Blaize's body before speaking, and for some reason that made me want to deck him.

"We have," he said finally. "At four seventeen this morning, a woman was seen running out from the alley, but the picture was too grainy to make out any distinguishing features."

"Probably the one who made the nine-nine-nine call." I wondered if she might also be the arsonist.

"Probably. And about ten minutes before that, a car drove into the lot. Never came back out. No doubt that's the missing car there." He gestured to the smouldering heap. The blaze had finally been put out. Firefighters swarmed over the gutted wreckage.

"So why have Homicide been called?" I asked.

"Approximately twenty minutes after the mystery female left the lot, the camera caught a second person coming out of the alley—someone who fits the description of a person of interest in your Oaksecutioner case."

If I had doggie ears, they would have pricked up. "Was it a tall, bearded man?"

Addams nodded.

I looked at Blaize. At Holloway. Their wide-eyed expressions probably mirrored mine.

We had evidence linking Mackenzie to the murders.

A rabble of excited shouts from the burnt-out car demanded our attention.

"We got a body in here!"

25

He'd watched as Kurt Lancer hurried out the front door, fumbling with his car keys, a slice of burnt toast, slathered in marmalade, clenched between his teeth. Dark circles coloured the underside of his eyes, and his cornrows were untidy, hastily braided.

As Lancer's Ford Fiesta rumbled to life, reversed out of the driveway and cruised away down the road, the observer moved from his hiding place. The windows into the Lancers' flat were drawn, but that didn't matter. He knew Lancer's daughter had been left with the neighbours upstairs. Her singsong voice wafted down from one of the first floor windows like she was reading aloud to herself.

He crept towards the front door. A twig snapped underfoot.
Shit.
A head flew out of an open window above him, forcing him to dive into the cover of the bushes. From a gap between the leaves, he spied a woman, hair wrapped up in a towel turban, leaning out the window. She scanned the darkened garden, neck swivelling like a radar dish, eyes wide like a startled rabbit's.

Who could blame her for being jumpy? Her daughter had been attacked on the doorstep of their home. She must feel like her private sanctuary had been breached, her sense of security shattered.

After a minute, the woman's head disappeared. The window slid shut with a *thunk*, and he let out the breath he hadn't realised he'd been holding.

That was a close one.

Being more careful where he tread, he tiptoed his way to the front door. He reached into his pocket, his hands closing around the smooth hardness of cool metal.

26

Holding my nose against the pungent odour of seared flesh and singed hair, I'd inspected the still-smoking corpse, destroyed beyond all recognition. Patches of pink showed where charred flesh had peeled away. White teeth smiled up at me where lips should have been. I stared into empty eye sockets on a head so badly burnt that the skull showed through chunks of flaking scalp.

Holloway had turned a peculiar shade of grey-green at the sight. I had to send him away before he hurled all over the evidence. Couldn't blame him, really. My own stomach did a queasy loop at the sight and smell. Even Blaize paled at the sight.

Forensic officers at the scene echoed my concern. No way could they ID the body using fingerprints or DNA. Fingers all but cremated, the arms of the victim ended in club-like stumps, curled and blackened like the tip of a used matchstick. "Pugilistic." The jolly term the coroners used to describe such fire damage to a body. As if the vic had died wearing a pair of boxing gloves, and the melted mitts had fused with the victim's burnt flesh.

I knew the fire was linked to the other murders as soon as I saw the chains around the victim's torso, and the sticky tarlike residue clinging to the front of the body in amorphous globs.

"I think it's melted rubber," one of the forensic techs said on inspection.

"From a tyre, maybe?"

The tech turned to me. "How'd you know?"

"Ixion," I muttered to no one in particular. The tech raised his brows at me like someone regarding a gibbering mental patient. I'd read the myth of how Zeus condemned Ixion to be tied to a fiery wheel, punishment for attempting to violate his wife Hera.

So who had our victim violated?

"Dad!" I jumped at the sharp cry. Meghan frowned at me through her bioptics. "You haven't been listening to a word, have you?"

"Sure I have," I lied. I glanced down at the book and realised she had flipped the page. I'd been so unfocused and tired when I returned from the fire.

Pursing her lips at me, Meghan appeared unconvinced but turned her attention back to her reading. "I need help with this word." She pointed to *Poseidon*.

"Pos-*eye*-don ..." she repeated. "Zeus got the heavens and earth, Poseidon the seas, and Hates ..."

"Hades."

"Hay-*dees*, ... who drew the short straw, became ruler of the ... Hm-deer ... Hm-duh ...?"

"Try the first letter again—and don't peek!" I said as Meghan's chin dipped down.

"It's such a long word ..." she said.

"Just break it down. Start with the first letter."

"*H* ..." Meghan's face scrunched up in concentration.

"It's not *H*. Try again."

"But it feels like *H*."

I took a steadying breath. "These dots are spaced further apart."

"You mean a *U*?"

"Yes, that's it. Now go on."

"*U ... M ...*"

I ground my teeth. "It's not *M*."

She huffed. "*Q*?"

"Oh, for God's sake! *N*, Meg, *N*! It says 'Underworld'! Dammit, it's not that difficult!" I tried to recall the words before they passed my lips, but my mouth clamped shut too late.

Meghan cowered against the pillow, gaping at me, a mirror of tears shimmering on the surface of her eyeballs.

"Sorry, I ..." I scratched at my head, rubbed my temples. "Daddy's tired. Just ... that's enough for today. Go to bed, sweetie. I'm sorry." I backed my way out of her room, stumbled down the corridor into mine, and shut the door behind me. Resting my head against the solid wood, I concentrated on my breathing, tried to stop the flower of frustration blooming within my chest, spreading through me like a rampant weed.

What kind of father am I? I'd left the poor girl all day, and the only time I had to spend with her, I ruined by thinking about work, by taking my anger and frustration out on her.

Kurt, you fool.

I slumped to the floor, my back against the doorframe. Something glinted between the carpet threads, drawing me like a distant lighthouse hailing a lost ship.

Another sequin. A pink one. Helen's craft materials sure got around. I flicked the tiny disc across the room.

My phone burred.

Go away.

I retrieved the handset from my pocket.

1 NEW MESSAGE
UNKNOWN NUMBER

My fingers didn't feel like my own as they pressed the button to open the text message.

CHECK UR DRESSER

My heart pulsed in my throat. *What is this, some cheap B-rate slasher horror?* I was already making my way to my dresser, my body on automatic pilot. With nothing new on top, I opened the top drawer with my foreign-feeling hand. Balled-up socks, squares of underwear, rolled up ties.

Something beckoned me from the folds of a handkerchief with

the glint of a faraway star.

My hands began to shake as my fingers closed around the white gold hoop.

It can't be.

The diamond winked as if privy to where it had been and revelling in torturing me by withholding the information.

That's not Angie's. It can't be.

I turned the ring over and over in my palms, read and re-read the inscription on the inside of the band:

28-08-2002

Our wedding day.

I rushed to the window and flung open the blinds. Warm summer air clung to my face as I leaned out, staring into the darkness. The balding grass, the malnourished apple tree with stunted fruit, the picket fence separating our house from the one next door—all remained the same.

I whipped my head round so hard something pinged in my neck.

Was he out there? Our stalker? Toying with us with some deranged way of demonstrating his power? By showing he could enter and leave our home with ease?

"*Fuck you!*" I roared into the darkness. "I know you're out there!" I didn't care who heard me as long as *he* did. Lights blinked on in the house next door. Curious, sleep-dusted eyes peered out at me, frowning with annoyance and a touch of trepidation.

The garden outside my window remained silent and still, keeping its secret—if he was still there—concealed.

The street bustled with activity. Vendors hawked their wares, their display stands spilling out of shops and onto the walkway. Shoppers toting carrier bags heaving with goods snaked through the crowds whilst others haggled with shopkeepers, demanding more value for their hard-earned coin. The melancholy notes of an *erhu* drifted from the speakers of one shop, its wailing strings competing with the upbeat rhythm of Canto-pop blaring from another outlet's stereos. The aroma of five spice and roast duck steamed out from busy restaurant kitchens, making my mouth water and my stomach rumble.

We were definitely stopping for lunch on the way home.

I loved Chinatown, loved the constant throng of people babbling in their musical dialects. Loved the fact that street signs were bilingual. Loved how entering the little slice of central London was like stepping into a different world.

Meghan insisted on stopping by a shop to pick up some *longan*. We ate them as we walked, splitting the brown skin of the grape-sized fruit and popping them whole into our mouths. After savouring the sweet juiciness of the translucent flesh, we spat the seeds back into the bag with the discarded shells. The shiny black orbs stared at us through their white scars like little eyeballs. No wonder the Chinese name for the fruit literally meant *dragon's eye.*

As we passed under the green-roofed pagoda arch, we took a sharp right, entering a narrow side street leading off from the main, touristy thoroughfare. Traffic was less manic but still busy. Holding Meghan's hand, I steered her onto the pavement to avoid colliding with a bicycle, its rear end balancing a tower of gurney sacks pregnant with potatoes and onions.

We weaved our way down the street until we arrived at an open doorway set between a Chinese apothecary and a shop selling mobile phone accessories and international telephone cards. Above the door, a simple, wooden plaque adorned with an etching of a plum blossom read in both English and Chinese:

SCHOOL OF WING CHUN

We entered the door and ascended a flight of steps, emerging in a spacious hall with laminate flooring. Mirrors lined an entire wall, the illusion from their reflections doubling the size of the room. Mounted on a wall, two broad-bladed butterfly swords crossed over a line of punch bags and wooden dummies. A handful of practitioners were dispersed across the training room, working on their forms or training in pairs.

"Kurt!" The familiar high-pitched voice of my teacher, *Sifu* Chen, approached me from behind. As a small, wiry, bespectacled Chinaman, in his mid-sixties but looking at least ten years younger, he wouldn't be what most people would envision when asked to picture a kung fu master. "How nice to see you!"

"Sifu," I held an open palm to my fist and bowed, "it's good to see you, too."

"And look at Meghan!"

My daughter giggled.

"So big now!"

I motioned for Meghan to sit in one of the chairs in the waiting area. "I'm sorry I haven't been in for training recently," I said, taking off my shoes.

"It's all right." Sifu Chen's inflection made *all right* sound like *all light*. "It good to have you back."

I removed a pair of black canvas slippers from my backpack, put them on, and joined Sifu Chen as he led me to a younger Chinese man practising his forms in front of the mirror.

"Hey, stranger!" the student said, his gaze holding mine in the mirror.

"You all right, Scott?" I asked.

We shook hands.

"Not bad, man." He ran a hand through his spiky black hair, his forehead glistening with perspiration.

Scott Long had been a regular sparring partner—and post-training drinking buddy—until my self-imposed hiatus. One of Sifu Chen's top students, he was training to become a professional fighter. When we sparred, he never pulled his punches. Just the way I liked to train.

He was tall for a Chinese, and he had blue eyes—unusual for

an Asian. He always joked that some white bastard must have jacked off in his family gene pool at some point in the distant past.

"Okay, Kurt," Sifu Chen said, "you and Scott, start warming up on your *chi sao*."

"Yes, Sifu," we said in unison. Giving each other a quick bow, we lowered into our stances and extended our arms. Our forearms connected and fell into a rolling rhythm, hands constantly searching for gaps in the other's defences.

"So what made you come back?" Scott asked after a period of silent concentration. He spoke perfect Queen's English with a touch of south London twang. In his own words, Scott was a 'BBC'—British-born Chinese.

"What else? I missed ya, man."

Scott laughed.

I meant it as a jibe—I didn't really want to go into detail about how I needed to feel better able to protect Meghan from a possible stalker—but there was a grain of truth in it; snapping at Meghan the night before was my wake-up call—the cold water in the face I needed.

I sensed an opening and pounced, but Scott parried my effort. He attempted a palm strike to my chest. I jammed his advance with my arm.

"How are things at home?" There was a drop in his tone, a heaviness in the way he asked the question that indicated he was expecting a serious answer.

"I'm coping, I guess."

"Life after Angie treating you well?" Scott had a habit of getting straight to the point. I found that refreshing. I was sick of how everyone I met tried to skirt the issue, sweep it under the carpet. How they pretended it never happened, that it wasn't happening.

I sighed. "Being a single parent is tough. I don't know how people do it."

"Doesn't Reggie help out?" We switched arm positions in midflow.

"Reggie's... moved out. He has his own commitments now." I focused on the movement of our arms: *attack, defend, swap... attack, defend, swap...*

"Well, if you ever need a shoulder to cry on—or a punch bag to vent your frustrations on—I'm your man."

I chuckled, my concentration dipping. Scott planted a one-inch punch to my chest that sent me reeling backwards.

"Shot," I wheezed. I signalled for a timeout and reached for my water bottle. As I chugged on my isotonic drink, I gave Meghan a wave. She waved back before returning to her book and half-consumed bag of longan. I cringed at the sight of her smearing sticky fingers over the glossy pages.

"Meg looks well." Scott mopped his brow with a towel.

"She's probably coping better than I am."

"Look at her whizzing through those pages! She's really gotten the Braille business down, hasn't she?"

"She's getting there, I suppose. Slowly."

"Isn't it amazing how visually impaired people can adapt and become completely self-sufficient?"

No, they can't, I wanted to say. *They will never be able to do things normal people take for granted: cook, clean, cross the road safely.*

Defend themselves from home invaders.

"Warmed up?" Sifu Chen said, interrupting my thoughts.

"As warm as we can be." Scott fanned himself with his towel. "Jeez, it's hot today."

Sifu Chen gave us a dark strip of cloth each.

"Put them on."

"Whoa," I said, "I've not trained for over ten months. I'm a bit rusty."

"Yeah," Scott said, "you think we're ready for this?"

The small man twitched his shoulders up in a shrug. "If you don't try, how would you know if you are ready?"

Fair point. Scott's eyes met mine as he moved to put the blindfold on.

"See you on the other side," he said with a wink.

I placed the cloth over my eyes, knotting it at the back of my head. The swathe of inky cotton swallowed up my vision. I blinked a couple of times, but whether my lids opened or closed, the same darkness met my eyes. My brain screamed at me. It knew it was daytime, but the premature night did not make sense.

"Ready?" Sifu Chen's voice asked from somewhere in the ocean of gloom.

"I guess," Scott said.

I merely nodded. Wherever I looked, the darkness was absolute as if I'd been suspended in the middle of a black void of oblivion.

"Begin," Sifu Chen said.

How? I didn't even know where to start. Hands groping in front of me, I shuffled forward with tentative baby steps, even though I knew full well we stood in the centre of the *kwoon*, with nothing lying around to trip us up. I tried listening out for Scott, but all I could hear were the noises from the other practitioners: the *thump-thump-thump* on punch bags, the *slap-slap* of padded feet, the drone of a dozen conversations. Noises my subconscious had always relegated into the background roared at me—a cacophony of random and disjointed sounds.

How was I supposed to find Scott in all the chaos?

Something touched my outstretched finger. A sharp intake of breath. The thud of a step forward. Instinctively, I leaned back. A rush of wind flew past my face. The tip of a knuckle grazed my chin.

Jesus! He nearly took my head off! I could hear nothing but the thundering of my racing pulse, the peals of my pumping heart, loud as an industrial pile driver. Moisture built up beneath my hairline. My blindfold began to take on a muggy dampness. Beads of sweat studded my upper lip. My mouth became dry as desert sand. I licked my lips, tasting the saltiness of adrenaline.

"*Oof!*" What had to be a fist connected with my chest. My

lungs deflated like a whoopee cushion. Something radiated heat beside me, something *close*. I stumbled back just as Scott attacked with a flurry of punches. I waved my hands frantically, managing to swat most of his shots aside, but the others got pretty close to their target.

"Kurt," Sifu Chen's reedy voice pierced through the fog of shadows, "focus. Try to see without your eyes."

I took a couple of deep breaths, attempting to pull the reins on my runaway heartbeat. Another *whoosh*—most likely Scott's fist—zipped by my face.

Calm down, I told myself, *try to feel, not see.* I forced all the white noise from my mind, banishing it into the background. My pulse still raced, but at least it stopped sounding like brass kettledrums. Bending my knees, I resumed my defensive stance, hands sniffing the air like the forked tongue of a snake. As the auditory turmoil died down, I discerned the rustle of cloth on cloth, the whisper of slippered feet gliding across the laminate, heading in my direction. This time, instead of backpedalling, I stepped forward, arms reaching out, preparing to meet the challenge head on. Our hands connected, sticking together on contact. Pressure—his arms on mine—probed, searching, seeking an opening, a chink in my armour. I pushed back just enough to give me a sense of my opponent's position, of where his hands were relative to his body.

He attacked, striking low. I defended by closing the gap. My other hand shot out in offence. It missed, but each time I deflected a blow and launched a counterattack of my own, my chest expanded with confidence, emboldening me to forge ahead.

As Scott lunged forward, I detected a weak spot, a breach. I threaded my arm through the gap. The blade of my hand sliced his neck. I heard a grunt. My other hand followed close behind for a follow-up strike.

"Stop!" The command rang out through the cavernous darkness. I obeyed, hands halted in mid-attack. Taking a few steps back, I tore off the oppressive blindfold. The sudden change in light levels dazzled me. I blinked several times, relieved to have regained my sight. Scott stood panting opposite me, eyes twitching from the unaccustomed brightness, his grey tank top stained dark with patches of sweat. I put a hand to my forehead. My fingers came away dripping.

We were both drenched in sweat.

Scott bowed. I returned the gesture.

"Good job, mate." I extended a hand, fingers still tingling.

"You too," he said, blue eyes buzzing. "Great workout."

"Very good, both of you." Sifu Chen interposed himself between the two of us. "Scott, too much strength at the end. Don't forget, hit too hard, and you leave big openings. Kurt," he patted my back through my sodden T-shirt, "too much hesitation. Trust your instincts." He jabbed his temple for emphasis. "Remember, you do not need eyes to see."

I nodded, still trying to catch my breath. I realised then that we had an audience. A few of the other students had stopped practising. With thumbs-up signs and murmurs of appreciation, they returned to their training.

Meghan still sat in the corner. From her position, I doubted she watched much of my martial art display. Even if she had, all she would have seen would have been blurred movements and swirling colours. Yet, when I turned to her, she smiled a dimpled smile and put her hands together in applause.

I dipped my head in a bow, my sifu's words still echoing in my head:

You do not need eyes to see.

The Reverend Patrick Mackenzie was officially a wanted man.

I beamed with vindication as I sat through the updates at our task force meeting, absently massaging a bruise on my right knuckle, a knock I sustained when training with Scott on

Saturday.

When officers arrived at Mackenzie's residence to question him about his car, he hadn't been home. In fact, he hadn't been home all weekend.

The bastard had gone into hiding.

A photograph of Mackenzie had been dispatched to the national press, his mug plastered on the front page of every newspaper. The media could be our worst enemy or our staunchest ally. In this case, they were the latter. The more people who saw his face, the better our chances were of finding him. We'd also issued an all-ports warning, circulating his description to airports, seaports and international railway stations, just in case he attempted to skip the country.

"Lancer," Chief Sutherland said. She had chosen not to sit down, opting instead to pace the room like a caged panther. "Give us an update on the latest crime scene."

I straightened in my seat, cleared my throat. "Mackenzie tried to incinerate all the evidence," I began, "but looks like he wasn't as thorough as he'd planned. Forensics found a strand of grey hair on the scene. They're typing it now."

"Any further information about the victim?"

"Our Ixion remains an unidentified male. Pathology is still working to ID him. Last I heard, they're hedging their bets on dental records. Oh, and guess what the coroner found in his mouth?" I held out the clear evidence bag containing an oak leaf with singed edges. Whispers and comments rippled through the room. Sutherland hushed them with her Medusa's stare.

Holloway raised his hand, a schoolboy trying to get the teacher's attention. "We got some good news on the oak leaves front. Forensic botanists have been typing the leaves and the acorn from the crime scenes. It's been confirmed they all came from the same tree. *And,* get this: they've pinpointed the *actual* tree."

Sutherland's eyebrows climbed towards her hairline. "They can do that?"

Holloway nodded. "Apparently, you can test trees for DNA, too. Anyway, the tree is situated in the East Reservoir Community Garden. Being the oldest oak in Hackney, it's a bit of a local celebrity in horticultural circles."

"Oldest oak in Hackney?" Sutherland echoed. "I guess that's fitting. Does Mackenzie live near there?"

I checked my notes. "It's not in his immediate neighbourhood. His home and church are about two miles away, as the crow flies."

"Right," the Chief said, "identifying the tree was a brilliant piece of detective work. Unfortunately, it isn't really going to help us find Mackenzie."

"Do you think he'd risk returning to the tree now?" somebody asked.

"He might, if he feels it's an integral part of his grand scheme," I said.

"In that case, we'll assign a patrol to watch the tree." Sutherland uttered a mirthless laugh. "I never thought I'd hear myself say that."

Dan Sykes, the young Detective Constable who fancied himself as a DCI, said, "Any word on the mysterious female seen leaving the lot around the time of the murder?"

"No," I said, "the footage was too grainy. We couldn't make her out. For now, we've launched an appeal for her to come forward. Do you think this mystery lady is our Hera?"

"She might be. She might not be." Sutherland shrugged. She didn't seem to care about the details of the killer's *modus operandi*. She just wanted the son of a bitch caught. "Can we link Mackenzie to any of the other crimes?"

"The computer techs are on that as we speak," Holloway said. "They've acquired Mackenzie's computer to see if he's made any recent online transactions of chains or anvils. As you can imagine, he didn't leave any receipts lying about."

"Well," Sutherland planted her hands on her hips, "I'm really hoping we're nearing the end of this blasted case. The Games officially kick off on Friday, and the Mayor has not stopped hounding me."

After the meeting, I left the conference room stoked. Like a shark homing in on its prey, I tasted blood in the water. Mackenzie's blood.

The son of a bitch was going down.

"You're looking cheerful today," Holloway said as I sat down at my desk.

"Had a good weekend." The sparring left me completely knackered, but it also helped unwind all my tension. Meghan enjoyed watching me practise—at least she claimed she did—and after the session, we enjoyed a leisurely *dim sum* lunch, the first uninterrupted meal out we'd had in months.

Holloway removed his glasses and rubbed the bridge of his nose. "I don't know about you, but I'll be glad to see the end of this case."

"What ... can't cut your first homicide? You have to admit, you picked a doozy for your first ever case." Leaning back in my chair, I stretched out my aching muscles, tilting my head to the side. My neck made a creaky *pop*.

Holloway cringed. "That is so bad for you! You're going to get arthritis."

I cracked my knuckles, delighting in Holloway's disgust. "That's an old wives' tale. It's been proven."

"Well, it can't be any good," he said with a shudder. "The human body isn't meant to make that kind of noise." He suppressed a yawn. "I swear, the first thing I'm going to do when we close this case is take a holiday."

"Where will you go?"

"Nowhere. Just some quiet time at home. Bit of reading. Might even do it outdoors if the weather is nice and the pollen count is low. You must be looking forward to your day off this Friday."

"Meg hasn't stopped talking about it. Will be interesting to see if the organisers can top Beijing." I sobered, remembering that

Reggie was supposed to be going with us. "Hey, I've got a spare ticket. Why don't you come with us?"

Holloway waved his hand. "Thank you, but I think I'll pass. Heaving crowds and screaming mobs aren't my cup of tea. Neither, for that matter, is watching a bunch of supremely fit people sweating it out against each other in battles of brawn and ego. Besides, I doubt I can wrangle a holiday at such short notice. Especially not if this case is still hot." He jabbed a thumb towards Blaize's unoccupied desk. "And especially if we continue being short-staffed."

I shook my head. "It's the fourth day this month she's been off," I said, careful not to let on that I knew what was wrong with her—kinda. "I hope she gets well soon. I think she's beginning to feel left out of the action."

"I'd feel that way if I were her." Holloway took out his mobile phone from the desk drawer. "Hello, I have voice mail. Somebody loves me."

"Message from a secret admirer?"

"I wish." There was a hint of wistfulness in his tone. "Cindy from the Coroner's office, actually. Let's find out what love she's sent my way." Pushing a button, he put the phone to his ear. After about a minute, he clicked off, dialled a number, waited as it rang. "Good afternoon, Cindy! Tom Holloway returning your call ... yup ... uh huh ..." His forehead wrinkled up. "You mean it was *synthetic*? You sure? Uh, okay ... That's not all?" I watched as Holloway's jaws slackened, his face dropping like the features of a melting wax doll. "You're fucking with me ..." I'd never heard Holloway swear before. "Uhm, thanks for being so quick, Cindy. Bye." He hung up, dropped the phone on the desk, his gaze off into the middle distance.

"Well?" I waggled my eyebrows at him.

"She had bad news and worse news."

"I kinda gathered that. Hit me."

"The grey hair found at the crime scene? Made from modacrylic fibre. A fake."

I frowned. "That's weird."

"That was just the bad news."

"So what's the worse news?"

"They've ID'ed the burn victim. Dental records."

"And?" How could identifying the body be bad news?

"We've found our suspect. The body was Mackenzie's."

27

The Oracle sat in the shade of his sacred oak, head resting against the firm trunk, the day's newspaper spread across his lap. The corners of his lips pulled up in a smile at the colour photograph under the front-page headline *THE FACE OF A KILLER?* Dressed in full church regalia, the man in the photo had one arm raised in mid-sermon. *Reverend sought in connection with Oaksecutioner murders* read the subtitle.

He wondered if the authorities knew yet what sort of a wild goose chase they'd been sent on, how far off they'd strayed in their investigations.

Ixion had been his most challenging conquest. The trickiest bit had been the timing—waiting until *after* the man's intent became clear, yet intervening *before* the act of violence occurred. It had also been the most *satisfying*. He studied the man in the photograph. Grey beard and tall stature, dressed in a purple and gold robe, finger pointed heavenward. The pompous mortal had truly believed his words divine, that they came directly from above. He was an impostor, another pretender to the jewelled throne of almighty Zeus.

But there is only one Zeus, and the world must remember that.

Had Ixion not been such an interest to the police, drawing their attention away from the Oracle, he would have been punished much sooner.

The Oracle read the entire news article, deriving pleasure from the prominence of his accomplishment. *Nationwide manhunt...*

public outcry ... considered armed and dangerous.

Front page news. His achievements were no longer news fillers beside the picture of a half-naked harlot.

His message was spreading.

He turned the tabloid sheet over to read the sports headlines. In the top right corner, a bold number *4* announced the number of days before the start of the Olympics. The news covered progress of final preparations, thoughts from the organisers, current status of medal hopefuls, opinions from athletes of the facilities at their competition venues.

All kinds of self-important bullshit.

They called the Olympics a "celebration of sporting excellence." *What blasphemy!* Had they forgotten the *original* intent of the Games? A festival in honour of the Greatest God of All? The pages bent and crumpled in his white-knuckled grip. With a disgusted snort, he flung the newspaper across the garden. It unfurled in mid-air, its pages scattering across the grass. The wind picked up some stray sheets, bearing them aloft like the ashes from a burning sacrifice rising to the heavens.

Ungrateful mortals. They have forgotten their divine provider. The name of Zeus was slowly being lost in the murky depths of their collective memory.

The Oracle stared up at the sky through a patchwork of sun-kissed, translucent leaves.

I will not allow them to forget, he vowed, sending his thoughts into the core of the sacred tree. He knew he was chosen for that very reason. He was the divine messenger.

He was the Oracle.

His ultimate task had always been to spread the message of Zeus, to *make* them remember His name.

And in four days, they shall *remember.*

28

I checked the flat number on the entry phone system against the address scribbled onto the Post-it note stuck to my finger.

This is the right place.

My finger hovered over the call button for a few seconds before I pressed it. As I waited, I shifted my weight from one foot to the other.

"Hellooo...?" someone chirped. "If you're the pizza man, you can forget about a tip. You're fifteen minutes late."

"Uh, hi," I hesitated at the unfamiliar voice. *Must be Blaize's flatmate. Lex, I think her name is.* "I'm Kurt," I began, "Kurt Lancer. I work with Sam. Don't know if she's ever mentioned me..."

"Oh!" the effervescent voice squealed, cutting me off. "*The* Kurt Lancer! Come on up! Top floor!" The door buzzed as it unlocked, admitting me into the apartment block.

'The' Kurt Lancer? I never saw Blaize as the kind of girl to enjoy a bit of juicy gossip over a manicure. *Especially* not if the topic of discussion revolved around someone she'd been regretting having a drunken fling with.

The door to Blaize's apartment was open by the time I reached the third floor landing. Standing at the threshold was Blaize's housemate and long-time friend, dressed in skinny drainpipe jeans, a figure hugging T-shirt and a checked bandana scarf.

It never occurred to me that Lex was a *man*. Leaning against the doorframe, he had his slender arms intertwined, appraising me shamelessly through trendy eyeglasses.

"You must be Kurt." He flashed me a crooked smile and extended a hand, palm down, as if expecting me to kiss it. "Alex Delaware. You can call me Lex."

I gave the limp wristed hand a ginger shake. "Pleased to meet you."

"*Enchanté*," he smiled, eyeing the box of chocolates under my arm. "Aww, you shouldn't have."

"They're actually for Sam … I mean, not that … y-you can have some too … if-if you want …"

Lex's eyes did a loop-the-loop. "At ease, soldier. I was just teasing. Besides, I can't eat too many of those. They go straight to the hips." He straightened. "Where are my manners? Come on in. Sammy B's in the lounge." He led me through a narrow hallway to the living room, where Blaize was sitting cross-legged on the sofa, a cushion clutched to her stomach. *Eastenders* was playing on the television set, the volume turned down low.

"Kurt, what are you doing here?"

"He came by to see you," Lex said. "Isn't that sweet? And you are so right, girlfriend. He's one *rrr*ough diamond!" He made the word sound like a growl, baring his teeth at me. I squirmed. *This must be how vulnerable a woman feels when a man mentally undresses her.*

"I … uh …" I waved the chocolates at her as a means of explanation.

"Thanks … I guess." Blaize shook her head. She looked pale. Even her hair seemed to have lost its fire. I noticed paracetamol and ibuprofen pill bottles on the coffee table.

"Just wanted to check you're all right."

"Would you like tea?" Lex offered. "We've got green, black or oolong. No coffee, I'm afraid. None of that evil sludge here."

"Lex," Blaize brought her hands together in a time-out gesture, "could Kurt and I, you know, have a quiet moment?"

"Ah," Lex winked, "gotcha. Don't want a third wheel hanging

about, do ya?" He pouted with mock hurt. "That's fine. I'm venturing into the wilds in search of sustenance. I'm tired of waiting for the bloody pizza guy. If he turns up, tell him to stick that cold pizza up where the sun don't shine, will ya?" Snatching up what could only be described as a handbag—or a 'man bag'—he loped towards the door like a gazelle. He stopped in front of the hall mirror, checking his hair, white-blond spikes protruding from a bed of darker roots, all held together by some form of indestructible hair gel. "You two lovebirds have fun now!" As the door slammed shut, I turned to find Blaize sunk deeper into the sofa, face half-buried in her cushion.

"Don't mind Lex," her voice sounded muffled from behind the pillow, "he's got OCB: obsessive compulsive bullshitting disorder."

"He is quite a character, isn't he?" I attempted what I hoped was a nonchalant shrug. "I was in the neighbourhood, so figured I'd drop by to see how you were getting on." I balanced the box of chocolates on her knee. "Belgian chocolate seashells. Your favourite kind."

"Thanks." She sighed, inspecting the chocolates before placing them on the table beside her medication.

"So ... how *are* you getting on?"

"I'm okay." She hugged the cushion tighter to her mid-section as she said it, thin lines creasing her forehead.

"No, you're not." I joined her on the sofa and patted her knee. "Please, Sam, tell me what's wrong."

"I told you," she insisted, "it's lady problems."

She'd once won her title fight against Tina "The Tornado" Wheeler despite nursing a cracked rib. If something was bothering her that much, it couldn't be any generic health issue.

"I know you, Sam. You're so tough, even childbirth probably won't make you flinch." She turned her head away from me. "It's not just any normal lady problems, is it?" I grabbed her chin, forcing her to look me in the eye. "Is it?"

Blaize's eyes shimmered like morning dew on a blade of grass. Her jaw clenched beneath my grip. For a moment there, I thought she was going to cry.

She pulled away, fixing her gaze on a water ring stained into the top of the coffee table. "It's endometriosis," she said, "do you even know what it is?"

"No," I admitted, not sure if I was prepared for the lurid medical details.

"In a nutshell, I have growths where growths shouldn't be, and it results in ... complications."

"Complications such as ...?" I nodded towards the painkillers on the table.

"The pain comes and goes. Today was a really bad day."

"At the risk of sounding ignorant ... how is it treated?"

Blaize fingered a tasselled corner of the cushion. "There's no cure, except ..."

After waiting for an answer that never came, I said, "Except what?"

She sighed. "Radical surgery."

The words hung in the air between us, damp and heavy and suffocating. "Just ... how radical are we talking?" I finally asked.

Blaize turned away again. "I wouldn't be able to have children."

"I-I'm sorry." My words came out as hollow and helpless as I felt. I put a hand on her shoulder. "I hadn't realised you wanted kids. You always seemed like such a career-driven ..."

She spun on me with such a searing glare that I shut up and released her shoulder.

"That's not the point," she snapped, green eyes wavering. "The point is ..." she huffed, slumped against the sofa and tilted her head back. "The point is I won't have that option." She gazed up at the plasterboard ceiling, blinking furiously. I sat at the end of the sofa, watching her in silence, wanting to say or do something to make everything better but feeling completely impotent. I'd never had Blaize down as the broody type. Then again, I suppose if I'd found I was shooting blanks, I'd have been pretty bummed, too.

We sat in silence in front of the TV. I watched the remainder of the soap without paying much attention. Blaize stared straight ahead, still clinging to the cushion as if it was the one thing anchoring her, keeping her from drowning in a sea of despair. She looked small. Of course, at five foot four, she wasn't tall to begin with, but she always carried herself with such assuredness, no one ever noticed she stood half a foot shorter than most of the thugs she dealt with. *The heart of a tigress with the build of a tabby cat.* Right then, though, she'd lost her confident swagger. For the first time in the two years I'd known her, she seemed helpless, like a lost little girl, one too proud to ask for help, to admit just how scared she was.

The credits began at the end of the episode. Gingerly, I stretched my arm across the back of the sofa, hooking it around her shoulders. Blaize stiffened. I half-expected an elbow to the ribs, but after a moment's hesitation, she relaxed into me, leaning her head on my collarbone. She smelled of peach blossom and magnolia, clean, light and fresh. The warmth of her body against mine fit just like it had two months before.

Walter Ellis's retirement party was one of the few occasions our entire team converged to let our hair down. It was also the first time I'd ever seen Blaize in a dress—a slinky black number that caressed every contour of her lithe body.

After a night of non-stop drinking games, I remembered offering to walk her home, remembered how she tried to kiss my cheek but got my lips instead. By the time we got to her doorstep, we were both in states of partial undress.

With the morning after came the sobering hangover. I wasn't ready to move on after Angie. She didn't want the stigma attached to an interdepartmental relationship. We swore each other to secrecy, but our once-easy friendship, strained under the burden of our shared illicit secret, had not been the same since. Sitting with her on the couch was the most comfortable I'd been with Blaize in a long time.

A pity it had to come as a result of bad news.

"You want to hear a secret?" she murmured, eyes dipping downwards. I grunted my assent. A lock of her cinnamon hair tickled the hollow of my throat. "I got pregnant once. At university. Stupid mistake." She blew air through her nose in an ironic laugh. "Too much partying, not enough sense. When the supposed 'father' found out, he ran a mile."

"What did you do?" Sensing difficulty, I held her closer, resting my cheek on the top of her head.

"I was in my final year. I had a job waiting for me. Plus, my mom would've killed me if she found out." Her voice wavered. She swallowed. "I had no choice. I had to get rid of it."

"I'm sorry."

"I wasn't. I mean, I felt kinda bad at first, but all it took were a couple of pills. Quick, easy, discreet. I never regretted it. At least, not until now." Another hollow laugh. "I suppose I deserve this, eh? Karma's come back to bite me in the arse." Her next laugh dissolved into a choked sob. Her shoulders shook. I stroked her head, running my fingers through her hair.

Blaize took a few steadying breaths. She placed a hand on my thigh, petted my knee. "This stays between us, y'hear?"

"I hear."

"If anyone finds out, I'll—"

"You'll cause me severe physical harm," I finished for her, smiling. "Yeah, yeah, I get it."

We lapsed into a long spell of silence. Not the stuffy, awkward kind we'd been having, but the warm, easy kind shared between good friends, friends who knew that sometimes words were just not necessary. Blaize rested her head on my shoulder, and I kept my arms around her. We stared at the TV as it droned on.

When Lex returned with what smelled like an Indian takeaway, I glanced at my watch; I'd been there nearly two hours.

Lex's grin could rival the Cheshire Cat's.
I took it as my cue to leave.

Back to the old drawing board.

I sighed, staring at the incidents board until all the photos, clippings and scrawled letters floated together into a swirling cesspool. Wistfully, I wondered if the answer would emerge from the mire if I stared into it hard enough.

It didn't.

I moved the photograph of the Reverend Patrick Mackenzie from the column labelled 'Suspects', to the growing 'Victims' column. We'd been so sure Mackenzie was our killer, we hadn't even entertained the possibility that the body in the car might be his. Everyone in the department felt like a complete noob because of the oversight.

The number of victims officially stood at five.

Number of suspects: *zero*

I uncapped a black marker pen and scribbled a note in a corner of the whiteboard: *Number of days to the Olympics: three*

My research into Zeus revealed the ancient Olympics used to be held as a festival in honour of the Greek god. Did the Games feature in the killer's plans? If so, did our man have something special planned? What could that be? Security for the Games was airtight, with all police units on standby. Contingency plans included everything from mass riots to a terrorist attack.

How could one man hope to get by all the security checks and precautions?

With a fake grey beard, maybe?
What the Hell is that about?

I banged my forehead on the board in an attempt to knock some revelation into my skull.

All I got was a headache.

"If you're trying to get a concussion, I'd recommend a brick wall."

I turned to Holloway with a defeated shrug.

"I'm lost," I said. "I'm at a total, complete loss. I was so sure Mackenzie was our man."

"And now we're back to square one." Holloway joined me at the board. "It is terribly exasperating."

I glanced at him. He was probably the only person I knew who used the word *exasperating* in a sentence. "What really gets me is we're back to having no links whatsoever between the victims. Mackenzie was our sole connection."

"Not entirely true," Holloway said. "The *church* was our sole connection. I've got people looking into the other employees at St. Margaret and All Saints. Perhaps someone else will jump out at us." He tilted his head. "Well, we can always hope."

I returned my attention to the incidents board, a jumble of pictures, papers and writings arranged as randomly as a child's scrapbook.

"I hate to be the one to ask," Holloway's voice dropped a few octaves, "your brother ... do you know where he is?"

"Reggie has nothing to do with this." I replied a little too fast, my tone a little too sharp.

"How can you be so sure? He was the last person to see one of the victims alive. If that doesn't make him a suspect, it at least makes him a key witness."

"He is *not* involved in this!" Passing eyes darted my way as my voice rose. I fought to level my tone. I didn't want to alienate Holloway, not when he'd been keeping my secret. Blaize I could trust. Holloway seemed burdened by the knowledge as if it weighed him down. Judging by the grey rings around his eyes, it might even be keeping him awake at night. It had to be hard for a straight shooter like him to keep quiet against his own solid principles. "Reggie was just pushing drugs in the wrong place at the wrong time." I tried to convince myself of the fact as much as I tried to convince Holloway. B-Dawg, our young informant, had dealt a major blow to the Ghetto Souljaz by revealing the names of key gang members. Reggie didn't make the list, suggesting he only functioned as a minor goon. Or, his reputed "police connections" probably made B-Dawg wary about naming him.

His one "police connection" was all that kept him from being wanted in suspicion of murder.

He's just a petty criminal, I told myself again.

He's not a killer.

"What you're doing goes against every major tenet in our code of ethics," Holloway whispered, his tone harsh with urgency.

I held his gaze so intently that Holloway made an involuntary gulp. "You can report me if you wish, Tom," I said, my tone remarkably calm and icy. "But it's not going to change the fact that I have no idea where Reggie is. Getting me kicked off the force will not help you solve this case."

"I-I'm not trying to get you kicked off the force. It's just …" He threw his hands up. "You know what? For your sake, I hope he doesn't turn out to be the killer." With a huff of disgust, he turned and left the room.

"Tom," I called to his retreating back, my skin prickling with guilt. He cast a tentative backward glance. "I'm sorry." I sighed. "It was never your obligation to cover for me. I do appreciate it."

He scrunched up his nose as if resisting my apology, but his shoulders slumped. "I'm sorry, too," he said. "It must be hard for you. He is your brother, after all."

"I may have an idea to bounce off you," I said, eager to change the subject.

"Bounce away." He looked oddly disappointed.

I removed an eight by six black and white photo from the board. The fuzzy image showed a figure hurrying out of a darkened alley in a blur of movement.

"Our mystery lady," Holloway said.

"She's the only lead we've got."

"We've already got an ongoing appeal for her to come forward."

"But no one has." I gazed at the hazy figure. Medium height and build, long hair, possibly blonde. Something that looked like a dark coloured scarf veiled the lower half of her face, obscuring her features. A deliberate attempt at concealing her identity?

"I think we should be a bit more proactive in seeking our mystery guest," I said.

"What do you suggest?"

"The parking lot belongs to a gentleman's club called Nympho Mania."

Holloway sniffed. "Hardly a gentleman's club. The place is seedy and rundown. Most of the girls are dumpy, glamour model rejects. Spearmint Rhino it is not." He hastened to add, "Not that I'm speaking from experience, of course. Anyway, you think our girl works there?"

"Why else would a woman be loitering about in the car park of a strip club?"

"True, but if she hasn't already come forward, what makes you think she will when you track her down at her less than admirable workplace?"

"I'm hoping to appeal to her sense of integrity and justice."

Holloway pushed his glasses higher up the bridge of his nose. "How much integrity do you reckon a woman who works in this sort of place would have?"

"You'd be surprised, Tom. Not all women who work in these places do so for the love of the job. So tell me, is tonight good for you?"

"Tonight?" He gaped at me until he realised I wasn't joking. "Go on then. What does it matter? I have no life …"

29

Crowds of people, young and old, lined the street, waving flags and sweaty T-shirts, bordered by uniformed police officers in fluorescent vests, their grim faces a stark contrast to the smiles of the spectators they held back. A tremor of excitement buzzed through the mob, their collective focus centred on the cordoned off road before them, where a young woman, blonde hair tied back in a ponytail, limbered up in her pink Nike trainers. Many among the crowd would recognise her as a popular model-cum-TV personality. Wolf whistles erupted when the woman bent over to stretch her calves, accentuating her Lycra-clad bottom.

Somebody further up the street shouted, setting off a domino effect of cheers and whistles. In the distance, flanked by police motorcycle escorts, a lone figure emerged from around a bend in the road. Heat from the afternoon sun rose from the baking ground in shimmering waves, blurring the figure's outline and bestowing on it a surreal, ghostlike quality. Held aloft in its right hand, an orange column of fire waved and danced, trailing a wispy stream of grey smoke.

As the runner drew near, the crowd whooped and applauded the prominent radio deejay. Smiling through the film of sweat slicking his pudgy red face, he shook hands with the waiting woman, holding out his burning torch to her identical but unlit one. The tip of the woman's sleek, silver cone ignited amid thunderous cheers and the lightning flash of a hundred cameras going off at once.

The Oracle snaked his way through the crowds, ignoring the celebrations around him and moving closer towards the blocked off road until all that separated him from the relay route were the extended arms of a policeman. He craned his neck to look over the copper's shoulder as the female torch bearer cantered past, ponytail swishing like the well-groomed tail of a show horse. She waved to the crowd and smiled, flashing bleached white teeth. Buffeted by winds, the Olympic flame twisted and pirouetted above her.

"Pretty awe-inspiring sight, isn't it?" the Oracle asked the officer in front of him.

"Hm? Oh yes. Very," he said without turning around, eyes fixed on the road.

"The fire that can never be put out. Do you know what the Olympic flame symbolises?"

"Doesn't it stand for purity, peace and freedom? A symbol of the undying human spirit?"

The Oracle hid his disappointment of the man's ignorance. "A romantic and poetic interpretation, but I'm afraid that's not what the original flame symbolises."

"Oh no? Then what does it stand for?"

He told the officer, who reacted with arched eyebrows and a nod as if he'd just learned a fascinating but useless fact, like how a flamingo has knees that can bend backwards.

"Interesting. I'll be sure to remember that," he said, his attention returned to the road, where the fat radio host milled around the police perimeter, high-fiving fans and offering autographs.

Oh, you will remember, the Oracle thought, stepping back and melting into the sea of people.

By the time my task is complete, everybody *will remember.*

30

Nympho Mania sat on a quiet side street just off Romford Road, in the heart of East London's red light district. Sandwiched between a licensed sex shop and an 'escort agency', the lap dancing bar's posters boasted an evening in the company of Stratford's most *"sensual", "seductive"* and *"titillating"* women.

I parked in the lot down the back, which appeared to have cleaned up well. With the discarded food boxes tumbling in the wind and stomped out cigarette butts smouldering near the back entrance into the club, the place looked like any other back alley car park in the inner city. No trace of the burning car wreck remained, save for a sunken patch of asphalt where the road had melted from the high heat of the blaze. A handful of cars sat in the lot, with one parked beside the entrance in a bay marked *RESERVED FOR CLUB DIRECTOR* written in spray paint on the brick wall—a Mazda MX-5 sports convertible in an ostentatious and eye-searing shade of tangerine. *Orange, the colour of choice for people who liked calling attention to themselves.* I cringed at the car's license plate:

N1 MFO.

Holloway met me as I climbed out from my Ford. "You planning on doing a number on stage as well?" he asked.

A habit from my undercover days, I tended to dress to suit the location of our investigation. Even if I weren't undercover, I believed it still helped me fit in, especially in cop-hostile environments. Back in Narcotics, my disguise often involved baggy jeans, hoodies, baseball caps, eye-catching bling, and even the odd transfer tattoo.

For our visit to the club, I'd opted for a pimp-drug dealer look, complete with a button-down shirt, exposed at the chest, testicle-constricting jeans, and patent leather shoes for our visit to the club. I'd added a gold chain around my neck, a thick one with a golden 'K' as a pendant. It had been a birthday gift from Reggie—one that matched his necklace.

I made a show of shooting my cuffs. The polyester in the shirt rubbed against the hairs on my arm, creating a static crackle. "Would you pay for a private show?" I asked.

Holloway fluttered his lashes at me. "I might do." He shook his head. "Oh, and darling, pink is so you."

I laughed. "Unlike some people, I'm a man comfortable with my own metrosexuality."

We walked up to the back door. The neon lights above brightened the area, its changing display showing a woman's legs spreading progressively further apart. A dark-shirted bouncer with a buzz cut and a perpetual scowl guarded the entryway.

"You're having a laugh," he growled as we approached. He pointed to Holloway's shoes as if they offended him. "You ain't coming in wearing them trainers." I got out my badge from my jeans pocket, and he snarled at it. His alpha male power display disrupted, he let us pass with a reluctant grunt.

"Trainers?" I asked Holloway as we passed by the sulky bouncer. "I told you to dress as if we're going clubbing."

"I did! I didn't know trainers weren't allowed."

I shook my head with a grin. "You don't get out much, do you?" Holloway dropped his gaze to the floor, cheeks flushing. We entered a dim reception area manned by a bored-looking clerk. Another muscle-bound doorman patrolled a winding stairwell leading downwards. Music boomed up from its depths, a siren's call luring hot-blooded males towards temptation and sin.

"Five pounds each, please," the receptionist droned, a rubber stamp in hand to initiate paying customers.

I handed her my badge. If the presence of two cops in the club surprised her, she didn't let it show. "We're here to speak to the director of this fine establishment."

"That would be Mr. Kosta." She gave bouncer number two a tired wave, instructing him to unhook the velvet rope across the stairs. "You'll find his office downstairs behind the bar." She returned to staring into the middle distance.

Damn, she'd make a good poker player.

We descended the spiral staircase, the music growing louder with each step. The beat of the bass consumed me, thumping its rhythm inside my skull. My heart sped up to match the saccadic tempo.

The main club hall was a photosensitive epileptic's nightmare, with flashing lights swirling across the walls and ceilings in pinks, blues and greens. Tables surrounded by plush looking seats dotted the floor. Most of the occupied chairs faced a glittering platform with three floor-to-ceiling poles. A trio of topless women frolicked on stage, bared hips swaying to the music as they rubbed themselves provocatively against the metal poles.

"Shut your gob," Holloway said beside me. "You're drooling."

I attempted a discreet adjustment of my crotch as we headed towards the bar in the far end of the room. A couple of middle-aged men, still dressed in the day's work shirts, ties dangling loose, sat nursing pints whilst ogling the performers and the other scantily-clad workers milling about. I bumped into a statuesque black girl, her breasts spilling out the unbuttoned front of her schoolgirl outfit. At first glance, she seemed like a stunner, but the lights shifted, revealing a too-square chin, hairy lips and an Adam's apple.

"Evening, handsome," he-she purred in a smooth baritone, pierced tongue running across painted lips. "Fancy a private lap dance?"

I mustered my most gracious smile and declined. Holloway,

looking flustered, brushed off the advances of a Korean girl in pigtails, who was all but popping out of her too-small sailor's costume.

I caught the eye of the bartender and flipped him my badge.

"Where is Mr. Kosta?" I shouted to be heard over the music. The bartender pointed towards a door at the far end of the bar, one which said *NO UNAUTHORISED ENTRY*.

Holloway and I crossed the bar, running the gauntlet of private dance offers from a horde of half-dressed strippers. I rapped my knuckles on the lacquered wood and waited. A few seconds later, it cracked open.

"Mr. Kosta?" I asked the short, swarthy man in the loud, silk shirt. He frowned.

"I wasn't expecting anybody." He huffed, preparing to shut the door until I shoved my badge through the gap and into his face. Without waiting for an invitation, I pushed the door open the rest of the way.

"Thank you for seeing us, Mr. Kosta," I stepped into his office. Holloway closed the door behind us, shutting out the deafening music. My feet sank into the cream shag carpet, no doubt a nightmare to clean. Cherry pink wallpaper with gold accents adorned the walls, along with framed photographs of half-naked women in flirtatious poses.

"Please," he said, not bothering to disguise his scowl, "call me Pluto." He sat in a lime green executive chair behind his white work desk. His shirt, swimming with even more psychedelic colours than his office, opened at the collar to reveal a thick gold chain. As we took our seats in matching green armchairs across from him, I recalled the man's orange car. Pluto Kosta was either colour blind, or he had absolutely no concept of colour theory.

Kosta swivelled in his chair, elbows on the armrests, fingers tented. I counted at least four rings on his hands.

"So, officers," he said. He spoke with a melodic accent I couldn't quite place. Judging by his olive skin, dark, greasy hair and angular features, I'd guess he was from somewhere in the Mediterranean. "What seems to be the problem?"

"What do you know about the fire in your car park last week?" I asked.

"Only that there was a man in the car. Terrible." He shook his head. "Other than that, I know nothing, just as I told the investigating officers."

I placed a photo of the Reverend Mackenzie on his desk, pushed it towards him.

"Do you know this man?"

Kosta's eyes dipped down towards the picture before flying back up. "You know, detectives, we have a strict policy on client confidentiality."

I narrowed my eyes at him. *If that's the way he wants to play...*

"This was the man who died in the burning car. In *your* parking lot. This is officially a *homicide*. Which makes this place a crime scene. If you would rather not divulge client information now, we will have to come back with a search warrant." I flicked my eyes towards the door. "I must warn you, though, with a warrant, we tend to be pretty *thorough*. Employee records, company accounts... we'll need to see the full Monty. Those girls out there? Some of them seem a little young. And others? The ones who can't speak much English? Have they got the proper work permits? Visas?" My eyes bored into his like twin augers, holding his gaze. I wanted to make the bastard sweat. I wanted him to shit himself.

After a few seconds, I broke off with a smile. "But I'm sure a reputable establishment like yours will have everything in order, hmm? You'll have nothing to worry about."

Kosta remained expressionless for a few moments. He smiled back, but the expression didn't reach his eyes. "Of course we don't," he said, "we have nothing to hide. Nevertheless, there is no sense in wasting both your time and mine with needless bureaucracy. I will try my best to lend you my assistance."

I had to admit, the guy was good.

Kosta held the photograph in front of his face. "Ah, I do know him. He is one of our regulars. Or *was*." He sighed. "Such a shame. The girls will miss him."

"How often did he visit?" Holloway asked.

"Mr. Shepherd dropped by at least once every other week."

"Mr. Shepherd?" I asked.

"Yes. Christian Shepherd. That was his name."

I looked at Holloway, who shook his head in disbelief. The slimy arsehole came under a false name. No wonder the flock at his church was never the wiser. The audacity of that pseudonym!

Good luck herding demons in Hell, 'Shepherd'.

"What did this … Mr. Shepherd … do here?" I asked.

"He would have a couple of drinks. Watch the live shows. And he frequently paid for private dances."

"And did he tend to, say, favour a particular dancer?"

"Oh yes. Our lovely Persephone was by far his favourite Nymph. She's got the most heavenly body. And the tightest ass. You know she only charges forty quid for a lap dance? For sixty, she even lets you touch her. A total bargain."

I smirked at Holloway, whose cheeks had turned as pink as Kosta's garish wallpaper.

"I think we'll pass on the lap dance, mate. But we'll need to ask her a few questions."

31

The observer glanced at the luminous hands on his watch.
Nearly midnight.

The neighbour's daughter had grown sick of waiting. After checking that the young girl was sound asleep, the teenager snuck out of the flat, turned out the lights and locked the door. She made her way upstairs, no doubt to her own bed.

The child was alone.

He slipped out from the hedges and crept up to the darkened window of the little girl's bedroom. A small top window had been left open for ventilation. On his tiptoes, he could just reach a hand in.

Too easy.

Knelt beneath the window, he snapped on a pair of gloves before extracting the half-filled wine bottle from his rucksack. The liquid inside sloshed with a syrupy consistency. As he uncorked the bottle, he caught a whiff of the fumes, the scent of a petrol kiosk.

He removed a length of cloth from the bag. Balling the rag up, he stuffed it over the mouth of the bottle before tipping the container upside-down. The cloth darkened as the material absorbed the oily liquid, and the smell grew more pervasive.

He unfurled the rag, placing one end inside the top of the bottle before fixing it in place by replacing the cork. From his backpack, he pulled out another cloth, wiped the bottle down, and removed his gloves. With the bottle in one hand, he fumbled in his jeans pocket with the other until his fingers closed round the hard plastic of his cigarette lighter. His pulse quickened in anticipation.

He stood from his crouch, shook off the pins and needles in his legs. With his thumb, he spun the wheel on his lighter. It sparked but didn't light. He tried again. Tiny starbursts vanished back into the ether as soon as they appeared.

Damn cheap shit.

He gave the lighter a shake, hoping it wasn't empty, wishing that he'd brought a spare. A gauze of perspiration dusted his upper lip.

With a *snick,* a little flame sprang to life, greeting him with a cheerful orange wave.

Finally.

A feathered throbbing pulsed in the hollow of his throat. He knew he had to work quickly. Holding the bottle at arm's length, he took a deep breath and moved the lighter flame towards the dangling end of the soaked rag.

"*Oi!*"

He jumped, nearly dropping the bottle. At the same time, the cloth fuse blossomed in a burst of blue and yellow flames.

Shit.

"Hey!" Another shout, closer than before.

I have to hurry.

He drew his arm back, preparing to hurl the flaming vessel through the open window and into the bedroom.

32

Persephone glided into the room wearing a red PVC corset and knee-high patent leather boots. She held a riding whip in her hand as she strutted to Kosta's blindingly white work desk and parked her pert bottom on the edge. Like any heterosexual male would, my eyes gave her a quick once-over. In her mid-twenties, she carried herself with an air of sexual allure, and she had curves in all the right places, but beneath the tonnes of makeup caking her face, she probably looked somewhat plain, with rounded cheekbones, thin lips, eyes set a bit too close together, and a slightly wonky nose.

Wait a minute. The cartilage holding up the bridge of her nose protruded in an odd angle, an *unnatural* angle.

"I will leave you gentlemen to it, then," Kosta said. He left the room, leaving us to interview Persephone in private. "Don't have too much fun," he said with a wink, "you'll have to pay for that."

I introduced myself to Persephone, my eyes wandering down to the cavernous valley between her breasts. When Holloway shook her hand, he kept his gaze fixed on the gaudy gold swirls on the fuchsia wallpaper.

I showed Persephone the Reverend's photo. "Do you recognise this man?"

"Oh, yes," she nodded. She had a bubbly, high-pitched voice, like one of those annoying fraternity girls in an American chick flick. "Christian. He's one of my regulars." With a coy smile, she dipped a bare shoulder in my direction. "I'm his favourite

Nymph, you know."

"So we've heard," I said. "Being his favourite girl and all, has he ever revealed to you his true identity?"

A shadow flickered across the surface of Persephone's eyes, but like a creature descending back into the depths of a still loch, it disappeared when she blinked. "What do you mean, true identity? Is he a masked superhero?" She really laid on the blonde bimbo act.

"The man you know as Christian Shepherd," said Holloway, "is actually the Reverend Patrick Mackenzie, a local church leader."

That surfacing darkness clouding her smiling eyes appeared again. She quelled it with a throaty giggle. "Oh, my! You serious? What a naughty, naughty man! He needs to be punished, he does."

"He already has been," I said. "He died in the fire in the car park last week."

Persephone gasped, but her shock seemed contrived. "Oh, my God. The poor man."

"What time do you guys close, may I ask?"

She frowned. "Three thirty in the morning. Why?"

"We got video footage of the Reverend driving into the car park at around four a.m. Funny that he'd hang around after the club had closed."

"Huh, that is kinda weird." She started to twirl the loop at the end of her leather whip.

"Do you have any idea why he would be here after hours?"

She tilted her head and stuck out her lower lip. "Nope." Her fingers continued to fuss with her riding crop.

I dug into my manila folder and removed the eight by six surveillance snapshot of our mystery lady.

"This woman was seen leaving the car park around the time of the murder." Colour leached out of Persephone's bronzed face as my gaze shifted from the photo to her. "She looks a lot like you."

"Er, ah … it's …" She wrung her riding crop, knuckles white

against the orange of her fake tan. "Could've been any one of the girls. In a blonde wig. We often wear wigs, you know."

"Miss Persephone," Holloway interrupted, "Are you aware that it is an offence to withhold information from the police?"

Her eyes darted back and forth between Holloway and me, a frightened deer cornered by two wolves. It almost made me feel guilty.

She dropped her gaze to the floor. "Fine. That was me." With a defeated sigh, all traces of her earlier airheadedness left. "And Chris ... erm, the Reverend ... he was there to meet me."

"May I ask why?" I pressed, although I had a pretty good idea.

She shrugged. "He wanted a bit more than a private dance."

"Does your boss approve of such ... transactions?"

She twisted the crop in her hands. "He is aware some of the girls offer ... extras. But he's no pimp. As long as we do our job, and he gets the agreed commissions, he doesn't care what we get up to when we're off duty."

I scrutinised the photo again. "Then why the secrecy?" I pointed to the dark shroud covering the lower half of the woman's face. "Why the scarf?"

Her gaze dropped once more to the floor. She gnawed on her bottom lip so hard I worried she'd draw blood. "That's not a scarf." When she spoke, her voice came out in a hollow whisper.

That was when I noticed the faint purple blotches marking her skin beneath the layers of concealer and foundation. Imperfections that would be easily missed under the spinning neon lights in the club, but exposed by the harsh fluorescent strip in Kosta's office. I chided myself for not noticing them before.

The bastard.

I leant in close and lifted her chin with my finger. Highly inappropriate behaviour on my part, but at that moment, I didn't give a fuck.

"Did he do this?" I asked her, gently touching the tip of her crooked nose.

All at once, what was left of her facade crumbled, revealing a broken, confused young girl underneath. She dropped her head and her riding crop. Her shoulders began to quake. Bringing her hands up to her face, she muffled a tear-choked sob, and the floodgates opened.

I stood rigid before the weeping woman, at a complete loss. I waggled my eyebrows at Holloway for help. He flung up his hands in a '*How the heck should I know?*' gesture. With a cringe, I extended a tentative hand and patted her stiffly on the shoulder. In response, she threw her arms around my neck and wailed into the crook of my shoulder. My hands tensed in mid-air, afraid of touching her, my mind already harking on a possible charge of misconduct. In the end, I allowed my arms to rest on her back and waited for her to cry herself out.

Her sobs eventually subsided, and she pulled herself away, leaving a smear of tears, powder and mascara on my shirt. I offered her a tissue. She blew into it gingerly, wincing as if the act alone hurt her broken nose. She tilted up to me with red-tinged eyes.

"Thank you."

I realised then that all she needed was to have someone show her a bit of kindness. Not salivate over her as if she were a hunk of rib roast.

"Why?" I asked. Not the most eloquent nor professional of questions. *Why did he do this to you? Why allow yourself to be treated this way? Why didn't you tell anyone? Why didn't you report the fucker?*

And how did you lose all your self-esteem?

"H-he knows my parents," she said, her voice thick with tears. "They go to his church. When ... when he turned up here one day, he recognised me. Threatened to tell my parents unless ..." she stared at her platform heels. Fresh tears, tinged with mascara, trickled down her blotchy cheeks. With the top coat smeared, her bruises stood out starker against the glitter of her makeup. She'd need to redo all her face paint.

"I'm sure your parents would stand by you." The words sounded lame even to my ears.

"You don't understand," she blubbered. "They're really strict Catholics. It's my word against his. They'd disown me! He ... he also threatened to go to the press ..."

"The press?" Holloway piped up.

Persephone gave a small nod, white teeth pressing down against the scarlet of her painted lips. "My real name is Denise Collingsworth."

"Collingsworth?" I gaped. "As in Collingsworth Toys?"

She cringed but gave a weak nod.

Collingsworth Toys was one of the biggest toy store chains in the world, with massive outlets on the high street of almost every town nationwide. They prided themselves on good old-fashioned playthings for children that nurtured their creativity and mental development. No dress-up dolls, plastic guns or video games—nothing that could glorify sex and violence in impressionable young minds.

"*Wholesome toys for wholesome kids.*" That was their catchphrase.

If Denise's occupation ever got out, it would ruin the Collingsworths.

"So why are you working here?" Holloway asked the question at the tip of my tongue. Surely the daughter of a business mogul like Edward Collingsworth would never be wanting of anything.

She drew up her shoulders before dropping them in a sigh, dabbing her eyes with the bobbling tissue. "I don't know. It's just ... my parents, they're so ... *prescriptive*. Down to the clothes I wear. *Nobody* notices me in maxi skirts and oversized sweaters. I just felt ... suffocated, I guess." She made a whimpering noise as she tried to blink back more tears. "I feel so stupid now."

I touched her bare shoulder. My next question seemed insensitive, cruel even, but I needed to ask. "The fire ... did you ...?"

Persephone—Denise's mouth dropped open. "No, of course

not! I may be desperate, but I'm no murderer! It ... it was a man. He ... he *saved* me."

Like Zeus saved Hera from Ixion's sexual advances.

"Who was he?" I pressed. "What did he look like?"

"It was dark. I couldn't quite tell. But he had a grey beard. Like Christian ... the *Reverend*." She spat out his title like a curse. "We were in his car when this guy opened the door. I think he hit him over the head. Then he told me to leave. That's all I know, honest."

"Were you the one who called the police?"

"Yes."

Holloway met my eyes. Our suspect with the grey beard. *Not* the Reverend.

Someone else.

"I realise this must have been difficult for you, but we do appreciate the information, and rest assured we will exercise the utmost discretion regarding your ... activities."

"Thank you," she whispered. She twirled a lock of bleached blonde hair, unable to meet our eyes.

"If you remember anything else ..."

"There is one thing." A crease formed between her eyebrows as she chewed thoughtfully on her hair. "The man ... he said something rather odd before I left. I couldn't quite understand it."

"What did he say?"

"He said something like, '*Be free, fair Hera. Spread word of the holy deeds of the Father, for He will rise again come Heca ...*'", she frowned. "It was a weird word ... *Heca* ... it sounded like *hack-a-tomb-* ... something like that."

I cut a glance at Holloway to see if he found the word familiar. He made a face at me but, nevertheless, scribbled down a phonetic for the word in his trusty notepad. Denise stuck out her tongue. "I'm sorry, I realise it's probably just gibberish from some raving lunatic."

"Trust me," Holloway told her, "when it comes to raving lunatics, it's only gibberish until you learn to decipher it."

The spinning lights and emergency vehicles in front of my home were becoming a distressingly regular feature.

I sprang out from the car and raced up the driveway. The garden glowed orange, illuminated by a lake of fire. The picket fence separating our house from the next was engulfed in a wall of flames. The hedge running along the side of the house crackled as tongues of heat and light ate away at its leaves and twigs. The window above the shrubs flickered and danced in the firelight, the reflections creating the illusion that the bonfire raged inside as well.

In Meghan's room.

"Daddy!" Meghan waved at me from where she sat on the front porch with Helen and her daughter, Lucy.

Thank God ... again. I fell to my knees and into her arms.

"What happened here?" I asked Helen.

"Someone tried to firebomb the house, that's what happened." Lucy answered instead. Huddled in her bedspread, she glared up at me as though I'd been the one responsible.

"I thought I heard someone shouting," said Helen. Her brown hair rippled about her face in a wild aura. Her eyes shimmered with so much fear that they appeared to glow in the dark. "Then there was this noise, like glass breaking, and a massive *whoosh*. I looked out the window, and the garden was on fire." She wrung her hands together, staring at a patch of dandelions between her slippered feet. "Firefighters said it was some sort of petrol bomb. A Molotov cocktail. They think the guy probably got interrupted. Lucky for us ... this time." I didn't miss the meaning behind the two words she appended at the end of her sentence.

She thinks this will happen again ... that shit like this will keep on happening.

As long as I'm around.

I'm endangering them all.

"What the Hell happened here?" Holloway asked, joining us on the porch. I'd forgotten he followed me in his car. "Is everyone all right?"

"As all right as we can be with World War fucking three kicking off in our neighbourhood." Lucy directed all her fear into anger towards me. Who could blame her?

"It's the Ghetto Souljaz, isn't it?" Holloway asked me. "'Crash and burn.' That's their signature."

I didn't reply, couldn't reply. *This can't be happening again.* Dread percolated through my veins and settled in the pit of my gut. Needles of panic pricked at my heart. The old fear returned. Fear of the unknown, fear of the hidden enemy.

Fear for my daughter's safety.

The last time a gang targeted my family, I lost Angie.

That petrol bomb was aimed at Meghan's room.

"The fire's under control now." A fireman gave us a thumbs-up through his bright yellow gloves. "It's safe for you to go back in."

I grabbed Meghan's hand.

"Go and grab a few things. Pack a bag." My voice sounded shrill to my own ears. "We can't stay here tonight."

This place isn't safe anymore.

"Where are we going?" She looked from me to Holloway to the fireman to the Jaimesons in frightened confusion. I had no answer for her, had no idea where we would go. We had no relatives in London. We might hole up in a bed and breakfast or a hostel for a couple of nights, but we wouldn't be able to afford that for long. I ran my hands through my hair, my fingers trailing through the exposed scalp between cornrows.

"You can stay over at mine for a bit."

I turned to Holloway, surprised by his offer.

"It's not exactly the Four Seasons," he said, "but I do have a large living room. You can probably squeeze a cot in there. One of you will have to crash on the couch, though."

"Tom," I said, "are you sure?" I didn't want to drag him into my mess. Should the gang be intent on getting us, they could easily track us to his place.

"Sure I'm sure." He gave a noncommittal shrug. "That is, unless you have somewhere nicer to go."

"No, just ... just give us a few minutes to fetch our stuff." Overwhelmed by the hospitality he extended us, I just stared at him. We barely knew each other longer than a month.

"I'll wait in the car. You can follow in yours." He turned to go.

"Tom," I called after him. He glanced at me over his shoulder. "Thanks."

He muttered something as he walked off. Probably, "No problem."

I entered our flat, snatched an empty suitcase from the store cupboard, and hurried to my room.

"Just a couple changes of clothes and your toothbrush, Meg," I said into Meghan's room. "And no toys!" I heard a muffled "Aww ..." before she poked her head out.

"How long will we be gone?"

"I don't know," I said.

"Can I bring a book?"

"Just one." Kicking my door open, I tossed the suitcase on the bed. I grabbed an armful of clothes from the laundry basket on the floor, clean clothes I never got the time to put away. Balling up some shirts and trousers, I stuffed them into the bag along with a bunch of socks, paired or otherwise.

Let's hope Tom's place has an iron.

My mobile phone vibrated against my thigh.

Another text.

I shivered in spite of the warm night. As I read the newest message from my mystery contact, the hairs stood up on my arms and on the back of my neck.

MEGHAN MAY NOT BE SO LUCKY NEXT TIME

They know her name.

I dropped the armload of clothes and rushed to the front window. The fire truck and a couple of firefighters still stood outside. One of them was speaking to a cop leaning against the door of a police cruiser. Three other officers were turning away rubberneckers who had appeared to watch the spectacle.

Sitting astride a motorcycle in the shadows on the opposite side of the road, I spotted him. A dark helmet obscured most of his features, but he was smiling.

The glint of his gold teeth mocked me before he sped off into the darkness.

"Please excuse the mess," Holloway pre-warned us as he fumbled with the locks on his door. "I didn't expect any visitors today." He led us into a small but tidy central living area with tasteful wood flooring. An open kitchen stood to our right, bordered by a granite-topped bar and a couple of barstools. On the counter, an empty coffee mug sat beside an open magazine. One of the stools had a jacket slung across the back. A pair of bookcases lined the wall to our left, housing a collection of tomes and DVDs. In front of us, a cream coloured sofa faced a flat screen TV, and through the French windows, a view of the glittering East London skyline. Set in a modern high rise overlooking the River Thames, Holloway's apartment made for a pretty impressive bachelor pad.

I looked around the spotless apartment in puzzlement, about to enquire "What mess?", when Holloway hastily snatched up the jacket from the bar stool and proceeded to remove the coffee mug and magazine from the counter top.

"Left for work in a hurry this morning." He looked almost embarrassed. He dumped the offending items somewhere out of sight before returning to our side.

"Let me give you the grand tour." He stretched out his arm. "This is the combined living and dining area. That," he pointed to the door beside the kitchenette, "is the bathroom. Behind door number two," he gestured to a door between the two bookcases, "is my room, and the last door there is just a storage closet. Feel free to dump your stuff in there if you want."

Meghan wandered over to the couch and plopped herself down. She wriggled and writhed like Goldilocks testing one of the three bears' beds.

"I call dibs on the sofa!" she called out.

I guess that left me with the floor.

Holloway moved towards the store cupboard. "I've got some spare pillows and blankets," he said, "and an old comforter you can use as a thin mattress." The interior of Holloway's store cupboard was as immaculate as the rest of his home, with everything stacked neatly on shelves or in boxes whose contents were clearly marked on their sides in permanent black ink. A vacuum cleaner, its hose coiled, stood in a corner beside a propped up, folded up ironing board. The linens on the top shelf of the closet were sealed in canvas bags to keep out dust.

He handed me an armload of sheets.

"*Mi casa es su casa.*"

Holloway left me to try to convert the floor into a passable sleeping area. Wary of the time—it was almost four in the morning—I tucked Meghan into the sofa and dimmed the lights. Undressing and crawling into my makeshift covers, I stared up at the unfamiliar ceiling, my mind whirling with a plethora of thoughts.

We were on the run. Forced from our home by a vengeful street gang. *How did it come to this? How could it be happening to us again?* A lump of ice formed around my heart at the thought of how close I'd come to losing Meghan. Those sick thugs had tried to get at me by the coldest means possible—targeting the people closest to me.

My thoughts flitted to Reggie, and a twinge of concern hit my chest. Was he all right? The Ghetto Souljaz would have no doubt discovered our fraternal link. Had I put him in danger with his own gang?

I recalled when I last saw him, slinking away into the night with a bloody nose, a bloody nose that *I* gave him. The memory gave me a pang of guilt.

We hadn't exactly parted on amiable terms.

Could he be in on these attacks? Could he be the main instigator? *No, he couldn't be. He adores Meghan. He wouldn't hurt her to get at me ... would he?*

"I'll be watching you."

Those were his parting words. Dark and icy, like rum on the rocks. Despite the mild and humid night, a rash of goose pimples erupted across my skin.

I checked the glow-in-the-dark hands on my watch. Four thirty. We had to get up for work in a couple of hours.

What's the point in sleeping? I rolled out from under the covers and padded towards the kitchen. The cool, hollow wood beneath my bare feet gave way to colder, harder stone tiles as I entered the kitchen area. I pulled open the refrigerator door, sending a cone of light splashing across the floor. Holloway's fridge was stacked neater than the display shelves at a supermarket. Every can and bottle had its label facing outward.

I cracked open a can of Pepsi, making a mental note to replace the drink as I plodded over to the bookshelves. Holloway didn't have curtains in his lounge, and the lights from the London skyline illuminated the room just enough for me to make out the book titles. I suppressed a wry smile when I realised they were arranged not just by genre, but also alphabetically by the author's last name. If Holloway had been asked to describe his taste in books, I bet he'd use the term *eclectic*. His fiction choices ranged from science fiction and fantasy to cosy mysteries and political thrillers, with a handful of the classics thrown in—Austen, Dickens, and the complete works of Shakespeare. Beneath a canvas print of the Milky Way galaxy, its spirals reflected in the chamber of a bisected nautilus shell in a glass display box beside it, Holloway had two entire shelves dedicated to non-fiction books. Charles Darwin's *On the Origin of Species* and Richard Dawkins's *The God Delusion* stood out among numerous works on Pantheism. *God is Everything, and Everything is God*; *All Things Bright and Beautiful: A History of Pantheism; Worshipping Nature.*

A thump off to my side took my attention. Light spilled out from Holloway's bedroom door, hanging ajar on its hinges.

Guess I'm not the only one having trouble sleeping.

It occurred to me that I hadn't yet offered Holloway a proper thank you for his generous hospitality. Tiptoeing up to the door, I rapped on the frame. It swung open from my knocking.

"Wait, don't—" the door had already opened the rest of the way. Dressed in a striped pyjamas set, Holloway stood halfway between the bed and the door, looking as if he'd jumped up to try and block my passage. I'd never seen a grown man who actually wore pyjamas before.

"Sorry, Tom, didn't mean to ..." My voice failed, my mind distracted by the saucy posters on the wall. They all depicted *men*. In cowboy hats, frolicking in the surf *Baywatch* style, posing in various stages of undress. A magazine lay open on the floor, perhaps the same one he had so swiftly swept off the kitchen counter. Naked men posed on the cover. *Attitude*, it read, *The UK's best-selling gay magazine.*

Holloway stood stock still before me, hands clenched at his sides, face glowering red, looking like a schoolboy who'd been caught spying in the girls' toilets.

Or in his case, the boys'.

"I ... never knew." To try and ease Holloway's embarrassment, I tried to sound unfazed by the discovery, but I detected the traitorous ripple in my own voice.

"I-I didn't want you to find out." He refused to meet my gaze. "At least, not this way."

I attempted a nonchalant shrug which probably looked more like a nervous tic. The tense silence in the room clung to my skin like cotton gauze. I scoured the room in search of a different topic of conversation. Beside Holloway's bed was another bookcase, a small, waist-high one filled with more books.

Highland Passion. Navy Blues. Night Stallion. The corny titles—and the illustrated covers of shirtless men snogging each other—suggested they were hot and steamy bedtime reads.

That explained Holloway's apparent discomfort back at the strip club. He wasn't being shy; he was completely and utterly put off.

All of a sudden, I grew acutely aware of the fact that I was standing in the middle of a gay man's bedroom, dressed in nothing more than a vest top and my boxer shorts.

"Hey, you know, I'm ... totally cool with this," I babbled. "I, ah, just popped in to say thanks. For letting me and Meg stay over. Sorry I barged in."

"Don't worry about it." Holloway's initial humiliation appeared to have given way to a sullen despondency. Arms wrapped around himself, he continued to stare at a patch of bedroom floor. I squirmed on the spot, wishing desperately that I'd kept my jeans on. As if reading my thoughts, Holloway smirked and looked up. "I thought you were a man comfortable with your own metrosexuality?" He kept his gaze fixed on me—in particular, the part of me covered in boxer shorts.

"Uhh ... I am! But ... you didn't, like ... invite us over because ... I mean ... you realise I have a daughter ..." I bumbled my attempt at articulating the awkward question.

He cast his eyes heavenward. "Stop fretting. I don't poach players who bat for the other team."

My relief did nothing to ease the clumsy silence crashing through the room.

"That doesn't mean I can't *fancy* someone straight, though." His eyes darted up to meet mine before dropping again. I remembered the day we stood outside St. Margaret All Saints, when he seemed disappointed, almost jealous, after my brief run-in with

Sarah Quinn.

Not because he didn't catch the girl's eye.

Because the girl caught *my* eye.

"Oh ... ah ... um ..." Mumbling something along the lines of trying to get back to sleep, I turned to leave.

"I would appreciate if you refrained from telling anybody at work about this."

I stopped at the threshold. "I'm cool with that. I understand if you don't want to, erm, come out."

"I *am* out." He sounded irritated. "Just not at work."

"Oh," I said again. Ever the conversationalist. "I ... guess that makes sense?" Despite the recent influx of female officers, policing remained one of the few professions that, by and large, retained its macho image. Fellow policemen still bumped chests, discussed conquests, and compared displays of bravado. If his pedantry hadn't already alienated him from fellow male members, the revelation of his sexual leanings certainly would have.

"I really don't want another transfer."

"Another ...?" I remembered when Holloway evaded my questions about his time in uniform, when he claimed he'd not gotten along well with his fellow officers. It wasn't because he was socially inept—well, not completely—it was because, like me, the men he worked with feared what they didn't understand, and they no doubt hid their insecurities behind hurtful jokes and cruel jibes.

Guilt stabbed at me for not making a bigger effort to get to know Holloway more when he first arrived. It must have been difficult having to hide part of his true nature from colleagues out of fear of ridicule.

"Hey." I gave him a tentative pat on the arm. "Don't worry. Your secret's safe with me."

Holloway glanced up at me and gave a wordless nod.

"So ..." I rubbed the back of my neck. "I'm your type then, huh?"

He snorted. "Don't flatter yourself, Kurt." He winked at me.

"I'd say you're *every* gay man's type."

Chief Sutherland's eyebrows disappeared up into her hairline when we turned up at work with Meghan.

"I must've missed the memo about Bring Your Child to Work Day," she said.

"She won't get in the way. You'll barely notice her. Promise." As Holloway took Meghan to my desk, I gave the Chief a quick rundown of events from the previous night—minus my discovery of Holloway's sexual leanings. Her eyebrows showed no sign of coming back down anytime soon.

"The text," she said, "did it come from the same number?"

I shook my head, making my neck twinge, and I winced. Holloway's floor didn't make a very comfortable bed. "Probably another one of those untraceable pay-as-you-go SIM cards."

"Give us the number, and we'll try to track it anyway."

"Is there anything your friends over at Organised Crimes can do about this?" I asked.

"Sadly, probably not." She pursed her lips together, her mouth puckering up like a wrinkled date. "The arson attack sounds like the Ghetto Souljaz all right, but with no evidence and no witnesses, there's nothing anyone can do."

"I saw one of them last night. The one with the gold teeth who nearly throttled me in the alley."

"You must mean Jamal Ashburn. He and his cronies were released on bail. His presence at the crime scene is purely circumstantial, unless you can place the smoking gun—or in this case, the smoking cocktail—in his hand."

I shook my head, my frustrations bubbling, rising up my throat like bile, leaving a sour taste in my mouth. "Surely you can bring him in for questioning? I mean, he was at the scene of the mad preacher's death as well. Perhaps the Ghetto Souljaz have some sort of vested interest in the killings. Perhaps that's the main reason they're out to get me."

Not to mention the fact they probably know I'm Reggie's brother. Reggie didn't seem like the kind of person to hurt his own family for revenge, but I'd learned in the last two weeks that I really didn't know him at all.

"Careful, Lancer," Sutherland said, "you may be confusing your case with your problems with the Ghetto Souljaz. I doubt the gang has anything to gain from such bizarre crimes, and even if this Jamal Ashburn could be brought in for questioning, we'll have to pin him to the other crime scenes as well, which will be difficult." She turned to where Holloway was trying to stop Meghan from spinning around on a swivel chair. "How long do you plan on staying at his?"

"Not long. I can't. It won't be fair on Tom. He's already gone so far out of his way." I managed a half-hearted chuckle. "I think our tendency towards organised chaos is already getting on his nerves."

Sutherland attempted a smirk that looked more like a grimace. "Where would you go then?"

I rolled my aching shoulders. *Somewhere with a bed.*

"We'll find a place. Maybe outside East London." I was banking on the Ghetto Souljaz not having much reach beyond their stomping grounds.

"Have you considered somewhere *outside* London?"

"No, that's too far to commute..." My voice trickled off as the realisation of what the Chief was implying hit me.

"It may be your safest option," she said, "at least until the heat is off. You'll drop off their radar in a few months. In the meantime, I can provide you with good references."

References. She wanted to transfer me. I shook my head, my mouth gaping open and shut in mute silence.

"What about the case?" I managed at last.

"Your primary concern should be Meghan's safety and well-being—and yours."

Like a fish out of water, I gulped in air that didn't seem to be sustaining my lungs. The Chief wanted me *off* the case. After all the time I'd put in, all the progress I'd made, I wanted to be the one to nab the bastard.

And what about Meghan? I couldn't just pluck her out of school, out of London, take her away from all her friends and everything she knew.

What if they learn about Reggie's connection? The thought turned my mouth to cotton.

"I . . . we'll be fine, Chief." I forced my voice level, to convince her as much as I was trying to convince myself. "Like you said, I'll be off their radar in a few months. We'll find somewhere to lie low till then."

"While on such a high-profile case?"

"I'll be fine." I returned Sutherland's gorgon gaze with a stony glare of my own.

The corners of her grey eyes crinkled as she squinted, regarding me with an inscrutable expression. Finally, she blinked, straightened her shoulders. "Seeing as you're planning on staying put, you may be interested in digging deeper into something one of the constables dug up last evening." She retreated into her office, motioning for me to follow. I waited as Sutherland foraged through the mound of paperwork on her desk until she came up with a computer printout.

"Sykes was going through a list of everyone entering and leaving the Empire on the day of the double murder. He came across a cleaning company, Hygienia. Crosschecking with the church revealed that they use the same cleaning company. Not much to go on, but we called up the company anyway. Asked for a list of employees sent to the Empire and the church in recent weeks. And guess what? Both places are maintained by the same cleaner."

I recalled the man in overalls mopping the church floor, whistling while he worked. He seemed a quiet, unassuming chap. I thought of how carefree he seemed, content with his lot, as if he had the best job in the world. Watching him, I'd half-expected cartoon rabbits and deer to turn up and help him with his chores.

"We met the cleaner in St. Margaret's," I said. "Seemed like a nice guy."

"From what I hear, Ted Bundy seemed like a pretty nice guy, too." Sutherland handed me the printout. It was a copy of Hygienia's employee record on a Mr. Quentin Gordon. The photograph on file showed a man with close-cropped, dark hair, not the floppy-haired, bespectacled worker we saw. I guessed Mr. Gordon had the day off when we visited—busy planning something nefarious, perhaps? That the pleasant young man we spoke to wasn't a murder suspect relieved me in a way.

"Probably another dead end," the Chief said, "but one I thought you may be interested in pursuing."

I looked down again at the photo. The man stared out at me with dark pupils. Perhaps it was my imagination, brought on by fatigue, but I thought I discerned a storm of intent brewing within those close-set eyes.

Could we truly be looking at a photo of our killer?

33

Being a chosen of the Thunder God hadn't always been easy. As a child, the Oracle struggled to understand his special talent, to harness its incredible potential. Before he discovered Zeus, his visions were nothing more than a jumble of disconnected thoughts. To his uninitiated mind, the messages were garbled, like a television set with poor reception—a chaos of swirling colours, jumpy quasi-images and throbbing sounds all inside his head. It used to frighten him, and it used to frighten Mother.

Mother used to try to see the visions, too. She sought to understand what he experienced. Although she did not possess the gift, she tried to recreate its effects by means of herbs and potions. Sometimes, they seemed to work. She would be happy, laughing, singing of the Elysian Fields of her dreams. Other times, her experiments would go horribly wrong, and when they did, she would cry, shudder and scream as if she had inadvertently transported herself into the depths of Hades, into Tartarus itself.

Mother was not a chosen one. Her mind and body were not made to receive such visions. As such, every time she induced one through her spells, it would weaken her, break her a little. The gods punished her for her insolent curiosity, and despite her best intentions, the secrets of Olympus remained out of her reach.

Those secrets remained out of the Oracle's reach, too.

Until his twelfth birthday.

That day, the Oracle experienced what the ancient Greeks called *epiphaneia*—an epiphany. He'd witnessed Pandareus stealing the sacred golden dog of Zeus.

He intervened and turned Pandareus to stone.

Just as Zeus decreed.

As if someone had toggled the antenna of the flickering television, his visions fell into place, fitting together as seamlessly as the pieces of a jigsaw puzzle. Free from background static, the voice of the Thunder God boomed within him, commanding him, filling the void in his soul with a resonant light. Liquid power flowed through his veins, the surge of it tingling his fingers and toes.

He knew.

In ancient Greece, oracles were special people blessed with a gift of visions, vessels for receiving the sacred word of the Many-Faced One. Charged with spreading the divine message of the Lightning Bringer, they enlightened the masses with the teachings of Zeus.

His purpose on Earth became as clear as still water after the mud has settled.

Through years of practice, he learned to channel his ability, to 'tune himself in' using purification rituals to prepare his body for divine possession, and libations and burning incense in honour of the Sky Lord. When the visions came, the exhilaration of the images still sent his pulse racing, but he no longer felt afraid.

He became honoured.

For a brief moment, the spirit of the Thunder God would inhabit the Oracle's body, filling him with the crackling power of his lightning bolt, with divine wisdom of the ages. Zeus would plant a seed within him, an acorn that would bloom into a divine quest, a crusade that must be completed in the name and honour of the Lightning Bearer.

The Oracle was on such a quest.

In the modern world, humans were growing more and more self-centred. They believed themselves capable of controlling their own destinies as if they could weave their own tapestry of life without guidance from the Fates. With their sun beds and ultraviolet lamps, they believed they had no use for Apollo. With their ocean liners the size of a small city, they believed they no longer needed to pray to Poseidon for safe sailing. With information so freely available on the Internet, they had forgotten to pay homage to Athena, the goddess of wisdom.

More and more, in a world where law, order and justice could be bought by the highest bidder, they lost their respect for the great Zeus Pater, Father of Gods and Men.

With the completion of his quest, sinful mortals would learn the error of their ways. The Olympians would not be forgotten; people would remember them, and they would worship them once more.

Pandareus. The Telchines. Salmoneus. Hera. Ixion.

Zeus's greatest conquest was next.

The people will *remember His name.*

34

"You want me to *what?*" Chief Sutherland's eyes came within a hair's breadth of popping out of her head.

"Just for a couple of hours until we get back," I said. "She'll be no trouble. Will you, Meg?"

"Uh huh …" Meghan sat curled up in one of the chairs in the Chief's office, oblivious to our discussion as she played on her handheld video game.

Sutherland's fingers clamped round my wrist in an iron grip. She dragged me out into the hallway.

"Lancer," she hissed, "you realise my only experience with children has been dinner with my sister and her kids?" Her eyes flitted to Meghan like an elephant would staring at a mouse.

"Don't worry, she's house-trained."

"No nappy changes required then?"

"Chief, she's eight. She can go potty by herself."

"What about snotty noses? And puking?"

"I can't guarantee she won't do either. Come to think of it, I might have given her too much Coco Pops for breakfast."

"Not funny, Lancer. Do you want me to watch your rug rat or not?"

I laughed. "Thanks, Chief." I popped back into the office to give Meghan a peck on the forehead. "Now, I want you to be good for Chief Sutherland, okay?"

"Okay, Daddy." Her eyes never left her handheld game.

"We'll have lots of fun together, won't we, Meghan?" Sutherland chirped in an uncharacteristically animated voice. "We'll get along like a house on fire ..." The words tumbled out. She cringed. So did I. Meghan stared up, blue eyes wide behind her bioptic glasses.

"That's a funny thing to say," she giggled. "A house on fire doesn't get along with anybody."

I wanted to kick myself when we parked beside the East Reservoir Community Garden. Towering above the other greenery, in the centre of the garden, stood a gnarled oak tree.

The oldest oak in Hackney. The tree from which all crime scene leaves had come.

"Why didn't we take a closer look at the local residents when we traced the leaves here?" I asked, checking the address again.

"It's frustrating, isn't it?" Holloway said. "Such an obvious clue, and we missed it because we got so preoccupied with trying to convict the wrong guy for the crimes."

We climbed out the car and walked across the road. Quentin Gordon lived on the top floor of one of the council tower blocks overlooking the garden. Blaize waited for us at the entrance to the flats. She ran forward, throwing her arms around my neck.

"I heard what happened last night," she said, squeezing me tight. "I'm so sorry. Is Meghan all right?"

"She's fine. Spending quality time with the Chief at the moment." Her closeness reminded me of that night at her place when we cuddled on the sofa watching telly in silence. Firm, yet soft under my touch. Despite her strength and her toned, athletic build, she still seemed vulnerable somehow, evoking in me a strong sense of protectiveness.

She pulled away. "I can't believe no one told me about it sooner!"

"You weren't around to tell," Holloway said.

Blaize shot him a glare dripping with so much poison, it surprised me that Holloway still stood.

"So, what info have we got on this Quentin Gordon guy?" I asked to defuse the tension. We started on the first of four flights of stairs leading up to the fifth floor. The stairwell reeked of piss, stale beer and old food.

"Not a lot." Blaize tore her glare away from Holloway. "Our man's clean. No rap sheets. Model employee, too. The cleaning company couldn't fault him in any way." We passed the third floor, and Holloway began to slow.

"Whew ... I gotta start going to the gym," he panted. "So anyway, we have nothing on this guy at all?"

"We do have some social care records. Gordon was in foster care for five years, between the ages of thirteen and eighteen, after his mother died of a crack cocaine overdose." Blaize walked ahead of us, tackling the steps like a woman on a mission—or a woman with something to prove.

"No dad?" Holloway clutched at his side as if he had a stitch.

"No dad," she said. As we started up the final flight of stairs, my own knees creaked, reminding me I was no spring chicken either. "Mom had a guy living with her for a couple of years. There were reports he was abusive."

"What happened to him?" I asked.

Holloway uttered an audible sigh of relief as we reached the fifth floor landing.

"Nobody knows," Blaize said. "Just up and left one day." She leaned against the top floor railing, arms crossed, waiting for us to catch up. Although it seemed like she barely broke a sweat, I noted the tension in her jaw as if she was biting back some form of pain or discomfort.

"Druggie mom, absent dad, abusive father figure, all around sad childhood ..." Holloway took a couple of breaths. "... that'd be enough to make anyone bitter."

"Bitter, yes," I said, "but outright sociopathic?" We reached apartment fifty-two. Holloway knocked.

No answer.

He knocked again, harder. "Mr. Gordon? This is the police. We have a warrant to search the premises." As Holloway waited by the door, I wandered to the window and peered through the grime and dirt caking the glass.

"I don't think anyone's home," I said, returning to the door.

Holloway's face sagged. "Should we come back?"

Instead of answering, I half-turned away from the door and launched a side kick right on the keyhole, following through with the rest of my body weight. With a *CRACK*, the door flew inwards, slammed into the wall and bounced back, coughing up pulverised plasterboard and splintered wood.

"Jesus Harold Christ!" Holloway shrieked, his shoulders arched up to his ears.

"What?" I held up my hands. "We've got a search warrant. We're allowed to break and enter."

"Yeah, but couldn't you have done it more ... subtly? This ..." he waved his hand at my handiwork, "borders on criminal damage."

"Stop nagging and come on in." Blaize stepped into the relative dimness of the flat. Holloway followed, tiptoeing over chips of wood and plaster as I took the rear.

"*Harold?*" I asked.

He flashed me a lopsided grin. "You know, 'Our Father who art in Heaven, Harold be thy name.'"

I laughed. Blaize rolled her eyes, but the corners of her lips twitched. Snapping on disposable gloves, we walked through the narrow corridor, poking our heads through every door we passed. The first door revealed a cluttered store cupboard with a coil of chains piled on the floor, chains similar to the ones used to hang Sarah Quinn from the tree, and to tie Mackenzie to the burning tyre.

The next door led to the bathroom. A cloud of sinus-clearing scents blasted outwards as we opened it—heady notes of frankincense and lotus mingled with the rich, creamy aroma of coconut. The concentrated odours forced their way up my nostrils, so strong they tickled my throat and left a bitter taste in the back of my mouth. I coughed.

"Woo..." Blaize fanned at her face. "Smells like our guy's into his aromatherapy and bath oils."

"Not quite bath oils." I indicated the ring of candle wax on the floor, arranged in a perfect circle. More half-burnt candles lined the sink, the edges of the bathtub, and on practically every available surface. Molten and re-solidified wax dripped from shelves like creeping stalactites. A bronze urn, filled with ashes, sat atop the toilet cistern, holding a stick of still smouldering incense. Propped against the base of the urn were a pair of glasses. I lifted them up by their thick plastic frame and peered through the lenses. *Barely any distortion at all. They must be very low power, perhaps only for reading.*

"Kurt," Holloway called from behind me, "look at this."

Behind the door hung a full-length mirror. A symbol had been drawn onto the surface at around the level of the chest. It resembled a curly number four or the number twenty-one, with the end of the 2 joined with the base of the 1:

$$\text{♃}$$

"That's the astrological symbol for the planet Jupiter," Holloway said. "The Roman name for Zeus."

"I wonder if this was intentional. If you stand right here," I adjusted myself until I was in position, "the symbol appears right over your heart."

"The kingdom of Zeus is within you," said Holloway.

I shook my head.

"This is juicy, real juicy." Holloway said, moving on. "I wonder what other goodies we'll discover."

We got our answer when we stepped into the living room—or at least, what *should* have been the living room in any normal home. Gordon's had no TV, no couch, no coffee table, chairs, rugs, no furniture of any kind.

Instead, he'd turned the place into a *shrine*.

A stone altar dominated the centre of the room—a slab of granite supported by a marble statue. As I drew closer, I whistled. The statue depicted a man, bearded and bare-chested, holding up the granite slab on his muscled shoulders. Bent over on one knee, his stone face was etched in pain, showing the strain of carrying his eternal burden.

I ran a gloved finger across the smooth granite. Cool to the touch, the black stone gleamed like polished onyx. Specks of inlaid quartz crystals glittered in its depths, twinkling like stars in the midnight sky. A pattern had been carved into the surface. I moved aside the incense urn, the earthenware jug and the bowl of fruit offerings. Concentric ellipses had been chiselled into the top of the altar, along with more arcane-looking symbols. I recognised the symbol for Jupiter among them, as well as the universal symbols for male and female.

"Atlas," Holloway said. He crouched under the altar. "Zeus punished him by making him hold up the Heavens for eternity."

I returned my attention to the drawings carved into the granite. Of course, it was an atlas, a map of the Heavens, the solar system. All those symbols had to relate to the planets.

"Why the male and female symbols?" Blaize asked.

"Ever heard the expression, 'Women are from Venus, men are from Mars'?" He pointed to the symbols, which had been carved in the correct astronomical positions. "Mars," he said, his finger on the male symbol, "and Venus." His finger scooted over to the female one.

I waved my arm over the entire altar. "But what does this all mean?"

"That our man is one messed-up molly. What else could it

mean?" He ran a hand over the carvings. "Hello," he said, pointing to the side of the slab, "we've got carvings along the edge, as well."

Blaize and I leaned forward. A series of Greek symbols ringed the sides of the granite slab, clustered together into twelve equally spaced groups.

"Do those spell out anything?" I asked Holloway.

"My ancient Greek is a bit rusty. I dunno . . ."

"You *know* ancient Greek?" Blaize asked. Shaking her head, she shrugged. "Not that it would surprise me much."

Holloway returned to examining the altar. Lips pursed, his gaze stayed fixed on the etchings, the brow between his glasses knitted. He looked like a scholar deciphering hieroglyphics.

"You know," he said, "there are twelve clusters of symbols—twelve *words*—carved around a map of the solar system. I kinda get the feeling this is some sort of calendar." He continued to circle the altar. "Look at this." He pointed out a notch in the granite, a chipped flaw against the smooth perfection of the slab.

"Ooh . . ." Blaize winced. "That must've pissed him off."

"I doubt it was unintentional." Holloway ran his fingers along the edges of the notch. "It's pretty hard to chip granite by accident. And this looks clean cut."

"Why'd you think he put it there?" I asked.

"Assuming we are correct regarding this being some arcane calendar, then . . ."

"This is some sort of date marker," I finished for him. My fingers ran over the symbols directly under the notch:

Ἑκατομβαιών

"What does this say?"

"I can't read Greek, but I know enough of the symbols to transcribe them into the modern alphabet." He took out his notepad and flipped to a fresh page. "The first symbol, the accented *E*, sort of sounds like our *H-E . . . He.*" He wrote down the letters on his pad. "The second symbol, kappa, relates to *K*. The next one's easy, alpha is *A* . . ." His voice dropped off, eyes darting back and forth between the etchings and his notepad. He chewed the end of his pen, frowning. When he finished, he showed us the 'translated' version of the word:

HEKATOMBAION

"Heck-a-tomb-aye . . . on?" Blaize said. "What does that even mean?"

"Do you think it's the same word that stripper claimed her saviour said?" Holloway asked.

"Sounds like it," I said. "We need to find out what it means."

"I'm on it." Holloway whipped out his phone, his fingers whizzing across the touch screen.

"I knew getting one of these new-fangled smart phones was a good idea." Blaize waggled her eyebrows at me as we watched Holloway access his web browser and type in the word in the search engine box. Within seconds, a list of links began to populate the page.

"Here we go." He tapped on the first link. He skim-read the entry, mouthing the words silently as Blaize and I craned our necks over his shoulders.

"I was right," he said finally. "This *is* a calendar. A festival calendar, to be precise. Hekatombaion is the first month of the ancient Athenian year."

"So it's January?" Blaize asked.

"No." Holloway pushed his glasses up his nose. "The year used to start in summer in ancient Greece. Hekatombaion corresponded to July-August."

"Which is right now." A feather stirred in my gut. "You said this was a festival calendar. What sort of festivals happened in this month?"

"Same festival we've been celebrating every four years since." Holloway's words sent a ribbon of chills twisting up my spine.

"The Olympics."

35

The Oracle admired the bowl-shaped structure of the Olympic Stadium. Steel beams criss-crossed its sides in a basket weave pattern. The floodlights had been turned on, casting the stadium in a fluorescent glow, boldly making it visible from miles around, a gargantuan flying saucer that had landed in the heart of the East End.

A magnificent feat of architecture.

Located on a manmade 'island' and surrounded by waterways on three sides, the stadium was set in a picturesque location with a commanding view of the rest of the Olympic Park. With a maximum capacity of eighty thousand people, the stadium even had a removable upper tier of seats that could be dismantled when not in use.

Truly a temple worthy of Zeus.
Nobody realises that.

The glittering stadium vanished as he let the curtain fall over the window. He turned to face his room with tasteful furnishings, neutral decor, a comfortable bed with its sheets tucked in with hospital-like precision. He missed his altar, his shrine. He wished he'd brought some candles and incense sticks with him, but the hotel had a strict no smoking policy, and the burning incense might set off the fire alarm.

He'd needed to move. The police were getting close. They called his workplace. He could tell from the shifty looks from his manager, suspicion flickering in his eyes like red flags.

Guilty until proven innocent.

It did not matter, though. The rituals may have expedited the induction of his trance, helped focus his mind to channel the word of Zeus, but he was capable of achieving the same results without them.

He sat down at the edge of the bed, fingering the beads in his hand, seeking comfort in their familiarity. The whiskers of the grey beard he wore tickled his nose.

Angelic strains of lyre music began—so beautiful and profound it could only have been performed by Orpheus himself. Light and colour danced at the edges of his vision, teasing him with promise.

It is time.

He reclined on the bed, eyes staring up at the light fixture in the cream coloured ceiling. Sweat dotted his forehead and upper lip, and his cheeks burned with a red heat. His stomach churned, making a gurgling noise. They could be hunger pangs brought on by his fast or flutters of excitement from the prospect of getting close to God.

The ceiling shimmered like the surface of a lake. It shattered, shards falling away from him, lifting up farther and farther into a sky the colour of lapis lazuli. The circle of light from the lamp began to grow, a warm orb of illumination that floated above him in a hypnotic dance. Clouds drifted into his peripheral vision, tiny fluffy ones at first. They darkened and expanded, fusing together until they blacked out the lamplight and blue sky in a blanket of roiling fog. Streaks of lightning tore through the storm clouds, bathing him in a silvery aura. His hair stood on end from the static electricity. Thunder rolled in from the distance like the sound of waves crashing on a rocky shore. The Oracle's heart beat faster as he recognised the rumbling voice of his Lord.

"O Zeus, Father of Gods and Men! Enter me, my Master!"

A jagged bolt ripped into his chest, right above his heart. His back arched as his entire body spasmed, but only a surge of delirious ecstasy filled him as the flash of light illuminated his soul. Divine power thrummed in his veins as the essence of the Lightning Bearer's spirit imbued his mortal blood.

He became one with God.

36

The garden resembled the landscape of an alien planet, black and barren and surreal. The picket fence, reduced to charred stumps, stuck out from the burnt earth at odd angles, like a row of rotting teeth over septic gums. Skeletal remains of bushes clawed at the peeled, blackened walls with bony fingers. Through the soot-stained window, Meghan's room looked untouched by the horrors outside the night before. The powder pink wallpaper smiled at me with its border of cheery daisies, her *High School Musical* quilt half hanging off her unmade bed.

In many ways, I felt responsible for what happened—like a criminal returning to the scene of a crime, which was absurd. As if I'd try to firebomb my own home.

I imagined the arsonist, crouched in the shadows under Meghan's window, lighting a Molotov cocktail and preparing to throw it into my daughter's bedroom. I realised just how lucky Meghan had been—just how lucky *I* had been—that the thug was interrupted. What if he'd succeeded? I shook my head and tried to banish the imagery from my mind.

Opening my car boot, I tossed in both suitcases, one with my clothes, the other with Meghan's, along with a black bin bag hastily rammed with assorted toys, books and toiletries. I couldn't bring everything with me; we were already cluttering up Holloway's spotless apartment. I could swear Holloway had developed a nervous tic in his right eye, one which twitched every time he passed his far from pristine living room.

"Thought I heard trouble," a woman's voice, husky in its familiarity, made me straighten up so quickly, I nearly hit my head on the trunk lid.

"Helen. Hi."

Even in her dressed down state, in an oversized rugby shirt and baggy track bottoms, she still looked smoking. Her auburn hair, darkened by moisture, hung in damp strands round her shoulders. As she stepped up to give me a hug, the floral scent of her lavender and rosehip shampoo enveloped me. We stood that way for a bit.

Helen pulled away first, leaving a yawning emptiness in my arms once more.

"So," she gestured towards the luggage in my trunk, "looks like you're shipping off."

"I need to lay low for a while. For everyone's sake."

"Uh-huh." She didn't attempt to change my mind, to convince me to stay.

I twiddled with my car keys, with my charity key chain from the Royal National Institute of Blind People. "I'm sorry I brought all this shit onto you and Lucy." I ran my thumb over the raised dots within the RNIB initials.

She smiled a wistful expression, one in mourning of the things that could have been. "You know, when you first moved in and introduced yourself as a police officer, I actually hoped you'd bring a bit of danger and excitement into my life. Suppose I should've been careful what I wished for, huh? After last night, I realise I can't quite hack a life of adventure and intrigue. It's just too ... stressful." She offered a self-deprecatory laugh, one that sounded hollow, fragile. "Guess I'm just a boring old maid who prefers a quiet, *uneventful* life."

Her gaze dropped to her sandaled feet. That was it, her goodbye. No *"Keep in touch"* or *"Call me."* Not even an *"I'll miss you,"* and that hurt more than it should have.

I kissed the top of her forehead, smelled her for one last time as her cool damp hair brushed my face. Silently, I wished her all the best, that perhaps one day, she'd be able to fill the hole in her heart. God knew I wouldn't be the one to fill it, and she wouldn't be the one to fill mine.

The last I saw of Helen was the swaying of her hips and the fluid chocolate cascade of hair down her back as she disappeared back into the house. Shoving my hands in my pockets, I surveyed the place once more—our home for just over a year. Though we hadn't settled long enough to develop much of an attachment, there were still memories connected to the worn brick and mortar, to the decimated garden. Meghan's first solo bicycle ride without her training wheels, the first time Reggie brought a girlfriend home, and I had balked at the idea of her staying the night. My attempt at making sushi that left everyone with a bad case of diarrhoea. Our first Christmas without Angie.

I noticed something twinkling in the blackened earth, a lone star in the middle of the midnight sky of a post-apocalyptic world. The crisped grass snapped beneath my feet as I squatted down, the odour of burnt vegetation still lingering in the air like a burial shroud. I picked up the shiny object, no larger than a bit of gravel. At first, I thought it was a small diamond, but as it sat in the palm of my hand, it weighed too little, and its facets didn't quite produce the same brilliance as a real diamond would.

A fake diamond. A rhinestone. I turned it over. Something pale and translucent, soft and gummy, crusted its underside.

Dried glue.

Another bit of Helen's craft materials? They seemed to insinuate themselves into every crevice she touched. The hazards of a maker of handmade greeting cards. I wished my occupational hazards were as benign. Briefly, I entertained the absurd idea that Helen had planted the petrol bomb. Maybe she wanted to get rid of me so badly, she staged an arson attack to force me into moving out.

Ludicrous speculations of a rejected heart.

I let the crystal fall from my hand. It disappeared from view, swallowed up by the carpet of scorched grass just like I swallowed my desire to love again.

"How's Meghan getting along?"

"Oh, she's *fine*." Chief Sutherland's voice sounded hollow and tinny over the hands-free speaker. "She's just spilled coffee all over my files, but other than that she's been just peachy."

I cringed. "Shit, sorry about that."

"My own fault, really," she said, cutting me off. "Should've known to leave the mug further away from my paperwork. It . . . wasn't in her line of vision."

"Where is she now?" I manoeuvred the car through the narrow residential streets as Holloway checked the street signs, an open *A to Z* on the dashboard in front of him. Blaize sat in the back seat, sorting through papers and documents in a large manila folder. Fine sprays of rain misted the windscreen but not heavy enough to warrant engaging the wipers.

"Sitting here playing Minesweeper on my computer. You wanna say hi?" Before I could reply, a high-pitched twittering came from the background. "Uh, she says she can't talk right now. She's about to break my best time."

I smiled. "Thanks, Chief. Really appreciate everything, you know. I owe you big time."

"You sure do," she said, her tone clipped, "and you can repay me by taking this bastard down." She hung up, but not before I overheard her say, "Right, who wants ice cream?"

"Somebody's made a new friend," Holloway said as he traced a map. "Turn left here. Number twenty-eight should be on our right." We pulled into an avenue lined on both sides by identical-looking, four-storey maisonettes, their whitewashed walls grey in the overcast gloom. As tourists from all over the world descended on London for the Olympics, I had no doubt each of them had their own preconceived notion of the city. The romance of Notting Hill and the Royal Family. The multicultural bustle of Chinatown and Brick Lane. Quirky London, with Madame Tussaud's and the guards at Buckingham Palace. A modern metropolis steeped in history, with superstructures like the London Eye and Canary Wharf soaring alongside the Tower of London and Big Ben.

Some may have found the city, with its sprawling city centre parks, unusually green; others may have found the weather a touch grey and wet. Whatever their expectations, I bet none of them would have pictured London as the underside of a carpet where the authorities had swept the forgotten people of the city. The poor, the immigrants, the unsavouries, all were hidden away in slums, located far from tourist haunts. Where we drove, London survived on benefits and dodgy deals, where residents were locked in an endless cycle of crime for survival. A London of young convicts and teenage mothers, of fourteen-year-old alcoholics and drug addicts, of forgotten war veterans slowly withering away in silence, like the dying poppies on a memorial wreath.

Larger drops of rain spattered the windshield. "Hope it won't rain at the Opening Ceremony tomorrow," I said, turning on the wipers. A rattling sounded from behind me. Peering into the rear view mirror, Blaize shook some pills out from a bottle. Her gaze met mine in the mirror.

I'll be fine, she mouthed, answering my silent concern as she popped a couple into her mouth.

I parked the car outside number twenty-eight, a mid-terrace maisonette which looked no different from all the others on the street, except for the overgrown lawn and mildewed walls.

"This the place?" Blaize leaned forward between the driver and passenger's seats. "Looks like no one lives here."

Holloway nodded. "Doesn't look like anyone's lived here since Gordon moved out." Holloway grabbed the manila folder from Blaize and opened the file in his lap. "Do you really think we'll find anything of use here?"

"It's not like we have any other leads." I reached for a document in the folder. My fingers brushed the inside of Holloway's thigh. "Sorry, sorry." I snatched the folder and buried my face behind a headed letter. I hoped he didn't think the touch was intentional. "I'm just hoping to dig up something from his past," I said quickly, "something that might help us predict what he'll do next."

"Huh," Holloway had some sort of medical report in his hands. "Apparently Gordon used to suffer from epilepsy as a child."

"Is that relevant?" I asked.

"It's interesting. Says here his particular form of epilepsy is complex partial seizures, particularly in the temporal lobe, the part of the brain that processes auditory and visual information. It's also involved in the development of long-term memory." He fell silent for a moment. "Seizures in the temporal lobe can cause a person to see, hear, even taste things that don't exist. And it may result in anomalies in memory development, such as *déjà vu* or *jamais vu*."

"*Jamais vu?*" French was never my strong subject at school.

"The opposite of *déjà vu*," Blaize said. "In *déjà vu*, you're convinced you've experienced something before, even when you haven't; in *jamais vu*, you are unable to recognise familiar experiences." She tapped the report in Holloway's hand. "In Gordon's case, his fits were so severe, he even had a seizure response dog."

"Seizure response dog?" I'd heard of seeing-eye dogs, even dogs for deaf people, but never seizure response dogs.

"It alerts people when its handler has a seizure and stays with the person to keep him or her safe," Blaize said.

"Wow. You think Gordon's hallucinations are a result of his epileptic fits?"

"It's a plausible theory," said Holloway. "And the problems with memory development might have contributed to his delusion."

"As could observations of his rather withdrawn personality," I added, pointing to a highlighted passage in the document I held.

"Aloof, awkward, unable or unwilling to socialise with other children, frequently in a world of his own …"

"Classic symptoms of autistic spectrum disorder." After scribbling a note in his pad, Holloway replaced the medical report into the folder.

"I don't get why there's no mention of epilepsy in Gordon's work records at Hygienia," Blaize said.

"Maybe he never went to a doctor about it," Holloway said, "so no one was aware of his condition, and the people who were assumed it was merely a case of childhood epilepsy he'd outgrown."

"Perhaps Gordon didn't see it *as* a medical condition." I thought about his victims, how they all seemed to have been punished in the name of Zeus. "Perhaps he saw it as a gift."

We stepped out of the car into the afternoon drizzle, the muggy air and spitting rain wrapping their clamminess around us like a second skin. The small garden gate, black paint peeling, exposing rotting patches of rust, creaked like the knees of a pensioner as we swung it open. We walked up the gravel path, choked with outbreaks of weed, pebbles crunching underfoot with each step. Waist-high grass licked at our legs with rain-drenched tongues, marking our trousers with slashes of darkened material like lash marks from a whip.

We climbed onto the front patio, a raised concrete platform still framed by warped wooden planks as if someone had gone through all the trouble of building a patio, only to move out as soon as the cement was poured. Rainwater spilled overhead from a blocked gutter hanging partly off the eaves of the roof. The grimy glass of the front window, spider-webbed with cracks, only afforded a murky view of grey shadows in the room beyond.

Holloway knocked on the door. "Police. We have a search warrant." Despite the obvious signs that the place was uninhabited, we still needed to follow procedure. After waiting a minute, I kicked the door down, the same way I'd kicked down the one to Gordon's flat. It exploded inward, sending up a cloud of dust and cobwebs. The tarnished door handle popped out from its fixings, landing with a thud on the mildewed carpet. "Crude, but effective," Holloway said, not showing nearly the distress I'd expected at my mess.

Light from the open door spilled into the front room, no doubt the first rays of illumination the place had seen in years. The lounge was small and sparsely furnished. A dusty, bile green sofa faced a short, wooden cabinet upon which a television set would have perched had it not already been stolen by opportunistic burglars. On the footstool, doubling as a coffee table, sat a crumpled can of beer and a plate that seemed to be supporting its own mini ecosystem. A narrow corridor led into the kitchen, dislodged mosaic tiles scattered on the floor like so many pieces of a massive jigsaw puzzle. One of the chairs around the table had toppled onto its side, three of its four legs acting as foundations for an intricate spider web.

"According to the report, Gordon's mom died here in the kitchen, at this very table," Blaize said. "Cocaine overdose. Gordon was barely thirteen at the time. He was the one who found her."

"Poor sod," Holloway said.

The kitchen stood silent and sombre, withholding its terrible secret from the unsuspecting observer. Dirty dishes still clogged the sink as if the house's occupants had left in a hurry, leaving the place in a sort of suspended animation.

"Let's check out the bedrooms." I led the way upstairs, rotting floorboards shrieking in protest under our weight as we climbed the aging staircase. The first door to our right yielded the bathroom, a mouldy cubicle with a yellowed tub and a toilet holding black, stagnant water. The next room housed a single bed, a chest of drawers, and little else. The greying bed linen, blue with fading yellow stars, suggested it had once been a young boy's room. I compared the neutral, off-white walls to Meghan's bright, wallpapered one. It did not look like a typical child's bedroom.

Searching through the drawers revealed nothing. Apart from the size of the clothes, nothing in the room pointed at its former occupant being a child. No toys, no games, no posters of his favourite movie or music band.

"Look at this." Holloway pointed at the corner of a hardcover book peeking out from beneath a dusty quilt. With a pen, he nudged the blanket aside.

MYTHS & LEGENDS OF ANCIENT GREECE: A STUDY OF ANCIENT HELLENIC TEXT

Not a child's picture book, either, but a serious, academic tome. The author's name even had *PhD* appended to it.

"Our chap started young." Holloway adjusted the frame of his glasses. With his pen, he flipped the book open, revealing yellowing pages of text. A card stuck inside the front cover had various dates stamped on it. The last date was *26 APRIL 1997*. "And looks like he's got a waaay overdue library book."

I wondered what it felt like to be obsessed over something for over a decade, to act on the compulsions. I imagined the vindication as years of delusion finally culminated in a chain of events that were logical only in one's own twisted mind.

He must be feeling pretty invincible right about now.

We searched the final upstairs bedroom, Gordon's mother's. Beside a double bed, the door to the built-in cabinet had come off its hinges, hanging limp like a butchered carcass. The inside of the closet smelled of dust and mildew, the clothes within tattered and pockmarked by fabric-hungry moths.

I gestured towards a rack of shirts. "Didn't the stepdad up and leave nearly a year before Gordon's mom died?"

"Ten months, to be exact. Why?" Holloway said.

"Don't you think it's odd he didn't take any of his stuff with him?" The shirts and trousers definitely belonged to a man.

Holloway shrugged. "If reports of Flynn Buchanan's penchant for cheap booze and violence against women and children were anything to go by, he probably wandered off after a drunken fight one night and just forgot to come back."

I fingered the sleeve of a disintegrating checked shirt. Although a size too small for me, it would still fit a rather large man. I envisioned being a child and having to face a drunk, angry bloke of that size on a daily basis. Would I try to fight back, or find somewhere to hide? Would I cry and whimper as the menacing shadow reeking of alcohol loomed over me, or would I just close my eyes and accept the inevitable punishment to come? I tried to imagine the child's reaction to the news that the horrible man was gone for good. Would I rejoice in my newfound freedom? Or would I quake in fear, in the knowledge that his disappearance would tip my already fragile mother over the edge, sending her spiralling into a self-destructive cycle of drugs from which she would never emerge?

We didn't find anything of note in the master bedroom, either. Descending the staircase, we were about to leave when I spotted the knee-tall door under the stairs. Crouching low to avoid bumping my head on the slanted ceiling, I knelt before it and pulled at its ring handle. The door screeched with resistance at first, but gave with a long, reluctant moan.

I jumped back so quickly I hit my head against the ceiling, my spine compressing against the base of my skull at the impact. I landed on my bum, shaking my head in an attempt to dislodge the stars swimming before my eyes.

"Kurt, you all right ..." Blaize's words trailed off as she knelt down beside me. My dizziness soon receded to a dull throbbing in my skull, and as my vision cleared, I convinced myself I hadn't been hallucinating.

I'd been hoping to find a skeleton in the closet.

What I hadn't expected to find was a *literal* skeleton.

The yellowed skull, strips of desiccated skin still clinging to the bone like grisly papier-mâché, stared at me through hollow eye sockets, its pointed teeth grinning at me from the gloom.

"What ... the *fuck* ... is that?" Holloway asked.

The case had turned him into a right foul-mouthed sailor. He covered his nose with his sleeve.

The fetid perfume of decay had rushed into the room with the opening of the closet. The odour was rank but faint, mellowed by the years but still carrying an edge, a putrid reminder of the stench when decomposition was at its fiercest. Blaize made a gagging, coughing sound. I wondered how anyone could have lived in the house without noticing the smell. They must either have been drunk, stoned, or deranged, or perhaps a combination of the three.

The top of my head still aching from its run-in with the low ceiling, I leaned forward to examine the petrified remains. The ribcage had collapsed in on itself. The bones were too small to have belonged to an adult—tiny bones the size of pebbles, many with tufts of hair still stuck to them, lay in a line, forming what looked like a disjointed tail; and the elongated skull bared its sharp canines at me.

A dog's skeleton.

"Looks like we found Gordon's seizure response dog," Holloway said, his voice sounding muffled from behind his sleeve. "Our culprit's first victim, you think?"

"Why would he kill his own helper dog?" Blaize held her hand over her mouth and nose.

"Why not?" Holloway said. "It might've made some sort of twisted sense in his mind. Plus, it satisfies one of the hallmarks of the Macdonald Triad."

The Macdonald Triad was a set of behavioural traits commonly associated with sociopathic behaviour. Apart from animal cruelty, the other characteristics were persistent bedwetting and pyromania.

From my seated position, I nudged at the remains with a foot. The carcass disintegrated where I touched it as if made from dust. Beneath the pile of bones and fur was an earthenware dish. A dog bowl with the name *Heracles* scrawled along the edge in a child's hand. I thought about all the programmes I watched on television about disabled people and their service dogs, about how human and canine developed a special bond of friendship and love. Gordon was an epileptic child living with violence and neglect, whose autism probably ostracised him from other children. That dog might well have been his only friend. I found it difficult to conceive why he'd kill the only thing that would have cared for him.

We stepped out onto the porch, grateful to escape the oppressive atmosphere and stench inside the house. The rain had stopped, but the sky remained the sombre colour of brushed steel. Puddles of rainwater dotted the yard and continued to drip from the leaking eaves overhead. Our little trip had yielded some interesting information, but it still didn't explain what triggered Gordon's psychosis.

More frustratingly, it hadn't offered any clues as to what Gordon would do next.

"Are you people police officers?" The voice was dry and brittle as winter leaves, yet it rippled with an undercurrent of authority, like an old school matron's. An elderly woman leaned across the fence from the garden next door. Wisps of grey hair, fine as spider silk, wafted free of the bun underneath a straw hat that looked like it had seen action in both World Wars. Dirty, yellow gloves clutched gardening implements as she scrutinised us with a squinty-eyed expression that seemed part curiosity, part suspicion.

"Yes we are, ma'am." Blaize said.

We showed her our badges and the search warrant. She examined both with the same Popeye-esque expression.

Holding out a gloved hand, she introduced herself as Mrs. Irene Fitzgerald. "My stars, what do you hope to discover here? This house here's not seen a soul in fourteen years! I've seen my grandson in Scotland more times than this house has seen people!"

"We've linked a previous occupant to an ongoing investigation," Holloway said.

"May I ask if you knew the previous residents?" I asked.

"I knew Elsie Gordon." The brim of her battered sunhat bobbed with conviction before swaying side to side in sympathy. "Such a sad story. Young people these days, they have no respect for their bodies, do they? Pumping themselves full of all manners of chemicals. And for what? An artificial high? Fewer wrinkles? Unnatural weight loss? I tell you, it's a sad state of affairs. The worst thing?" She clucked her tongue. "She had to go and leave a son behind. Poor little tyke had to go into care."

"What were they like?" Blaize said. "Elsie and her son?"

The lines around the old woman's mouth deepened as she pursed her lips. "I didn't know them all that well, mind you. I tend to keep myself to myself, ever since my dear Gerald passed away. God bless his soul. We weren't exactly close as neighbours. Just said hi when we saw each other, chatted about the weather, things like that. I think the word I'd use is *acquaintance*. We were acquaintances. Nothing more." She waved her muddy trowel as she spoke. I had to step back to avoid a flying clod of dirt.

"They were nice enough people, I suppose," she continued, "when the mother wasn't stoned, that is. I could tell when she'd had a bit too much the night before. She'd look like death warmed over in the morning. And the son ... what was his name again? Q ... Quinn? Quincy?"

"Quentin," I said.

"Was that his name?" She seemed doubtful. "I suppose it was. Quiet boy, in any case. Came across a little shy. Withdrawn. He had the fits really bad, poor thing. I saw him once in the garden. Just fell over and started twitching as if he was being electrocuted. Got himself a nasty gash on the head from the fall. Wet himself, as well, in the process. Must've been scary for the poor child. It certainly scared me. Probably scared Elsie, too. She was a young, single mother. I think she had trouble coping with her son's condition." She lowered her voice to a conspiratorial whisper. "Now

I'm not one to gossip, but word in the neighbourhood in those days tended to spread. Some people thought Elsie took all them drugs to … to get away from it all, you know? Escape reality. But that just left the poor child to deal with his problems alone. That is, until they got him that lovely helper dog. Beautiful creature, and so gentle and intelligent. It knew how to keep the boy safe when he seized. Stopped him falling anywhere dangerous. Pulled him to safety. Even knew how to run and get help. The child adored his little helper. Spent all his time with it. They say a dog is man's best friend. Well, that dog certainly was Quinn's best friend." I didn't bother correcting Mrs. Fitzgerald's name confusion. Instead, I glanced at Blaize, and at Holloway, who scratched at his temple with the end of his pen. I could see my question reflected in their frowns.

Would a kid be delusional enough to kill his own best friend?

"Did you know Elsie Gordon's last boyfriend at all?" I asked the old lady. "A Mr. Flynn Buchanan?"

Mrs. Fitzgerald screwed up her face with such vehemence I half-expected her to spit in disgust. "I always said if I never heard that name again, it'd be too soon," she said. Her glare accused me of ruining her day with unsavoury memories of an unsavoury character. "The man was poison. Pure hemlock. Never a kind word to anybody. Such an angry man. Always scowling, especially after a drink." Her shoulders jerked up in an exaggerated shudder. "He used to hit her, you know. I heard the shouts in the night coming from inside the house. The sound of breaking glass was an unusually common noise in the Gordon household. I saw the bruises and cuts on the poor woman. Sometimes even on little Quinn. For the life of me, I don't know why Elsie put up with him; he was a violent drunkard and a parasite. Sadly, the woman was probably too drugged up half the time to notice." Dropping her gardening tools, she patted the dirt from her gloves as if brushing her hands of the matter. "To be perfectly honest, I didn't know the man personally. I'd never spoken to him. But I knew him enough to keep my distance."

"Do you know what happened to Mr. Buchanan?" Holloway asked.

"For society's sake, six feet under, I hope."

I marvelled at the venom spewing from this kindly old lady, who looked the spitting image of Betty White's character in *The Golden Girls*. She must really have disliked the man.

"Sadly, I can't be certain of that. He sodded off after a particularly rowdy night, in more ways than one. A storm was brewing, but even amid all that lightning and wind, I could hear him, clear as day, swearing and shouting. The crashes from inside the house were louder than the crashes of thunder. I heard some screaming. Even the dog was howling. Goodness knows what he was doing to the poor animal. I didn't see him the next day or the day after. Come to think of it, I never saw the dog after that, either. After a week, I remember trying to broach the subject of his whereabouts with Elsie. But she wouldn't hear of it. She looked like a ghost, she did. Folded in on herself, as if his leaving wasn't the best thing in the world to happen to her, as if her world had actually ended without him!" Mrs. Fitzgerald threw her hands up. I couldn't dodge the spray of mud in time. Specks of loam dotted a shoulder of my pale blue shirt.

"She went downhill fast after that," she sighed. "Wasted away before my eyes until she was just skin and bones. Passed within a year of his disappearance, don't you know." I noticed Holloway gazing purposefully at his watch as if telling me that whilst small talk with the resident Miss Marple was all well and entertaining, it wasn't giving us anything we didn't already know. Yet, something about what Mrs. Fitzgerald had said nibbled at the back of my consciousness.

"You said there was a storm the night he left?"

"Oh, yes, a mighty one. Cracks of lightning, thunder, howling winds. But the odd thing was, it never rained. Not a drop. As if the sky exhausted itself on the light show and sound effects, and just couldn't deliver the goods."

Lightning and thunder. Both associated with the god Zeus. If Gordon was already obsessed with Greek myths, could he have taken their presence as some sort of divine sign?

"And you said the dog was howling?" I asked. The arched eyebrows from Holloway betrayed his confusion at my line of questioning.

"Yes," Mrs. Fitzgerald said. "At first, I thought it just didn't like all the hoo-ha from the storm, but it wasn't so much howling as *yelping*. It sounded as if the animal was in pain."

"And this dog . . ." I continued, "what sort of dog was it?" Holloway looked completely gobsmacked. Blaize, who knew me better, leaned forward.

"It was one of those generic helper dogs. You know, the yellow types with long hair blind people always have. Can't quite recall the name of the breed . . ."

"Chihuahuas?" Holloway suggested, but quickly retracted his sarcasm. "Labradors?"

"Labradors. That's it. Gorgeous creatures. I'd get one myself if they weren't such a handful. The poor dog. I don't want to know what that beast did to him."

Come on, Kurt, think. Something I read about Zeus and the legends surrounding him mentioned something about a dog.

A golden dog.

"Well if you ask me, only one remotely good thing came from that awful night," Mrs. Fitzgerald continued. "At least Elsie got a finished patio out of the horrible man before he left."

I frowned, looking from the old woman to the cement patio we had stood on mere minutes before. "What do you mean?"

"*Flynn*," she spat out his name like hacking up phlegm, "he built that patio there the night he left. Which was kind of strange, now that I think about it. After all that shouting and raging and fighting, why would he stop to pour concrete before leaving? And in the middle of the night? In what was threatening to be a torrential downpour? If it had rained, the concrete wouldn't have set. So in some ways, Elsie was lucky it stayed dry that night."

"Kurt ..." Blaize's eyes bored into me with urgency, but my own remained fixed on the simple cement patio, still encaged within its wooden frame.

A stormy night. An odd time to be building a patio. No builder in his right mind would pour concrete while there was a chance of rain.

It hadn't rained. Good luck for some.

Good luck that might have been perceived as a godsend by others.

A yellow dog.

In mythology, something happened involving Zeus and a golden dog.

"Tom, get Chief Sutherland on the phone. Sam, we'll need Forensics, and maybe some sort of industrial digger." Irene Fitzgerald had claimed that, for the sake of society, she hoped Flynn Buchanan was six feet under. She might have gotten her wish, although she may have been a bit off with her estimate.

I glanced again at the simple concrete patio.

He was more like *two* feet under.

37

The wind howled through the open window, sending the curtains flapping like mast sails. An electric buzz imbued the air with a dry static. The low-hanging clouds were black, swollen with rain, threatening an imminent downpour.

The Oracle stood with his forehead pressed to the glass, admiring the light show outside, performed by no other than the supreme ruler of the Pantheon Himself.

People always warned him to stay away from the window during a lightning storm. He wondered why, why anyone would choose to distance themselves from the mighty Lightning Bringer, to stay away from this inspiring display of true power. When the great Thunder God descended to the Earth, giving mere mortals the honour of His presence, why would they lock the windows, draw their blinds, and shut Him out?

It was on such a night that Zeus visited him, when He deemed the Oracle worthy of becoming the chosen one, and bestowed on him the power of the God.

Another peal of thunder bellowed overhead, shaking the foundations of the house. Despite the deafening noise, the boy did not cover his ears. He stared out his bedroom window, mouth wide as he watched the sky being torn apart by lightning, bright and jagged like serrated blades.

To think that all the might and power came from just one god, a god who not only wielded the lightning bolt and thunderclap, but who also ruled over all beings, mortal and immortal. Such would be a god to be reckoned with. Not one of those half-baked gods, who would let his own son get crucified, or the airy-fairy ones preaching peace and love to all. No, the god demanded respect.

He was one god that should be feared.

His gaze of awe dropped back down to the open book in his lap. The chapter he'd been reading dealt with the ancient Oracle at Dodona, where priests used to converse with the great Thunder God. The priests, called Selloi, *would lie on the ground and hear His voice in the rustle of oak leaves and branches.*

Perhaps, *thought the boy,* I could be a Selloi. *He certainly did a lot of lying down and hearing things, though not by choice. His episodes scared him—the colours, the sounds, the strange emotions, the feeling of not quite being in his own body. He'd woken up from spells with gashes on his head, a bloody nose, even a broken leg once, and never remembered how he got them.*

Could it be that he just had not learned to control his ability?

Lightning lit up the bedroom in a blinding white, followed seconds later by another deafening crash. Heracles whimpered, pushing his shaggy body closer against the boy. He soothed the dog by hugging him and scratching the back of his floppy ear. After all the times Heracles had been there for him, comfort was the least he could offer in reciprocation. The dog licked his cheek in gratitude, and the boy laughed a rare laugh.

Heracles was the only one who came closest to understanding his ability. Not his mother, not the doctors, and definitely not the other children at school. When his visions frightened him, Heracles would be by his side, soothing him with his mere furry presence. Whenever he awoke from his blackouts, he'd find Heracles waiting for him patiently. Since he got the dog from the epilepsy charity, he'd suffered fewer injuries during his episodes. Except when the boy had to go to school, Heracles never left his side. He became the boy's protector.

More importantly, he became his friend.

Another bang rang through the house, but it wasn't thunder. It sounded like the front door.

The boy stiffened, his heart gripped in an icy fist. Every night, he would pray for Flynn not to come home, pray for him to crash over at 'a friend's', to fall asleep in a gutter somewhere, or to just decide never to return.

Some days, the boy would get his wish.

Other days, he was not so lucky.

Turning off his bedside lamp, the boy dove under the covers, pretending to be asleep. A pair of industrial boots stomped up the stairs, their rhythm unsteady.

The boy was well acquainted with the steel toes of the boots. They shambled onto the landing. Each footfall echoed the boy's thundering heartbeat. They grew louder as they approached his room. He prayed for them to keep on walking past his door.

The footfalls moved on down the hall, and the boy let out a sigh of relief. The door into the room next door burst open with a loud bang. Flynn said something, his voice gruff and treacly with alcohol. Mother replied, sounding equally stoned. A roar from Flynn, followed by a sound like a whip being cracked and Mother let out a pained gasp.

Please let Flynn go to sleep ...

The footsteps shuffled back out onto the corridor.

Each plodding step intensified the boy's dread, like the legs of a spider inching up his spine. Pulling the blanket up to his eyes, he imagined the wearer of those boots, a hulking brute with stretched tattoos and a red face. Like the boys' schoolmates, Flynn did not understand the boy's condition, and like them, he compensated for his ignorance with cruel teasing.

The only difference was that he was over three times older—and bigger—than the kids at school. Flynn was someone who saw fit to impose his dominance over the boy and his mother by means of physical violence and verbal abuse. He reminded the boy of the giant in the story Jack and the Beanstalk—*big, clumsy, cruel, and more than a little dim-witted.*

"Fee-fi-fo-fum..."

Perhaps Mother would call for Flynn, to urge him to go to bed, but he knew his mother was probably experiencing visions of her own, visions of the drug-induced kind, leaving the boy to face Flynn alone.

The door to his room flew open with a crash louder than the thunder outside. Flynn's bulk loomed in the doorway, framed by the yellow light streaming in from the hallway, a shadowy demon stepping out from a portal to Hell. He held a half-finished vodka bottle in his hand.

"Get up!" Flynn hollered. He kicked the bed frame, making the boy's world rock. "Get up, you lazy spaz!" He tried to swig from the bottle, but most of the clear liquid ended up dribbling down his chin. The boy slithered deeper beneath the covers.

Maybe if I pretend I'm asleep he'll go away.

A manacle-like grip clamped down on the boy's ankle, yanking him off the edge of the bed. He had the sense to lift his head so it didn't hit the laminate floor, but he landed heavily on the back of his shoulders, causing the air to leave his lungs in a painful whoosh.

"I shh-aid, get the fff-uck up!" Flynn slurred. "Ya gotta help me with the patio!"

"I-it's one in the morning!" the boy managed to wheeze. In response, a boot burrowed into the tender flesh under his ribs. The boy yelped, curling up into a ball. No amount of ragged breathing seemed to be getting any oxygen into his lungs. Something hot gurgled up his throat, leaving a sharp, bitter aftertaste on the back of his tongue.

"Don't be shh-o lazy, you little prick!" Flynn shouted, spittle hanging from his hairy lip. "I don't give a fff-uck if it's-sh yer birthday. You're helping out!" Rough fingers stinking of alcohol grabbed the boy's hair, forcing him to his feet, but something warm interposed itself between him and Flynn. Heracles growled deep from his belly, the vibrations from the dog's tension passing into the boy's body.

Flynn kicked the dog aside. Heracles yipped.

"Fff-uckin' mutt." Flynn dragged the boy downstairs by his hair, swaying so much as he descended, he ricocheted alternately from wall

to banister in a side-winding dance. The boy feared that if Flynn fell, he'd bring the boy tumbling down the steps with him. Outside, the thunder continued to rage. Lightning lit up the house at erratic intervals, like strobes of light on a disco dance floor. Yet, there was still no pitter-patter of rain, as if the great Zeus was too angry for tears.

The boy stumbled on the last step. Flynn's grip on his hair kept him upright, but he banged his shin on the stairs and slammed into the man's side.

"Watch it!" A stinging slap whipped his head to the side. A bloom of heat spread from his right cheek. "Clumsly oaf!" With a bark, Heracles shot down the stairs, his trimmed claws tapping at the wooden boards in a precipitation of clicks. Quick as a streak of yellow lightning, the dog launched himself onto Flynn's hand, the one still holding the boy's hair, and latched on with his teeth.

Flynn screamed, letting go of the boy, who scampered to the relative safety of the far wall. With his free hand, the man gave the dog a vicious punch in the snout, and Heracles let go, snuffling and licking his injured nose. Flynn bellowed, his features twisted with drunken rage. A vein throbbed in his temple. His face was the reddest the boy had ever seen—almost a livid purple. He half-hoped that the man's head would explode like it did in cartoons when someone got too angry.

Flynn's head didn't explode. Instead, he fell on Heracles, his immense bulk pinning the dog to the floor. Hurling a litany of curses, he circled both hands around Heracles's throat and squeezed. He shook the dog, smashing its head again and again onto the floorboards. Heracles whimpered. He began to howl—not the long, mournful howl he sometimes emitted when baying at the moon, but a blood-curdling, high-pitched wail that would give the boy nightmares for years to come.

"Stop it!" the boy pleaded, pushing himself off the wall. He threw himself on the man's back, wrapping both arms round his thick neck, hanging on to Flynn like a cowboy on a bucking bronco, or a fly trying to stop a stampeding rhino. "You're hurting him!" Heracles's cries began to sound strangled. Out of fear and desperation, the boy bit

Flynn on his ear. Flynn roared and reared backwards, throwing the boy off. A ripping sound preceded the taste of copper coins on his palate. He spat out a chunk of flesh just as a black shadow eclipsed him.

The backhand across the temples sent the boy hurtling into the wall. Stars exploded in his vision, his world spinning into a vortex of shadows. Flynn stood in the fading light, reaching out for him with a beefy hand as a blur of yellow bounded up behind him.

The boy surrendered to the sea of darkness.

He could have been out a few seconds, a few minutes, or perhaps even a few hours. The first thing the boy became aware of was the grogginess, like waking from a deep sleep. Next came the pounding in his head, like the time a bully placed his head in one of those C-clamps in the school Design & Technology workshop. He gingerly touched the tender swelling on his head. His fingers came away sticky.

Sitting up slowly to avoid jarring his head, he was momentarily confused as to why he lay at the bottom of the stairs. Had he fallen down them? Did he have an episode again? Thunder rolled. Lights flashed in the darkness.

The storm was still brewing, and rain had still not arrived.

The grey mist clouding his mind evaporated, replaced swiftly by chilling horror.

Heracles lay beside him in a spreading puddle of blood, the dog's beautiful, golden fur matted with dark crimson. His midsection was criss-crossed with red fissures, still weeping blood. Brown eyes that used to gaze so lovingly at the boy stared straight ahead at a patch of peeling wallpaper, dead and glazed like a pair of marbles. Beside the body, still gleaming with malicious intent, was a stained kitchen knife.

The boy yowled, a long, keening noise that came from deep within him. He had never been one to understand the emotions he and the people around him projected—never knew why someone would be happy or sad, never understood why his heart sometimes felt light, other times heavy. The grief bubbling up within him was something more primal, something that preceded mere joy and sadness and anger. It consumed him from within, tearing at his heartstrings with black tentacles, filling his eyes with burning tears. Clutching handfuls of the dead dog's fur, he buried his face in Heracles's bloody chest, sobbing and moaning until he went hoarse.

His emotions spent, the boy slumped back against the wall, his hands marked with Heracles's blood. Beads of perspiration weighed down his upper lip. Detached from the situation—like someone watching a bad movie—swirls of colour invaded his peripheral vision before completely swallowing his world. He smelt something green, like fresh mown grass.

He was having another episode.

There was no Heracles to help him through.

Fighting down the fear that always rose, the boy laid himself down beside Heracles, still gripping the dog's limp form for reassurance. His muscles tensed up, his small body going rigid. The images, colours, the phantom noises and smells invaded his mind like a raging flood. However, they seemed less disjointed, more coherent somehow. A rumbling voice reverberated deep inside his thoughts. He could not make out the words, but he understood its language. White-hot strobes flashed intermittently, giving his visions a jerky quality, like the moving pictures from an old movie reel. He saw Heracles, alive, tail wagging, pink tongue lolling. Yet, there was something different about him, in the colour of his fur. Instead of his usual custard yellow, Heracles's coat shone a lustrous gold as if spun from flaxen silk.

Flynn appeared next, the collar of his polo shirt turned up in that despicable way. In the boy's vision, Flynn grabbed Heracles by the collar and dragged him away. The dog struggled, whining, but both he and Flynn faded into a wispy cloud of colours. A name appeared to the boy, not spelt out like a billboard, nor was it spoken. Rather, it was felt*:*

Pandareus.

The boy woke, staring up at a darkened ceiling illuminated briefly by a flash of light. His ears still rang with rumbles, and for a moment, the boy wondered if he was experiencing some form of residual aura. He remembered the gathering storm, still angry, yet still not releasing rain. Each crash of thunder pulsated through his veins, each lightning streak electrified his blood.

Zeus continued to speak to him.

The god had given him a sign.

The boy sat up with renewed purpose. Through the wind and thunder, he detected the lazy whirring of a cement mixer. The front door flapped in the stiff breeze, banging against the wall. The Lightning God cast a bolt, lighting up the sky. The boy caught a glimpse of Flynn's lengthened shadow.

I have been chosen.

The boy rose to his bare feet and picked up the bloody kitchen knife beside the dead dog.

I will not disappoint.

38

I stabbed a German supporter with the corner of my cardboard hotdog sleeve.

"Sorry, sorry," I said, as he wiped his face with a corner of his flag. Holding my food and drink above my head, I inched sideways along the crowded row of seats, stepping over legs, bags, and discarded food wrappers, muttering my apologies as I passed. The plastic carrier bag swinging from my wrist narrowly missed a woman's head.

"Here we are!" Meghan shouted above the tens of thousands of voices in the stadium. She traversed ahead, navigating the cramped aisles with relative ease, her tiny frame squeezing neatly through the seated masses. She plonked herself down in one of three empty chairs and held our tickets up to her nose—checking we were in the right seats, I presumed. I sat down beside her, dumping our shopping bags in the spare seat beside me.

Reggie's seat.

My heart tugged at the reminder, but I drove it out of my mind just as the background music cut off. "See, told you we'd make it in time!" I said, passing Meghan a cup of lemonade and carton of chicken nuggets.

"We still nearly missed the beginning!" Despite the admonishment, she slurped from her straw. "Because *you* got home late from work!"

"We would've made it in plenty of time if you hadn't insisted on queuing up for souvenirs and snacks," I said in a mock childish tone.

"*Shh!* It's starting!" Meghan stood up in her seat. Atmospheric music filled the air as the crowd hushed, the centre of the arena commanding the attention of every spectator.

Almost every spectator.

I found it hard to concentrate on the proceedings. I tried to, for Meghan's sake, but my mind kept harking back to Quentin Gordon, to our gruesome discovery at his childhood home the day before.

When the digger cut through the patio, we discovered yet more skeletal remains buried beneath the concrete.

Human bones.

Mr. Flynn Buchanan had not deserted them after all.

We consulted the ancient myths for one where Zeus punished someone by burying him under a layer of cement. Nothing came up, but we found a story about some guy called Pandareus, who stole a golden dog from Zeus's temple. The god punished him by turning the man to stone.

It didn't take too many leaps of the imagination to deduce what happened on that stormy night almost fifteen years ago.

Flynn Buchanan was Gordon's first victim.

Were there others through the years? Or had Gordon been lying dormant since, waiting for the advent of the Olympics, the festival traditionally held in honour of Zeus?

Why hadn't he surfaced during the other Olympics? Could the proximity of the one, being in London, have triggered his killing spree?

"Daddy, Daddy! Here comes Greece!"

Startled from my thoughts, I looked down. Troops of athletes, attired in the colourful outfits of their countries, marched through the arena. The blue and white of the Greek flag waved proudly at the forefront of the team filing across centre stage.

We're on the parade of nations already? I checked my watch in disbelief. *Flipping Hell. How long had I been daydreaming?* I glanced at Meghan. Mouth open in awe, she clutched her paper cup in both hands, eyes riveted on the procession. Guilt ate at my heart. It seemed like only the week before I held a squalling pink baby in my hands, amazed at the fragility and innocence of the precious bundle in my arms. Even as a newborn, her eyes shone bright as pearls, and straight away I knew her name.

Meghan.

Little Pearl.

My little pearl was not so little any more. The last eight years had flown by. *Especially* the last year. The days seemed longer and darker post-Angie.

How much time with Meghan had I lost forever, because I'd retreated into my own thoughts? How much of her childhood had I missed because I just hadn't been there, because I'd selfishly chosen, instead, to lose myself in my work?

Absent-mindedly, I took a bite of my hotdog and spat it back out. The sausage had gone cold, with blobs of congealed fat and condiments—the bread dry and spongy. I shoved the rest of the hotdog under my seat. Opening the ceremony programme in my lap, I resolved to enjoy the special day with my daughter, with no distractions from work.

A cacophony of cheers and whistles rang out through the crowd. Supporters leapt from their seats as the Great Britain team entered the arena. I rose to my feet as well, picked Meghan up, and lifted her onto my shoulders so she could watch the spectacle. The national team marched in to near-deafening roars from the crowd. A sea of Union Jacks, along with a handful of St. George's Crosses, fluttered amid the spectators, waving proud in a rare display of solidarity. Meghan bounced up and down on my shoulders—well worth the strain in my neck to hear her squealing in excitement. Swept up in the tidal wave of mass exhilaration, I forgot all about my case for a good two minutes.

The audience settled down as the British athletes took their place on the field. Meghan and I took our seats. I placed one arm around her as I checked the souvenir programme.

"What's next?" she asked.

I made a face. "Speeches." Meghan mocked a wide-mouthed yawn. She took the programme from me and flipped through the glossy pictures. I watched her as I half-listened to the speech by the head of the organising committee, applauding in the right places, but by the time the President of the International Olympic Committee took to the podium, my attention span had been exhausted. As the speaker droned on, my mind, like a gambling addict drawn to a roulette wheel, once again wandered to the Oaksecutioner case.

Everything points to Gordon striking today.

He doesn't stand a chance—does he? Security was tighter than at Heathrow airport and Prince William's royal wedding put together. Gordon wouldn't get within a couple of miles of the stadium without being recognised. The net was tightening around our man. Catching him would only be a matter of time.

The polite silence in the stadium erupted into cheers at the end of the final speech. I clapped along with everyone else.

"Look, Daddy!" Meghan jumped up from her seat. "Here comes the Olympic flag!" The crowd rose to its feet as eight flag bearers entered the arena, holding aloft the white flag, its five interlocking, coloured rings so synonymous with the entire Games—a symbol of a world united, if only for a few weeks of sporting competition. As the flag was raised, a symphony orchestra began playing the Olympic Anthem, an uplifting score with an accompaniment of powerful cymbals, stirring trumpets, and a harmonious choir.

> *Olympian flame immortal,*
> *Whose beacon lights our way.*

A strange sensation prickled at my gut, an overwhelming sense of *déjà vu*. The tune resonated with a haunting familiarity, and I didn't know why. I tried to dismiss it, but somehow I got the notion I hadn't just heard the anthem before in previous Olympic opening ceremonies.

I swear I came across this tune more recently.

> *Emblaze our hearts with the fires of hope*
> *On this momentous day.*

Think, Kurt, think ... why is this nagging at me so much? I grabbed the programme, flipping through the pages until I found information about the Olympic Hymn.

Composer: Spyridon Samaras

Samaras.

"*He's relatively obscure, but I like his work.*"

The cleaner in the church, the jolly one who was whistling while he worked.

He had been whistling the Olympic Anthem.

The realisation struck me with such vehemence my knees nearly gave out. My mouth went dry, my tongue floppy.

I'd met the killer face to face—and I let him get away.

I'd seen photos of Quentin Gordon. He had dark hair, a crew cut. The guy I met looked like a pop idol wannabe, with wavy blond curls and glasses.

Glasses ... like the ones I found in Gordon's bathroom. Glasses with lenses that appeared to have no corrective index at all.

As I thought about it, both Quentin Gordon and the blond cleaner were the same height, the same build ... and I believed they both had dark coloured eyes.

Had we all been tricked by a disguise as simple as a pair of spectacles and a wig? The only way to confirm my suspicions was to call up the cleaning company. Check if they employed a blond cleaner by the name of ... I tried to remember the name. It was something simple, I knew. Common, beginning with the letter *J* ... Jack? John? Joseph?

That's it. Joseph. Joseph Peter.

Reciting the name in case I forgot it again, I dialled Holloway's number. I could get him to check the guy up.

Joseph Peter... Joseph Peter... I frowned. Something bothered me about the name. I got the feeling I'd heard a familiar word uttered by a foreigner, like how tourists frequently mispronounced Leicester Square '*Lei-sester' Square* instead of '*Lester' Square*.

"Holloway. What's up, Kurt?"

"Joseph Peter..." I whispered his name aloud. There was a certain ring to it, but like seeing the world through distorted lenses, I couldn't place why it seemed so familiar. I tried contracting his first name: "*Joe* Peter..." The sensation in my gut grew stronger, telling me I was on the right track. I mumbled the name, faster and faster. "Joe Peter... JoePeter... JoPeter..."

"Hello? Kurt? You there?"

"*Jupiter.*"

Son of a bitch. There would be no need to ring the cleaning company.

I was sure we had our man.

"Kurt! What's going on?"

"Jupiter," I murmured into the phone. "Jupiter's the Roman name for Zeus."

39

The Oracle stood in the shadows, hidden from the spectators. Just as Orpheus's lyre music had pacified Cerberus, the three-headed hound of Hades, the majestic notes of the Olympic Hymn lulled the crowd into an awed, respectful silence.

Music hath charms to sooth the savage beast.

Mouthing the words softly, the Oracle sang along in time with the choristers as the Olympic flag rose up the central mast.

Wings of anticipation fluttered in his stomach like anxious butterflies. Their flight made him so light-headed, he wanted to take off. He took deep, heavy breaths in an attempt to steady himself, to keep himself grounded.

He had every right to be nervous. The great god Zeus had assigned to him his biggest quest yet. The last twenty-six years, the odyssey that was his life, it all led to that day.

Just how many people present remembered the original intent of the Games? How many witnessing the events unfolding actually understood what the Olympic flame symbolised?

The flag reached the top of the pole amid an explosion of cheers. Its five rings appeared almost fluid as the flag flapped in the warm currents, waving proudly from its lofty perch.

"O Zeus," he whispered, "bestow on me the strength and courage to complete my task, such that your name will once again be remembered among these ungrateful mortals."

"Extended coffee break?"

The Oracle started at the voice that seemed to have snuck

up from behind. A man in security uniform stood behind him, thumbs hanging from his belt loop.

The Oracle straightened. The man wouldn't have heard his prayer amid the crowd's thunderous din. "Yeah," he managed to sound almost apologetic, "just had to see it all for myself, you know."

"I don't blame ya," the security guard said in his Cockney accent. "Having the Games on home soil and all. I say enjoy what you can."

"Thanks." The Oracle turned his attention back to the arena. "I might stay to watch the torch ceremony."

"Yeah, you should. I hear they're pretty confident about besting Beijing."

The Oracle smiled. "Do *you* know the original meaning of the Olympic flame?"

The guard shook his head. "Can't say I do, mate. Enlighten me."

Oh, I will enlighten you. In a few minutes, I'll make sure every-body in the world is enlightened.

40

"What are you yammering on about?" Holloway asked. I could barely hear him over the noise in the stadium. "You're not making sense!"

With my hand cupped over the phone, I told Holloway all about my suspicion—my *conviction*—that Joseph Peter was Quentin Gordon. I could've kicked myself for missing it before. Olga Petrov, the street preacher Nicholas Kemp—he picked them out whilst working at the church. As for Sarah Quinn—his 'Hera'—and her tendency to hit her stepson, he must have eavesdropped on her confession. I pictured the blond Joseph Peter beside the photograph of a close-shaved Quentin Gordon. The same height, the same build, the same intense brown eyes disguised behind Peter's thick eyeglasses. I imagined Gordon's angular cheekbones and prominent ears hidden beneath Peter's yellow wig.

It was so obvious.

How the heck did I miss it?

Holloway said something drowned out by the booming voice of the announcer saying something about the athletes taking a vow to play by the rules.

"I can't hear you!" I put a finger to my other ear to block out the noise, straining to listen to Holloway. All I managed to catch was:

"... Hygienia holds the cleaning contract for the Olympic venues."

The bottom fell out from my gut. Gordon's employers were contracted to clean the stadium. Disguised as Joseph Peter and wearing the Hygienia uniform, Gordon would easily slip past security.

Quentin Gordon could be inside the stadium right now.

My eyes scanned the arena. Where would the bastard be? What was he planning? The noise from the crowd peaked once more as the disembodied voice of the commentator announced the arrival of the torch relay. The stadium erupted in cheers and whistles as a lone figure appeared on the track, bearing a trailing ribbon of fire.

All at once, the answer came to me.

I knew what Gordon would do next.

"Tom," I shouted into the phone. "Get over here right now—and bring backup!"

"What?" Holloway's voice was a whisper struggling to be heard above a chaotic medley of screams, claps and piped-in music.

"Get here now!" I repeated, louder. "With backup!"

"On my way."

I ended the call and rose to my feet. The crowd did the same as the first torch bearer passed the flame to a second runner, who began jogging at a leisurely pace. The announcer introduced her as a former national gymnast.

I had to get down to the field before the end of the torch relay.

"They're going to light the flame!" A little voice chirped at me.

I'd forgotten my daughter was there.

Guilt stabbed at my heart as I gazed from Meghan to the arena. I couldn't just leave her alone in the stands, and I definitely couldn't bring her with me.

The torch passed from the second bearer to the third as the applause from the spectators reached fever pitch.

What can I do?

I sensed a presence beside me. Turning, I looked down to find someone sitting in the vacant seat next to me. His baggy basketball jersey did nothing to hide his sizeable bulk. The baseball cap, its rim pulled down low over his brow, concealed his face, but I didn't need to see his face to recognise him.

As the fourth torch bearer gained possession of the Olympic flame, Reggie lifted his head and smiled up at me.

"Awright, bruv?" He tipped the brim of his cap at me. "Did ya miss me?"

I couldn't answer. My heart stuck in my throat, obstructing my breathing, keeping the words, the questions, from tumbling from my mouth. *What are you doing here? Where have you been? What have you been up to?*

What part do you have to play in all this?

"*Uncle Reggie!*" Meghan barged past me with a squeal and barrelled into his arms.

"Hey, Goggles. I missed ya."

I gaped as Reggie propped Meghan on his lap and returned her hug. He'd cut his hair since the last time I saw him, swapping his cornrows for a buzz cut. The right side of his face was peeling, mottled with pink patches of healing skin. His right eyebrow looked thinner than his left, as if he'd had it trimmed.

Or as if it'd been singed by fire.

My eyes fell to the *R* he wore round his neck. The faux diamonds studding the initial glinted in the orange evening light, but a dull gap near the base of the letter stood out like a broken bulb in a chain of Christmas lights. An empty indentation broke the *R* where a rhinestone should have been.

A rhinestone like the one I found in the remains of the scorched garden.

He was at the house during the arson attack.

"You ..." I started but didn't know how to continue. I didn't want to make a scene, particularly not in front of Meghan.

Did Reggie try to firebomb Meghan's bedroom? Did he attack Lucy's daughter and steal Angie's wedding ring? Did he send me those threatening text messages? What was he doing next to us? Was he somehow involved in the Oaksecutioner case, just like

Holloway had feared all along?

The unanswered questions pinballing through my mind made my head spin. I plopped down in my chair. Down on the field, the flame passed to the fifth torch bearer. Meghan returned her attention to the torch relay. I grabbed the chance to lean towards Reggie and speak in his ear.

"Why are you here?" I asked, my voice just above a whisper.

"Same reason you're here," he said with a shrug. "To enjoy the spectacle."

"Stop fooling with me," I hissed. "You know about the arson attempt. I know you were there when it happened."

"And a good thing, too." Reggie eased Meghan further towards his knee, keeping her from overhearing our conversation.

"What?" I wasn't sure I heard right.

"Ain't no random good Samaritan who foiled your fire attack."

I blinked, my mind raging with conflicting thoughts.

"You've made some enemies, bruv," he went on. "I can't watch out for you forever. A guy can only do so much to protect his brother from vengeful gangsters and thieving babysitters."

"Thieving babysitters?" I frowned.

"Wasn't easy gettin' that ring off her. Bitch kept screamin' bloody murder. Them emo kids with purple hair should never be trusted. They'll rob you blind and slit their wrists." He leaned in towards me. "If you intend to hang on to the past, you best put it somewhere safer than your boxer drawer." He returned his attention to Meghan as she bounced on his knee. The flame had moved on to runner number six. Meghan was hopping so much she nearly tipped over. Reggie shot out a protective hand to steady her. His eyes gleamed as he brushed a ringlet of hair off his niece's face, but when he turned back to me, his gaze hardened.

"I suggest you guys move a bit further out of East London. Least for a few months." He stroked Meghan's wavy brown hair. "Like I said, Goggles may not be so lucky next time."

Another roar rang out, but it didn't come from the stadium

crowd. The roar came from inside my own head as if a massive tidal wave had slammed into my mind.

I'M WATCHING U

MEGHAN MAY NOT BE SO LUCKY NEXT TIME

Had Reggie been the one who sent those text messages? Not as threats, but as *warnings*?

I looked at my brother as if seeing him for the first time. I remembered him as a pudgy kid, one with a penchant for penny sweets and shoplifting. I remembered all the times I'd had to bail him out of tight spots—from the police station after he hotwired a car for a joy ride, from the local drug dealer after he pinched a bag of weed from the man, from a Vietnamese street gang wielding kitchen cleavers after he racially insulted one of them in a drunken tirade.

The tables had turned.

He was bailing me out.

"Reggie," I choked out. "How?"

He waved a hand. I noticed some new bling on his fingers. "I gots my connections," he said, his tone nonchalant. I wasn't sure if I should feel grateful or mortified at his 'connections'. Before I could decide, he narrowed his eyes at me. "Ya don't trust me, do ya?"

I chewed the inside of my cheek, afraid of giving voice to my doubts.

Dude, he's your brother.

He was also a possible suspect. He was at one Oaksecutioner crime scene that we knew of. I let him go once before. Could I do it again?

Reggie snorted. "Figures." His gaze dropped to the accumulating litter at his feet. "Sorry, man."

I frowned. "For what?" For getting involved in street gangs? For dragging us in with him? For thoroughly confusing me by turning up at our shared event?

"For not being the brother you always wanted me to be." His

gaze stayed fixed to the floor.

I opened my mouth, closed it again when I couldn't find anything to say. A Mexican wave undulated towards us, arms thrown up in a roughly orchestrated fashion. Meghan jumped up with a whoop, arms flailing. Neither Reggie nor I joined in as the wave rippled past us. More cheers as the flame moved to the seventh and penultimate runner.

The penultimate runner.

I remembered my more pressing concern.

Gordon.

A war of indecision raged in my head. Should I stay with Meghan? Should I wait for Holloway to arrive and let him deal with Gordon? Or should I leave Meghan with Reggie?

Could I trust him?

I stared at Reggie, tried to read his intentions. Deep-set eyes the colour of liquid chocolate gazed back at me.

Eyes that looked much like mine.

Decision made, I jumped to my feet. "Stay with Meghan."

"What?" He blinked several times. "Where you off to?"

Meghan turned as well, eyes wide behind her bioptic glasses.

"To end this case." I didn't want to bog him down with the details. "Once and for all." I ran a finger down Meghan's cheek. "Sorry, little lady. I'll be back soon—promise." I found Reggie's eyes again. Something shimmered in their depths. There was no need to come out and say it.

I trusted him enough to leave Meghan in his care.

That was all that mattered.

I pushed through the spectators.

"Oi!" I heard Reggie shout. I glanced at him over my shoulder. Flashing a crooked grin, he gave me a thumbs up. "Do what you gotta do, Kurt."

I nodded, turned back, and resumed shouldering my way through the celebrating crowd. The heat from the cram of bodies made me sweat. I smelled the sour odour of a thousand perspiring armpits.

"Make way!" I called out. "Police business!" I started running when I hit the aisle, taking the steps two at a time as I made my way down to the front row of seats.

I was preparing to leap over the barriers and onto the track proper when I got stonewalled by a pair of security guards.

"Let me through!" I shoved my badge up one of the uniformed gorillas' nose.

"What's this about?" The other muscle asked, the collar of his shirt straining against his trunk-like neck. Over the PA system, the commentator named the final torch bearer, Sir Benjamin 'the Bullet' Brighton, three-time Olympic gold medallist and national record holder of the two hundred metres sprint, igniting a thunderous applause.

"I'm here on official police business!" I tried again to cross the barrier, but the brutes kept me back. "I have reason to believe somebody in the stadium might be in danger!" The guards exchanged uncertain glances. Their hesitation offered me the chance to hop over the barrier, but the men, both of them built like Olympic weightlifters, still blocked my passage.

"You need to speak to the Head of Security," one of the guards finally said.

I wanted to punch the guy in the face. "We don't have time! This is a matter of life and death!"

"Sorry sir, but we must abide by procedure." Tweedledum and Tweedledee hemmed me in while they summoned a third minion to join us. He spoke into a walkie-talkie, no doubt communicating with headquarters. I wanted to yell at them, to tell them I wasn't a terrorist, that I wasn't the bad guy. While we stood about twiddling our thumbs over some bureaucratic pile of bullshit, the killer roamed free inside the stadium, probably casing out his next victim.

Over their massive shoulders, I saw 'the Bullet' approaching the giant unlit cauldron, flaming torch held high.

The Neanderthal on the walkie-talkie approached me.

"Please come with us, sir." All three goons escorted me down one of the tunnels off the track, leading me into the bowels of the Olympic stadium. Behind me, a jubilant roar echoed as 'the Bullet' lit up the Olympic cauldron, officially signalling the start of sixteen days of athletic competition. Loud explosions of fireworks sounded in the sky like thunder. The walls of the tunnel lit up in brief flashes of colour, alternating between red, yellow, green, blue and purple, in time with the pyrotechnic show outside.

As they herded me towards a door marked *SECURITY*, I had a feeling I might already be too late.

41

Ben 'the Bullet' Brighton shook one final outstretched hand before waving to the crowd and jogging into the tunnel. He felt like he was running on air, and it wasn't because of his new pair of running shoes, fitted with the latest in cushioning technology, courtesy of his sponsor.

The honour of igniting the Olympic cauldron—the dream of every athlete. To reach the pinnacle of their sport, and to be recognised for their efforts.

He snatched a towel from an attendant at the end of the tunnel and made his way towards the locker area. *A nice cold shower, followed by a couple of drinks within the Olympic Village with some old running mates.* It seemed odd not to have a training schedule and diet regimen during the Games—the perks of retiring from professional competition. He looked forward to experiencing the track events, as a spectator rather than a participant, for the first time in years.

Littered with used towels and unattended gym bags, the locker room was otherwise empty. Everybody else was outside watching the spectacle. As he settled onto a bench to unlace his trainers, Brighton wondered who would be staking claim to his two hundred metres title. Unlike many old dogs who'd run out of tricks, and who kept tarnishing the reputation they'd spent years building up by losing to the younger guns in their later years, he'd had the good sense to quit whilst still at the top of his game.

That young Jamaican runner seems like a good bet for gold.

The door to the locker room burst inwards. Brighton jumped. He pulled his track bottoms back up. A young man in the blue overalls of a cleaner stood at the threshold. His eyes flashed with urgency behind thick eyeglasses.

"Oh, thank God somebody's here," the young man said, flipping a lock of unruly blond hair off his face. "You gotta help me, mate. My colleague, he fell off a ladder. Hit his head. I can't find a phone anywhere!"

"Okay, okay, calm down," Brighton rummaged in his backpack for his mobile phone. He checked the screen as it lit up.

No signal.

Damn it. They were too far underground.

"Do you know first aid?" Panic made his voice quaver. In his dark eyes, Brighton saw a frightened young man way out of his depth. "He's bleeding really bad. I don't know what to do."

"I know some basic first aid." Brighton moved around the benches and towards the door. The socks on his feet slipped along the tiled floor, but he decided against wasting time by putting his shoes back on. "Where is he?"

"Oh, thank you!" the young man huffed relief. He started walking ahead at a hurried pace. "He's this way."

42

I paced within the confines of the small office like a caged panther, cursing under my breath as the Head of Security, a burly black man named Nathan Young, spoke with Chief Sutherland over the phone. We were losing precious time, a fact highlighted by the noisy wall clock above the bank of monitors. Each tick sounded like the tap of an impatient fingernail against a metal surface, maddeningly counting the wasted seconds.

After what seemed like an eternity, Young hung up the phone and turned to me.

"Detective Sutherland has confirmed your identity. She's sending over some backup as we speak."

Halle-fucking-lujah.

"So," Young continued, "what do you need us to do?"

I needed you to let me through fifteen minutes ago.

"I need to find Ben Brighton," I said.

"The runner?" Young looked perplexed.

"He's Prometheus," I explained. "He stole fire from the gods. *That's* what the Olympic flame originally symbolised—the theft of fire. In the legend, Zeus punished Prometheus by chaining him to a rock and sending an eagle to eat his liver."

Four pairs of eyes stared at me, regarding me as they would an escaped inmate from Broadmoor, complete with straitjacket. Young wore an expression that seemed to show regret at having offered me his team's full cooperation.

I decided to rephrase my statement.

"I think he could be in danger. Our investigations strongly suggest that he may be the next victim of the Oaksecutioner."

"He'll be in the showers," one of the security guards piped up. He pointed to one of the monitors. It showed the entrance to a men's locker room. For obvious reasons of privacy, there were no closed circuit cameras inside the changing rooms.

"How do I get there?"

"I'll come with you," a guard offered. His name tag read *Davidson*.

"In the meantime," I said to Young, "keep your eyes on the monitors. Look out for a Hygienia cleaner with long, blond hair and glasses. Or one with short, dark hair and no glasses. Or any combination of the two. Our perp might be in disguise."

"Got it," Young said, although his face betrayed that he didn't.

"Oh, and when my partners turn up, let them through immediately. Their names are Sam Blaize and Tom Holloway."

Davidson led me out from the security office and down a maze of corridors, all illuminated overhead by strip lighting, passing offices, bathrooms, staff rest areas and store cupboards. I wondered if the Christians in ancient times had to wander through similar twisting labyrinths in the Coliseum before they were fed to the lions.

"Here we are." Davidson stopped before a swing door prominently labelled with a male stick figure. We stood on both sides of the entrance and regarded each other. For a moment, and one of few times, I wished I'd been a cop in America. What I wouldn't do to have the comforting weight of a firearm in my hands at that moment.

After a mental count to three, Davidson and I both moved. Throwing the door open with my shoulder, we barged into the locker area.

Empty.

Banks of metal lockers stood facing each other, separated by rows of low wooden benches. Gym sacks and sports shoes were stowed underneath the benches, and a couple of damp used towels had been dumped on the floor.

"Ben?" I called out. "Ben Brighton?" No answer. Davidson and I treaded softly, looking behind lockers and in hidden corners. I moved into the shower area, searching every stall.

Deserted.

"Detective," Davidson's voice echoed off the tiles. I found him knelt before a bench in the locker area, staring at a pair of running shoes—red, orange and gold swirls decorated the sides, depicting a pair of flaming wings. *Attractive, if a bit too loud for my taste.*

"Bullet-Proofs," the guard said. "The latest shoes endorsed by Brighton."

"So they're his shoes?" I spied a pair of dressier loafers under the bench. They were the same size as the trainers. Did the guy walk out barefooted? What could have prompted him to do that? Or did he get surprised?

Davidson radioed in. "Brighton's not here. Can you see him on any of the cameras?" After a few seconds of static, a voice crackled back, tinny and distorted.

"No sign of him. No sign of the cleaner, either."

"Son of a bitch," I muttered.

How did our killer and his victim both just disappear?

The atmosphere in the security room reeked with despondency as we sat about, deflated. After the build-up and anticipation, finding nothing had been a bit of an anticlimax.

We were still worried about Ben Brighton, though.

Where could he be? And where could Gordon be? Is he even here? I had been so sure of his motives, I wondered if perhaps I'd jumped the gun.

Young finished talking on his two-way radio. "No one's seen Brighton outside, either. Last anyone saw of him was when he lit the Olympic flame."

"Rewind all your video footage up to that point," I said. "I want to see where he went." As Young began typing in commands on a keyboard, the phone in my pocket vibrated.

Holloway.

"Hey. You here yet?" At first, I heard nothing and wondered if the line had gone dead.

Holloway's voice filtered through in spasmodic snatches. "Kurt ... I ... you ... found ... here ..." He sounded excited.

"Sorry, mate, you're breaking up ... Hello?" I stood up and started pacing in the hope it would improve my reception.

"Hurry ... blood ... he's ... somewhere ..." He sounded far away, on the other end of the galaxy.

Did he say 'blood'?

"Sorry? What did you say? Hello? Tom!"

I checked my screen.

No signal.

Damn.

"Sorry, mate," Davidson said. "This stadium's like a black hole when it comes to phone reception. That's why we use these." He tapped the walkie-talkie hooked to his belt.

"Detective." Young brought my attention to the monitors. "We found him." He pointed to a monitor on the lower right corner. "This is Brighton entering tunnel C right after the torch ceremony." On screen, a man in his late thirties, built like a cheetah—wiry and light, with long powerful legs—reached the end of the tunnel, took a left turn, and disappeared from view.

"Where did he go?"

Young hit a key before pointing at a different monitor. The screen showed Brighton walking down a corridor before stepping through a door into the locker room.

"So he did make it back there," I said to no one in particular. "Are there any other exits in that locker room?"

Davidson shook his head. "One way in, one way out."

"He must have left at some point. Can you fast forward it?"

A shower of snowflakes dotted the screens as Young sped the recording up. What looked like two figures amped up on caffeine flitted past the camera.

"Stop!" I said. "Go back." The scene raced backwards before Young let it play out again at normal speed. A blond man in overalls opened the door. He stood at the threshold, his back to the camera. He appeared to be speaking to someone inside. When he backed out, Brighton exited the room with him.

Both men walked away together.

"How the heck?" I wondered what Gordon said to Brighton to convince the man to follow him. The two figures, moving at a brisk, urgent pace, walked out of view of the camera. "Where'd they go?"

"There they are!" Davidson jabbed a finger at a screen. "Camera fourteen!"

Jesus. We were playing spot the killer on a bank of computer screens. I stared at the feed from camera fourteen. Gordon led Brighton down a corridor—I had no idea which—they all looked the same to me. Gordon gesticulated, his movements hurried. He pushed the frame of his glasses higher up the bridge of his nose.

Good actor.

They disappeared again.

Now where did they go?

"They should show up on camera seventeen next ... Huh, that's weird."

"What?" I didn't like the concern dripping into Young's tone.

"Camera seventeen. It's been moved." He pointed at a monitor. The camera feeding it appeared to be pointed at a portion of wall.

"Cameras eighteen and nineteen appear moved as well," Davidson said. "Hold on, *and* twenty-two and twenty-three. Son of a bitch."

Dread built in the pit of my stomach as I turned back to the bank of monitors. The corridor in camera seventeen was partly out of view. Someone could have walked underneath without being seen. Camera nineteen showed what appeared to be a staff rest area, with paisley couches and a coffee table, but the periphery of the room, including the entrance, was off-screen. Each of the sabotaged cameras had been moved subtly enough that it still seemed to be pointing at something, yet angled in such a way that not the entire area was in focus.

No wonder security hadn't noticed anything wrong sooner.

"What sort of area do those five cameras serve?" I asked.

"A stretch of corridor on the other side of the stadium," said Young. "Two of the cameras should have been trained on the corridor. Three are installed in rooms off the corridor."

"Brighton and our man must be somewhere there." I leapt off my seat. "Let's go."

Young, Davidson and I left the security office. The two gorillas who held me up earlier stayed behind to monitor the security cameras.

We jogged through the winding corridors, Young barking into his radio, summoning backup. Our footfalls echoed through the empty hallways. Everyone else was either enjoying the last of the festivities outside or wrapping up and preparing to go home. A thought flickered through my mind. I hoped Meghan was all right with Reggie. He might have to take her home—but he didn't know we were shacking up with Holloway. I wondered where Reggie would take her, what kind of place he was staying at, if it would be somewhere suitable for a little girl. I prayed she wouldn't be spending the night under a fog of cannabis smoke, on a mattress stuffed with dirty money.

"This is it," Young panted.

By the time we reached the corridor patrolled by camera seventeen, even I had run out of breath. The hallway stretched out before us, the bright lights from the fluorescent strips overhead deceitfully hiding the lurking darkness. Three doors stood to our left, two to our right. I found camera seventeen perched high up in a corner, close to the ceiling. The lens piece had been angled a little bit too high.

"Dammit, where's backup?" Young grumbled. "They should be here by now."

"We can't afford to wait for them," I said. "Split up and check the rooms. Shout if you find anything." As Young and Davidson moved further down the corridor, I opened the door immediately to my right and found a store room, perhaps six by six feet in size. Sealed boxes stood stacked in a corner like a cardboard Jenga tower behind a canvas laundry cart filled with all sorts of junk, from bottles of cleaning fluids to sheets of tarpaulin. A pair of subwoofer speakers sat beside a Henry Hoover and a mop bucket with wheels.

After clearing the room, I picked up the mop and unscrewed the head. With the pole gripped in both hands, I stepped back out into the corridor. Young and Davidson were nowhere in sight—probably in one of the other rooms. I crossed the hallway, tried the first of the three doors on that side.

The door led into a staff rest area. I stood at the threshold, holding my makeshift weapon in front of me. A counter ran across the far wall, equipped with a kettle, a sugar jar, and a small portable television set. A tall, narrow dresser, perhaps a cloak cupboard, stood in the corner beside the counter. A door to my left was signposted *TOILETS*. In the centre of the room, I recognised the gaudy fabric settees from the security footage. I looked for and found the camera. It, too, had been moved in such a way that the entrance and the door to the bathroom lingered out of view.

I made my way across the room towards the toilets. A whiff of something in the air, something too intangible for me to identify, wafted past me. Wiping the sweat off my brow with the back of one hand, I pushed the door open with the other.

Blood spattered the tiles on the wall in gruesome patterns resembling sinister Rorschach inkblots. Between the two washbasins and the toilet stalls, Brighton lay in a spreading puddle in the centre of the room, his midsection oozing like a ruptured pipe. I finally recognised the odour as the coppery scent of blood, mixed in with those of loosed bowels.

I gagged, bitter bile tainting the back of my throat. Rubbery legs froze, rooting themselves to the floor.

Not because of the sight and smell of the massacre.

From seeing my partner, Tom Holloway, kneeling over the man's body.

Covered in Brighton's blood.

I stared at the blood on Holloway's hands, seeping into his sleeves, staining the front of his shirt. A streak of red ran down one cheek like a lick of war paint. Wild eyes stared back at me from behind thick glasses that had slipped down the bridge of his nose. At his feet, Brighton's body continued to seep blood from a grinning wound in the centre of his torso, a weeping crater of pink flesh, yellow fatty tissue and white bone.

Prometheus. *Sans* liver.

"Kurt!" he called to me. "Get over here!"

I hesitated, unsure what to think. Holloway would normally pale at the sight of a paper cut. He'd turned green at all the other crime scenes. Yet, he knelt, up to his elbows in somebody's chest cavity.

Could his queasiness have been an act all along?

I recalled Holloway's strange religion—naturalistic pantheism—of his broad knowledge of pagan rituals and theology.

As a key member of the murder investigation team, it would have been easy for him to throw us off his scent.

Had he been getting us to chase wild geese all along?

"Kurt!" he said again. "Don't just stand there! The man's going into shock!"

He's still alive?

I stepped closer, my hands still wrapped round my staff.

"What happened?" I asked.

"I was signing in with security when they got a call over the radio. Something about a security alert. I tagged along with them, but then we split up to search the rooms. That's when I found him." Holloway used paper towels to staunch the bleeding—in vain—as Brighton's complexion had taken on a yellow-grey pallor. Only the pulsing of blood from his wound gave any indication that the man still lived.

"Have you called for help?"

"I tried to call you, but can't get any reception in here. I just about managed a nine-nine-nine call. Paramedics are on their way, but with the traffic outside from people leaving the stadium, it's gonna take a while for them to get here."

"There must be some sort of medical team around." The smell of blood and urea was overpowering. I was amazed Holloway seemed unfazed.

"I didn't want to risk running off and not remembering how to get back here. This place is a maze. Also, I was worried Gordon might come back and finish the job."

Or were you *trying to finish the job before I interrupted you?*

I forced the thought from my mind. Brighton was my top priority. After a few seconds of deliberation, I roused myself to action.

"Stay here," I told Holloway, "I'll go get help." Gladly turning my back to the bloody scene, I ran out the restroom, cutting across the lounge area on my way to the door.

Davidson and Young should have been just down the corridor. I could use their walkie-talkies to radio for help.

Without slowing down, I reached out a hand, grabbed the door handle and pushed.

My forward momentum sent me colliding into the door.

I rattled the handle again, tried pulling the door open. It shook in its frame as I yanked at it. The handle would not turn.

What the fuck?

I hadn't noticed an auto-lock mechanism on the door on my way in.

"Hey!" I shouted, about to start pounding on the door. A noise behind me, one that sounded like the click of a lock sliding in place, took all my attention.

With a growing lump in my throat, I turned. Slowly. In front of the bathroom door, which had a key sticking from the lock, stood the cleaner I knew as Joseph Peter. He wore a fake beard over his face, the grey of the whiskers a stark contrast to the youthful gold of his wig. Bloodstains on his blue overalls turned the material a maroon-purple colour. Something glinted in his right hand.

It looked like a blood-splattered scalpel.

"Phineus, betrayer of secrets!" His voice boomed with a hollow, resonant quality as if echoing from somewhere deep within his soul. I hadn't expected such a powerful baritone from such a skinny man. "You shall not reveal the plans of the great gods to mere mortals!" Behind the thick frames of his glasses, his eyes flashed with a glazed, almost feral quality. He reached into the open cloak cupboard—no doubt where he'd been hiding all along—and pulled out what looked like a bottle of cleaning fluid. He unscrewed the cap with his thumb, letting the lid fall to the ground.

What, he's going to start performing his cleaning duties now?

He advanced towards me. I gripped my mop handle, holding it in front of me in a defensive stance. Behind Gordon, Holloway thumped on the locked toilet door, shouting to be let out.

"Your prophecies have revealed too much of the secrets of Olympus," Gordon said, "For your treason, almighty Zeus deprives you of your vision!"

What the hell is he talking about?

Gordon lunged forward—quicker on his feet that I expected. I glimpsed the flash of his scalpel and hopped backwards.

Right into the path of the hand with the bottle.

With a flick of his wrist, he thrust the container forward. A stream of clear fluid sloshed out. The liquid seemed to come at me in slow motion—a clear amorphous globule more viscous than water floating through the air. It splashed me in the face. The cold made me gasp, the liquid tasting astringent on my tongue, like detergent. A sharp smell stung my nose.

My eyes began to burn—an incredible, searing pain as if someone had shoved glowing hot pokers through both my eye sockets.

I cried out. My hands shot to my face as I tried to wipe the fiery chemical away, but every brush of my fingers left a blazing trail of hot coals across my corneas. My eyes watered. As my vision descended into a red haze of pain, my cheeks and lips started to tingle.

My whole face was on fire.

Something hit the back of my knees, like a boot—a heavy one. Arms flailing, I fell forward, sprawling onto the floor. Lost in my own world of pain, I was nevertheless aware of a presence beside me. Gordon's voice pierced through the veil, a disembodied booming from above.

"And the Lord of Thunder commands that you be besieged by harpies for all eternity."

The first cut caught me across the cheek, sending more pain spreading across my already raw face. The next sliced through my clothes and dug into my shoulder. I tried opening my eyes, to see the danger, but my eyelids refused. The caustic chemical had sealed them shut.

Harpies. Winged bird-women with blade-like talons.

He was going to stab me to death.

As the cuts rained down on me from the heavens, slicing through my flesh like razor-tipped hailstones, a terrible realisation struck.

I was about to become the Oaksecutioner's seventh victim.

Meghan. No!

I couldn't allow it to happen, couldn't let her lose another parent in the line of duty.

My hands stretched out before me in the fiery darkness as I attempted to fend off the unrelenting blade. They withdrew just as quickly when the scalpel bit deep into the back of my left hand.

Another slash from the scalpel caught me across my forearm. I forced my eyelids open, but all I made out through the burning haze was a blur of light and colours. A blue smudge lunged towards me, and I stumbled backwards, my bottom landing heavily on the floor. A whizz as Gordon's blade cut the air in front of my face. I rubbed my eyes with the heel of my palm, but it only intensified the pain. I opened them again. Still nothing but a meaningless blur. Blood thundered in my temples. Somewhere in the background, Holloway yelled and pounded on the locked bathroom door. The pungent smell of bleach stung my nostrils, the chemical burning my skin, dripping into my open wounds and searing like lava.

Too much noise. Too many stimuli. Paralysed by panic, my mind shouted at me, but nothing made sense. I couldn't think, couldn't see, could hardly breathe as my breaths grew quick and shallow, like the thudding of my heart.

I yelped as Gordon's scalpel bit into my collarbone. Like a slap to the face, the sharp pain snapped me out of my panic. *"Remember, you do not need eyes to see."*

Sifu Chen's words rang with such clarity it was as if he stood in the room with us. I forced myself to take deeper breaths and clamped my eyelids together, shutting out the confusing chaos of shifting lights. Darkness enveloped me, rendering me completely sightless. One fewer sense for my overloaded brain to worry about. As I crawled along the floor, my hand groped a wall of fabric behind me. One of the settees. In my mind's eye, I pictured my position in the room—sitting almost dead centre, with what felt like an armchair against my back. I tuned out the mess of noises around me. Holloway's cries and the banging on the door faded into the background.

I only needed to listen out for Gordon.

The soft squeak of rubber soles approached. The sound of chafing clothes. An intake of breath.

He's almost on top of me.

I rolled onto my side, thrusting a foot forward in an arc. My kick connected with something bony. Gordon uttered a gasp. Something hit the floor with a thud. No clattering, though, no sound of metal hitting the linoleum tiles.

Gordon still has hold of the scalpel.

Reaching up, my searching fingers found the chair's arm. I used it to haul myself up. I ran around it, putting the armchair between Gordon and me. A growl resounded from somewhere in the near distance.

"Do not fight the Fates, Detective." Gordon's calm tone carried a chilling edge, the voice of a man teetering at the precipice of sanity. Steps came towards me. Something dragged along the floor. I must have hurt one of his legs when I kicked. "Your role has been chosen for you, and by the will of Zeus, you shall fulfil it."

"Listen," I moved the chair in front of me as a shield, "we have guards nearby who are on their way now. That camera feeds directly to the main security office. The police will be here shortly." I tried to keep him talking, not only to help me pinpoint his location, but to also stall for time.

Where the hell are Davidson and Young?

"That does not matter," Gordon said. "Your fate has been woven with mine into the great tapestry of life. Your past, your present, your future ... they cannot be changed. The great Thunder God has decreed your punishment, and there is no escape. Accept it." Commotion came through the door behind me, the one leading out to the corridor. Muffled voices raised in alarm called to each other. A two-way radio crackled with static.

Davidson and Young.

Reinforcements on their way.

I just had to stay alive for long enough.

"We can help you, Quentin."

"*Do not call me that!*" he roared with such sudden vehemence that I cowered behind the chair, afraid he'd lunge for me. "That was my name *before* I was chosen by the Lightning Bringer. Now, I am the Oracle."

"Oracle." I held one hand up in a gesture of submission. The other remained gripping the back of the armchair, in case Gordon tried any sudden moves. "Your epileptic seizures—they're not incurable. We can get them under control, find you the right doctors. Your mom, Flynn ... we can help you come to terms with them, too. Let us help you."

An odd noise, as if Gordon blew air through his nostrils.

I cracked an eyelid open to chance a peek. The small movement was like hot sandpaper rubbing across my corneas. I could make out a fuzzy blue shape before me. What I gathered to be Gordon's shoulders twitched up and down. The noise came again.

He's laughing.

"You talk about my visions as if they are a curse." He snickered. "They are, in fact, one of the highest gifts Zeus can bestow on any mortal. The ability to speak with the gods—who wouldn't want such a gift?" Another laugh. "Why are you so quick to condemn history? Everything that has ever transpired happens for a reason. It is the way of the gods. My past, my childhood, they were divine tests, and through them Zeus has found me worthy. You speak as if you can change the past. Even if that were possible, I wouldn't change my past for anything. This is my destiny, Detective, and I have embraced it. Why don't you embrace yours?"

A blur of movement.

Before I could react, Gordon ripped the chair between us from my hands and flung it across the room.

Christ, he's stronger than he looks.

Gordon charged at me. I staggered backwards. The blade of Gordon's scalpel zinged past, inches from my neck. The small of my back slammed into the kitchenette counter. I fumbled for a weapon. My hand closed around a curved handle.

The kettle.

Judging by the weight, it was filled.

As Gordon advanced again, I swung. He grunted as it hit him, the vibrations from the impact riding up my arm. Tepid water sloshed everywhere, mixed with the blood, sweat and bleach on my face.

The bastard stayed standing.

Jesus, he's tough …

Knuckles smashed into my temple, knocking me sideways. My body slumped over the counter before sagging to the ground. The sensation of floating in a murky darkness took hold. I wasn't sure if it was the chemically induced blindness, or if I was fading out of consciousness.

A presence hovered over me. Heat radiated from Gordon's body along with the metallic tang of Brighton's blood and the rhythm of his breathing. Calloused hands gripped my chin and forced my head back. The back of my skull connected with the cupboard door behind me. Something cold, hard and sharp pressed into the flesh over my Adam's apple.

"In the name of Zeus." Gordon's breath tickled the exposed skin on my neck—sour, with a hint of copper.

The stench of a madman.

The scalpel dug deeper into my throat, piercing my skin. A trickle of warmth oozed down my collar.

A deafening crash shook the room. The blade jerked away from my neck. For a split second, in my blinded, disoriented state, I thought the noise was thunder from Zeus himself, a roar of triumph from the Greek god in appreciation of his latest sacrifice.

Me.

"Kurt!" A shout rang out. Footsteps advanced towards us before two bodies collided with a hollow clash, followed by the sound of a messy scuffle. Holloway squeaked as something smashed hard into the counter beside me, but amid the chaos of the skirmish, I caught one very promising noise.

The clang of the scalpel dropping to the floor.

I crawled on my hands and feet towards the source. My searching fingers found the cool metal handle of the blade.

Got it.

The heel of a shoe came down hard on the back of my hand. I gasped as Gordon put his entire weight on my fingers, but the shift in his mass told me he was poising for a follow-up strike. I raised my free hand in time to block the anticipated kick from his other leg, one that had been aimed at the side of my head. My arm hooked round the back of his knee. I jumped off the floor, bringing his leg up with me.

A gasp.

A surprised intake of breath.

Gordon's head struck the linoleum floor with a *thwack*. His leg went slack in my arms. Seizing the opportunity, I fell on him, flipping him by the shoulders so that he lay face down. I found his arm by touch, and I snaked my own arm around his, putting him into a lock hold.

"Tom!" I yelled when I got my breath back. "You all right?"

"Y-yes ... I think so ..." he sounded shaken. "My God, Kurt. Your face ..."

"Never mind that. Let security in." I didn't want to dwell on *why* Holloway seemed so shocked about my face. He rushed across the room. The door rattled. Cool air from the corridor rushed in, along with the anxious voices of Davidson, Young, and what sounded like a whole army of guards. Gordon squirmed under my grip. With a feral growl, he bucked his body. I responded by tightening the arm lock, applying a none too gentle pressure on his shoulder. Multiple hands brushed mine as someone eased me off Gordon and led me to an armchair. Walkie-talkies squawked with excited chatter. Somebody emptied his guts into the kitchenette sink, no doubt after having glimpsed the carnage in the staff toilets.

"Tilt your head back," Holloway said.

I complied as fingers pried my eyes open. They might as well have applied wax strips to my eyeballs and ripped them off. Cold liquid ran over my face, flooding my eyes, not quite putting out the fires, but at least keeping the burning pain under control.

"You need to go to hospital. An ambulance is on the way."

"What about Brighton?" Through my hazy vision, Holloway shook his head.

"I think he's gone."

I nodded grimly. No way would he have survived long without his liver. I slumped into the chair. In the background, security guards bustled about, shouting into radios. The noises were far away, surreal. As my adrenaline rush wore off, my limbs grew leaden, my swollen eyelids heavy. The lumpy settee felt soft and cosy all of a sudden. My head hurt. My entire body hurt. I wanted to just curl up and fall asleep.

A chilling noise snapped me back to a dread-filled wakefulness. Gordon was laughing, a low, sinister cackle that echoed through a room plunged into a sudden silence. The laughter grew louder, harsher, as if amused by some inside joke none of us were privy to.

"Well done, Argonauts. As prophesied, you have spared Phineas from the harpies. But the wrath of Zeus is not over."

"Will someone shut that son of a bitch up?" one of the guards, perhaps Young, shouted.

"Wait!" I held up a hand. Twisting around in the chair, I turned to Gordon, a blue smudge lying prone on the floor. I was becoming increasingly concerned as my eyesight had still not returned. "What do you mean, it's not over?" We had him tied up, in custody. How could it possibly *not* be over? A flesh-coloured oval turned to face me. I imagined Gordon with a crazed grin on his blood-smeared face.

"Prometheus is not the end. He is the beginning."

"Kurt, lay back." Holloway pushed me back into the chair. "You're hurt. Stop wasting your energy on that madman. He's just babbling crazy talk."

"No he's not." Fingers of dread clawed at my gut. Something from the piles of literature I ploughed through on Greek mythology screamed at me.

"What?" Holloway brought his face close to mine. "What are you talking about?"

"He's right. Gordon's right. This isn't the end." The realisation drove an icy dagger through my chest.

"This is just the beginning."

43

Sam Blaize popped two ibuprofen caplets before exiting her car, gritting her teeth against the twisting pain in her midsection. It was a bad day, even by her standards. Blaize was no stranger to pain—she'd had her fair share of hard knocks. She'd broken her nose twice in the ring and had taken a knife to the shoulder blade during her time as a uniformed officer. Still, the agony she experienced made her title fight against Tina "the Tornado" Wheeler seem like a kid's pyjama party pillow fight.

She took deep breaths before making her way through the car park towards the stadium entrance, walking briskly and checking her watch. Despite turning on her flashing lights, she'd still taken forever to arrive. The end of the Opening Ceremony had unleashed a mad rush of people clamouring to get home, and the lack of exits had resulted in a bottleneck. She'd had to fight through a stream of crawling traffic just to get into the car park.

She crossed a pedestrian bridge spanning one of the waterways surrounding the stadium. A couple of squad cars were parked beside one of the entrances, lights spinning. Overhead, an air ambulance whirred as the helicopter prepared to land on the athletics field inside the stadium. Blaize fought off a stab of concern for Kurt. She didn't know the details, but the latest from the police radio reported one civilian and one officer down. She prayed he was all right as she pushed her way through the onlookers gathered around the main entrance. News crews were already setting up their cameras at the fringe of the crowd.

Jesus, these vultures are fast.

"Awright, darlin'," someone patted her on the shoulder, his hand resting a fraction too long on her collarbone. The man perched atop what looked like a cleaner's trolley, no doubt to get a better view. Dressed head to toe in brand new official Olympics merchandise, a price tag still dangled from his cap. "You mind tellin' me what 'appened here? Why all the cops and medics?" He slurred his words, swaying as he spoke. She detected the sour tang of beer on his breath.

Blaize shrugged his hand off her shoulder and kept going.

"Can I at least have yer number?" he called after her.

"Don't these people have homes to go to?" Another wave of pain crashed down on her. She winced, biting down on her bottom lip, and forged ahead. The flash of fluorescent vests told her she was nearing the front of the mob. She ducked beneath the arms of a uniformed officer, joining fellow team member, Detective Constable Dan Sykes, at the ticket barriers.

"What's the news?" she asked.

"We got him," Sykes said, eyes gleaming. "We got the bastard." The words brought a rush of triumph surging through her. An arrest. The highest point in any cop's career. The sensation beat any sense of achievement she ever got in the ring, even when beating her opponents by knockout.

"And the victim? The officer? Who was it?"

"Vic didn't make it." He gave a casual shrug as if that was no longer important. "Lancer got done. Not sure how badly he's hurt. He got some chemical in the face. They think it's concentrated bleach."

The twinge of concern wormed its way deeper. Blaize wanted to deck Sykes for acting so blasé about it all, but another crushing spasm sucker-punched her in the gut. She clamped her mouth shut to keep the grunt from escaping her lips, but it whistled out through her nostrils instead. Crossing her arms across her abdomen, she tried to mask the pain, forcing herself not to double over in agony.

"You okay, Sam? You don't look too comfortable."

Comfortable? She felt as though her intestines had been twisted into a sailor's knot, and some psychotic Popeye, high on spinach, was using her stomach as a punch bag. Still, she couldn't, *wouldn't*, let that on, not to the rest of the team, and especially not to Sykes. The man had that chauvinistic air about him—lads' mags stashed in his desk drawer, throwaway sexist comments, and about as much charm as a Neanderthal preparing to club her over the head and drag her by the hair back to his cave. She never liked the way he treated her, as if her sole purpose on the team was to provide eye candy for the men, as if she was completely dispensable in any investigation.

His gaze strayed further south of her face, down towards the V-shaped collar of her shirt.

Holloway saved her from having to answer by bursting through the barriers.

"My God, what happened to you?" Sykes's eyes bulged.

Holloway's hair stuck out in wild curls, his shirt had come untucked, and his glasses hung from his face at a wonky angle as if the frame had been bent out of shape.

Worst of all, he was covered in blood.

"Shit! Tom, are you hurt?" Blaize asked.

"Huh?" His flashing eyes flitted wildly before settling on the front of his stained shirt. "Oh, the blood. It's not mine. It's Ben Brighton's. His liver, it was cut out. He didn't make it, unfortunately. Kurt, he's fine ... kind of. Bit beat up. He's being taken to hospital by air ambulance. Quentin Gordon's in custody, but he's going on and on about it not being over, and I think we figured out why. It's big, really big, and we have to find—"

"Whoa, whoa, whoa!" Blaize held her hands up. "Slooow down!"

"Yeah, Speedy Gonzales," Sykes said. "Why the *ariba ariba*?"

Holloway took several heaving gulps of air whilst leaning

against a barrier for support. "Pro-prometheus." He sounded the name slowly, the strain of being forced to relay news so achingly slow showing on his face. "He's not the end. He's just the beginning."

"What are you talking about, new boy?" Sykes scratched his temple.

"It didn't occur to me, either," Holloway sped back up, "but Kurt made the connection. Yes, Zeus punished Prometheus for giving the sacred fire to man. But he didn't stop there. He intended to punish mankind for accepting and using the gift. So he created a vessel…"

"Right, time out." Sykes formed the letter *T* with his hands. "We got the guy. Why should we care what happens next in this fairy tale?"

"Just shut the fuck up, Sykes," Blaize said.

"It's not a fairy tale, it's a *myth*," Holloway said, "and we have grounds for concern."

"Why?" Blaize asked. "What's in this vessel?"

"Misery, disease, despair … all the sufferings known to man."

"Wait a minute…" A flutter of recognition passed. "You don't mean…"

"… Pandora's Box," Holloway finished for her. "Yes."

"Uh, guys," Sykes said, "You've lost me."

Blazie ignored him, her concentration fixed on Holloway. "Do you really think…?" The implications were terrifying.

"This guy's been living in his own psycho dream world for nearly twenty years," Holloway said. "I'm willing to wager that he's capable of anything."

Blaize looked up at the bowl-shaped stadium. The arena had an eighty thousand capacity and a sweeping track and athletics field, not to mention numerous changing rooms, bathrooms, medical rooms, offices and a warm-up track. With Gordon's access as a cleaner, he could have gotten anywhere in the massive complex.

"So, you're saying there's a box in there somewhere, waiting for some Pandora to find?" She grappled with the logistics. It would take hours, if not days, to find a suspicious parcel amongst all the tools and equipment in all the rooms.

"It may not be a box *per se*," Holloway said. "The concept of the vessel being a box is a relatively modern one. It could be anything... an urn, a jar, a sack... any form of container."

"That narrows things down. *Oof!*" Sykes earned a backhand to the chest from Blaize. "But seriously, you think the guy planted a *bomb* somewhere in the stadium?"

"A bomb is the most likely and logical option," said Holloway. "He wants something that can unleash misery and despair on a large number of people, so I gather it'll be somewhere public."

"The stadium's pretty much empty. Everyone's either gone home or they're leaving." Blaize glanced over her shoulder at the crowd of onlookers. "That is, if they weren't so bloody nosy."

"Maybe it's somewhere someone will find tomorrow, when the stadium fills up again," Sykes said.

Holloway tried to wipe blood off his glasses but only succeeded in smearing it across the lenses. "We need to think outside the box a little, pardon the pun. The bomb, or whatever it is, might not be planted inside the stadium."

Not only did they need to search *inside* the stadium for their 'Pandora's Box', they needed to search *around* it as well. "Finding it will be like looking for a needle in a haystack. We better get started now."

This is so not going to wash out. Holloway picked at a rusting scab of dried blood on his sleeve as he, Blaize and Sykes organized how to begin their search. He tried to ignore the curious stares from the crowd, wondering if they thought *he* was the Oaksecutioner. Bathed in the blood of the killer's sacrificial victim, he certainly looked—and smelled—the part.

I need a bath. A long, hot one. And a sponge. No, a scouring pad.

He was certain he would never feel clean again.

A commotion behind him made Holloway turn around. Flanked by two burly policemen, Gordon was led out of the building in handcuffs.

The deranged bastard was *smiling*.

"That's him!" someone called out. "The Oaksecutioner!"

Blinding explosions of light burst forth from every direction as a hundred cameras went off at once. Some were big, professional-looking SLRs toted by hungry newshounds, but most of them were camera phones, whose sad owners were no doubt already posting their photos and updating their statuses on social media sites across the Web.

With his fingertips, Gordon extracted something from the waistband of his trousers, something that exuded a dim glow even within his cuffed hands behind his back.

Is that a mobile phone?

He appeared to push a number on the keypad. Just one.

What's he doing? Who's he trying to call? The answer came to Holloway in a blaze of horrific realisation as dizzying as the camera flashes. Holloway's gaze darted to Blaize.

Jesus fucking Christ! His eyes returned to Gordon as the man's thumb moved slowly across the keypad area.

"His phone's a detonator!" Holloway said, running at Gordon. "Stop him!" He flung himself at the man just as the two police escorts snapped into action. They collided in a tangle of arms and legs. All four men fell to the ground. The resultant pile was as close as Holloway ever got to a rugby scrum.

Holloway extricated himself and grabbed Gordon by the shoulders, but the other man lay on his back, his hands—and the phone—out of reach beneath him.

"Help me turn him!" With combined effort, the two officers hauled Gordon to his feet. Reaching behind him, Holloway pried the phone from Gordon's fingers. A jagged crack spread across the still-lit screen like a mini lightning bolt, underlining the name of the 'person' Gordon was trying to contact.

Pandora

Holloway's heart sank to the bottom of his gut at the flashing word beneath the name.

Calling

Scanning the scratched-up keypad, he found a hole where the 'Cancel' button should have been.

Fucking bastard. Gordon had gouged out the key, leaving an exposed circuit panel. The 'Off' button was also missing.

From the depths of the battered phone, Holloway heard the faint, tinny beep of a ringing tone.

The call had connected.

The cleaning trolley began to ring.

Near the front of the rubbernecking mob, the drunken guy who hit on Blaize balanced precariously atop it. Crushing an empty beer can in his fist, he reached for the waste bin lid.

"Stop!" Holloway shouted, waving his arms. His shrill cry snapped Blaize into action. She dove through the crowd, pushing her way towards the trolley.

"Move aside! Sir! Get away from that trolley!"

The man froze, his hand resting on the cover of the waste sack.

Blaize shoved him off his perch, sending the man reeling backwards with a startled yelp. "Everybody back!" she ordered, flailing her arms. "There's a bomb in here! Get back!" At the mention of the word *bomb*, a chorus of panic rippled through the gathered crowd. Those closest to the trolley took a few steps back, but hemmed in by the rest of the mob, they could retreat no further.

"Make way!" she shouted, grabbing hold of the trolley handle.

The black bin bag rustled with the vibration of the phone within. The radio signal would soon initiate the bomb's firing circuit, and all their lives would be extinguished in a hail of flames and flying glass.

As Blaize pushed it, the trolley gave a sudden lurch. The heavy bin bag swayed, its insides clinking together. There was no time to try to defuse the explosive, especially not without any bomb disposal expertise. Blaize eyed the canal over twenty yards away.

Downhill.

Gripping the trolley handle with sweaty palms, Blaize hunched over the cart and started to run. Bottles of explosives clinked together as the trolley gathered speed, bumping and swaying. The crowd parted before her, with people screaming and darting out of her path. The distance to the canal closed to fifteen yards. Ten. The muted ringing inside the bag grew more insistent, or perhaps it was her imagination.

The trolley pulled away from Blaize as it hit the steepest point of the incline. With one final push, she let go and dove to the ground. The cart rumbled downhill, the ringing fading into the distance. Its front wheels slammed into the low barrier before tipping over into the canal.

The bomb went off as the trolley hit the water, the shockwave spreading across the surface of the canal and spitting up a shower of hot water and mud. The explosion jarred Blaize deep in her bones, rattling her teeth and skull. Shards of broken glass rained down on her, and the deafening thunder threatened to split her eardrums. Sizzling water vaporised from the heat of the blast. Her nose stung with the pungent odour of burnt chemicals.

Is that damn phone still ringing? Blaize swore she was still hearing it. *Everything* seemed to be ringing at that moment.

She lifted her head. Mangled remains of the trolley bobbed in the canal—scraps of metal, bits of melted plastic. Wisps of ash, purple-grey smoke and shredded bin bags floated in the air. Darkened stains from water droplets and bits of broken glass dotted the ground around her like scattered mosaic tiles. She turned her head. Glass fell from her hair. The people in the crowd had flattened themselves to the ground, arms over their heads, eyes bulging with shock. Stunned into a collective silence, nobody

spoke, save for some frightened murmurs, tearful whimpering.
Gordon's maniacal laughter carried as officers hauled him away.

44

"R ... N ... I ... B." I ran my thumb across each set of dots on my key chain. "See? Nothing to it."

"Daddy," Meghan said, "you're holding it upside down,"

"Ah, phooey." With an exaggerated show of frustration, I tossed my keys onto the bedside table, but they grazed the edge with a chink and clattered to the floor. Meghan laughed again.

"Throwing your toys out of the pram already?" Blaize's unexpected but welcome voice lilted with a tone of amusement.

"Hey, Sam, didn't hear you come in."

"Uh, I'm here, too," announced another voice. "Tom."

"Yes, Tom, I know it's you." I held a hand up in front of me. First Holloway, then Blaize, grasped it in greeting. My fingers lingered on Blaize's for a touch too long.

"You look like a reverse panda with those bandages," Blaize said.

"A reverse panda?" I asked.

"Yeah, black with white eye patches."

I laughed. "Doctor says they can come off in a few days. I can even go home tomorrow."

"And by 'home', you mean my living room." Holloway sighed. "A blind man in an unfamiliar flat. You'll be doing a lot of finding furniture with your shins."

"Nah, I think I'll just stay put on the couch. Put my feet up." I groped for and found Meghan's head, mussed up her hair. "Peaches here can wait on me hand and foot. Can't she?"

She blew a raspberry at me.

"Yep, we can spend some time together watching—or listening to—the Olympics on TV while she feeds me grapes and massages my smelly feet."

"Ew," Meghan said, "I think I'm gonna be sick."

"Speaking of being sick." I angled my face towards where I guessed Holloway was standing. "How come you didn't get sick when you found Brighton?" I marvelled at how he'd fought to save the dying man, his hands stained with blood and waste, when the smell alone had made me queasy.

"Don't remind me. I think the main difference was that this time, the man was still alive. As a first-aider, I figured I had to try to help. It did freak me out a little when I found out he was dead, though."

A roar from the television interrupted our conversation. The commentator announced a British medal hopeful taking to the balance beam. "Did you know that gymnastics was one of the original events at the ancient Olympics in Greece?" the sportscaster asked.

I rolled my eyes behind my bandages. Since Gordon's capture, everybody talked about Greek myths and the history behind the Games.

Perhaps the Oracle had succeeded in his quest, after all.

"You're missing all the fun, Daddy," Meghan said. "Janet Pringle's in the all-round final tomorrow. It's a shame you won't be able to see."

I mocked a disappointed pout, and she kissed my puckered lips.

"Speaking of which, would you like to swing by tomorrow?" After a few seconds' confusion, I realised that Holloway was talking to Blaize. "We can all watch the Games with a couple of beers and a takeaway."

Looks like Tom's slowly coming out of his shell.

"Sounds great," Blaize said. "Can I bring my housemate?"

"Of course," Holloway said.

"Oh, you'll like Lex," I said with a knowing smile. I would have winked at him if I could. "I bet you two will hit it right off."

"Right," Holloway said. I detected the chafing of cloth as he fumbled for something. "As much as I'd love to stay and chat, *some* of us have incident reports to file."

"Gee, you know I'd love to help if I could." I smiled my smuggest smile. Holloway patted me on the shoulder, and Blaize added a kiss on my cheek. Her hair brushed my face. I breathed in her peach blossom and magnolia scent.

"How are you getting on?" I whispered to her.

Blaize stayed silent for a beat before whispering back, "I'll call you." She gave me another kiss on the cheek. I listened to her footsteps as she walked away. They sounded lighter, her feet dragging less. Perhaps she'd come to terms with her endometriosis. Whatever the case, I vowed to be there to help her through.

As a friend.

"I hope we're not having Chinese again for takeaway," Meghan said after the door shut with a click.

"What do you mean, 'again'?" I asked. "When have you had Chinese?"

"Uncle Reggie got me chicken chow mein and sticky spare ribs yesterday."

I smirked. Chinese food constituted one of Reggie's five-a-day, the others being kebabs, burgers, Doritos, and a Mars bar. I hadn't seen him since the Opening Ceremony, although he'd dropped Meghan off at the hospital that morning. To my relief, he shacked her up at a Travelodge. I could think of worse places for a little girl to spend the night.

"Let's read a book together." Meghan bounced up and down on the edge of the bed. "I've got *Perseus and Medusa*."

I groaned. "Not more Greek mythology."

"Don't worry, this one has a happy ending." She shoved an open, hardcover book into my hands. "See if you can read the first sentence."

"How hard can it be?" I traced a finger across the page, frowning at the smooth paper erratically interspersed with raised dots. I tried forming a mental image of the positions of the dots. All I got was gobbledegook. "It says ... er ... *Once upon a time?*"

Meghan snorted. "Not even close!"

"I give up. Why don't you just read it to me?"

"Aw, come on," she said. "It's not *that* hard." She launched into full reading mode, sounding each word aloud. Her voice tinkled with growing confidence, with the assuredness in her own ability.

You do not need eyes to see.

My phone beeped. A text message. Meghan leapt from the bed.

"Who's it from?" I asked.

"I dunno, some number ..." her voice trailed off. "I think it's Uncle Reggie."

"What does it say?"

"'Get ... well ... soon, bro. Don't ... forget, I'm watching you.'"

I settled deeper into the pillow, fingering the stitches on my hand.

Thanks, bro.

Epilogue

"O holy blessed father, hear my prayer ..." The Oracle stared up at the featureless ceiling. His lips fluttered in fervent prayer as he took slow, deep breaths, willing his body to relax.

"Disperse the seeds of life-consuming care ..." As much as he tried to ignore them, to focus on his incantation, every lump in the thin mattress beneath him seemed intent on distracting him from his task. His throat was parched, his mouth woolly and dry from hours of prayer.

"Zeus was the first. Zeus will be the last. All things are from Zeus."

He smacked chapped lips together, shut his eyes and waited. Waited for the haunting strains of music, the dancing colours and lights, the aura that always preceded his audience with Zeus.

Zeus did not come.

O holy Lord, why do You forsake me? All he had ever done was to fulfil his God's wishes.

With a roar of frustration, he sat up. He reached for the glass of water beside his bed, knocking over an empty Styrofoam cup, the cup that held those colourful pills he'd taken—medicine, claimed the doctors, elixirs to clarify the mind.

Curse those foul wizards! They had deceived him, tricked him into ingesting poisons that tainted his soul. Soiled and impure, his body was no longer an acceptable vessel for the Thunder Bringer.

He shivered and rubbed his shoulder. He scratched at the skin, raking his fingernails down the length of his arm. His flesh prickled as if reacting to the toxins. The poisons coursed through his system, repressing his latent ability, cutting him off from his God.

I must purify myself.

The scratching intensified. Red welts began appearing on his arms. The poison pulsed in his blood, right beneath the skin on the inside of his wrists. With a small cry, he clawed at the throbbing, tearing his way towards the green blood vessels underneath.

I will restore my body to purity, O Zeus, so that I may serve you once more.

The Oracle sank his teeth into his wrist, ripping out chunks of flesh. When the blood flowed freely, he lapped at it, sucking it up and spitting out the poison. As he worked, his head grew light, his vision dancing before him.

It is working. I am cleansing myself.

The reinforced door to his cell swung open, and a couple of orderlies rushed in. Seizing him, they pinned him to the bed. One of them plunged a needle into the Oracle's arm. *More poison?* He didn't know, but it turned his limbs to lead as heavy and unresponsive as the legs of the lame god Hephaestus. Night shrouded his vision, dimming his senses. In the darkening room, another figure appeared in the doorway. Dressed in a white robe, the bearded man's imposing silhouette appeared illuminated in a halo of light.

Zeus.

"You," the Oracle managed, as his consciousness ebbed away, "are you my saviour?"

The Lightning God smiled as he held his clipboard.

"I can be."

Acknowledgements

The evolution of this book was a long and oft-interrupted journey, an odyssey I could not have possibly completed alone. To list everyone I owe a debt of gratitude to would fill up the pages of a whole new book, but I would be remiss if I did not mention at least the following:

All my friends and family, who did not laugh when I announced I wanted to be a writer. Your support and encouragement were the fuels that saw this project through.

Fellow writers, whether I have met you in person or only in the realms of cyberspace, thank you for sharing your tales of trials and tribulations. Knowing that others are walking the same path made my journey a far less lonely one.

Thanks to Rob Mewis, my personal oracle, for invaluable insights into the structure and running of units within the Metropolitan Police Specialist Crime Directorate; also, thanks to Donna Mewis for her constant hospitality, and for the many barbecues.

My critique partner-in-crime, fellow mystery writer Lisa L. Regan: thank you for casting your eagle eyes over my manuscript while it was still in its primordial form, and for your brilliant feedback.

To the amazing team at J. Taylor Publishing, especially Aimée, Julia, Julie, and Ron, thank you for turning my manuscript into a real, live book.

While all those mentioned above have contributed to an improved final manuscript, none is, of course, responsible for any remaining errors or shortcomings, to which I claim sole responsibility.

J.C. Martin

J.C. Martin is a butt-kicking bookworm. When she isn't reading or writing, she teaches martial arts and self-defence to adults and children.

After working in pharmaceutical research, then in education as a schoolteacher, she decided to put the following to good use: one, her second degree black belt in Wing Chun kung fu, and two, her overwhelming need to write dark mysteries and gripping thrillers with a psychological slant.

Her short stories have won various prizes and have been published in several anthologies. *Oracle* is her first novel.

Born and raised in Malaysia, J.C. now lives in south London with her husband and three dogs.

Lightning Source UK Ltd.
Milton Keynes UK
UKOW050634280712

196703UK00001B/4/P